WILD SCOTTISH MAGIC

THE ENCHANTED HIGHLANDS
BOOK NINE

TRICIA O'MALLEY

LOVEWRITE PUBLISHING

WILD SCOTTISH MAGIC
THE ENCHANTED HIGHLANDS SERIES
BOOK 9

"The fault, dear Brutus, is not in our stars, but in ourselves." – William Shakespeare

GLOSSARY OF SCOTTISH WORDS/SLANG

- Bloody – a word used to add emphasis; expletive
- Bonnie – pretty
- Hen – woman, female
- "It's a dreich day" – cold; damp; miserable
- Lorry – work truck
- Luch - Celtic version of Luke
- Och – used to express many emotions, typically surprise, regret, or disbelief
- Scran – food
- Shoogly – unsteady; wobbly
- Tatties – potatoes
- Tetchy – crabby, cranky, moody
- Tea – in Scotland, having tea is often used to refer to the dinnertime meal
- Wee – small, little
- Wheesht (haud your wheesht) – be quiet, hush, shut up

CHAPTER ONE

LIORA

"T he Heartbreak Witch?" Zara screeched through the phone, and I collapsed back against my scratchy hotel pillow. Covering my face with one of my hands, even though Zara couldn't see me, I tried to push back the panic that was wrapping its ropes around my chest.

"I know, Z. I knoooow." Humiliation washed over me, my skin flushing with the heat of it.

"How did this even happen? You're viral? On *WitchTok* of all things?" My older sister, Zara, was almost blind, far better at magick than me, and Had Her Life Together. With capital letters, like that. She'd just taken a job at the local vet's office in Loren Brae—a small town I'd briefly lived in and run away from—but Zara had insisted on moving back there despite my reputation. In her words, she was there to "un-sully" our name.

1

I'd left Loren Brae after a particularly chaotic astrological disaster, determined to never look back, and now I feared I had no choice but to return.

"Everyone is talking about you," Zara hissed, and I winced.

"I ... I know. Or so I heard before I logged off *WitchTok*. And every other social media app that I have."

"I thought you weren't going to do readings anymore." Zara's voice held more sympathy than censure, and that somehow stung even worse.

She knew, more than anyone else, how much I hated with every ounce of my being that I couldn't seem to make my magick work. Not like hers, at least.

Maybe the internet was right—it was time for me to hang up my hat, so to speak—and finally admit the one truth that I'd been avoiding for a very long time.

I was an absolute shite astrologer.

Even thinking it made my gut churn in pain, because somehow, somewhere, along the way I'd become convinced that astrology was where my magick was meant to manifest. I loved it. And it loved me, I was certain of it, but something hadn't quite clicked yet for me. At least to make accurate predictions, that is.

I'd spent endless hours poring over charts, reading astrology books, researching Astro cartography and other iterations of astrology, and still ... somehow I managed to land myself in hot water.

"But she was so excited, and she was offering so much money," I said, groaning as I tugged at my mousy brown hair. "Rent was due. I swear, Z, I've been working really hard. I know astrology inside and out. It's not my fault that the prediction came out the way that it did."

"You ..." Zara took a deep breath before continuing. "You told the girlfriend of one of the most popular rugby players in the world that he wasn't her soulmate and she was destined for unhappiness."

"I would never!" I sat up, outraged. "That's an exaggeration. I swear people don't listen when I tell them what I see."

"Liora." This time it was a sigh of resignation, and my shoulders hunched. "Astrology is meant to be used to look for personal traits or forecast good times in the year ahead to make a move or start a new job. You know, to look at when the planets are favorable to act. You can't predict a love match from astrology."

"I mean, you can see if someone is a good match or not based on their birth chart," I mumbled.

Zara sighed, again, and I pinched my nose. A horn sounded outside, and shouts carried through the grimy window of the only hotel I could afford to stay at after I hadn't been able to make rent and my roommates had ousted me from our tiny flat in Glasgow.

"Even so, it doesn't determine love. You know that, Liora. People can be horrific matches but still decide to work it out. To figure out a way to love. It's not on you to predict the outcome of a love match for someone. When will you learn? I thought after ..." Zara trailed off.

My stomach roiled. I knew what she was referring to.

The entire reason I'd left Loren Brae.

I'd been younger. Convinced I knew the way of things.

And I'd given an impassioned reading, certain I was in

the right of it, and had ruined a relationship with the blame landing squarely on my shoulders. It had been the talk of Loren Brae for months.

"In fairness, it's not my fault she ran back to her boyfriend and told him he wasn't her soulmate," I said, pulling my thoughts away from memories past. "I never said that."

"What, exactly, did you tell this WAG?" Zara asked, referring to the term for wives and girlfriends of sports stars in the UK.

"I told her, that based on her chart, it looked like she might be destined for more than one great love in her life."

Zara gasped. "Liora, you didn't."

"It was true though."

"But you can't say that to someone who is head over heels for her boyfriend. They've had a big row now. Broken up over this."

"Well, in theory, wouldn't that make me right?" I pulled my stubbornness around me like a cloak. I hadn't been wrong in my reading. "If they were so much in love and perfect for each other, an astrology reading shouldn't have been able to tear them apart, right?"

"Be that as it may ... it's landed you in hot water, again, and without a place to live from what I can gather."

I glanced to the pile of luggage in the corner of the room. It wasn't much, but it was mine.

Tears welled.

"Aye," I said, defeat filling me.

"Come home, Liora. We'll sort it out. It might do you some good to take a break from this and focus on what you really want out of life."

I gulped back a sob. It wouldn't do to cry to Zara. She'd always known exactly who she was and what she wanted out of life, while I'd clung to astrology because it was what I loved. But it appeared that it didn't love me back. Maybe it was time to admit defeat and set my sights on becoming employable in a different profession.

"I can't—"

"You can. I'm delighted to be back in Loren Brae. And you will be too. Things have changed, Liora. It's a good place to land, at least for a little while. Come back. Mitch misses you." I grinned as Mitch, her guide dog, barked in the background when he heard his name.

"I ..." I looked around the tiny hotel room, largely taken up by my luggage, and sighed.

"Okay, Z. I'll take some time off. I'll come back to Loren Brae."

Loren Brae. The incredible town I'd once thought would be my forever home until I'd royally screwed that dream up. Surely, nothing like that would happen again though. History couldn't repeat itself. *Right?*

CHAPTER TWO

Liora

It wasn't Loren Brae I'd hated, specifically, that had sent me running. The wee town set on the rocky shores of Loch Mirren came into view as I crested the hill in my ancient Fiat, and I couldn't help but smile at the postcard picture it made. Colorful buildings toppled over each other, the loch spread out at their feet, with a charming castle tucked in the hills in the backdrop. Clouds bunched together on the horizon, the sun spearing through the gaps, highlighting the perfectly round island centered in the middle of the loch.

I shivered when I looked at the island. It had always given me the heebie-jeebies, and much like my ability to screw up my life, nothing had changed. Awareness prickled over my skin as I tore my glance away from the island and kept my eyes on the road, following the instructions my sister had given me. She lived smack dab in the middle of the wee downtown, in a ground-floor flat that we were most definitely not going to share for any longer than necessary. In fact, Zara already had a line on a place for me to stay and given my budget constraints, which were heavy, I'd be happy to take anything at this point.

Somehow I needed to figure out how to make money.

I suspected my old fallback, waitressing, was about to come firmly back into my life. If I wanted to get back on my feet and figure out what I wanted out of my future, I needed some space to deal with the basics first. A place to live, enough money to pay my bills, and only after that would I be able to deal with the heartbreak of having to accept that my astrology career had finally spiraled and crashed in flames.

I'd once thought I'd have my very own shop, pretty shelves lined in crystals and tarot decks, a cozy room for private readings, and a function space to host classes. I truly believed, down to my pink sparkly painted toes—though the paint was well-chipped now—that everyone could benefit from learning more about their birth chart. It was self-help in its most elemental form, a tool that could be used to understand oneself more deeply, and a way to help center a decision-making process.

And yet.

Here I was, blinking back tears of frustration, as I shifted into park and heaved in a deep breath, and then another, as I stared at my sister's front door. Painted a bright red with a scruffy pad to wipe muddy boots at its foot, it was both serviceable and welcoming. Just like Zara. My no-nonsense sister always seemed to have the answers to everything, and she navigated the world in almost total darkness. It was hard living up to her expectations at times.

Still. I would get through this. As I had every other speed bump in the past. Taking another deep breath, I pulled from my endless well of optimism that had fueled me through many a crisis in the past.

"It's just a new adventure. You'll maybe even meet some new friends. Z says she loves her new boss." I quietly cheered myself up as I unbuckled my seat belt and got out of my car. "Plus, you get to see Mitch."

My sister's guide dog was a bouncy golden retriever that adored cuddles when he wasn't working. I was much the same.

Heaving my backpack out of the back seat, I left the other luggage in the boot and went to knock at the door. Barking sounded, and Zara's stern voice admonished Mitch, before the door swung open.

"Z!" I beamed at my petite sister and drew her in for a hug. We rocked back and forth like a metronome, and I breathed in her scent. She'd worn the same perfume forever, a spicy mix of anise and cocoa, and it instantly soothed me. Being back with Zara meant everything was going to be just fine. We were a team against the world, not that I particularly enjoyed depending on her to solve my problems, but somehow things always seemed less complicated when I was with her. Which, admittedly, was at times annoying. I didn't want to lean on her as my crutch through every big disaster in my life. Hopefully, this time, I wouldn't need to ask too much of her.

Mitch bounded around our feet, clearly not in work mode, and Zara sighed and pulled back.

"Mitch. Sit."

Mitch sat, instantly, though his bum wriggled in excitement at seeing me. His mouth lolled in a doggy smile, and his eyes were alert as he looked up at me.

"Free for a cuddle?" I asked Z, waiting for her permission.

"Aye, he's off work." Zara smiled gently as I dropped to my knees and wrapped my arms around a delighted Mitch, who dragged his tongue across my face as his whole body vibrated in excitement. He was a great dog and he'd made an enormous difference to my sister's mobility and independence.

"Cuppa tea?" Zara asked, moving confidently through her space, which was set up to her own exacting standards. I'd learned long ago to keep things neat and tidy when I was with her, lest she inadvertently trip over something I'd carelessly left out.

"Please, thanks." I stood and crossed the room—an open-style lounge and kitchen space—and put my bag on the couch and off the floor. "I'm just putting my backpack on the couch and then I'll deal with the rest of the luggage later."

"I've already got your place lined up." Zara filled the kettle and clicked it on, pulled out two sage green mugs, and a box of Twinings. Her movements were methodical and precise, much like her personality, and I smiled. Being with her was like the cup of tea she was making for me—warm and soothing.

"That's shockingly fast. I wasn't sure you'd be able to swing anything in my budget," I said, raising an eyebrow. *Of course* she'd already sorted out my accommodation.

"Loren Brae has had some struggles the last few years, it seems. There are a lot of people heading out to the cities. But I managed to find something serviceable enough. It's small, but clean and warm. It's just a wing of a house, and you'll have to share the kitchen, I'm told, but you'll get your own bedroom and lounge room. Faelan said her client's friend is renting the space for a little extra income. He's watching after the property for his mum who has moved into assisted care and could use the extra money. Parkinson's, I believe. Such a shame."

"That's ... a lot of information," I said, instantly being reminded what living in a small town is like. "I guess that will work. I don't really cook much anyway, so I'm sure the shared kitchen won't be a bother."

"I don't know the lad, but he's coming by with keys tomorrow. I paid the security deposit and first month's rent for you." Zara's tone was as measured as the water she poured into the mug, and my stomach twisted.

"Z. You didn't have to do that. I have savings. Not much. But some."

"An early Christmas present," Zara said, turning to me with a small smile. "You know I hate frivolous gifts. It makes me feel good to be able to help, and I know you can use the help. Win-win."

"Only if you're certain." I crossed the room and took my mug from her, pressing a quick kiss to her cheek. "Love you, Z."

"You too, L."

Mitch sat hopefully at the counter, his eyes going from us to a cabinet door.

"Does Mitch want a treat?"

"Mitch lives for treats." Z's smile tugged up the corners of her lips. "But go on, he can have one."

"Yay!" Digging into the cabinet, I found a bone for him, and retreated to the couch, mug and treat in hand. Mitch followed closely and then sat, his eyes staring at my hand.

"Who is the best boy in all the land?" I asked, and Mitch wiggled, but stayed in place. "You are!"

I handed him his bone, and he took it gently, then dropped to the floor to chew happily, clearly agreeing with my assessment.

"I've got work in the morning, so you'll have to meet the landlord, but I figured you'd be fine with that since you'll be living there." Zara settled onto a lounge chair with a side table next to it. "You know I'd have you here but..."

"I'd clutter up your space, make you break a hip, and you don't like sharing your bed," I deadpanned and Zara laughed, shaking her brown hair back from her shoulders.

"You're not wrong. But I am so happy you're back here. I've missed you. I mean, I don't want to live with you, but I *have* missed having you around."

"The feeling is mutual. You're far too uptight for me," I said, blowing on my tea and taking a sip. Easing back into the cushions, I crossed my legs and grinned as my sister made a rude gesture at me.

"Try navigating the world in darkness and see how you feel about rules," Zara said.

"Ugh, playing the blind card once again," I murmured and she laughed.

"Only with you because you're a pain in the arse," Zara said.

"But I'm your favorite pain in the arse, aren't I? Admit it."

"Aye, my bubbly, sunshiny, chaotic, messy whirlwind of a sister. You are my favorite pain in the arse. Though I certainly have some opinions on your latest snafu. Have you heard what they're saying about you on TikTok?" Zara shook her head, pursing her lips.

"Och, you have to ignore them." I'd removed the app from my phone to avoid hearing hurtful things. Denial is thy name and all that.

"I try, but my algorithm keeps serving it up. Don't you think it's ... it's time?" Concern flooded Zara's pretty face.

"I mean, I'm not going to give up on astrology. I love it, Z. You know that. But I do need to figure out why I just can't seem to make it work. Clearly something's off if I keep giving bad readings, well at least what people feel like, are bad readings."

"I mean, there's a common denominator here." Zara raised an eyebrow and sipped her tea.

"Bitch," I gasped, holding a hand to my chest. "Betrayed by my own sister."

"Never, but I'm also not going to sugarcoat things for you."

"Och, that much I know." Sugar and Zara were not friends.

"Maybe just ease back for a bit? Or if you're dead set on astrology, maybe we need to go through some of our old books and see why it's not working for you? I think your life will go much more smoothly when we get this sorted."

Zara's abilities ran more to empathic and aura readings. She could instantly tell a person's character by the colors she saw in her mind's eye. She could also speak to plants. Her gifts were unique to her, and none of our family had her magick, at least that we were aware of. I'd always thought my gift had landed firmly in astrology, latest catastrophe notwithstanding, while Mum's had run more to empathic readings. I couldn't remember what Gran had as a gift because I only had blurry memories of her from when I was quite young. It had been a while since I'd done a deep dive into our history.

"Do you have any of Mum's stuff here?" I asked. After our mum and dad had split when we'd both been just out of school, Mum taking off for London and Dad for the States, there wasn't much in the way of physical memories left behind. With Zara being a neat freak, I wouldn't be surprised if she'd sifted through and tossed most of it.

"I do, actually. A few boxes she left for us in storage. I haven't gone through it because I figured I'd wait until we were settled somewhere and then we could pick a few pieces each for our place." Zara shrugged. She was pragmatic to a fault and had been recently living in Edinburgh until she'd decided to return to Loren Brae, craving nature and the small-town life. Like me, she hadn't yet fully planted her roots, but it was beginning to sound like Loren Brae might be just the spot for her.

And maybe, just maybe, it might be for me as well.

"I'll pull the boxes out and have a look." I laughed at Zara's look of dismay. "And I'll make sure there's nothing on the floor or in your way when you come home. Promise."

Zara's shoulders relaxed and she put her tea down on the side table and drew her feet up to snuggle into the chair.

"That's fine then. The boxes are in the cupboard at the end of the hall by my bedroom."

"I'll take a look tomorrow. For now, I just want to catch up. Tell me … how is it being back?" I danced around the reason I'd left, though I still felt the prickly threads of shame twining around my gut as I thought about the situation that had driven me from Loren Brae before.

My friend, Avery, had come to me for a reading. Specifically of her boyfriend, Torin. She'd been convinced they were perfect for each other and had become enraged when I'd shown her the differences in their charts. In my effort to explain that a mismatch in charts did not mean the end of a relationship—it usually just meant more work for the couple—I'd inadvertently shown her how neatly his chart lined up with mine.

I'd meant to use it as an example, since I could see the complementary angles in our charts, but she'd exploded.

Suddenly, I'd become a green-eyed witch, desperate to steal her man, determined to break them up. She'd left that day, refusing to speak to me, and their relationship had imploded shortly thereafter.

Rumors had quickly spread that I was the reason for the breakup, with the heavy implication that it had been my prowess in bed and not in the astrological charts that had torn them apart. Avery refusing to speak to me only fueled the fire, so instead of sticking it out, I ran to Glasgow and started my life over. Maybe it was a bit dramatic, but I'd been ready for a change anyway, so the move had come at a good time. Still, I wasn't overly excited to run into anyone who still thought of me as a homewrecker.

"Honestly? It's great. I mean, it's changed, like, *a lot,*

since we were last here." Zara shifted in the chair, tapping a finger against her lips. "A lot of people that we once knew have left. There's been an influx of new people moving here. Many from overseas. And, well, there is just one little problem. Loren Brae is in trouble."

"What?" I almost dropped the mug I'd just picked back up. "What do you mean by that?"

"The Kelpies have risen from the loch. They're terrorizing the town." Zara's eyes stared into nothingness, but I knew she saw more than I ever could. I flinched at the concern on her face.

"What the actual hell, Z? The Kelpies?" My heart hammered in my chest. My sister shrugged one shoulder, her lips tightening, her expression suggesting we were just meant to live with these pesky mythological beasts. "But ... you ... and Mitch. Will you be safe? And your new job?" I asked, faintly, as I gripped my mug more tightly and took a bracing sip of the tea. This didn't sound like a *little* problem. This sounded like a big, fat, magickal problem that could seriously hurt someone. No wonder people were leaving Loren Brae.

"Aye, it's fine enough, I suppose. There's a group of women here who are fighting to protect the town. Or so I've gleaned, as I'm fairly sure my boss is one of them. I listen, you know. I think they just might be successful in defeating this. But until then, don't stray too close to the loch."

"Too close ...?" I gulped. "Z, the entire town is literally *on* the loch."

"I know it. But I think you'll be okay. Just be smart." My almost blind sister, who needed a guide dog to navigate the uneven streets of Loren Brae, dismissed angry Kelpies as casually as swatting away an annoying fly.

"Be smart, she says." I rolled my eyes. "Like I have any clue how to fight a Kelpie. What are they, anyway?"

"Water horses. Biting ones."

"Och, that's grand. Just fecking grand." I sighed and buried my nose in my cup of tea. Did I manage to trade one set of problems for another? Taking a calming sip, I shook off my worries.

No. This is your new adventure and you are going to make it amazing. Water horses be damned.

CHAPTER THREE

LIORA

The next morning, a lad of about sixteen had dropped off keys and instructions for me regarding my new home, and I decided to not burden Zara any further with my move. After a morning cup of tea, a quick tidy up around the flat to make sure I hadn't left anything out that could be in Zara's way, I loaded a few of the keepsake boxes from the cupboard into my car. It would be easier to take my time going through family heirlooms where I could lay them out and have a proper look at them, and knowing me, I'd get distracted and leave them out for a while, which just wouldn't do in Zara's place. Instead, I found myself following the lad's directions to a stone cottage on the outskirts of Loren Brae.

Turning up a gravel drive, I inched down a lane shrouded by trees, the wind shifting the branches, and sunlight dappled the forest around me. The nights were drawing closer now, the daylight hours shortening, and I was just happy to have some sunlight as the icy wind brought the promise of winter with it. I let out a small sigh of happiness when the cottage came into view. It was exactly as Zara had described. With one main building, and two small wings flanking either side of the cottage, it looked cozy, well maintained, and the perfect spot for me to take stock of the mess of my life. A place for healing, I supposed, if that was what I really needed. Except I still wasn't entirely convinced that I was the one who needed healing.

Maybe to hide from the spotlight for a bit.

But to heal? I wasn't sure that I was broken. Even though everyone else seemed to think that I was. Shaking my head, I laughed at myself. Those were thoughts for another day. What I needed to do was check out my new living situation and make sure that I didn't disrupt the other tenant too much. I'd try to keep my chaos carefully contained in my own wing, while hopefully not disrupting the flow of the other person's life too much.

Resolved, I took the keys the lad had given me, the paper with a neat list of instructions, and exited the car, tugging the strap of my pocketbook over my shoulder. I just wanted to get the lay of the land before I fully unpacked. Following the instructions to go to the side door on the right wing of the house, I bypassed the front door and made my way to a small door painted a deep evergreen color.

An acorn bounced off the roof with a sharp thud, before knocking me on top of the head.

"Ow!" I said, looking up to where a red squirrel sat on a

branch above me, chattering at me. Or laughing, if a squirrel could laugh. "Sir! That was *very* rude."

The squirrel chattered some nonsense at me again and then darted away, clearly pleased with himself.

Unlocking the door, I pushed inside the house, automatically reaching for a switch to flip the lights on.

"Och, well, this is nice, isn't it then?" I breathed a sigh of relief. The door had opened directly into a lounge room, which had two doors on either side, one open and one closed. The closed door presumably led to the rest of the house, and I was pleased to see a bolt on my side, ensuring my privacy as needed. The lounge itself was serviceable, if not a bit spartan. Not that it mattered much, as I could make any space homey and welcoming in a short matter of time.

A draft of wind, sharp with scents of the loch and the damp forest, pushed me further inside, and I closed the door behind me against the cold. Crossing the room, I flipped on the switch in the next room to reveal a bedroom that just fit a standing cupboard, a dresser, and a double bed. Attached was a tiny en suite bathroom, which was more than serviceable for my needs. Nodding, pleased with the space, I returned to the lounge and eyed the door to the main room.

I hadn't spied a car outside, so I assumed my landlord was still at work, as the lad who had dropped the keys off had indicated. Now would be a good time to just take a quick peek at the rest of the house.

Dropping my pocketbook on the couch, I crossed the room and unbolted the door, swinging it open to see the main room of the cottage. Clearly, this part of the house had been the main building back in the day, and the wings had been added on to it through the years. I smiled, charmed at the idea of a hodgepodge cottage gradually evolving the years, and nodded my approval at the landlord's decor. It was a touch sparse but not unwelcoming. A leather sofa dominated one side of the room, facing a wide-screen television, with deep set cushions and a faded blanket folded over the back. A grey stone fireplace laid with wood, ready to be lit, and a neat pile of perfectly chopped logs sat next to it. A large rug, in muted blues and greens, was tossed across the wood floor, and windows on both sides of the house looked out into the surrounding forest.

"A perfect wee retreat in the woods," I said, out loud. "Yoo-hoo? Anyone home?"

I figured it was best I call out in case someone was here but didn't own a car. When nobody answered, I ventured farther into the room to explore the side with the open kitchen. A long wood table separated the kitchen space from the lounge, and I admired the roughhewn edges, the carefully sanded wood, and the matching chairs that looked like they were lovingly carved by hand.

"Och, this is stunning," I said, running my hand across the tabletop. It was a work of art, and I could see why someone would want to have such a magnificent piece in their home. I could imagine sitting here, working on my charts, drinking tea while staring into the fire. Shaking my head, I turned to the kitchen, which had all the basic accoutrements a kitchen needed. After a quick perusal, I noted the Post-it Note attached to one cupboard.

"'Welcome. Sorry I couldn't be here but will be back late tonight. Please feel free to use this cupboard for any food items. I've also cleared two drawers in the fridge for you,'" I read out loud. "Och, well that's just fine then, isn't it?" I hadn't even thought to stop at the market and get food, but when my stomach growled loudly at me, I realized I would need to eat at some point today.

"There's time enough for that," I murmured to my stomach, and turned once more, taking a deep breath and letting it slowly out. The house felt good to me, lived in, but not cluttered. Somebody obviously cared enough to keep it clean, and aside from making food, I could have my privacy as needed. I was used to living with roommates, so this wasn't an unusual situation for me, though I typically liked to meet the landlord or roomies before I signed a lease. But I trusted my sister, and surely she wouldn't put me in a position that was unsafe for me.

"This is Loren Brae," I reminded myself as I dug my car keys from where I'd tossed them in my purse. "Small towns are different from big cities. You'll be just fine with whomever this roommate is."

Pleased to have my own space again, particularly one that gave me a separate bedroom and a lounge, I hurried outside to narrowly miss getting hit with another acorn.

"Hey!" I said, putting my hand to my head and peering up at where the squirrel chattered at me again. "Watch out!"

The squirrel bounced around on the branch and then jumped to the roof, where he ran across quickly, and then he jumped down to the ground. There he scampered across the grass and astounded me by leaping on top of my car.

I froze.

We were in a standoff, it seemed.

The squirrel tilted its fuzzy head at me, his dark eyes gleaming, and I tilted mine in response.

"Sir. Why are you chucking acorns at my head?"

"To get your attention, duh."

I almost leapt out of my skin when I heard a voice, a touch rough around the edges in my head. My mouth dropped open. Had I just really heard a squirrel? Or was my imagination running away from me as it often did?

"Was that you who just spoke?" I planted my hands on my hips. I'd never heard animals speak before, but it wasn't an entirely unheard-of concept for the people of my family to have latent powers of sorts. Our whole bloodline had been touched by the fae, or so my mum had always said, and I'd been told we all had some sort of powers or another. Talking to animals might just be mine.

Or maybe stress was getting the better of me. The silence drew out as the squirrel tilted its head the other direction, and I mimicked him.

"Aye, lass. That was me."

"No way," I breathed. "Wait. How come I couldn't hear you when you chattered at me before then?"

The squirrel made a chattering noise and no words formed in my mind.

"So you can communicate with me if you feel like it? Is that what you're saying?" I lifted my chin.

"Aye, that's the way of it. I'm Bracken, by the way."

"Bracken? Well, that's a cool name. It's nice to meet you. I'm Liora." I glanced over my shoulder at the front of the cottage and was relieved to see there wasn't a Ring camera doorbell on the front. I could only imagine how my new landlord would think of me if he was watching his new tenant talk to a squirrel out front.

"I know."

At that, my attention snapped back to Bracken.

"How do you know that?"

"Because you're mine." The squirrel ran across the top of my car and leapt to a nearby branch. *"I'll be around, Liora. Welcome home."*

"Wait, what does that mean? That 'I'm yours?'" I called, but Bracken was already bounding through the trees, like a ball ping-ponging through a pinball machine, and I gaped after him. "Well, that was weird."

I looked up at the now empty branches.

"But cool," I amended, not wanting to offend Bracken if he could still hear me. "Really cool. New talent unlocked, I guess. Yay for me!"

Would I be able to hear all the squirrels now? Or just Bracken? What about dogs? I brightened as I thought about being able to communicate directly with Mitch. My sister would love that. He'd become such an integral part of her life, and I knew she'd get a kick out of hearing his thoughts. Humming to myself, my mind focused on all the ways I might be able to communicate with animals now, as I quickly worked through unloading the car and setting myself up in my new space. By the time I'd finished, leaving the boxes from Zara's house on the table in front of the couch, my stomach was growling.

Grabbing my purse, I locked up and glanced around the trees to look for Bracken. The light was dimming, the sun already dipping toward the horizon as night came early in the late fall in Scotland. With no sign of Bracken anywhere near my car, I hopped in and drove to the supermarket. Briefly, I debated stopping at The Tipsy Thistle for a meal, but I looked a mess and since I'd likely be applying there for work, I needed to be at my most presentable. Instead, I dipped into the market, bought a few basics, and was back home before full dark.

Home.

It felt weird, moving into a house where nobody was home, but I wasn't a stranger to weird situations in my life. Instead, I just needed to be grateful that I had a roof over my head and a small space of my own while I figured out what came next.

I kind of hated that I needed to work out what came next for me. In novels, it always made it sound like the heroine just sat down and sorted out her life in an afternoon. But the reality was, life just wasn't that cut and dried, was it? What? I was suddenly going to have an epiphany and have it all figured out? Maybe life was just a series of taking small steps forward until you blundered into where you were meant to be. But I guess that probably didn't make for fun reading, so I could see why authors left the ugly bits out of their stories.

But here I was, thirty years old. Sitting in my torn and faded pajamas, an empty sandwich plate on the table in front of me and clutching an almost empty bag of crisps, silence stretching out around me and filling the room until it almost made my head hurt. Was now when I was supposed to suddenly have all the answers come to me? If so, I could use a manual. A set of instructions.

Hell, even an acorn thrown at my head would feel better than this yawning emptiness inside of me.

Never one to settle into uncomfortable feelings all that long, I decided to distract myself from the whole *what should I do with my life?* problem, so I cut into the tape on one of the old cardboard boxes from Zara's cupboard. Sliding it open, I pushed the packet of crisps aside and dusted any crumbs from my hands before opening the lid.

The first picture, right on top of a pile of old books, made me laugh out loud. It was Z and me, probably around seven years old, at Halloween. She was dressed as a witch, and I was grinning widely, a front tooth missing, in a fat orange pumpkin suit. I'd always been the more ridiculous of the two of us, and I took the picture out and set it aside, knowing I'd want to keep it.

I busied myself digging around and sorting items into piles. Old pictures, letters, and birthday cards went on one side of the box. Notebooks, recipe books, and other books that needed further investigation on the other side. At the bottom of the box, my hand touched soft velvet, and I pulled out what looked to be an old pouch. Opening it, I gasped at a beautiful leather-bound book, with an intricate Celtic and floral pattern stamped into the cover. Taking it out of the protective bag, I leaned back onto the couch and tried to ignore the hum of excitement that had zipped through me when my hands touched the book. It was just me over imagining things, as I often did. I was sure of it.

Gently, I opened the cover, and tears immediately sprung to my eyes as I saw my name written across the front page, under a line of women who had come before me.

Liora Webster.

Ailis Webster. My mother.

Beatrice Baxter. My grandmother.

Senga Durnell. My great grandmother.

Why wasn't Zara's name on the list? Tapping a finger against the page, I felt that zing of energy again, and tilted my head, studying the book. Was there something more here? Turning the page, I let out a soft sigh of pleasure.

The celestial charts stared back at me, drawn with intricate detail, and with lovely penmanship. Slowly, I paged through the book, and gasped when I realized what I was holding.

It was a spell book.

But it was also so much more than that. The women of my family had made notes in the margins, adjusting spells, adding their insights, or even, like on one page, making a joke about another's cooking. It was a journal. It was a grimoire. It was a family history of shared magick and love.

What a gift.

I couldn't believe it had been tucked away for so long, and being the curious sort that I was, I was desperate to try a small spell. Just to see if any of this worked...

Just to see if I actually had this kind of magick.

I mean, I should, right? My name was right there, added to the book.

Paging through the various spells, I landed on one that seemed innocuous enough. A spell for truth-telling. I wasn't sure who I'd use it on, but maybe I could just practice it? Just to see if anything, I don't know, shifted in the air around me as I did.

Humming to myself, I studied the spell. It seemed simple enough. I needed to pick a small item to anchor the spell in the middle of my circle, and then do the incantation. If the person I needed to be truthful stepped inside the circle, the spell would activate.

Thinking, I popped up off the couch and picked up the acorn I'd taken inside with me after Bracken had thrown it at me. Laying it on the floor, I crossed the room and picked up the book. I then traced a large circle around the acorn with my foot, just setting the parameters of the spell even though I didn't mark anything into the floor.

"Right, so the acorn roots the spell," I murmured, standing there with the book in my hand. "I've got my circle. Now I just need to do an incantation?"

Reciting it to myself several times to make sure I had it straight, I stared down at the acorn, my back to the door, and began.

"Root of witness, bell of clear, bind the tongue, let truth be near."

I repeated the spell, slowly and with intention, focusing on the words. Just as I was finishing the third round, a sound caught my attention.

A man stepped into the room, directly into my circle, and stared down at the acorn on the floor, a question on his face.

"No." I gasped, my eyes widening as his face turned up from the floor, his eyes meeting mine.

"What are you—"

"Torin." I gawked.

"Not you," Torin Cattanach, the man whose relation-ship I'd seemingly ruined, gaped at me in surprise. "Bloody hell, Liora, but you've gotten even more beautiful than the last time I saw you."

"What? You think I'm beautiful?" It felt like a record

scratching as awkward silence filled the room. The last time I'd seen Torin he'd been berating me for destroying his relationship with Avery.

"Wait. What?" Torin looked down at himself, askance, dismay on his face. "Did I just say that out loud?"

The truth spell. *Shite, shite, shite.*

"Um, aye, you did." I pressed my lips together, suddenly very nervous. Torin wasn't the type of man to play around with, if I remembered correctly. He was gruff, terse, and often downright short with people.

"That's... odd. Damn it, why are you here? And what am I supposed to do with a freaking goddess living under my roof?" Torin's face filled with horror, and he slapped his hand over his mouth, looking down at the acorn on the floor to where I stood, gaping at him, a thousand emotions running through me. "Bloody hell, woman, what have you done to me?"

CHAPTER FOUR

TORIN

Liora ... *bloody* ... Webster.

My new tenant.

The universe must hate me. Not only did my favorite chainsaw break today, but I had to come home to... whatever *this* was.

A mess I'd created.

It had seemed simple enough. I'd let part of the house to a roommate, make a bit of extra cash for my mum, who refused to take any money from me, so I had to come up with a harebrained scheme of sharing her house with a renter to get her to accept help. She'd moved into an assisted living village, one where she could still be independent, but also have care if needed. Her Parkinson's was progressing, but she was hanging on to her independence for as long as she could. I'd offered to get her in-home help, but she'd decided she preferred the social atmosphere of a community, and so far her updates had proven she'd chosen well.

I was also lying about what I was charging for rent to my new tenant. I was giving my mother quadruple what I was charging, simply explaining that was the cost of rent these days, and she was happy to have the cash. It was easier that way, for both of us, but I hadn't expected Liora Webster to be my new tenant.

Why hadn't I asked more questions? My mate had told me about a lass moving back to town, she'd been here before, and I hadn't much questioned it. I was rarely home as it was, so it didn't much matter to me who moved in.

I could kick myself now for not having asked for more details.

This woman was a walking disaster. She'd singlehandedly exploded my relationship with Avery, which, at the time, I had thought was going well. Dating in a small town was hard enough, so I'd been actively trying to make things work with Avery, until she'd come home one day slinging accusations about me being in love with her good friend, Liora.

I mean, hell, I wasn't blind. Of course, Liora was stunning. But I was never one to look outside my relationship for excitement. Being accused of cheating had stung me to my core, not to mention having to live with the false accusation long after Avery had broken up with me and moved out of Loren Brae. That's the thing about rumors, they stick to you like a cobweb, and years later I was caught, still trying to untangle myself from them.

And now sexy Liora was here? Living with me?

Bloody hell, this was not going to look good.

"You can't stay here," I said, rubbing my hand across my chin, as I studied the gorgeous chaotic mess of a woman standing in the middle of the room, gaping at me, an acorn on the floor between us. I didn't even want to know what she was doing with the acorn. If I asked, it would be some long-winded confusing explanation that would end up annoying me even further. As I recalled, it had always been like that with Liora. She'd always been involved in some mess or another, and many a night Avery and I had stayed up late with her, talking her through whatever mess she'd landed herself in that week.

Which was certainly not the energy I needed in my life.

No, what I needed, right now, was for her to leave.

Liora sucked in a breath, and despite my frustration with the situation, I couldn't help but notice how the deep inhale made her generous breasts rise. Tearing my eyes away from her lush body, I looked around the room.

Several boxes lay open, books and photographs scattered about, and a lacy bra in vibrant pink hung from the doorknob to the bedroom. Images of my hands cupping Liora's breasts flooded my mind, that soft pink mouth of hers hot on mine, and I swallowed, pushing the thoughts away.

It had been far too long since I'd been with a woman.

That was all.

This desire certainly had nothing to do with Liora and must have everything to do with the fact that I'd been in a dry spell of all dry spells. After Avery and I had broken it off, I'd dated lightly, until I'd fallen into another relationship with a sweet woman who was a teacher two towns over. Liz had been nice enough, but nice didn't carry a relationship, and it had fizzled out in a natural and comfortable way for the both of us. We'd parted amicably about a year ago, and I hadn't seen or heard from her since.

And suddenly my desire for a woman's touch had to come roaring back when Liora of all people stood in the middle of my house, nervously chewing on her full lower lip.

I wanted to be the one to bite into her lip.

Shocked at my thoughts, I scowled down at the acorn.

"What... is that?" I pointed at the acorn, since Liora didn't seem inclined to address my statement about her needing to leave.

"That is an acorn," Liora said, carefully. She slanted a look up at me. Her eyes were the light blue of summer sky just after the sunset fades. Soft and searching, framed by spiky dark lashes.

"I'm aware that it's an acorn. Why is it in the middle of the floor?" I asked.

I'd felt *something*, when I'd walked through the door.

I hadn't meant to intrude, but the door to her wing was wide open, and I wasn't used to having a roommate yet. So I'd just walked in without knocking, and I'd felt something weird. Like a rush of energy across my skin. Maybe it had been my senses trying to warn me that Liora was here.

Or maybe she was up to something.

Something ... unusual.

Loren Brae was steeped in magick. It was impossible to live here and not be aware of that. But I'd worked as a forester most of my life, and when I immersed in the forest, it was hard to ignore the things I would hear and see. There was more to this world than I could ever possibly understand, so I always made sure to stay on the good side of whatever magickal folk roamed our woods.

"Um, decorating?" Liora suggested, and I made a rude noise.

"You can't stay here," I reiterated, in case she hadn't heard me the first time.

"You don't want me to stay?" Liora looked up at me, her expression crestfallen, her soulful blue eyes watering.

"Of course I want you to stay, but you can't." I jerked and slapped a hand over my mouth. Had I just said that out loud? What was happening to me?

Amusement danced across Liora's pretty face and was quickly dashed when I glowered at her.

"I'm confused. Do you want me to stay or to leave?" Liora tilted her chin up at me.

"I want you to stay." Again, shock filled me. Where were these words coming from? What she needed was to leave. I wasn't remotely in the mood for being the source of town gossip once again. And yet here I was, my mouth saying what logic was telling me would be a bad decision.

"Great, then I'll stay." Liora beamed at me, like sunshine spearing through the trees, and I gaped at her.

"What is happening?" I demanded. "Why am I saying exactly what I shouldn't be saying? What I should be saying is that I don't want you to stay because I don't want to become a part of the village gossip mill once again. Yet all I can seem to say is that I want you to stay."

"That's nice, isn't it then?" Liora toed the floor in fuzzy purple socks, looking everywhere but at me.

"Liora," I growled, and her eyes snapped back to my face.

"Oh, um." Liora shrugged one shoulder, sheepish, and her eyes darted away again.

"Bloody hell, woman. You've done something. Haven't you?" I pointed at the acorn. "This isn't here by chance, is it?"

"No, not entirely."

"Not entirely or not at all?" I demanded, my pulse picking up. I *knew it*. Liora had always been one for witchy things, leaning hard into her astrology and tarot, and God knows what else.

"Um, not at all?" Liora asked.

I closed my eyes and counted to ten, though every ounce of me wanted to throttle her.

"Tell me, exactly, what you were doing."

"Is that part of the lease agreement? That I have to explain everything I do in my space?" Liora crossed her arms over her chest, a stubborn look crossing her face, and she pushed that full lower lip out in a small pout.

"Of course not," I said. "If I'd known it was you signing the lease, I'd have written a spanking clause into it."

Liora's mouth dropped open.

I froze.

This was not good. Whatever was happening to me was *so* not good. At all. I couldn't possibly have just suggested that I wanted to spank Liora for violating any terms of the lease. Yet the image of bending her over the couch and dropping her jeans made me just a touch dizzy.

I needed to focus.

"Is that ... is that something you like to do to women?" Liora asked, her voice breathier than normal. Her eyes had widened.

"Yes." I slapped a hand across my mouth and shook my head. Removing my hand, I took a deep breath. "No. Yes. It depends."

"Depends on what?" Liora's eyes narrowed.

"I don't know." I threw up my hands. I couldn't believe I was having this conversation. What was happening to me? "The woman. What we're doing. If she likes it. If she asks for it. Probably a million other factors that I can't think about right now because all I can think about is the fact that I'm pretty sure you've done something to me. Have you?"

"Ummmm..." Liora drew the word out, her teeth working into that full bottom lip again, and I groaned.

She *had*.

She'd done something to me.

"Just tell me," I said, hands clenched at my sides.

"I was just trying out a wee spell from my gran's book. It was meant to be—"

"A spell?" I groaned, closing my eyes. "I bloody well knew it. I knew it. The energy was just different when I walked in here."

"You did?" Liora sounded more delighted than worried, and I opened my eyes to glare at her. "I mean, och, *that's* interesting."

"What kind of spell was it, Liora?" I gave her a look that I sincerely hoped would make her be straight with me.

"Um." Liora gulped. "A truth spell."

"A truth spell?" A prickle of warning went down my back. Surely she didn't mean...

"Aye. As in ... you always tell the truth." Liora's voice dropped to a whisper, and she grimaced.

"I don't lie, anyway. So that shouldn't be a problem. Right?" I raised my voice slightly. Worry pinged through me. I didn't like the idea of not being in control of my words.

"Well, there's not lying, and then there's inside thoughts that should best be kept ... inside." Liora's teeth dug into that plush bottom lip of hers again and heat flashed through me.

"Like how I'd love to see your mouth wrapped around—"

"Aye, like that," Liora said, hurriedly interrupting me, her skin flushing a delicious shade of pink. "Also, *really*? And why? I thought you hated me."

I started to say that I *did* hate her, but the words physically wouldn't come out of me. Instead my mouth opened, and a small guttural sound came out, but no words.

Bloody hell. I couldn't say that I hated her because I didn't.

Even if I thought that I did. Even though I blamed her for the breakup of my relationship. I didn't, at my core, really hate Liora. She'd been an easy person to blame, particularly when rumors had followed me for years after, but I didn't hate her. It took a lot for me to *actually* hate someone.

"I don't hate you," I admitted. "But I hate what your actions left me with. A broken relationship and everyone in town thinking I'd cheated on Avery. It was right shite."

"I'm..." Liora's face fell. "I guess I didn't think about how that affected you."

"Well, it wasn't great, was it? And then you left. So did Avery. And I was here. Left to deal with the aftermath." I raised a hand, cutting off whatever she was going to say next. It didn't matter. She might have magick, but she couldn't change the past. At least not that I knew of. What I needed to know was how to fix the spell I'd walked into.

Damn it all to hell and back. How had I gotten myself into this situation? Not only was I sharing my home with Liora, but she was actively practicing magick. Surely I should be able to boot her out for breaking some type of clause in the lease.

"Torin, I—"

"Just fix this. I don't even know how I feel about you doing magick in my house, but so far it doesn't seem to be going well. Which tracks for you, if the past is any indication of how things will go."

Liora winced, and I immediately felt bad for my words. But not bad enough to take them back.

"Listen, let me just see what I can find in the book to reverse this. Surely there's a remedy and we'll get you sorted in no time."

"I would certainly hope you have a remedy." My mouth dropped open as Liora's gaze shifted away from mine. "Tell me you can fix this."

"Um, I'm not quite sure. I just sort of picked it at random. I've only just discovered this book, you ken? It was in a box with my gran's stuff, and I saw my name written in it. Look!" Liora grabbed a leather book from the table and paged to the front. Turning, she showed me her name scrawled next to a list of others. "See? It's meant for me. I just ... I haven't quite had time to read it yet. I only just found it."

"So instead of reading it through you just decided to

flip to a page and try out a spell with zero preparation or research?" I raised an eyebrow at her, and she swallowed, her face growing pinker by the minute.

"I'm sorry! I ..." Liora bit her lip again and I almost groaned.

"Stop biting your lip. It's distracting." I blanched as I realized I'd spoken my inside thoughts out loud again.

"Distracting, how?" Liora's eyes widened and she licked her lips.

"That's even worse." I pointed at her mouth in frustration.

"Wait, but, why?" Liora genuinely looked confused, and I groaned out loud as I realized she didn't understand that I was finding her both wildly distracting and desperately attractive.

"Just fix this. Now." I needed to get away, to think, to clear my head so I could figure out what the hell this meant for me.

Not just the fact that I was blurting out inappropriate comments at my tenant, but the fact that Liora was living in my house. I couldn't have picked a more distractingly chaotic person if I had tried.

Not to mention, what was Loren Brae going to think of this? It certainly wouldn't paint the past rumors about me in a good light.

Growling with frustration, I stormed out, slamming the door behind me, and stomped across the kitchen to my bedroom.

I was going to kill Ross for putting me in this situation.

LIORA

I reached for my phone to call my sister and then stopped, dropping my hand back to my side. I couldn't keep calling Zara to rescue me from every situation I stumbled my way into.

Nope, this one was all on me.

And I needed to find a solution fast, or Torin was going to boot me out on my bum. I was surprised he hadn't already, if the fury in his expression was any indication of how he felt about having me as his new roommate.

Not to mention that wee truth spell that had knocked him back a step when he'd crossed into my circle.

Stupid, stupid, stupid.

What had I been thinking?

Of course the spell needed a subject to work on. What?

Why was I even trying a spell that had nowhere to go? Nowhere to land? I'd been caught up in the excitement of finding my name in the book and maybe, just for once, having an answer to why my magick couldn't ever seem to work. And instead, I'd just made the situation worse.

Per usual.

Sighing, I slumped back onto the couch and pulled my feet up, cradling the book in my lap.

"Bloody hell, Liora, but you've gotten even more beautiful than the last time I saw you."

My body flushed with heat as Torin's words came back to me. Had he really meant that? Obviously he had, as the truth spell was working, and he seemed furious about what had come out of his mouth. Which meant, Torin, a man who could easily be a cover model for Lumberjack Monthly or whatever manly magazines were out there, thought *I*, Liora Webster with the mousy hair and messy magick, was beautiful.

Honestly? The thought didn't even compute. It was so at odds that someone as visually stunning as Torin—I'd just leave out his abrasive personality—would find me beautiful.

Last year I'd stumbled across a woman on TikTok who watched videos of this man chopping wood with his shirt off and pretended to be solely interested in his axe-wielding technique and not the muscles rippling down his bare chest. It had made me laugh, but then I'd found myself thinking how much the man had reminded me of Torin.

Broad, strong shoulders.

Thick muscly arms.

Dark chestnut hair, searing blue eyes, and the swagger of a man used to carrying an axe around.

Or a chainsaw, for that matter.

Sighing, I let my head fall back on the cushions and closed my eyes. Torin was a forester, used to walking among the trees, and not one for idle chitchat if I recalled. I wished I could remember his birth date, but I was betting he was a Taurus or at least had a Cancer Moon. Avery had been head over heels for him, or so I'd thought, until she'd been willing to let the relationship break up over an astrology reading. Or perhaps there'd been more, but she hadn't spoken to me about it.

She hadn't spoken to me at all.

It had hurt to lose one of my only good friends in a town as small as Loren Brae, and when she'd packed up and moved on, I'd done the same, needing a fresh start elsewhere.

Apparently, Torin had been left to deal with the brunt of our choices. Sympathy filled me. Frankly, it wasn't fun to be the center of gossip and rumors, that much I knew, and when he hadn't even done anything to deserve them? Well, I guess I could understand why he wasn't exactly thrilled to see me standing in the middle of his house.

I looked around the room. The furnishings were somewhat simple, but still comfortable, and the house itself exuded warmth. It was a place to start fresh, a safe haven to ground myself, and I didn't want to leave. What I needed to do was find a solution to the truth spell, fix Torin, and beg him to let me stay in the flat.

An hour later, I was still paging through the book and not finding anything about how to undo that particular spell. Sure, there were ways to generically reverse a spell, but I'd lost my confidence. What if, in the undoing, I made the situation worse? Already Torin had next to zero patience with me. I was certain he wouldn't allow me to keep practicing unknown spells on him.

Plus, I'd discovered two more books in the boxes, both of which held numerous spells, recipes, journals, and other words of wisdom. It would take me days to get through it all.

I stared off into space, my mind whirling, as I tried to come up with a solution that would suit us both and not leave me homeless. My eyes landed on my open duffle bag on the floor, a tattered romance book tilting out of the open top.

My eyes widened.

Could it work? Or would he throw me out of the house?

From what I'd remembered, Torin had been more bark than bite. Though he was intimidating, both in manner and physical form, I also remembered the time he'd helped bottle-feed a kitten that Avery had rescued from behind a garbage bin on the street.

Standing, I went to the small bathroom and sighed at my appearance. Dust smudged one cheek, and my hair was tousled in a messy knot on my head. If I was going to propose what I thought would be a viable solution to buy me some time, I needed to at least make myself presentable. Grabbing my makeup bag, I dashed some blush onto my cheeks, lined and smudged my eyes to make them a touch bigger, and ran my fingers through my hair to detangle it and leave it softly floating around my shoulders. I changed into a soft, siren-red jumper, one of my favorite vintage finds, and slicked clear lip gloss across my lips. When finished, I studied my face in the mirror. Subtly sexy, well at least as sexy as I could get, approachable, and hopefully sufficiently put together to convince this man to let me stay in his house until I got my shite together.

When I eased the door open and peeked out, I found Torin eating soup and a massive sandwich at the big table, a fire dancing in the grate. Rock music, turned low, played in the background, and he scrolled through an iPad in front of him. Edging closer, I saw it was stock reports.

Of course the man was into investing.

It was so adult of him.

Which in fairness, he was.

As was I.

He had to be in his early thirties by now, though I couldn't quite remember his exact age. I'd turned thirty earlier this year. Which was why I knew that I needed to figure out what I was doing with my life. At times I still felt like a kid, fresh out of school, the whole world in front of me. Yet many of my friends were married, even mothers now, and well into their careers. While I floundered, latching myself to, apparently, the wrong career path. Everyone always said to do what you love and the money would follow, unfortunately, I just hadn't found that to be the case for me.

"Are you just going to stand there staring at me, or are you going to come in?"

I jumped at Torin's gruff voice, the sound sending a shiver of awareness down my back, and I edged closer to the table.

"Um, so I was thinking…"

Torin glanced up, his gaze slicing through me, and gestured to his pint glass.

"Beer?"

"No, I just—"

"Wine?" Torin stood and I watched, flabbergasted, as he went to an actual wine cabinet and pulled out a bottle. "Red suit you?"

"Um, sure." It wouldn't hurt, that was for sure. "Thank you." Why was he doing a one-eighty and serving me wine now? Confused, I bit my lower lip and stood, hands linked behind my back.

"Did you eat?"

"Eat?" I couldn't follow what was happening. An hour ago he was shouting at me and now he wanted to feed me?

"Aye. Food? The stuff that gives you sustenance and keeps you alive." Torin angled his head toward a pot on the stove. "I've plenty of soup left. Potato leek. Help yourself."

My stomach grumbled in response, and Torin sighed and put the wine bottle down next to a glass on the counter. Moving to the stove, he ladled out a bowl of soup, sliced off a thick hunk of crusty bread, and plopped it down at a seat across from him on the table.

"Sit."

I did as I was told, my heart hammering in my chest, as he poured me a glass of wine and then returned to the table, sliding into the seat across from me. He'd changed into loose grey joggers, and a hooded sweatshirt, and I wanted to crawl onto his lap and wrap my arms around his neck.

Shocked at the thought, I reached for my wine and took

a healthy gulp, needing to think about anything else than just how freaking gorgeous this man was.

"Slàinte," Torin said, dryly, raising his glass to me, and I winced. I tilted my glass at his and swallowed against the awkwardness that now clogged my throat.

"Sorry, I should have thanked you first. It's been … an unsettling day."

"I'd say." Torin sighed and picked up his spoon, gesturing at me with it. "Eat."

"Oh, aye. Thanks." We ate in silence for a few moments, until Torin had finished his meal, and I'd made my way through most of the soup. My nerves were scrambling as I searched for a way to propose my, admittedly, outlandish temporary solution to the truth spell problem.

"I need you to stay."

I blinked at Torin's words, my head coming up from where I'd been staring forlornly at my soup bowl, and took in his tense expression.

"You do?" I asked, incredulous.

"Aye, you're a solution to a problem I have."

I waited and a log snapped in the fireplace behind me. Torin's face was all angles and shadows, the firelight flickering over the sharp edge of his jaw.

"That's it? You're not going to tell me more?" I raised an eyebrow at him. "What's the problem?"

Torin opened his mouth to speak, and then glowered at me, and I realized he'd been about to put off answering my question, but the truth spell wasn't going to allow him to do so. He, seemingly, had come to the same realization and raked a hand through his hair as he leaned back in the chair.

"This was my parents' house." Torin gestured with his

pint glass to the room. "My dad passed a few years back and my mum needed to move into assisted living for her Parkinson's. I rent this from her, but she refuses to take much from me. She also won't let me help with the cost of the assisted care community she's chosen. The only way around that I've found is to have a tenant that I can collect rent from. Since she hasn't asked to see the lease, she hasn't questioned the amount of rent I'm giving to her."

Understanding filled me. "So you're giving her far more than I'm paying, aren't you?"

"Indeed." Torin's expression was inscrutable, but I couldn't help but warm toward a man so willing to go to uncomfortable lengths to help his mother. He clearly didn't need a roommate but had been willing to open his home to one if it meant helping his mum.

"But..."

"But I don't know if you're the answer. I don't know how I feel about Loren Brae knowing you're living here. And frankly, I'm not sure how much your chaotic energy will disrupt my life." Torin squeezed his eyes shut as he realized what he'd said. "Sorry. That whole truth spell thing."

"It's okay." I slumped back into my chair, deflated. "You're not wrong. Chaos seems to follow me wherever I go."

"I like a simple life," Torin said. "Quiet. Unbothered. I like to be in the trees. I have more work than I know what to do with. I'm not home much. But when I am ..."

"You want peace and quiet." I understood what he was saying. Which meant he was also going to flip when he heard what I had in mind. "But don't you get lonely? Do you go out much?"

"Here and there. I'll grab a pint with the lads when I've got time. But until you can fix this spell issue, I'm not sure I'll be going out much, no."

I noticed Torin didn't answer my question about if he got lonely or not. I guess that was one way to get around the truth spell. He could just choose not to answer a question.

"So..."

Torin pinned me with his gaze, and I gulped, nerves pinging around in my stomach and making me fidget in my chair.

"Spit it out," Torin ordered.

"I wasn't able to find a direct solution to the truth spell issue. Yet." I winced as Torin's face hardened. "I did find some options for reversing spells, generically, but I'm worried that I could inadvertently make the situation worse. I'd like to proceed with caution."

"Then I'm stuck? How am I meant to go out in public? What do I say when Mrs. MacPherson at the shops asks me to go on a date with her daughter, who I'm fairly certain isn't into men at all?"

"Um, you can say you're busy?" I took a deep breath. It was now or never. "Or, you could say... that you were already dating someone."

"Who? That would be lying." Torin looked at me like I was not the sharpest knife in the drawer.

"Um, me?" I suggested and Torin jumped out of the chair, shocking me with his movements.

"You?" he shouted and I winced, gritting my teeth together. "Do you have any idea how that would look?"

"Admittedly, not great, but I'm sure it would be fine. In

time," I said, folding the paper napkin he'd given me in half. And then half again as he paced.

"How does that even make sense, Liora? Please. Make it make sense for me."

"It wouldn't be real dating," I rushed to explain, folding the napkin faster so I could get my words out. "It would be fake dating. Just until we get the truth spell turned around."

"How does that even make sense?" Torin scoffed, and tears stung my eyes.

I'd never been great at keeping my emotions in check when someone was mad at me.

"I mean, it sounded like you find me attractive. So you wouldn't have to worry about saying the wrong thing to someone else. You could just say you were dating me, and nobody would be the wiser, right?"

"Of all the wild ideas..." Torin stopped his pacing and gaped at me. "You want to fake date? After the whole town thought I cheated with you years ago? Simply because you think that I'm attracted to you?"

"I mean, not only because of that. It was just ... you said some pretty explicit stuff about me earlier ... so it seemed like ... and it could explain why I was living here ... and I ... it was just a thought ... I don't know..." Helplessness reared up in me, and then a tear spilled over, streaking down my cheek, and I sniffed, furious with myself for even proposing such an idea.

"You're crying?" Torin shouted, incredulous, and I hung my head, another tear dripping down my cheek.

"Aye," I whispered, unfolding the napkin to dash at my cheeks.

"Bloody hell, woman." Torin rounded the table and surprised me by dropping to his knees by my chair. "Please don't cry. I can't handle it."

"I can't help it. I don't do well with people getting mad at me." I sniffed and tried to hold my emotions back as a sob welled in my throat. It was more than just Torin shouting at me. I'd had a shite few weeks. How had I even gotten myself into this position?

"I'm not mad ..." I looked down at where Torin's face contorted, and then he stopped as the truth spell prevented him from completing the sentence. Then he sighed and tried again. "Right. I *am* mad at you, but not in the way you probably think. I'm just not super pleased with this situation, okay? It's messy and I like neat and orderly. All of a sudden I can't control what I'm saying, I have the most beautiful woman I've ever seen in real life living in my house, and now you want to pretend to date."

My mouth fell open at the same time as Torin's and he swore roundly, standing back up to pace the room.

"What the hell, Liora? How am I supposed to live around you when I say things like that?"

"I mean, I'm not mad about you saying those things," I admitted, wiping my eyes. "It's nice to hear someone actually thinks I'm pretty."

"What's that supposed to mean?" Distracted, Torin whirled and braced his arms on the table, glowering down at me.

"It's just ... I'm not conventionally pretty." I shrugged and stopped myself. The last thing we needed was to parade all my faults this evening. I'd already had enough embarrassment for the day, hadn't I?

"And who, in their right mind, wants conventionally pretty?" Torin's brow furrowed in confusion. "Your beauty is unusual, eye-catching, like the sun creating a rainbow in the dew clinging to a spider's web at dawn."

I froze, physically unable to speak, as he stared at me, his eyes unreadable.

Was that really what he thought of me? Nobody had ever compared me to such a fragile and delicate beauty before and I had no idea how to respond. My heart hammered, and I heaved in a breath, unsure of how to proceed.

Torin swallowed and visibly composed himself.

"So. There's that. I see how this truth spell situation could cause quite a problem." Torin turned and began to pace again while my thoughts scrambled to come back from being called beautiful. By him.

"I just thought fake dating might cover the situation for a bit, but it was probably a stupid idea." I laughed at myself and took a wobbly gulp of my wine. "Just another hare-brained scheme, I guess."

"But it would have to be real, for it to work."

I froze and turned to where Torin now stood, his back to me, staring at the fire. Had he just said he wanted to really date me? I stood, and taking my wine glass with me, walked over so I could see his expression as he stared into the fire.

"What do you mean by that, exactly?" I asked.

"It's just that if anyone asked me if we were dating, and I couldn't lie, I'd have to tell them we were fake dating. So it doesn't really help, does it? Unless we date. For real." Torin lifted his head and looked at me, and I could see the flames flickering in the reflection in his eyes.

It mirrored the flames flickering in my tummy.

Was he proposing we actually date? No, he couldn't possibly be. He just needed to word it that way so he would not lie to anyone. But I would know it was fake. And surely, on some level, he would know that as well.

"But ... what would that look like? How would it be real? If it's ... not." I stopped, feeling awkward. Turning, I plopped down onto his couch and finished my glass of wine, leaning over to put the empty glass on the table. Torin snapped to attention, and without asking, he picked up my glass and crossed the room. I turned, watching how he moved through the space, confident and comfortable, even though his body radiated tension. Opening another beer, he poured it into a pint glass and filled my wine glass before returning to the couch with our drinks.

"I don't know." Torin sat across from me, and I cradled my wine glass, watching as the fire lit the warm liquid in the glass. "But it might work. It would explain you living here without me having to discuss my mum's finances and medical woes with the world, and it would be easy enough to explain anything untoward I said about my attraction to you."

"You're really attracted to me?" I couldn't help but fixate on that last part. My stomach twisted, but not with nerves this time. Something else pulled at me, long and liquid and lovely, and I couldn't help but shift on the couch, crossing my legs more tightly. It had been a very long time since I'd dated anyone. *Years?* No one had taken me, my work, seriously. So, I'd stopped trying. I hadn't realized until this moment how I'd missed feeling as though I was attractive to a man.

"It's impossible not to be." Torin shrugged away my question as if it was a given.

I honestly had no words. I could not believe that this gorgeous, confident man, was attracted to *me*. I had so many more questions. I opened my mouth to ask if he'd always been attracted to me but stopped when Torin held up a finger.

"Don't, Liora." Torin's voice rasped, and he took a sip of his beer. "Don't ask questions you don't want the answers to."

"But what if I do want the answers?"

Torin leveled a look at me from across the couch and desire speared inside me.

"I'd ask that you respect me, as a person, who'd like some privacy with his thoughts and feelings. It's not fair that I can't protect what I'm thinking and saying because of a spell that you've wielded. It wouldn't be right of you to take advantage of that by digging into all the corners of my brain, would it?"

"Och, Torin." I gasped and put my wine down. Leaning over, I patted his arm. "I'm *so* sorry. I didn't even think about it like that. Of course, I shouldn't be asking invasive questions if you have no choice in how you answer them. That's entirely too intrusive and, bloody hell, what was I thinking? I'm sorry. I'll have to get adjusted to the idea that I have to be careful in my line of questioning since you've got no filter now. I'm sorry. I am. Truly. I'll do better."

"Thank you. It's a bit of a mind fuck to not be able to filter my thoughts right now."

Torin met my eyes and silence filled the room and something warm and heavy hung in the air between us. I realized I was still touching him, my hand curved partly around his massive bicep, and I eased it off, breaking the contact.

Though I was definitely going to spend the rest of the evening thinking about how he said he was attracted to me. Because, holy hell, how could I not? He was the type of man bound to invade my deepest fantasies, and I knew I'd have a hard time falling asleep later with his image branded on my mind.

"So. It's agreed then?" Torin pulled me from my thoughts, and I blinked at him, confused.

"Agreed?"

"We're dating." Torin put his beer down on the table. "At least until we figure out a solution to the truth spell."

"What if it takes a long time?" I asked, worried. Leaning over, I set my glass on the table and sat back, twisting a sterling silver and amethyst ring I wore on my thumb.

"Then we date for a long time." Torin startled me by sliding across the couch and putting an arm around the back of the cushion behind me.

My eyes widened and my breath caught as I turned to look up at him. Every nerve ending in my body came to life, and I was equal parts terrified and excited by his closeness.

He smelled like newly chopped wood and soap, a fresh intoxicating scent, and I bit my lower lip, nerves working their way through me.

"Och, that lip." Torin glowered, his eyes on my mouth.

"What... what are you doing?" I asked, surprised at his nearness.

"If we're dating, we have to get comfortable with being close to each other. And usually, I would kiss my date at the end of the night."

"Wait," I said, slamming a hand on his chest. My hand met a wall of steel. *Bloody hell but the man was ripped.* "You haven't taken me out to dinner yet."

"Aye, but I did. Didn't I feed you?" Torin leaned closer, a devilish smile dancing on his lips, and I sucked in a small breath, torn between laughter and anxiety.

"You did but ..." His mouth hovered over mine.

"Say, thank you, Torin."

"Thank you, Torin," I whispered and then his lips were on mine.

The kiss shocked me. As in, sent a physical shock straight through my body. I jolted against him, and his hands came to my shoulders, steadying me, as his lips explored mine. Softly, he pressed against me, his teeth scraping my lower lip, and he sucked gently. Desire pooled low in my belly, molten and slow, and my fingers curled helplessly into the front of his shirt.

Torin kissed like he spoke—controlled, sure, but with something unruly simmering underneath. His mouth brushed mine again, softer this time, as if savoring the taste of me, and the gentleness of it undid me far more than any wild, demanding kiss could.

"Torin ..." I breathed into his mouth, not even sure what I meant to say.

He hummed, a low sound that vibrated against my lips, and his hand slid from my shoulder to cradle the side of my neck. His thumb stroked just under my jaw, guiding me closer, and he let the moment stretch. His lips parted such that a whisper of breath mingled with mine, the tender press of him coaxing me into leaning in for more.

I kissed him back. Carefully at first, then with a helpless, aching hunger I didn't mean to reveal. His lips curved against mine, as if he felt the same, and that tiny, wicked smile made nerves swoop low in my stomach.

When he finally pulled back, it was only by a breath. His forehead rested lightly against mine, our noses brushing, our breaths tangling in the inch of space he'd left between us.

"Liora," he murmured, voice rough, "you're trouble."

I swallowed hard. My heart thudded too fast, too loud. My whole body felt tuned to him, aware of every point of contact, every shared breath, every inch of him still caging me in that easy, devastating way.

He wasn't just attractive. He wasn't just charming. He wasn't just a man temporarily without a filter. He was a danger to my attempt to get my life together, to finding out who I was and what I wanted.

I eased back so I could meet his gaze.

"I think," I whispered, my words faltering, "I may be in over my head with you."

Torin's smile was wicked and yet, unbearably tender.

"Aye," he murmured, thumb brushing my lower lip where his teeth had been seconds before. "That makes two of us."

I took a deep breath to steady myself as he eased back and then stood, looking at me like I was dinner and he hadn't eaten in days. He shook his head, clearly arguing with himself, and stepped farther back from the couch.

"Och, and Liora?"

"Aye?" My breath caught.

"The fake dating idea is dumb."

"Then why did you kiss me?" I asked, indignant.

"Because I've been wanting to for years now." Torin's grin flashed wide in his handsome face. *He had?* Confused, but at the same time, interested, I watched as he whistled his way down the hallway toward his bedroom.

Bloody hell. What had I gotten myself into now?

CHAPTER SIX

Liora

Despite being certain that I wouldn't be able to sleep a wink the night before, I'd fallen into a deep sleep filled with aching dreams where Torin carried me away over his shoulder like a caveman and had his way with me against a tree deep in the shadowy privacy of a thick forest.

I'd woken, aroused and certain I could still feel the press of rough bark at my back as he'd taken me with abandon, his strong arms keeping my legs braced around him.

Seriously, just what had I gotten myself into?

When I'd peeked out into the kitchen this morning, nerves humming, I'd been happy to find a note from Torin with his phone number, telling me he had appointments most of the day and wouldn't be home until late. It was sweet, and somewhat cozy, and so what if I'd folded the note and tucked it into my handbag to save for later?

I'd always been one to fall hard and fast for my boyfriends. It was another thing that Zara took issue with about my choices. I just didn't know any other way. Maybe it was my impulsive nature, or maybe it was my natural optimism, but I typically blew past red flags like a race car at the starting line and didn't look back until everything had imploded in my face.

So, maybe I really need to take stock of what had happened yesterday and figure out how to calmly maneuver this new wrinkle in my life with Torin. *And work out how to tell Zara.* There was no need to proceed too fast, since we technically weren't really dating, even though he was telling himself we were. It just helped him with telling the truth, was all. This wasn't real.

Even though the kiss had felt very, very real. *Why had he kissed me like that?* I hadn't seen Torin for years and yet within moments of seeing him again, he kissed me. Kissed. Me. Even though he'd been so angry with me. This was strange, right? *Because I'd wanted to for years.*

I hoped he'd be okay today, out in the world with no filter. Luckily, he worked largely on his own, at least that I knew of, but I realized I needed to ask more about what he did for his job. If we were to be dating, publicly, then we needed to know what the other did for a living.

Which meant ... it was also time for me to try and seek employment.

But first, coffee.

Torin had left the coffee pot on, a serviceable no frills style coffee maker, and I poured myself a cup and wandered to the back door to stare out into the forest. Was he working in the woods today? Or did appointments mean he met with clients? I remembered how in demand his services would be after an intense storm, so I was guessing that appointments meant private clients. Instead of commercial? I truly had no idea the scope of his job, which I would need to remedy soon enough. Maybe I needed to create a dating quiz of sorts for him, like fifty first date questions, so we could answer any questions about the other if it came up in public.

A squirrel ran out into the yard and stopped, looking directly at me.

Was that Bracken? I unlocked and opened the back door, stepping quietly outside so as not to scare the squirrel away. The morning air was crisp, the promise of winter ever closer, and I shivered.

"Bracken?" I asked, cupping both my hands around my coffee mug for warmth.

"Aye. It's me." Bracken tilted his head inquisitively, like I'd been the one to stop him mid-task with a question I needed answering.

"So, um, how's it going?" I winced, slightly embarrassed. I really wasn't sure how I was meant to be communicating with a squirrel.

"I am well, Liora." Bracken made a soft chittering sound, and I couldn't be sure, but it sounded like he might be laughing at me.

"Listen, I have no idea what to ask a squirrel. Like, how's the foraging going?" I asked, amused.

"It's well, thank you. I've got quite a good store for winter."

I immediately felt chagrined. I'd been teasing a bit, but the reality was the squirrel was needing to put food away to feed himself for months at a time. I couldn't even plan out my next week.

Even Bracken had his life together.

"What did you mean when you said that I was yours?" I decided to cut to the chase, as the wind had picked up slightly, and my pajamas were threadbare.

"I've been waiting for you, Liora. I'm here to help."

"Help how? With what?"

"You." Bracken made that soft chittering sound again and his fluffy tail bounced behind him.

"Is it a tiny oracle you are then?" I tilted my head, amusement filling me. "You've got the answers to all my problems?"

"I might. I might not. Answers are like acorns."

"Is that right?" I laughed, delighted with the way my morning was going already. How could I be glum? Here I was having a cup of coffee that I didn't have to make and talking to a squirrel on a crisp autumn morning. "And just how are answers like acorns?"

"You see … every winter I have a problem. How will I eat through the long, cold, dark days? And so, as I learn and grow through the year, I hide acorns. Every year, I find better spots to hide them. And they're only known to me. When the time comes, when I dearly need my acorn, only I know where to find it."

I blinked at him, slowly unpacking his words, and then smiled with delight.

"You are a wee oracle!"

Bracken bowed.

"At your service, madam."

"So I gotta find my acorns. And then I'll have the

answers I need." I raised my cup to him as Bracken scampered to the edge of the yard. "Hey, Bracken?"

"Aye?"

"What if you forget where you hid your acorns?"

"Then you find new ones." Bracken ran up the side of the tree and I laughed as he bounced from branch to branch, chittering at me, before turning and going back inside.

"Schooled by a squirrel first thing in the morning." I sighed and finished off my coffee. "And he's not wrong. I do need to find new acorns." Because whatever answers I'd buried deep inside myself currently weren't surfacing, and I needed solutions to problems.

The first being, gainful employment.

I wasn't going to touch astrology, no matter how much I longed to pull out my charts and have a look at the current state of affairs surrounding my life. What I did know was that it was a new moon today, so a perfect time for new beginnings, and even if waitressing wasn't my passion in life, at least it would give me stable income and a chance to immerse myself back in the community.

And to set some past rumors straight. *But now you're "dating" Torin.* How do we explain that we reconnected as soon as I arrived back in Loren Brae, and despite "the past," we felt like a good fit? *But never cheated?* Goddess, what a mess.

After a quick shower, I plaited my hair neatly back, put on my siren-red jumper again, topped it with a deep purple woolen trench coat, and shoved my feet into slouchy suede boots. With a tumble of my favorite crystal necklaces around my neck, and a malachite bracelet at my wrist, I locked up and decided to walk into Loren Brae. Torin's house wasn't all that far out of the village, and I'd tucked my brolly in my handbag in case of rain. I needed some time to center myself, to recalibrate, I supposed, as I adjusted to these new developments in my life.

I was back. In Loren Brae.

And living with my boyfriend, it seemed.

Fake boyfriend, I quickly amended, though my heart did a funny little dance at the word boyfriend. It sounded odd, like I was a teenager excited after her first kiss. At what age did we stop calling them our boyfriends? Was he my fella? My man?

Amused at myself, and trying to ignore that delicious wiggle of desire in my core as I thought about his kiss again, I turned down the lane and onto the main road that hugged the rocky shores of Loch Mirren. MacAlpine Castle held court in the hills above the village, a dowager countess watching over her people, and the sun struggled to shine through the grey clouds that clung to the horizon. Wind shifted across the loch, bringing it into a light chop, the surface looking cracked and wrinkled like a balled up piece of paper smoothed out again.

Did the Kelpies really live there?

I eyed the island, a perfect circle of land with a fortress of trees, imposing as ever. Was that why it had always made me unsettled? Because magick lived there? There was nothing untoward to be seeing at the moment. For all intents and purposes, it looked just like any other wee island in any other loch in the country.

But I could feel that it wasn't. I had always felt that way. And now that Zara had confirmed my suspicions, I took a small moment to feel validated in trusting my intuition. I hadn't had a lot of wins lately, so having the affirmation that my gut had been correct about the wee island helped boost my confidence as I made my way toward the local pub.

The Tipsy Thistle was the heartbeat of the community, a place to go to watch a match, laugh with friends, and catch up on the local gossip. If I could get a job here, it would be the fastest way to integrate myself back into Loren Brae, dispel any rumors about mine and Torin's past, and put down roots.

Even though this is meant to be temporary, I reminded myself as I opened the door to the pub. *You aren't staying.*

Technically, it was early enough that the pub wouldn't be open yet, which I realized as soon as I stepped inside to find the room empty, and a handsome man wiping down bottles and making notes in a notebook at the curved wooden bar that dominated the room. A beautiful stone fireplace was stocked with wood and ready to be lit on the other side of the room, and vintage pub signs mixed with photos of Loren Brae on the walls. Long wood beams crossed the ceiling and worn wood planks covered the floor. Music thumped softly in the background and the man grinned at me as I walked towards him, nerves tightening my throat.

"Liora!"

"Hiya, Graham." I smiled. It was impossible not to. The handsome pub owner had a wicked grin that broke the hearts of women of all ages. Endlessly charming, he was a notorious bachelor, and the town's golden boy. I wasn't sure if he'd remember me, as I hadn't been in the pub all that much, and hoped he only remembered good things.

"What brings you back to Loren Brae? I saw your sister is working at the vet's office now."

Graham reached over and offered his hand and I shook it, blinded a bit by his bright smile and cheerful countenance.

"Aye, she is. That's kind of why I'm back." No need to fill him in on any astrology drama, grabbing on to the lifeline he'd thrown me. "I wanted to be closer to Zara and Mitch."

"Are they doing all right then? They seem well enough." Graham's face creased with concern.

"Och, aye, they are. Just missing family, I guess." I shrugged one shoulder and glanced around the pub. "Say, Graham. Is there any possibility you're looking to hire servers? I ... I could dearly use the work." I hated admitting the last part, but there was no other way around it. I needed a job.

"Well now, let me have a think." Graham's eyes studied the expression on my face and I tried to appear like a hardworking, resourceful individual, and not someone desperate for a place to work. Any place to work. "Have you worked in the service industry before?"

"Aye, for years now." I smiled brightly at him. "Off and on, that is. But I've worked in everything from fine dining to a coffee shop. I never miss a shift and I make friends with everyone."

"I don't doubt it." Graham's smile widened. "You've always been a cheerful sort if I recall. You used to do readings too, didn't you? Astrology, was it?"

"Och, well, I did that a bit. Here and there." I hated dismissing my career like it was of no importance, but I'd learned that not everyone viewed astrology in the best light. Which was silly, considering how helpful it could be to others, but I'd grown used to the way people's faces would take on a knowing look when I told them what I did for a living.

"I don't know if you've heard, but things have been a bit … quieter around Loren Brae the last few years," Graham said, moving back behind the bar. "I'm not sure I'd even have enough for full-time work."

"Part-time works too," I rushed out, moving to the side of the bar and leaning against it, a plea in my voice. "Anything you could give me, really."

Graham's eyes met mine again, his gaze carefully assessing.

"I promise, I'm a hard worker," I whispered, as close to pleading as I could allow myself to get.

"I can take you on for the weekends. We still get a few tour buses through to see the castle, and they often stop by for a pint if they're not having a meal at Grasshopper."

I blinked at him, confused.

"Grasshopper is the new restaurant at MacAlpine Castle. You could also ask there for work, to make up for extra hours I cannae give you," Graham explained.

"Ah, right. I didn't know they'd opened a restaurant." Last I'd been in Loren Brae, the castle had been suffering, with interest in tours falling off and a potentially new owner on the horizon.

"There's been a few changes since you were last here."

Graham held up a hand. "Hold on a second, while I go grab the application form."

Sighing in relief, as it sounded like he'd be willing to give me work, if even for a few days a week, I settled onto a bar stool and closed my eyes. Taking in a deep breath, I dropped my guards, and let myself listen and feel the vibe of the pub. It had always been a friendly and welcoming spot, but I'd never been inside when it was almost empty before. Now, I felt like I could get a read on the energy of the place. The building, much like many of the places in Loren Brae, was several hundred years old and as far as I was concerned, every place held energy.

Not getting any bad vibes, I opened my eyes to find Graham staring at me, a bemused look on his face, a form in his hand.

"Sorry." I flushed. "Just taking in the space."

"And? How did it rate for you?" Graham asked, sliding the form across the bar to me.

"It feels good in here," I answered honestly, taking the pen he handed me. "A place for community."

"That's why I've always loved owning it," Graham admitted. "It can be a home away from home."

"Which is exactly what I'm looking for," I blurted out, and flushed again when Graham raised an eyebrow at me. "Sorry, I just meant, you know, in work. I like working at places that actually care about their clientele, their product, and the space they create."

"I can't offer more than minimum wage, at the moment, I'm afraid."

"That's fine, I'm happy to have the work."

"You'll get some tips, depending on whether tourists

come through. Those are yours to keep. The weekend shifts are long, if you get here before lunch to help set up. Food's done around nine at night, so that'll be about ten to twelve hours a shift. You reckon you're up for that?"

"No problem. I've got a good pair of trainers. They'll suit long days on my feet." I beamed up at him, doing a quick mental calculation. Three shifts a week at minimum wage should be just enough to cover rent and groceries for the month. It wouldn't leave much extra for literally anything else, but I knew how to work with a lean budget. I could walk to work, I had enough clothes, and I was excellent at making dried beans and lentils stretch into many meals.

"Your meals are covered while you're working. Lunch and dinner," Graham added, seeming to read my mind as I filled in my information on the form.

"Oh really? That's generous of you." I amended my mental calculation for my food budget. "I promise not to eat you out of the pub."

"Are you staying with Zara then? Or do you need a line on a place to rent?" Graham asked, and I froze. This was the first real test of my new "fake" dating situation I'd set out for Torin and me, and I needed to just pull the plaster off fast and get on with it.

"I'm staying at Torin's actually," I said, realizing it would be weird if I said I was renting from Torin, but also his supposed girlfriend. Though couples split rent, didn't they? I wouldn't know, I'd never moved in with a boyfriend before, but my thoughts were scrambling too fast to come up with the best answer in this moment other than to say that I was staying at his house. It answered the question without elaborating too much.

"Torin's?" Graham's eyes sharpened, and my spirits fell. It wasn't likely that Graham would have forgotten. Not when it had been the hot gossip for a while. "I haven't seen him in a while. How's he getting on?"

"Oh, um, he's grand." I blew out a small sigh of relief that it seemed that Graham was going to give me some grace and not poke too much into my personal life.

"Tell him I said hello, would you? And bring him in for a pint sometime. He's a nice lad."

"Aye, he is." That much was the truth at least. I quickly finished filling out the form and passed it back over to Graham. He took his time reading it over, nodding once or twice, and then looked up at me over the paper.

"I'll get this sorted and add you to payroll. See you Friday at half ten in the morning."

"Thank you, Graham." I hopped up and held my hand out. He shook it, his grip confident, and I smiled, relieved that something was going well in my life. "I can't tell you how much I appreciate it."

"Nae bother, hen. I could use some help around here. I've just been stubborn about adding anyone else on. You popped in at a good time. The holidays always pick up a bit."

"Great. Really looking forward to it. I'll see you on Friday." Waving goodbye, I almost ran from the pub before he could change his mind.

Thank you, new moon. I nodded my head to the sky, sending up a quick thanks, and then hustled down the street to see if I could poke my head into the vet's and tell Zara my good news. If it wasn't too busy, that was.

Rounding the corner of where the main street met the loch, I stopped in front of the vet's office. With a wide front window that looked into the practice, I could see Zara at her desk, Mitch laying on his dog bed in front of the counter. The waiting room appeared empty, so I decided to pop in.

A bell sounded my arrival, and Zara immediately stopped talking into the recorder she held in her hand. She had many tools to transcribe her voice into text, and I assumed this one would help with her notes on charts. Mitch popped his head up, and his tail wagged when he spied me.

"It's me, Zara," I said, before she could speak. "Can I greet Mitch?"

"Aye, he's off work."

"Hey, boy," I said, and Mitch jumped up and ran over to me, his butt wiggling as I rubbed my hands through his shaggy fur. Thinking about Bracken, I decided to see if I could talk to him. "Can you say hi back? Speak?"

Mitch barked, but nothing came into my mind.

Hmm, maybe I could only just hear Bracken then.

"I come to you with good news," I said, glancing around the office. It was clean, but with warm touches like a vase with flowers on the waiting room table.

And a fox sitting in the open doorway that led to the rooms behind Zara.

I gasped.

"Um, Z," I whispered, and Z stiffened, hearing the warning in my voice.

"What's wrong?" Z hissed, not moving.

"There's a fox sitting in your hallway."

"Oh." My sister visibly relaxed. "That's fine, then. That's Gloam."

"Hello, Liora."

I froze, staring as the fox prowled closer to me. Had I really just heard his voice? Glancing from my sister to the fox, and back again, I swallowed. Had I imagined his voice in my head? Were the threads of reality unraveling for me?

"Zara, is someone here? I didn't think we had any more appointments this morning." A pretty woman with dark hair and a confident air, dressed in green scrubs, poked her head out of the doorway behind the fox. "Oh, hello." An unreadable look crossed her face when she looked down at the fox and then back up at where I stood, frozen, in the waiting room. "Oh, the fox? He's harmless. Just a patient we're treating. You don't have to be scared."

"I'm not. It was just a surprise is all." Who had a pet fox? Was that even legal? Tilting my head, I tried to figure out how to attempt to communicate with it without the other two women questioning what I was doing. "He's very handsome. Aren't you? I wonder if you know how handsome you are?"

Gloam's eyes slitted, and his mouth fell open like he was laughing. *"Aye, I well know how handsome I am."*

My eyes widened. He'd really spoken. I'd heard his voice, clear as a bell, in my mind. Unsure of what to do, and not wanting to freak out in front of Zara's boss, I planted a bland smile on my face.

"Liora, this is Dr. Faelan Fletcher. Faelan, this is my sister, Liora."

"Oh, Liora! Of course, it's lovely to meet you." Faelan stepped forward, her hand out, when Gloam intercepted her. He wove himself between her legs, almost like a cat, and Faelan faltered, glancing down from him to me. "What do you mean..."

"She's one of us."

"Um." I looked desperately between the fox and Faelan, unsure of what to do. My sister's head bobbed between the two of us, a faint line forming on her forehead as she tried to figure out what was happening that she couldn't see.

"Welcome, Liora." Faelan stepped forward and reached out a hand. "I think you're just the person we've been waiting for."

CHAPTER SEVEN

LIORA

An hour later, I was walking up the hill to MacAlpine Castle, nerves pinging around my stomach like a bucket of bouncy balls tossed into the street.

It had been an enlightening hour, to say the least.

After I'd stared at Faelan in shock, she'd thrown the lock on the door and pulled Zara and me into her office. Faelan was a member in the Order of Caledonia, much like Zara had thought, and was tasked with helping protect the magickal Truth Stone that lay buried out on the island in the middle of Loch Mirren.

The Clach na Fìrinn.

It was why the Kelpies had been terrorizing Loren Brae, apparently. The Order of Caledonia, when complete, was meant to consist of nine members, all of whom were gifted magickal powers of sorts for protecting the Truth Stone. To be worthy of those powers, each member needed to pass three challenges, unknown to them, to complete their acceptance into the Order.

It was all very fairy tale and mythological to me, but when Faelan and Zara spoke of the Kelpies, the fear on their faces was very, very real. Even though it sounded fantastical, Zara was one of the most pragmatic people I knew. If she agreed with Faelan about what was happening in Loren Brae, I'd believe her. If anything, I'd always been the more naïve one of the two of us, always wanting to believe the best in people.

Lost in my thoughts as we followed a long line of carefully trimmed hedges that lined a road that led up to the castle, I barely heard what my sister said.

"What was that?" I tuned back in to the conversation from where I'd been daydreaming about a knight rescuing a princess from a room in the castle.

"A ghost coo is about to jump out of the bushes and scare you," Zara said and I scrunched my face in confusion at her.

"A what—ahhhhhhh!" I shrieked as a massive slightly transparent ghost coo leaped out of the hedges and ran at me. I ducked as it trampled through me, a wash of frigid air making the hairs on the back of my neck stand up, and I gulped for air. Bringing my hand to my hammering heart, I whirled to find the ghost coo racing back up the lane, tossing its head back and forth.

"Is he... is he laughing?" I asked, incredulous, as I took in the almost delighted expression on the coo's face.

"It's his favorite." Faelan sighed. Raising her voice, she

called to the coo. "Brilliant job, Clyde. You really got us this time!"

The ghost threw his head back and bellowed in delight before winking out of sight.

"I'm sorry, but what ... what was all that?" I was torn between shock and amusement.

"That was Clyde. He's the resident ghost coo at MacAlpine Castle, and his very favorite thing in the whole world is scaring people. He's basically an overgrown toddler that we all have to clap for every time he successfully scares someone," Faelan said, affection in her voice.

"But you saw him, didn't you, Z? Before he even got close?"

"Aye," Zara said, shrugging her shoulder, one hand clasped on Mitch's handle on his harness. "He has a very particular aura. I can see him coming from quite a way away."

"He's not been able to surprise Z yet. No matter how much he keeps trying." Faelan laughed.

"I might pretend to be scared one of these days just to keep his morale up," Zara said and we all laughed.

I couldn't believe what my morning had become. I'd gone from returning to Loren Brae, scared for my future, to newly employed and laughing about a ghost coo with a new friend. Och, and not to mention the whole magickal Order thing and the new fake boyfriend in my life.

Opening my mouth to bring up the dating situation to Z, I paused as a cacophony of barks met my ears as we rounded the edge of the hedges to the castle.

A chihuahua led the charge in a fuzzy fair isle jumper, his teeth bared as though he would rip our throats out.

Behind him, a corgi mix of sorts with a big floppy bow at her neck followed at a more sedate pace, and behind her loped an aging brown lab with a tartan collar.

"Sir Buster, that's enough," Faelan said, and the chihuahua skidded to a stop, his little body vibrating with rage.

"He's a tiny fierce beastie, isn't he?" I tried to hold back a laugh, not wanting to insult the wee lad.

"He's all bark, that one." I looked up to see an older man with a shock of white hair tucked under a green knit hat, thick eyebrows, and kind eyes following the herd. "Thinks he's king of the castle, isn't that right, Sir Buster?"

Sir Buster lifted his nose in the air, as though agreeing with the man.

"That's Lady Lola." Faelan pointed to the corgi mix. "And this distinguished gentleman is Harris."

Faelan bent to pet the brown lab who'd wandered over and pressed his nose to her thigh. "Harris belongs to Orla, the head builder on the Common Gin site, and he comes to work with her most days."

"And I immediately take custody." The man studied me over the rake he carried in one gloved hand. "I'm Archie, caretaker of MacAlpine Castle, along with my wife, Hilda."

"Orla's part of the Order, too." Faelan glanced to me and my gaze darted between Archie and Faelan's face. Did he know about the Order?

"Ah. You've found our next one, is that right?" Archie leaned on his rake, his eyebrows drawing together as he studied me. I hoped what he saw met with his approval. A flicker of movement caught my attention and I glanced to the right to see Gloam slip quietly into the row of hedges.

The dogs all turned, scenting something, but stayed where they were. They must know Gloam.

Sir Buster bolted to me and pawed at my boot, his body trembling as he looked up at me and growled.

"You're giving very mixed communications, sir," I said, torn between picking him up and easing gently away from the vibrating mini rage beast.

"Go on, pick him up. He'll settle down," Archie advised, and I bent and scooped up Sir Buster. His growls increased, but once he was tucked in the crook of my arm, he relaxed. "So, lass. You've come to join the Order then?"

"Um." I glanced down at Sir Buster who looked up at me with warm brown eyes. "I'm not sure? I've only just learned about it."

Look at me, not jumping into things immediately. I gave myself a mental pat on the back. Zara couldn't fault me for ignoring red flags on this one.

"If Loren Brae needs you, then you should join," Zara said, admonishing me, and the bubble burst. Here I thought I was doing well to be cautious and now Z was all about me diving right in? I never seemed to be able to win with her.

"Let's go bother Lia for a cuppa tea," Archie interjected. "The restaurant's closed on Mondays, but we often take our lunch there. I'll round up a few of the others."

The others? Why did that make it sound like a cult? Torn between amusement and suspicion, I followed Archie and the dogs around the corner of the castle, and past the entrance to a manicured walled garden. Though it was largely trimmed back and tucked down for the upcoming winter, the garden was still vast and beautiful, with tall trees and hills rising in the back to cradle it. I could imagine wandering through the paths, smelling each bloom, and setting my crystals out to soak in the energy of the full moon on a warm summer night.

"Kitchen's through here," Archie said, knocking smartly on two wooden arched doors with heavy iron hinges. They were propped just slightly open, and Irish rock music sounded from within. "I'll go get Hilda."

A woman with a pretty face, curls bound back by a bandanna, popped her head out of the door.

"Oh, hi! Hold on." She pushed the door open and then went to her phone, lowering the music that blared out of the speakers. "Sorry. Dropkick Murphys. For some reason the loud music helps me focus and create my lists for the week."

Behind her, a large wooden table dominated a massive kitchen, which was equal parts quaint and old-timey and modern and industrial. Stone walls and high ceilings with thick beams reminded you that you were in a castle, but slick stainless steel prep tables showcased modern features. At the wooden table, several notebooks lay spread out and opened, and a laptop was shoved to the side.

"Lia, this is Liora. She is Zara's sister and Gloam believes she's next in the Order."

"No way." Lia's face lit up. A New York—or was that Boston?—accent tinged her words. "Welcome. When did you arrive?"

"Um, two days ago," I said.

"Archie was hoping you'd have a spot of lunch for us, so we could chat." Faelan checked a slim watch at her wrist. "And I've got to get back to clients shortly."

"No problem. I've got a chili in the pot. Does that suit everyone?" Lia gestured to where a large stainless steel pot simmered on the stove. "In the dining room?"

"Perfect," Faelan said. We waited as Zara commanded Mitch forward and they navigated through the kitchen and into a sort of setup area that housed stacks of plates, cutlery, linens, and tableware. I gasped as we stepped out into the dining area.

The restaurant was both overwhelming and cozy at the same time.

"This used to be the ballroom," Lia said, seeing my expression as I looked up at the tall ceilings with massive ornate wooden and iron chandeliers, beautiful stone walls with votive candles tucked in the crevices, and tall windows overlooking the gardens. "We made it smaller by creating these walls on either side with faux greenery and adding lighting."

On two opposite sides of the room, tall greenery walls closed in the dining area, making it feel more intimate, and tables of various sizes were scattered through the room.

Movement whirled, and I gasped as a ... *creature* ... in a red hat with big eyes dashed through the room with a tablecloth in hand. In seconds, a table was set, and I was left clutching Sir Buster so tightly that he began to growl.

"Sorry, sorry," I whispered, easing my grip on the dog. Had anyone else seen that? Why was nobody reacting to the fact that a goblin had just raced through the room? Was this something to do with my powers? Confused, and more than a bit unsettled, I eased toward the door. Maybe it was best if I left altogether.

Lia turned and must have seen something on my face that had her throwing her head back with laughter.

"I forget. That's Brice. He's my kitchen broonie."

I blinked and pressed my lips together, tilting my head at Lia. She seemed mostly sane, but I'd only just met her.

"I know, I know." Lia laughed again. "Trust me, it took me a moment to wrap my head around it, too. Particularly as I'm not from Scotland and not as in tune to all the magickal elements that come with the history here."

"A broonie?" I swallowed, uncertain if this was some sort of hazing that went along with initiating people into the Order of Caledonia.

"Aye," Faelan said, smiling as she took a seat at the freshly made-up table. "We've got a kitchen elf, garden gnomes, my fox, a talking crow, a ghost coo, hedgehogs ... honestly the list goes on. It's quite a magickal hodgepodge of creatures and witches we've got here, isn't it?"

"What about a squirrel?" I blurted out and then flushed when Zara swung her head toward me.

"A squirrel?" Zara asked.

"Och, have you met your familiar already?" Faelan asked in delight, and Zara's face crinkled with concern.

"Her familiar?"

"Many of us have a familiar. Gloam's mine. I know I've told you he's just a recovering patient, but he's actually my familiar. Many magickals have familiars. They help when doing spells or just act as a companion as needed," Faelan explained, beaming as a bowl of chili landed in front of her.

"What the—" My mouth fell open. I hadn't even seen the broonie this time, but clearly he'd delivered the chili.

"I know. He moves fast," Faelan said, acknowledging my look of surprise.

"What happened?" Zara asked.

"Um, the house elf moved like the speed of light and delivered a bowl of chili to Faelan at the table." Automatically, I took Zara's arm and helped her to the table, and she bent and unharnessed Mitch so he could be off duty for a bit. Mitch immediately bounded over to where Harris and Lady Lola lounged in the corner and made his introductions. Sir Buster squirmed in my arms, so I put him down so he could race off and lord his importance over Mitch.

"I can sense him. He's got a pleasant aura," Zara said, settling back into her seat. Her eyes took on that dreamy expression they did when she looked inward. "He's a sweet soul."

A soft sound at Zara's side had her turning, and my eyes rounded as Brice appeared. He moved slowly as he put the bowl of chili in front of Zara, and then took her hand, placing it on the bowl so she could feel where it was.

"That's him, isn't it?" Zara asked, smiling down at the house elf who had the type of face that only a mother could love.

"It is," I whispered.

"See? He's sweet. I could tell." Brice reached up and put a spoon in Zara's hand and she smiled again, before leaning over to spoon some chili into her mouth. "Mmm, delicious."

Seemingly satisfied with the compliment, Brice disappeared in a blur of motion again, and before I knew it, the table was set with eight bowls of chili, and two baskets overflowing with thick hunks of crusty bread.

"Hello, hello." I turned as a curvy woman with strawberry blond hair and a hooded jumper strolled into the dining room. Behind her, a short woman in coveralls followed, along with Archie and who must be his wife, Hilda.

Harris jumped up and bounded across the room, nuzzling his nose into the leg of the shorter woman.

"Och, there's the best lad. I've missed you, darling." The woman cooed down to an equally adoring Harris.

"You must be Liora." The woman in the hoodie smiled down at me and offered her hand. "I'm Sophie, owner of MacAlpine Castle, though I still really don't believe it's mine. This is Orla, head builder at the Common Gin distillery site, and one of the Order as well. You've met Archie, and this is his wife, Hilda."

The trim woman with kind eyes and short-cropped grey hair smiled at me from where her arm was looped through Archie's.

"Sit, sit. Faelan and Zara have to get back to work." Lia bustled back into the dining area with two jugs of water in hand. In moments we were all tucked around the table, the dogs circling and hoping for a snack, and I looked down at my bowl of chili and then up at the group of people. It all just seemed so ... normal.

Yet this was anything but normal.

"Delicious chili, Lia," Sophie said. "But is there..."

A bowl of shredded cheese appeared in front of Sophie and she beamed. "Thanks, Brice!"

"I'm sorry... I hate to be rude," I said, unable to shake the overwhelming feeling that I was being put on. "But this has to be a—"

"Joke?" Zara finished for me, angling her head toward me in accord. "It does feel pretty surreal. Even for us."

"Aye. We're not strangers to the magickal world," I explained as everyone at the table looked to my sister and me. "But our powers tend to run more toward auras, empathic readings, astrology, that kind of thing."

"Nothing wrong with that," Archie barked at me, and I raised my eyebrows. I hadn't said there was something wrong with that, had I?

"It's just that this all seems a little…"

"Out there?" Sophie supplied and I nodded, pleased that someone else agreed with me.

"It is," Orla said, picking up a piece of bread and dunking it in her chili. "There's no denying that."

"But it's also really fricking cool," Lia added. "I mean, trust me, when I moved from Boston to start a restaurant here, I certainly wasn't expecting to have a kitchen elf as my sous chef. But, here we are."

"Do you get used to it? Having familiars?"

"Is that what you meant about a squirrel earlier?" Zara intervened, turning to me. "Do you have a magickal squirrel?"

"I, uh, I mean, kinda?" I asked, uncertain how to proceed.

"Oh, that's grand. Your familiar has already found you." Hilda beamed at me and nodded toward my bowl. "Eat up, dear. It's not poisoned. Promise."

"That's exactly what they'd say in the movies if it was poisoned," Sophie said, shaking her head at Hilda. "Listen, Liora. It's wild and out there and I totally get it. I moved here not having a clue about any of this, but what I did have was a strong belief in the mythological. My uncle had spent countless hours going over these legends with me, and so to see them come to life? Well, I was pretty jazzed, I guess. But at the end of the day, when the Kelpies come for you, you don't have a choice but to believe. Because you need to know how to protect yourself and those around you."

"Oh, great." I swallowed, my nerves making it difficult to talk. I was supposed to fight a Kelpie?

"I, too, thought it sounded a bit cult-ish. I think everyone did, no?" Lia looked at Orla who just nodded and kept eating.

"But in the end I've learned it's about something more than all of us," Sophie continued, glancing to Archie who just gestured with a piece of bread for her to go on. "The Order of Caledonia was contrived to protect the Truth Stone, to make sure it stays where it is, and doesn't land in the wrong hands. Through the years, it has grown too powerful. Without the Order protecting it, which is what is currently happening, it has called upon the Kelpies as the last line of defense. Unfortunately, the Kelpies don't distinguish between friend or foe. They've become a terrifying menace and the longer we go on without completing the Order, the more they attack the town."

They attack the town?

"It's no joke," Lia said, catching the look on my face. "You'll hear them. In the night. The sound alone will send shivers down your back."

"I'm terrible in a fight," I rushed out, nervous they'd landed on the wrong person to help them. "I always just want everyone to get along. I'm not tough or fierce or any of that. I'm like ... sparkles and fun and let's all go hug trees together."

Faelan smiled at me. "I'm one for the flowers, my friend. I'm more than happy to go hug all the trees you want to, but you'd be surprised what comes out of you when you need to protect those you care about."

"That sounds ... terrifying." I looked across the table, wary. "I'm not sure I want to sign up for your club if it means that I have to fight."

"You'll have to either way, eventually. If you stay here." Archie's voice cut through me. "None of us has a choice, not really. It's just that some of you will have more tools at your disposal. Like your magick."

"I'm not sure how reading people's charts will help in a battle against Kelpies," I said, nonplussed.

"You might have other powers." Zara surprised me when she turned to me. "It would make sense why your astrology never really clicked for you. There might be something else that you don't know about."

"I..." I looked at her and then down at my hands. "I did find my name in a family book. A spell book."

"You didn't tell me," Zara burst out.

"Listen, there's a lot that has happened in the last day," I exclaimed. "The family spell book being the least of them."

"Well, that sounds promising, doesn't it?" Sophie beamed at me across the table. "At least you might have some information to guide you."

"Not all of us have that," Orla added, looking up at me over her bowl of chili. "I had no family to speak of, let alone a book to read about my past. You're lucky to have it."

"Oh." I gave her a soft smile, understanding what she was trying to tell me. "I haven't had much time to go through it, but I'll look more deeply later."

"I think you need to do this." Zara turned to me and reached out to find my hand. "Seriously, Liora. This may be the answer you've been looking for. Why you've been so lost these past few years."

I winced at her words, my skin flushing as she revealed my vulnerabilities to the group of people I'd just met. "I wouldn't say lost exactly."

"Floundering. No direction," Zara continued on, ignoring me. "And maybe this is why. You're meant to be here. In Loren Brae. Helping others. Maybe your magick will finally make sense and it will all come together for you. I have a good feeling about this."

"And these people?" I asked, not even caring if I was being rude. If Zara was going to lay my weaknesses out for everyone, what did it matter if I was being blunt back? But I wanted to get a read on everyone from Zara's own take, with her empathic powers rarely leading us wrong.

"They're good people. I wouldn't be sitting here, eating this food, if I didn't think so," Zara insisted, squeezing my hand harder. "Even Sir Buster has a good aura."

"Told ya he was all bark," Archie said, his tone gruff.

"Like someone else I know," Hilda murmured, squeezing Archie's hand.

"So what then? I just join a *magickal Order*? And then go on with life? How does this work, exactly?"

"We'll take you through a ritual to induct you into the Order."

I blanched at the word ritual.

"And, you'll pick your weapon ..."

I shrunk into my chair even more.

"And then when you complete three challenges, you'll be a part of the Order," Archie finished.

"It sounds intense. And it kind of is. But you also get used to it and you'll be fine, I promise," Lia said, looking across at me. "If I can get used to a kitchen elf, you can get used to whatever your powers may be."

"That's the truth of it. Though I'm not sure any one of us will ever get used to Clyde," Sophie laughed.

A long wailing "moooo" was our only warning before Clyde burst out of a wall, trampled across the table, and sent the dogs into a fit, chasing him as he looped the room.

"Bloody hell, Clyde. That's enough!" Archie barked and Clyde disappeared, and the dogs skidded to a stop, looking around in confusion.

I held my hand to where my heart hammered furiously.

"Does that happen often?"

"Too often." Lia glowered into her bowl and Sophie snorted out a laugh.

"He made Lia pee her pants once."

"Damn it, Sophie, do you have to tell everyone?" Lia rounded on Sophie, and despite my misgivings, I was smiling.

"You're sure?" I lowered my voice and leaned into Zara.

"Aye. This feels right, L. I don't know how else to explain it, but I think you should do it. I truly think you could make a difference here."

"Okay, I trust you." And a part of me really wanted Zara to be proud of me for once. Looking up to where

Sophie and Lia bickered, I raised a hand to interject. "All right, ladies. I ... I agree. I'll do this. I'll join the Order."

"Well done, lass." Archie gave me a nod of approval. "Welcome to the Order of Caledonia. Loren Brae needs you."

My stomach twisted at his words. I hoped they were true, because I wasn't even sure what I needed, let alone how to help a town in need. But, per usual, I decided to jump without looking. At least Zara wouldn't begrudge this choice.

CHAPTER EIGHT

LIORA

"Welcome to the Order of Caledonia," Archie repeated again, two hours later. Sophie and Hilda had joined us as we'd walked the castle grounds, going to each cardinal direction point, where a small plaque lay almost covered by moss in the ground.

I'd taken an oath at each plaque, the words reverberating through me as I looked out across the hills and down to the loch, where the Stone was nestled on the island.

"I accept the responsibility of protecting the Clach na Fìrinn and promise to restore the Order to its fullness. In doing so, I show myself worthy of the magick of Clach na Fìrinn."

I'd even chosen a weapon, though I had to admit, as weapons went, it was probably fairly useless.

I glanced down at the brooch in my hands.

I almost always carried it with me, as it had been my great grandmother's. A gold brooch, with two dragons twisting together in a Celtic pattern, surrounding the stars and moon. From the bottom, three pearls dripped. It had a long pin, which I supposed in a pinch, I could stab someone in the eye with. But other than that, I wasn't sure what kind of weapon it would make.

Hilda had assured me it was a symbolic choice, and that my weapon would likely come out in my magick.

"Thank you," I said, clutching my brooch tightly in my hand. It did make me wonder what weapons the other women in the Order had. Surely something useful and ... frightening perhaps. The wind whistled down the hills, carrying something ancient and unheard with it, and I shivered as the surface of the loch kicked up, the white caps forming across the water. "Now what?"

"That was pretty much my question too." Sophie laughed, and hooked an arm through mine, and dragged me back toward the castle. "I'd like you to meet the other women, when you can. I'm not sure how busy you are or what you do, but it helps to meet the others. We're a team, really, but it's also just nice to have friends in a new town."

"It's not new," I admitted. "But it has also changed. I lived here once before, and to be honest, I wasn't exactly wanting to come back."

"Oh, is that right? Why?" Sophie turned to me, her eyes wide and curious. Friendly. Not judgmental. Could I trust her with my past? Did it even matter anymore? I couldn't change what had happened and I hadn't done anything wrong. "Um, there was some drama around when I left. I gave a reading to my friend that didn't go well. She, um, kind of freaked out, broke up with her boyfriend, and then the whole town thought he was cheating on her with me."

"Och, I remember that nonsense." Hilda turned to me, rolling her eyes. "That's why you looked familiar to me. Och, that was a whole bunch of kerfuffle for no reason. Torin's a good lad, and I never could see him being a cheater."

"He wasn't. At least not with me. Or anyone else that I'd heard of." I bit my lower lip. Would I be able to be open with these new friends? Could I tell them about how I'd screwed up and enchanted him into not being able to tell lies? Indecision warred. I know Zara had said to trust them, but I also didn't want them to immediately regret asking me to be a part of their magickal Order.

"I don't think I've met Torin," Sophie said, scrunching up her nose as she thought about it.

"He's a forester. He's done some work here, though not recently," Archie said. "Good lad. Fair prices."

"I'm renting from him," I said, unable to bring myself to tell them that we might be even dating? Maybe not. He hadn't quite taken to my fake dating idea. And his kiss had felt real. Confusion roiled through me. I probably needed to talk to my sister about it first before the rumor went around town. "He's given me a fair price for rent as well."

"See? A good lad. Not a cheater." Hilda made a tsking noise with her mouth. "Such a shame really. Nasty rumor. Your friend moved away, didn't she?"

"Aye, she did. Not that we speak anymore."

"Let me get your number. I'll get something together this week. Just us girls. You can give us readings," Sophie exclaimed, pulling out her phone. It all seemed so innocuous and normal, and not like I'd just taken part in an ancient ritual to protect a magickal Truth Stone. The dichotomy in situations was giving me mental whiplash.

"I'm not sure that's a good idea," I began, but she waved my concerns away.

"Oh, hush. It will be fun. Plus, you said you loved astrology. If your powers are there, don't you want to work with it more?"

"Maybe? I guess." My stomach twisted. I hated turning my back on astrology and even speaking poorly about something I loved made me feel ill. "But I'd love to meet the others. Honestly? I could use some friends right now."

It grated to admit it, but I had always been a creature who craved companionship. I loved going to parties, making friends, and being in the thick of things. Living in Glasgow had been fun, but I'd also found it tricky to make new friends at my age. Without a shared interest like being in school together, it was harder to meet groups of friends to join.

"Aw, I get that." Sophie casually looped an arm over my shoulder and gave me a quick squeeze. "I know what it's like to be a stranger in a strange land and all that. I'm more than happy to help you meet people."

"Thanks, I appreciate that. I just got a job at the pub, too, so I'm sure that will help."

"No way!" Sophie said, tugging me toward the castle. "Are you bartending? Serving? You should ask Lia. I'd bet she'd put you on some shifts too."

"Why would she need to? Brice seems to be able to do the work of twenty," I pointed out, laughing.

"Yeah, but he can't be seen by regular people," Sophie said.

"I think I just need a little time. I'm happy I got the job at The Tipsy Thistle, but a lot has happened in the last two days, and I really just need to process for a moment, I think. Get my feet under me." I still didn't have it in me to tell her that I'd screwed up a spell and made it so Torin couldn't tell a lie. Well, technically I hadn't screwed up the spell—it had worked, hadn't it—but it was just not for the intended recipient.

Which was the problem, really. I'd picked a random spell and had just jumped into it without bothering to think about needing to have a recipient for said spell. So, yeah, I guess I had screwed it up.

"You've only been here two days? Damn girl, yeah, you need a little time." Sophie shook her head at me, and then her smile widened as she looked at something over my shoulder. "Though, I'll admit, things do tend to move fast in Loren Brae."

I glanced behind me to see a handsome man dressed in a kilt and a thick woolen jumper striding across the lawn toward us.

"Oh my," I said.

"Hands off. This one's mine." Sophie blew him a loud air kiss, and he detoured to us, and grabbed her around the waist to dip her low in a steamy kiss. When they came up for air, Sophie's face flushed, and eyes dreamy, I almost sighed.

"Sorry about that. This one gets a little demanding when she sees me in a kilt if I don't immediately pay attention to her." The man grinned at me, and I felt a little woozy myself.

"This is Lachlan. He tried to kick me out of the castle when I first came here. But we sorted that out, didn't we, honey?" Sophie fluttered her eyelashes at him and he just laughed and poked her in the side.

"I'm Liora."

"She's Zara's sister. Faelan's new assistant? And, she's just joined the Order."

Lachlan's mouth dropped open. "Och, lass. Congrats to you. That's fabulous you found the next one so fast."

"I didn't. It sounds like Gloam did, actually."

"Smart little fox." Lachlan held out his hand and I shook it. "Welcome to the Order, Liora. If you need anything, just let us know. There are a whole lot of us around, and we are all tuned in to what's happening in Loren Brae. You're not alone here."

"Oh, thanks." For some reason, those words made tears prick my eyes and I had to turn away for a moment and collect myself as Sophie chattered something about marketing photos to Lachlan.

I wasn't alone here. I'd known that, when I'd decided to come back to be closer to Zara, but it meant even more to hear it from someone else. Particularly because I still wasn't entirely sure what to do if a Kelpie attacked me. Clearing my throat, I turned back around.

"And if a Kelpie attacks?"

"Reach for your power," Sophie said, automatically. She brought a fist to her solar plexus. "You can feel it. In here. You might not know how it will manifest. Mine is my voice.

I'm the Knight. So I'm one of the most powerful against the Kelpies. I try to be available and as close as I can be at all times, but it's a large loch and there's only so much I can do."

"You do a great job, darling." Lachlan brushed a finger under Sophie's eyes where I now noticed the dark smudges, presumably from lost sleep. "More than is expected of you."

"I accepted the duty, didn't I? When I became Knight?" Sophie shrugged him off. "Liora, is your car here, or do you need a ride?"

"Nope, I walked. All good. I'll head on back now and I think the walk will clear my head." I nodded to Lachlan. "Nice to meet you."

"Same to you."

I waved goodbye and squatted to pet Sir Buster and Lady Lola, who had come charging around the house after Lachlan but had been distracted by chasing a bird across the lawn.

I tried to clear my head as I walked down the lane toward the loch, but my thoughts refused to be manhandled into place. I still had to tell Z about my job and about how I'd screwed up the spell on Torin. And how was I supposed to tell Torin that I was now a part of an ancient magickal Order? He was already unhappy with me for doing magick in his house, and on the first day out on my own, I'd gone off and joined some sort of mystical cult?

Aye, I was in for it.

But maybe—*maybe*—he wouldn't mind. It was hard to say with him.

Frankly I didn't know the man all that well.

What I did know was he kissed like he had all the time in the world to savor me, as though I was the only woman that mattered, and even just thinking about his mouth on mine again brought heat to my cheeks.

At the end of the lane, I glanced toward Zara's work, but knowing she was likely busy and it wasn't the time to get into what had happened with my spell, I turned away from Loren Brae and headed toward Torin's, I mean, our house. I was used to sharing a space, as most of my life I'd lived either with my sister or roommates, but still it felt odd to think of Torin's gorgeous two-wing cottage as my home as well.

A horn honked lightly behind me, and I turned to see a lorry, with big wheels and dirt on the bumper, pull to the side. The front window rolled down, and Torin, his thick hair covered by a navy knit hat, poked his head out.

"If it isn't the bonniest lass in Loren Brae walking home. Can I give you a lift, darling?"

You can give me a lot of things.

My cheeks flushed at my thoughts, and I ducked my head away as I rounded the bonnet and hopped up into the passenger seat.

Be an adult, Liora. Just because the man kissed you once doesn't mean he's going to do it again. Last night was an anomaly brought on by frustration and confusion. He's had all day to think it over.

"Hiya, beautiful." Torin shocked me by gripping the front of my coat with both hands, hauling me forward, and laying a searing kiss across my lips. I pushed at his chest, out of reflex more than anything, but then my fingers curled into his jacket.

God help me, but I may have moaned before he released me.

"Um, hi," I said, flopping back into my seat. "You don't have to do that, you know. The whole kissing thing."

"Just gotta get something out of this shite situation you landed me in."

I winced at his words and gritted my teeth as he pulled back onto the road.

"And I'm not talking about the dating you part. Though, to be clear, fake dating is still a dumb idea. I'm talking about the whole not being able to filter my words. It's significantly more difficult than I thought. I was always certain that I wasn't much of a liar, but now I realize that while I might not be a liar, I also heavily filter my thoughts around people."

"Which is probably a good thing, no? Don't we all do that? Not all thoughts need to be spoken out loud." *Like how he thinks I'm beautiful.* I had no idea what to do with that or figure out how that made me feel. Because it definitely made me feel some sort of way.

"I've had some time to think."

Here it was. I knew once Torin had a moment away from me and had some time to digest what would happen, he'd be kicking me out of his house. It was what made the most sense. My track record with tossing him into shite situations wasn't great.

"I'm not sure I care what people in Loren Brae think anymore."

I turned to him, my mouth dropping open, surprised at his words. What did he mean by that? Was he talking about the whole cheating rumor with Avery? Or about telling people how I screwed up a magickal spell and he could only tell the truth now? Or about the fact he'd kissed me? My mind whirled with questions, and when he glanced at me, a lightning-quick smile dashed across his face.

"You should see your face right now."

"I mean, it's a loaded statement, no?" I dropped back into my seat as he turned off the main road and bumped up the lane to his cottage. Our cottage. As we pulled in, a red squirrel ran across the roof and stood on its back legs, as though waiting for us. Narrowing my eyes, I zeroed in on the small tuft of white fur at the tips of Bracken's ears. It was how I was identifying him now, just so I didn't try to launch into conversation with every random squirrel I met on the street.

Not that I met a ton of squirrels, but they were around.

"Hello?"

I jolted and turned to where Torin grinned at me, having turned the engine off and opened his door. I'd clearly just blanked out on everything he was saying, so focused was I on if the red squirrel staring me down was Bracken or not.

"I'm sorry, I floated away."

"Glad to know I can keep your interest."

"No, I swear, I am interested. It's ... been a day."

Instantly, Torin's mood shifted. He closed his door and rounded the bonnet, popping open my door and unhooking my seat belt before I could do anything else. I gaped up at him as he leaned in and hauled me out of the car.

The man was clearly used to lifting heavy things. I wondered if he even realized that several times now he'd just pulled me to him, or in this case, lifted me. It must be second nature to him, what with picking up logs all day long, but I certainly wasn't used to being handled like this.

Not that I minded it.

Not at all.

"What happened and who do I need to beat up?"

My insides went all warm and gooey. He leaned over me, one arm braced over my head on his truck, and I suddenly felt all faint and fluttery. Like a damsel in actual distress. Not a woman who had taken a magickal oath and was supposedly going to help defeat mythological water beasts. A part of me desperately wanted to fan myself and ask Torin to take his shirt off while he chopped wood for the winter.

Settle down, woman. The whole forest is watching.

My gaze flew to where Bracken chattered at me from the roof. That little shite! And I couldn't respond to him because then Torin would really have to decide whether he'd gotten himself in too deep with me.

"Long story. Shall we go inside? I'd love a cup of tea."

"Aye, lass. I hope you're hungry as well. I stopped at the market on the way from my last appointment." Torin surprised me by opening the back door and pulling out a market bag full of food.

"You cook?"

"Of course, I cook. I'm a grown man, aren't I?" Torin looked at me like I'd said the silliest thing in the world and whistled his way up to the front door before unlocking it and heading inside. I followed more slowly, waiting a moment until he was fully inside before looking up at Bracken.

"Did you know? About the Order?"

"I did. It's why I said you're mine. I'm here to help, lass."

"Can we talk? Later or tomorrow? I need some help, I think."

"I will come by in the morning after the man leaves."

"Thanks, Bracken. See you then."

"Are you talking to someone?" Torin appeared at the door, his coat off, and I smiled brightly at him.

"Just a cute red squirrel up on the roof."

"Cute? I'm handsome," Bracken chattered at me.

"Aye, I love those little buggers. They're so fun to watch, aren't they?"

"The best." I trailed inside and closed the door behind me, realizing, belatedly, that I'd walked into the main room of the house and not my wing. I needed a moment alone, just to think about what I was going to say to Torin about my day.

"I've got the kettle on. Is lasagna okay? It's easy enough to throw together."

"Sounds great, thank you." I couldn't remember the last time anyone had cooked for me, let alone a man. It felt oddly comforting, to have someone to take care of me that way. "I'm just going to be a moment."

Ducking inside my side of the house, I closed the door behind me and took a deep breath and then another. Dropping my handbag on the table by the couch, I made use of the toilet, changed into some comfortable clothes, and then studied my reflection in the mirror. Even my comfy clothes needed an upgrade. I'd been budgeting for so long that it was easy to overlook the state of my clothes, but there wasn't much I could do about it now. When I did shop, it was typically at vintage stores, and I picked pieces thoughtfully, hoping they would last a long time. My joggers and hooded jumper didn't exactly fall into that category.

Indecision warred, but the need to feel comfortable after an emotional day won out, and I left the bedroom. My gaze landed on my handbag where my now-magickal brooch was tucked away. Did I bring it with me? Was I supposed to have it on me at all times? Hilda had said it was more symbolic than useful, and I truly couldn't imagine wielding a brooch in an attack, so surely it was fine where it was. Decided, I left the brooch behind and slipped back into the main room to the scents of garlic simmering and music turned low in the background. Torin had changed as well, looking just as rumpled and cute as he had yesterday, and I realized that I wanted to go over and give him a hug.

Stifling the urge, I wandered closer to the kitchen.

"Anything I can do to help?"

"Nope, just browning this meat to add to the sauce, and then I'll layer the lasagna, and the food should be ready within the hour. That should be enough time for you to tell me whatever it is that has that line across your forehead. How do you take your tea?"

Automatically, I reached up to touch my forehead. Damn it, there *was* a line there. It must be because I furrowed my brow when I was concerned.

"Um, milk and light sugar. Thanks." I accepted the cup of tea he offered and smiled faintly at him. This was a touch too surreal. Last week I was hiding in a dodgy hotel room wondering what to do with my life. This week I had a purpose. Direction. And the possibility of new friends who had simply ... accepted me. *Welcomed me.*

At least Mercury wasn't in retrograde. Because this new moon was mooning hard.

I closed my eyes.

Duh. This wasn't just a new moon. Uranus was transiting my first house. Of course this was all happening at once. I'd known it would all happen at once. I'd done my chart for the year, hadn't I? I knew big changes were coming.

But that was the thing about knowing and preparing, wasn't it? I'd known something big was coming. The problem was, I hadn't done anything to prepare for it. Instead, I'd kept myself too busy, buried my head in the sand, and when everything had boiled over, I didn't have a backup plan in place.

As I was about to mentally berate myself, yet again, for feeling like a constant failure, a funny thing happened. Something tugged in my chest, and I reached up to rub my solar plexus, remembering how Sophie had done the same earlier that day.

"Reach for your power. You'll feel it."

Light bloomed softly inside me, gentle and soothing, a soft wash of water on a pink sand beach as the sun set in the distance.

Maybe I hadn't needed a backup plan because I was exactly where I needed to be.

It was such a startling thought that I plopped down into a chair and took a bracing sip of tea as an entirely new perspective entered the game.

"You have the most expressive face."

I glanced up in surprise to see Torin watching me from

where he layered the lasagna in a casserole dish on the counter.

"I'm sorry. Just woolgathering. It's been a day."

"Tell me about it?"

"First, tell me why you no longer care what Loren Brae thinks. What did you mean?"

Torin reached in the fridge and pulled out a Guinness. Popping it open, he upended the can into a pint glass and let it sit like that until it emptied, and then took the can out and brought his glass to the table. Letting the beer settle, he sat and steepled his fingers on the table in front of me.

I gasped at the long cut on his finger.

"Torin! You're hurt. Och, let me put something on that." I stood up and reached for his hand, turning so I could see the cut on his palm. It was red and angry, and looked like something was buried in the skin. "Is this a sliver? Shouldn't you be wearing gloves?"

"Och, it's nothing, lass." Torin tried to tug his hand back, but I pursed my lips and kept his hand in mine, studying the wound. "Be right back."

Dropping his hand, I went and grabbed my first aid kit that I always kept well stocked. Being a classic Pisces, I frequently hurt myself due to constant distraction, and I'd learned to patch myself up through the years. Returning to the main room, I took Torin's hand and cleaned the wound and then held his palm closer to my face.

"I think there's something in here."

"It's a sliver."

"It needs to come out."

"Och, it will work itself out eventually."

"But why wait? Doesn't it hurt?"

"It's annoying, but it's fine."

I tilted my head to look at Torin. Was he really just happy to live with discomfort? His face was so close I could kiss him again, and my pulse kicked up.

"Will you let me take this out?"

"If you promise to tell me about what happened today that has you so stressed out."

And I realized that I did want to tell him about my day. Just as much as I wanted to ease his suffering with a massive sliver in his hand. Was he really just going to walk around in pain? Why hadn't he been wearing his gloves?

"Aye, I'll tell you. But first, tell me why you don't care what Loren Brae thinks anymore." This was the third time we'd circled around to this conversation, and I dug in the first aid kit for the needles I kept there. Taking one out and wiping it with alcohol, I picked his hand back up and made quick work of pulling the sliver forward enough to switch out the needle for tweezers. I tugged, twice, and then I had the small chunk out. Holding it up to his face, I glared at him. "You were going to let that sit in your hand?"

"I would have taken it out eventually." Torin shrugged and took a sip of his Guinness. "And to answer your question, I realized that I don't care what Loren Brae thinks about me and Avery because I know the truth. And anybody who knows me, or cares about me, will know the truth as well. Nothing else matters, not really. You ken?"

I still held Torin's hand in mine, but my eyes were glued to his. He was so steady. So certain of who he was and what he cared about.

"How can you do that? Just brush aside what people

think?" It seemed like I'd been ruled by what other people thought for most of my life.

"It doesn't much make a difference. Does it? Not really." Torin curled his hand so his fingers held mine. "Not when I'm out with the trees all day. Did you know they talk to each other?"

"The trees?" I asked, faintly, my eyes fixated on his.

"Aye, the trees. They work together. As a community. If you look up into a canopy? You can see the lines of where they make room for each other. So everybody can get some light. And I was thinking about that, today, when I was worried about the gossip coming back and people thinking I was a cheater. I just realized it doesn't matter. My community? My people? They talk to me. They make room for me. They let me have light."

Holy shite, but this man was taking my breath away. My heart trembled at his words. I had no idea Torin could be so thoughtful, but he meant every word of it. He had to. He was under a truth spell.

"And me?" I asked, softly. "Am I a part of your trees?"

"You're newly planted." Torin turned my hand and placed a kiss in the center of my palm. My skin tingled, his lips seeming to sear an imprint into my hand, and then the oven timer dinged. I jerked and he released my hand and stood.

"Let me just slide the lasagna in the oven and then you can tell me about your day."

CHAPTER NINE

TORIN

It had been a hell of a day.

Week, month, year even. But that was just life. There was no use moaning about what had happened. I always found it best to crack on with what needed to be done. And what needed to be done was not fall head over heels for the impossibly beautiful Liora Webster.

It didn't miss my attention that every time I told her she was beautiful she looked shocked. Who had she been dating that hadn't complimented her? Eejits, probably. Stupid eejits who didn't realize what they'd had.

Just thinking about having Liora's lush body in my hands again was enough to make lust drive through me, and I had to take a deep breath and count to ten while I put the lasagna in the oven and pulled out the bottle of wine I'd opened yesterday. Pouring Liora a glass without asking, I busied myself with getting plates out while I thought about my reaction to her.

Particularly because I couldn't trust myself to speak right now without blurting out every nonsense that popped into my head. Like how Liora was a freshly planted tree in my forest. What kind of ridiculous poetry had spewed out of my mouth? I could only imagine the lads taking the piss if they ever caught wind of the way I was carrying on with Liora.

But, bloody hell, I'd meant every word of it.

Last night, after we'd kissed, and after I recovered from the shock of just *taking* her like I did, I'd lain awake for quite a while, drumming up the memories of Liora and Avery together. Memories of Avery were mostly unpleasant, at least once I'd unpacked our relationship in the fall-out of our breakup. We'd never really been a great fit, if I was honest. But when I thought about Liora and Avery's friendship, I realized they'd never been particularly close friends— at least not from the way Avery had spoken about her. We only saw Liora occasionally at the pub or when she was over for a glass of wine every now and again. But of all of Avery's friends, I'd liked Liora the most.

Avery had complained about her a time or two. Liora this and Liora that. *She's always in some sort of mess or another. Why can't she get her life together?*

Sure, from what I'd remembered, Liora had always seemed to have a problem that needed fixing, but she'd never really asked anyone for help either.

Where Avery had been Type A and well-ordered, Liora had sort of drifted at a whim, and I'd always wondered how the two had managed to stay friends. In fact, I'd kind of hoped some of Liora would rub off on Avery, who ran her life ruthlessly on a schedule, which everyone, including me, had been meant to fall in line with. Along with when I was meant to propose, give her children, and settle down.

It had all been a touch too scarily efficient for me, and when she'd flipped out over some astrological reading that Liora had done for her, it tipped our relationship over the edge to where we'd been heading anyway. Rock bottom. Avery had manufactured the whole cheating idea, likely because it was easier than looking at her own faults, and had blasted both me and Liora with it. She'd left Loren Brae, a trail of insults and accusations behind her, and Liora had followed shortly after.

I'd only been sad to see Liora leave.

They'd both left me to clean up the mess they'd made. At the time, it had stung, largely because I prided myself on my reputation in town and didn't want clients to think that I wasn't trustworthy. Eventually, over time, the rumors had faded away and life had returned to normal. But now that Liora was back, I was certain the rumors would surface again.

Particularly since we were dating now—whether Liora realized it or not. Her fake dating idea was ridiculous, but that didn't mean I couldn't lean into *really* dating her.

I'd spent some time today after a few chaotic meetings with clients where I'd said the wrong things—like how I thought Mr. Smythe shouldn't cut down a perfectly beautiful oak tree simply because he was too lazy to rake the leaves—decompressing among the trees. One of my jobs, among many, was trail upkeep in a national park close to Loren Brae, and I'd spent several hours trimming back branches, clearing wood, and basically, talking to my trees as I worked myself through it. What I'd landed on, after a few hours of introspection, was that I just didn't care if people thought that I had been unfaithful to Avery. *My* people knew that cheating and lying wasn't in my nature. And most people I'd worked with since that time knew that I did a good job, priced my services fairly, and delivered results on schedule.

Once I'd come to that conclusion, peace with the situation had settled within me. It had also given me freedom to admit that maybe, just maybe, one of the reasons that the cheating rumor had stung so much was that I *had* always fancied Liora. Not that I had ever planned to do anything about it. I wasn't one to cross lines. But since it was impossible for me to lie now, even to myself, I had to admit that I'd always been very attracted to Liora.

She was just so wildly different from anyone else that I knew. She'd been endlessly optimistic—a stark contrast to Avery who was measured and pragmatic—cheerful and bubbly, where Avery had been regimented and ruled by schedules. Sure, Liora had been chaotic, but she had also been a lot of fun to be around.

Maybe, even though nothing had ever happened between Liora and me, Avery had picked up on an undercurrent that I hadn't even realized was there at the time. It would certainly explain her anger, as well as how quickly she latched onto the idea and gave me no room to defend myself.

Seeing her again had solidified what I'd always thought —Liora was mouthwateringly beautiful—and she'd always been a unique and vibrant person who had interested me.

I watched, now, as Liora curled into herself, her teeth digging into that sexy lower lip of hers, her eyes wide and dreamy as she got lost in whatever she was thinking about in the moment. She did that, I noticed, drifted away on some thought or another. I didn't mind, as it gave me time to observe her beautiful face freely, and it was always fun to see her reanimate when she realized that she'd floated away from the conversation.

"What's your sign, Torin?"

This time, it was me who had to be pulled back into the conversation. Smiling, I brought her over her glass of wine and slid into the chair across from her. Her hair was plaited back from her head, and I missed it being all messy and loose around her shoulders.

"I'm a Taurus."

"That's right, I remember now," Liora murmured, a pleased expression flooding her face. "What's your rising sign?"

The only thing rising on me was something that wasn't polite to bring up in conversation, but I couldn't help my body's response to that kissable mouth of hers.

"You can't possibly expect me to know that," I said, laughing, and she laughed along with me.

"No, I don't suppose you would. If you could just give me your birth date, where you were born and time—"

"Liora. Tell me what happened today." I nudged the glass of wine across the table at her.

"Och, right. I mean, it wasn't a bad day necessarily. It was just a day. But a *big* day. A momentous day. I think. It's hard to say. It's just that..." She trailed off as I grinned at her. "What?"

"I'd just forgotten how fun it was to listen to you talk."

"Fun? Most people find me exasperating." Liora twisted a silver ring at her thumb, and I wanted to take that sad look off her face.

"I find you fascinating. And incredibly sexy."

Surprise flooded her face followed by that soft wash of pleasure that I desperately wanted to see on her face again. In my bed, preferably.

Was I moving too fast? Maybe. It wasn't entirely in my nature to be this resolved in moving forward with dating someone, particularly someone new. But Liora was old-new. I knew her, I liked her, and I was happy to see her again. I hadn't been lonely per se, but her arrival felt timely. *She fits this place.* She was familiar, but at the same time, I still had so many layers to peel back. Either way, she was the most interesting thing that had happened to me in ages, and I had to admit, if even just to myself, I was captivated.

"Um, thank you." Liora took a gulp of her wine, and I was happy to see she wasn't entirely unaffected by me.

"So... your day?" I smiled when she faltered, and realized she'd been looking at my hand where I'd been absently tracing a finger up and down my pint glass. Picking it up, I took a sip, just to calm myself down and stay focused.

"Well, the good news is... I got a job! I'll be waitressing at The Tipsy Thistle." Liora beamed at me, but I furrowed my brow, as confusion filled me.

"But I thought you were an astrologer. Or is that not what you're doing anymore?"

"I mean, I am. But also I'm not. I mean, I was, professionally. But that's not ... it's just..." Liora waved a hand in the air and then went back to twisting the ring at her thumb. "I ran into some issues there. So I'm just ... taking a break. For a bit. And Graham was great. He said I can help on weekends and that should be at least enough for me to make rent."

"Wait, you're worried about making rent?" I tapped a finger on the table. I was feeling all sorts of sensations at the moment, not the most of which was annoyance that she'd be working with Graham regularly. Not that Graham wasn't a nice lad, it was just that most women fell head over heels for him. Secondly, I was confused. I'd named a fairly low price for rent, one which most people shouldn't struggle making. If it was such a problem, I'd be happy to get rid of it altogether. It was just a cover, really, for me to help my mum out.

"I mean, of course, I am. I have to pay the bills somehow."

"Liora, I don't want to put you in a tough spot. I'm happy to cover the rent."

"That's ridiculous, Torin." Liora's mouth gaped open in shock. "You barely know me. You can't have me just move in for free and live off you."

"But you're my girlfriend, right? It's weird to make your girlfriend pay rent."

"I'm not ... it's not. First of all, no, it's not. Plenty of people split finances with their partners. As a feminist, I take offense that you'd think you'd need to provide for me when I can provide for myself perfectly fine, thank you very much. And secondly, I don't need your charity."

"It's not—"

"So, I'll be working at the pub, which is a great way to make friends in the community again and dispel any previous bad rumors anyone had about me. Or you," Liora finished off, lifting her chin and giving me a stubborn look.

I knew that look.

Every man should know that look and respond accordingly.

"Well, then, I'll say congratulations. It's a grand place, as you know, and I'm sure you'll enjoy your time working there." I mentally sighed. It looked like I'd be going to the pub more often now. Like I'd let her drive home late at night in that ancient tin can of a car of hers. Not with the way things had been in Loren Brae of late.

"Thank you. I think I will too."

"But you'll still do your astrology, right? Don't you love it? I feel like I remember you being obsessed with it." Though those were Avery's words, not my own.

"I do. I love it. It's just not been the most ... lucrative of late." Liora's face shuttered, and I wanted to ask her more about why she loved astrology so much, just because her expression lit up with joy when she talked about it, but she continued on. "But there's something else that happened today. Something big."

"Hit me with it."

Liora narrowed those gorgeous blue eyes at me.

"It's magickal related."

"I can take it." I shook my head when her eyes narrowed even farther. "Promise. I told you. You can't live in Loren Brae and not understand that there's magick afoot. It's everywhere, isn't it?"

"Is it? Where do you see it?" Liora's eyes lit, but I waved a finger at her.

"Uh-uh. Stay on topic. What big magickal thing happened today?"

"Och, right. Um, well, it turns out that Loren Brae might just need me."

I tilted my head at her and picked up my beer again, gesturing for her to go on.

"At the castle. There's a magickal Order. The Order of Caledonia. Um, I'm not sure if I am meant to tell you everything, but basically it's just that I took an oath. To help protect Loren Brae."

"From..." I raised an eyebrow at her.

"Um, the Kelpies. And bad people who want to do bad things with powerful items that don't belong to them."

At that, both eyebrows went up to my hairline.

"That sounds dangerous, Liora."

"Och, I'm sure it's perfectly fine." Liora waved my concerns away. "Sophie says that our powers will help us."

"Your powers." I took a deep breath. Right, I'd known Liora was magickal of sorts, but this was really driving it home. "And what, exactly, would those be?"

"Great question." Liora beamed at me. "I asked the same. I guess they're meant to come to me and I'll just figure it out as I go."

This entire scenario would have made Avery break out in hives. I found my lips twitching at Liora's impossible optimism.

"And this doesn't freak you out?"

"Och, no, it one hundred percent does. But I'm in it now. And I think it's going to be grand. There are other women in the town who are part of it. I've met a couple of them already. They're really nice. I think... I think it's what

I'm meant to be doing, Torin. I'm meant to be here. And maybe that's why I've felt like a key that hadn't found its lock for so many years now."

At the sadness that filled her eyes, I reached across the table and held her hand.

"I have so many questions. But for now, I'll just say... ceud mìle fàilte."

One hundred thousand welcomes.

When Liora beamed at me across the table, I chuckled. *That smile. She brings me joy.* And maybe she was the one extending to me *one hundred thousand welcomes.* Maybe she was what *I* needed in my life.

Maybe this was the beginning of something very good.

CHAPTER TEN

LIORA

It was my first shift at The Tipsy Thistle, and I'd hit the ground running. Despite Graham claiming that business had slowed, I certainly couldn't see a difference. There was a busy lunch rush where I'd just done my best to keep up and do as I was told, and now I was taking a break to tuck into my own late lunch in the lull before happy hour started.

I was buzzing though, just buzzing, as excitement consumed me. A few locals had remembered me, and were cheerful about me working for Graham, and I realized that maybe I'd given the rumor Avery started far too much weight in my own life.

Maybe I was giving a lot of other people's opinions too much weight in my life.

It was definitely something I needed to think about,

more seriously, as I had to admit I was itching to get back to my astrology readings. It would take time to build up any local business, but I still had a functioning website and enough of a following that I could re-open my bookings anytime. Particularly as we were approaching a new year. It was always a wonderful time for people to get a reading and plan ahead for any significant changes in the year ahead.

"I'll take it that's a yes?"

I blinked at Graham, who must have spoken to me while I was daydreaming about my business.

"I'm sorry, I missed that."

"I asked if the food suits." Graham gestured with the towel he was using to wipe down the bar.

"Och, aye. It's grand, thanks." It was simple enough—coronation chicken sandwich and vegetable soup—but the servings were hearty and I could use the sustenance to get me through the dinner shift. "People seem really chuffed with the food here."

"Aye, I've got a new lad in the kitchen. He's been a real treat to work with. Shows up on time, cooks hearty simple meals that are fan favorites, and so far has been able to manage the workload. Though I may need to get a sous chef on board during busier times."

"Is there anything I can do to help there?" I was eager to please Graham, hoping at the very least, to keep employment as long as possible.

"Do you have kitchen experience?" Graham lifted an eyebrow at me.

"Sadly, none. Actually, now that I think about it, best to keep me out of the kitchen." Graham and I both laughed as the outer door opened and a woman walked in.

"Agnes!" I exclaimed, jumping out of my seat. I hadn't seen Agnes in years, but we followed each other on socials and occasionally dropped each other a message. "You look great."

"Do I?" Agnes glanced down at her jumper dress, the fabric wrapped softly around her trim body. A necklace with a book charm on it hung around her neck, and small sparkly hoops hung at her ears. "Thank you, I've got a date later."

Graham slammed the stock notebook he'd been writing in and glowered at Agnes.

"Is that right?"

"Aye, that's right." Agnes shot Graham an unreadable look and took the stool next to me. "Mind if I crash your lunch?"

"Nae bother." I glanced to where Graham continued to glower at Agnes and tried to gauge the energy bouncing off the two of them. "Just enjoying a bite after my first lunch shift."

"Are you working here then? Och, that's grand. I'll see more of you then. I heard you were back in town, and I've been meaning to reach out. It's been a busy week."

"Sounds like it," Graham muttered, rounding the bar to go wipe tables across the room. Agnes cast him a look, again, her eyes shuttered, and then turned back to me.

"It's been busy for me as well. Just needed to get settled a bit. It's only been less than a week since I've been back." I spooned up some veggie soup and swallowed, enjoying the light hint of heat in the added spice, and thought about the last few days.

Nothing had happened since I'd taken the oath.

It had been four days, and I'd only managed to see my sister once, as she was so busy with work, but in that time I hadn't quite been able to admit to her that I'd screwed up a spell. Instead, I'd focused on the good news of me finding a job and joining the Order but had stayed away from any magickal screwups. I didn't like when Zara furrowed her brow and concern settled on her face whenever she spoke about my latest mishaps. Better to just keep everything on positive news for now.

But still, I was waiting to see what would happen when it came to the Order and these supposed magickal challenges.

Yet nothing had happened.

Crickets.

Nada.

I was still a little too nervous about trying another spell, at least at Torin's house, but maybe that would be the key to unlocking whatever level of power I had. I was taking my time going through the books I'd taken from Zara's flat, but so far nothing I'd read had given me any further inclination about my powers. Sure, the books themselves were chock-full of recipes and magickal spells, but that didn't necessarily lead me any further down the road to understanding what my particular magick was.

"And you're living at Torin's then?"

I looked at Agnes in surprise but then shook my head with a small laugh.

"Small towns."

"Aye, get used to it. Everyone knows everyone else's business. Isn't that right, Graham?" Agnes raised her voice as Graham came back across the room, his arms full of dirty glasses.

"I'm not sure what you're referring to, darling. You know all of my business." Graham deposited the glasses by the cleaning station.

"Do I? What's that I heard about you helping a pretty lass from Linlithgow the other day?"

"You'll have to be more specific. There are loads of bonnie lasses coming through here." Graham held up a glass and Agnes nodded. Filling it with ice, he topped it up with sparkling water and a lime, and then he slid her a bottle of cordial to add flavor.

"The one who you personally showed how to locate her accommodation?" Agnes sniffed and a wide smile split Graham's face.

"Och, darling. Are you jealous?"

"Not in the slightest." Agnes rolled her eyes. "I'm just getting Liora up to speed on how small towns work and how quickly news carries."

"And did the gossips also tell you the lass was my cousin's girlfriend?"

"Ah, no." Agnes sniffed. "They may have failed to mention that."

Amusement fluttered through me as I watched the two, who were clearly besotted with each other, try to pretend like they didn't care in the slightest what the other was doing.

"So, Torin?" Agnes turned to me, dismissing Graham. "How's it living with him? Are you two…"

Agnes left the comment dangling, and I shrugged.

Torin was all in on us dating. Or at least, that was how

it seemed. He'd brought home the makings for dinner each night after work, and we'd talked long into the night about everything and anything. And then he'd give me a lingering kiss that had every nerve ending in my body on fire, before I'd push him away and hightail it for my room. I was grateful to have the space this weekend because what I needed to do was get my head on straight.

We *weren't* dating. At least *I* didn't think so.

But he was acting just like a devoted boyfriend, and his kisses were hot enough to make me forget any resolve I had about not jumping into things headfirst. The more we cozied in together, the more I was likely to ignore every red flag fluttering cheerfully around this fake relationship.

We'd also said we were committed to this act until I resolved Torin's truth telling issue, which meant this was my first test. Did I say we were nothing? If so, I'd be throwing Torin under the bus because he was convinced we were actually dating. Or at least he'd convinced himself enough so that it wouldn't come out as a lie if anyone asked him about it. Frustration filled me, because the lines were murky now, and I had no idea how to navigate it.

"Um...it's..."

"Complicated?" Agnes said, shooting a look at Graham.

"The best things usually are, darling," Graham drawled and there was enough heat in his look to make my face flush. I noticed Agnes's cheeks pinken too and she visibly swallowed before looking back at me.

"Be that as it may, I won't pry. Yet." Agnes smiled at me. "I'll get the details out of you over wine one night this week. Come by the store? Books and a wee gossip?"

"I'd love that." I meant it, too. I was craving connection

and friendships. And, as much as I loved Zara, her relationship came with some strings. Largely that as the older sister, she felt she had to always look out for me, so I didn't always feel I could talk as freely with her as I liked. I wanted her friendship and love, but it was often served with a side of censure.

I couldn't blame her, necessarily. It wasn't like I always made the best decisions.

But they were my decisions.

I really needed to get better at my self-talk.

"Graham, Liora is the next member of the Order."

I dropped my spoon back into my soup hard enough to have it splatter outside the bowl and gaped as Agnes casually mentioned the magickal Order I'd been silently freaking out about the last four days.

"Is she? Och, that's grand then. We're getting close then, aren't we?"

"Aye. If we can fill the seats, we'll finally be able to put the Kelpies back to rest."

"About damn time." Graham and Agnes shared a mutual look of relief while I continued to gape at them in surprise.

"Seriously? Is this just a known thing in Loren Brae?" I asked, dropping my voice lower as a few new customers wandered in.

"Hiya, folks. Anywhere that suits you," Graham called to a couple with their small son, and they wandered toward a table across the room.

"Do you need me to—"

"Nae bother. Enjoy your lunch." Graham grabbed menus and rounded the bar.

"Wait, I'm confused," I said, keeping my voice low and turning back to Agnes. "How do you know that I joined the Order? I've only told one person." Was Torin already gossiping with his friends? He didn't strike me as the type to run to them with stories. Frankly he didn't strike me as the type for talking much. About anything. With anyone.

Actually, that wasn't fair. After I'd gotten him to warm up a bit, he'd spent quite a bit of time each night talking to me. So maybe I'd only ever seen him as being gruff because I hadn't known him all that well.

Not that I knew him well. Yet.

But I knew his kisses.

Which was definitely a problem. I needed to put some space there. It would be unfair of me to lean too far into ... whatever ... this was simply because I couldn't undo a spell I'd put on Torin.

Who wasn't even complaining about it, mind you.

Sure he blurted out random things like how I sometimes snorted when I laughed and that he thought it was adorable.

What was a girl supposed to say to that?

"I'm sort of their unofficial helper," Agnes said, drawing me back to the conversation. "Because I have a deep love for research, and own a bookshop, I've been able to uncover a lot of the history of the Order and sort of determine why things have been the way they are. Or kind of. I'm helping where I can."

"Are you..." I glanced around and whispered, "Magickal?"

"Not that I know of." Agnes's laugh was a pretty trill that had Graham glancing over.

"Honestly, I'm not sure if I am either," I said, glum, and finished my soup.

"Och, surely you are. What happened to your astrology? I thought you were ace at doing readings." Agnes's expression changed as she seemingly remembered some of the issues I'd had in the past. "Oh, right."

"Aye, that," I said, pushing my plate away and sighing. "My readings seem to have a way of backfiring on me, and I'd promised my sister that I'd take a break and just let it go for a while."

"But ... don't you love it?" Agnes's brow furrowed.

"I do. But maybe I'm just not meant to be a professional reader."

"That's ridiculous." Agnes shook her head at me. "Of course you're meant to be a professional reader. Just because someone interprets a reading wrongly doesn't mean you're shite at your job."

"But it does affect reviews. And bookings," I pointed out, embarrassment washing through me. I'd read a few of my recent reviews after the WAG incident and they hadn't been great. Which was unfair, really, since the reviews were coming from people I hadn't even given readings to.

The door to the pub opened and another woman around our age walked in, looking timidly around the room until her gaze landed on me and her face brightened. A delicate woman, with dark hair pulled back from her face, and soulful eyes, she seemed on a mission.

"Greta. Hi!" Agnes exclaimed, turning to welcome the newcomer. "Och, I haven't seen you in ages. How are you getting on then?"

"Well enough, Agnes. Thanks for asking." Greta smiled

shyly. "It's been a real struggle looking after the kids and work, so I haven't had much time to socialize."

"If you need anything..." Agnes began and Greta waved it away.

"I know, I know. I've just got to figure this out on my own."

Agnes squeezed her shoulder and gave her a compassionate look.

"Liora, this is Greta. She lives just outside Loren Brae."

"Actually, I was kind of hoping to see you," Greta surprised me by saying when she took the hand I offered.

"You were? Have we met?" I asked. I honestly couldn't remember the diminutive woman. Instantly, I felt bad. "I'm sorry...I don't recall."

"No, we haven't. I just heard..." Greta leaned in and lowered her voice. "You give readings, right?"

Over her head, Agnes raised her eyebrows and nodded furiously at me.

"Um, I do, yes. Astrological readings. Tarot as well. But I'm not a psychic, if that's what you're needing."

"No, I just need..." Greta took a deep breath. "I just need some guidance about a few decisions I'd like to make. In the coming year. For myself." Her eyes held a plea and between her expression and the way Agnes was trying to telegraph something to me over her head, I relented.

"That's fair. It sounds like an astrological reading for the upcoming year might be a good fit then. But, keep in mind, they don't tell you what to do. It's just a guide to be used to help know when it might be a more prosperous time to make changes, or when the energy might get a bit murky or sticky for you...that kind of thing."

"Understood." Greta's face lit. "Would this weekend work? My mum has the kids in the morning tomorrow."

"Oh, already? Um." I thought about it. I wouldn't have to be on shift until eleven tomorrow morning, so I could make it work. "Sure, would nine suit? I have to be here by eleven."

"Perfect. I'll come to you then?"

"She's staying at Torin's. You know where his place is?" Agnes leaned in.

"Och, aye. Not too far then. That's grand. Just grand. Thanks, Liora. I'll see you tomorrow." Before I could say anything else or even give her a price, Greta all but ran from the room as though it had taken all of her courage to speak and now she had none left.

"That's fantastic news," Agnes breathed and leaned in, a delighted look on her face. "This is such a big step for her."

"Was that Greta I just saw?" Graham asked, coming across the room from where he'd been taking the order from the couple having an early dinner.

"Aye, it was."

"Nice to see her out," Graham said, before ducking into the kitchen.

"Greta's widowed. She lost her husband last year and has two young kids just on her own. She really had a tough go of it, but Shona, one of the Order, helped her to learn to live within her grief a bit. I'm happy to hear she's looking for some advice on her life. That means she's probably putting herself out there more."

Now I understood why Agnes had been silently urging me to accept the booking behind Greta's back.

"That's sad. Must be tough." I couldn't imagine navigating grief and single parenthood at the same time.

"Such a shame, it really is. We've all done the best we can to help, but she's a bit stubborn about not letting people in. Hopefully this is a good sign."

"I won't be able to tell you anything about the reading, you know." I stacked my bowl on top of my plate and stood. "I do keep the confidentiality of my clients."

"Och, goodness, no. I would never ask. I'm just happy to hear she's making some decisions for herself. Whatever they may be."

"I've got to get back to work," I said, picking up my empty bowl.

"Give me your number and I'll text you about a wine night." Agnes pulled out her phone and typed in my number as I recited it. "Sooner rather than later."

"Please, I'm gasping for some girl time," I admitted.

"We'll plan it. I'll see if the others can join too." Agnes stood. "That's me off then."

"Oh right. On your date."

"Date with my auntie," Agnes leaned in on a whisper. "But he doesn't need to know that, does he?"

"Ah, right." I smiled as Agnes picked up her handbag and headed toward the door as Graham came out of the kitchen. "Have *so* much fun tonight."

"Och, I will. Thanks, Liora. Good to see you again. Later, Graham."

"Agnes, wait. Damn it." Graham looked down to the bowls of soup he had in his hands and then to the door, frustration blooming on his face as it closed after her. He delivered the soup in a hurry and by the time I had finished washing my dishes in the kitchen and wrapped my serving apron back around my waist, he'd worked himself into a tizzy.

"Did she tell you where she was going tonight?" Graham demanded and I raised both eyebrows at him.

"Did who tell me?" I asked, looking around the room.

"Damn it, Liora. Agnes."

"Is it part of my job requirement to tell you what she tells me?" I asked, sweetly, and Graham's eyebrows drew low on his forehead.

"Is it?" I asked, using the same tone I would to scold a naughty child.

"No, it's not." Graham sighed and raked a hand through his hair.

"Is everything okay?" I asked, sweetly, as I straightened the bar stools and looked around the room for things to do.

"No. Nothing's okay. It's never okay," Graham grumbled and then nodded toward a tray of ketchup bottles. "Tomato sauce needs filling."

"Thanks," I said, and ducked into the kitchen to get the big jug of tomato sauce. Working quickly, I filled the bottles while Graham muttered and cursed under his breath, until it was impossible to ignore him anymore. After I topped off the last bottle, I capped it and turned to him. "If you fancy her, why don't you ask her out on a date?"

"Och. I have. I've asked her to marry me too."

"Have you really?" I asked, surprised.

"Aye. Just like that too." Graham turned to me. "Will you marry me?"

"It's a bit improper for the boss to be proposing to his staff, wouldn't you say, *mate*?" a voice growled and I whirled to see Torin standing by the bar, his eyes simmering with fury.

Graham took one look at Torin's face and then glanced over to me, before lifting his chin and letting a slow smile slide across his face. They looked like two dogs bristling for a fight. I pressed my lips together and bit back a sigh. Men.

"It depends. When you have such lovely staff as I do, it makes the idea of marriage a touch more palatable, don't you think?" Graham gave Torin a smug smile, and I rolled my eyes.

"If he's—"

"He's not," I said to Torin who had turned to me. "He's taking the piss. Stand down. Graham, tell him you weren't talking about me."

"Alas, though you are, of course, mouthwateringly beautiful, my heart belongs to another," Graham said, clasping his hands to his chest.

Torin relaxed, and slid onto a stool, though his face was still annoyed.

"Could've just said that, mate."

"I wasn't the one jumping to conclusions," Graham said. "Pint?"

"Irn-Bru. I'm driving."

I glanced up as a group of people walked in and I reached for a stack of menus.

"So when did you and Liora start dating?" Graham asked and I skidded to a stop as I was about to greet the guests.

"We're not—"

"This week. It's new." Torin slid me a glance and gave

me a sultry smile that had enough heat in it to send my insides twisting into knots.

"Nice. That's always the fun time, isn't it?"

I shook my head at the two men and went off to greet the new customers, and then I didn't have much time for anything else. I couldn't believe that Graham had been handling the dinner shift all on his own. The Tipsy Thistle did more than a steady business for dinner, it was fully packed. I barely had time to stop and ask Torin how his day had been before I was needed at another table again.

But, by the time my shift had ended, I'd padded my apron pocket with a few tips, and I'd made strides in reintroducing myself to some of Loren Brae's long-time locals. I noted a few curious looks between Torin and me, but otherwise, nobody said anything untoward about us.

"That's me off, then," I told Graham, ready to be off my feet for the day. "Honestly, I can't believe you've been doing this shift on your own."

"I've had some help, here and there, but nothing regular. It makes a difference. Nicely done, Liora. I think you'll be a grand addition to The Tipsy Thistle."

"Thanks." I beamed at him and then looked at Torin as he rose from his stool. "Are you leaving too?"

"Of course, I'm giving you a ride home." Torin looked at me like I was speaking a different language.

"You are?" I asked, incredulous, and Torin put his hand at the small of my back and ushered me toward the door. It was a clear signal to the pub, and a part of me wondered how much he was doing this to keep up the ruse, and how much was because he genuinely wanted to be with me. Once we were outside, the crisp night air causing our breath to come in small wafts, I paused in front of where he'd parked his lorry next to my car and turned to him. "Torin. You don't have to drive me home, you know. I've lived in a big city for a long time. I know how to take care of myself."

"Aye, I don't doubt it." Torin shrugged and looked around.

"And it doesn't make sense for you to sit through every one of my shifts and wait for me. In fact, it reads a little possessive."

"It does?" Torin looked at me, surprise on his handsome face. "It's just … I don't know. What you said about the Kelpies the other day … and having to fight them and all that. It's in my head, all right? I'd be gutted if something were to happen and I wasn't here to help."

At that, some of my annoyance with him eased. Pressing my lips together, I stepped forward and patted his cheek.

"You're an incredibly thoughtful man, aren't you?" I asked, peering up at him. Standing on my tiptoes, I went to place a kiss on his cheek, but he turned at the last second, capturing my lips with his own.

Heat speared through me, and as much as I wanted to remind myself that this was just fake, it certainly felt real.

A shriek split the night and Torin lifted me in one movement, turning to press my back against the wall of the pub, covering my body with his. My heart hammered in my chest, as my thoughts scrambled.

"Is that the Kelpies?" I hissed. I hadn't heard them yet, and the hair lifted at the back of my neck.

"Aye," Torin said, looking over his shoulder as he protected me. "Get in the car."

"No, I should do something."

"Do you know what to do?"

I blanched and then shook my head. I couldn't move, he had me so thoroughly pinned against the wall of the pub, and it was both soothing and incredibly maddening at the same time.

"Let's just wait a moment and see if we hear them again. Sometimes they just scream in warning."

"They do?" How did he know that?

"Aye, I've heard them enough."

The moment drew out and when another shriek didn't come on the icy evening air, Torin's body relaxed. Finally, he turned his head and looked down at me, the light from the streetlamp reflecting in his eyes.

"We're probably okay, no?" I asked, my body on fire from being pressed against his. It was like being smushed between two rock-hard walls, and despite the very real fear I had from hearing the Kelpies for the first time, my body, traitorous bitch, seemed to have other ideas.

I rocked my hips subtly, and desire flared in Torin's face.

"Careful, darling." Torin bent his head and nipped lightly at my lower lip. "Though I'd dearly love to see your face when your legs are wrapped around my hips, now is not the time or the place."

Of course it wasn't. I was literally plastered to the wall of my place of employment. What was I even doing? Shaking my head, I put a hand to his chest and shoved lightly, until he moved back and I could breathe normally again.

This was ... getting out of control. I needed to keep in mind the end goal. Get my life together. Undo the truth spell that made Torin say things like *that* to me and help Loren Brae with the whole pesky Kelpie problem. *Although, there was no way the truth spell affected him physically, right?* His kisses left me breathless and if he kept pinning my body with his, I would not survive that sort of heat.

Falling for Torin was nowhere on that list.

Which was my typical pattern once I slept with a man. It was impossible for me to separate emotion and sex, and because of that, I'd ignored too many red flags and gotten my heart bruised in the past.

It didn't matter that he kissed like a god.

"Let's just go home," I said, putting space between us. I got out my keys. "I can drive. It'll be fine. Promise."

"I'll follow right behind you then. Take it slow and stay alert."

And when we pulled out and followed the road past the loch, I couldn't be certain which was more a danger. The Kelpies or the man in the lorry behind me.

CHAPTER ELEVEN

TORIN

There were several lacy pairs of pants hanging in my laundry the following morning. I froze and blinked at them, surprised at the visceral response my body had to seeing the delicate fabric hanging from the drying rack in front of the washing machine.

It wasn't like I hadn't known that, naturally, Liora would be doing her washing in the house. Of course she would. People had to clean their clothes, didn't they? It was just that I hadn't envisioned what that might actually look like.

And, apparently, it looked like neon pink and purple lace thongs.

I bet she looked incredible in them.

As the image of her draped in vibrant lace flashed through my mind, I turned away from the drying rack and took several deep breaths. I needed to work on controlling myself. It was this damn truth spell. No matter what, I couldn't seem to filter the things that I thought or said. In some ways, it felt like I'd resorted to caveman-like needs. Torin hungry. Torin horny. Torin tired.

It was deeply annoying.

Yet it had also allowed me to start dating Liora, and even though she'd been in my house just under a week, she had managed to infiltrate every part of my life. I wondered if she even knew how much her presence trickled over into the entire house.

A dish of crystals at the windowsill to "charge" in the moonlight.

A few glass bottles with sprigs of greenery on the fireplace mantel.

A scented candle by the kitchen sink.

A threadbare blanket folded across the back of the couch by the fire.

Pieces of Liora sprinkled all over the house, not to mention her mindless humming, or how she argued with herself seemingly all the time, unbeknownst that anyone was listening to her conversations. She was endlessly intriguing, and I'd started coming home from work earlier than usual to spend more time with her.

Watching her work at the pub had actually been fun, once I'd warned Graham away, that is. Liora was captivating to watch in action, making connections with everyone she spoke to, and bringing a breath of fresh air to the pub. I'd been able to connect with a few people I hadn't seen in a while, since I didn't go out much, and though the truth spell made conversations tricky to navigate, I was getting better at pausing before I spoke. I needed to take a moment to filter through my thoughts and then pick the comment that made the most sense for the conversation with the lowest possibility of offending anyone.

Movement caught my eye and I moved to the window in the door that led outside. I smiled as I saw Liora, in her joggers and a puffy coat, seemingly having a very serious discussion with a small red squirrel. The squirrel sat back on its haunches, bobbing its head as she spoke, and I quietly opened the door and stepped out into the crisp air of the sunny autumn morning.

The squirrel tracked me right away, but it took a moment for Liora to finish speaking and realize that I had joined her in the backyard.

"Bracken, I'm going to need you to help with this, you understand?"

I swear the squirrel gestured one paw to me, and Liora turned and blanched.

"Make a new friend?" I asked, surprised that the squirrel hadn't run away.

The squirrel looked between Liora, who suddenly had a guilty look on her face, and me. It was then that I realized there was potentially something magickal going on here.

"Och, Liora. Is this another spell?" I asked, stepping closer. The squirrel stayed where it was, confirming my suspicions that something else *was* going on.

"I guess it's only fair that I'm honest with you, since I've kind of put you in the same boat," Liora muttered.

"Oh gee, that's grand. Glad to hear you were thinking of lying to me."

Liora grimaced and straightened, turning to look at me.

I sighed. The soft morning light speared through the trees, illuminating her face.

"This light makes you look like a magickal wood nymph," I muttered, unable to lie to her, but annoyed she was keeping things from me.

"I think that's one of the grumpiest compliments I've ever received," Liora said, amusement lighting her gorgeous face.

"Well, I can't help that you're standing here looking drop-dead gorgeous in the stupid morning sunlight while hiding things from me," I said, shoving my hands in the pockets of my hoodie.

"Thank you? I think?" Liora said. I didn't respond, having learned that sometimes it was just best to wait her out, and she sighed and dug at the ground with one toe of her trainers. "I can hear him speak."

"Who?" I paused and then looked at the squirrel.

He waved at me.

"Holy shite." My mouth dropped open and the squirrel chittered at me, before racing across the yard and bounding up a tree. "Did he just wave at me?"

"Aye. He did. That's Bracken. It appears he's my familiar."

"Right." Okay, so she had a familiar. What the hell was a familiar? "What the hell is a familiar?"

"A magickal animal or creature who bonds with their witch to help them with things in the magickal world. Or just to be a companion, really."

"You're a witch?" I asked, trying to sift through all the questions I had, but zeroing in on the most important part.

"Hello? Earth to Torin? I'm the one who put a spell on you, remember?"

"Aye, I do at that. But I didn't realize that made you a witch."

"In your world, who are the people who typically cast spells?" Liora raised an eyebrow in question. Bracken chattered from the tree, seeming to have a laugh at my expense.

"I thought you were an astrologer."

"I am. But it appears I'm also a witch. Of sorts. I don't know, Torin. Truly. It's more like a word used to cover magickals, okay? I've still got a lot to learn. And, not much time to talk this morning, I'm afraid. I've got a reading shortly."

"Wait," I said, before she could turn and go back inside. "How are you? After last night? Did you have bad dreams or anything?" Liora had insisted she was dead on her feet after her shift and had gone right to bed after we'd gotten home, while I'd stayed up for quite a while just in case the Kelpies had shrieked again or if she needed me for anything. But there hadn't been a sound from her side of the house, so she must have done as she said and tucked into bed.

"I'm okay. It was a bit of a white-knuckle ride home, but I have to admit I'm glad that we didn't see the Kelpies on the loch or anything like that. I really can't say what I would have done."

"You would have done nothing but kept driving. I would have gotten out if needed."

Liora sighed and tilted her head, bringing her fists to her waist.

"Torin. It's not your job to protect me."

"It will be a cold day in hell if you think I'd actually let you get out of a car and face down a Kelpie by yourself. That's madness, woman, madness." I shook my head at her.

"And what is it you'd plan to be doing then?"

"I don't know." I threw up my hands. "But I sure as hell wouldn't stand by and let my woman get attacked, would I now?"

"Torin. I'm not..." Liora trailed off and shook her head. "We need to talk about this whole 'us' thing."

"No, we don't," I said, feeling my stubbornness kick in. There was no way she got to walk into my life, create total upheaval, and then create distance from me. I wouldn't allow it. "You feel something for me. And I for you. Don't deny it."

"It's not ... I can't ..." Liora wrung her hands.

I stepped forward and cupped her chin. Leaning down until my mouth hovered over hers, I lowered my voice.

"Tell me you don't feel anything when I kiss you and I'll back off."

Liora's breath caught, and for one suspended heartbeat I thought she might actually say it. Might actually deny what simmered between us.

But her eyes flicked to my mouth. Her lashes fluttered.

And that was my undoing.

I closed the whisper of distance and kissed her.

It wasn't fierce. It was a slow, seeking, an almost reverent brush of lips, like I'd been waiting all damn week for her to exhale just so I could breathe her in.

She gasped softly against me, her lips parting so that the kiss deepened, warmth sliding through me like a sip of whisky. Her fingers curled into the front of my hoodie, gripping tight.

I angled my head, lips coaxing, asking without words.

Liora made a small sound threaded with want.

And she leaned in.

Her body fit against mine as if she'd been carved for this exact moment in my arms. The truth spell hummed under my skin, pressing every unfiltered thought to the surface.

God, she tasted like morning.

Like possibility.

Like a beginning and an ending.

I pulled back only when the need for air insisted, resting my forehead against hers. Her breath came out in soft pants, plumes of white in the cold air.

"Tell me," I murmured, voice ragged. "Tell me you feel nothing."

Liora swallowed. Her hands slid from my hoodie, dropping to her sides as if it took every shred of willpower to let go.

"I..." Her voice cracked. She shut her eyes, regrouped, opened them again. "I can't say that. Because it's not true."

A fierce bolt of satisfaction cut through me, hot and bright. "Aye. That's what I thought."

"But that doesn't mean I know what to do with it," she whispered, stepping back, retreat already in her posture. "Torin, everything in my life is upside down. I'm barely keeping my head above water. And if I fall for you, like, really fall—"

"But you are, aren't you? Already. Just like I am," I said. I wasn't trying to win. I wasn't gloating. It was simply the truth, pulled raw from the spell.

Liora let out a shaky breath. "I need ... space. To think. To breathe."

I nodded, even though every part of me wanted to pull her back in and kiss her senseless again. "Take it. But don't run from this. Or from me."

She bit her lip—traitorous mouth—and then turned toward the back door.

I let her go.

She paused only once, hand on the handle, and said without looking back, "That kiss ... I felt it, Torin. I felt everything." *Whatever you do, Torin, do not fist bump the air.*

And then she was inside, the door clicking softly shut behind her.

I stared after her, heart hammering like a bloody drum.

A rustle above me made me glance up.

Bracken hung upside down from a branch, tiny paws pumping the air like he was celebrating a championship win. He let out a chirping cheer, then did a little spin, tail flicking in triumph.

"Oh, sod off," I muttered, though I couldn't stop the grin tugging at my mouth.

Bracken chattered something that sounded suspiciously like, *About time, lover boy*, and scampered higher into the tree.

I scrubbed a hand over my face.

Liora felt something.

She'd admitted it. *I felt everything.* She wasn't the only one. Liora just fitted. She fitted me. I wanted more with her, which again, should terrify me, but it wasn't terror I felt.

And now?

Now I just had to make damn sure she didn't talk herself out of us.

CHAPTER TWELVE

LIORA

How the hell was I supposed to focus on giving a proper reading when my insides were scrambled in knots and my heart was pumping wildly? Glancing at the clock, I swore, and then dove into the shower, needing a moment to calm myself.

Water always soothed me, and so after I'd scrubbed the important bits, I took a moment to sit, my hair piled on top of my head and my back to the hot spray of water.

How had we gotten here so fast?

Was it possible to feel something for someone after a few nights of long conversations and hearty meals by the fire?

I mean, it wasn't like I'd just met Torin. I knew him from years ago, and we'd also gotten along. But I'd never looked at him in a romantic light. Even though he was dead sexy. But he just wasn't on my radar in that manner because he'd been with Avery. Still, I was remembering more about him, now that we were spending time together, and I realized just how much I had genuinely liked him back in the day.

I could already hear Zara lecturing me about moving too quickly.

Which I wasn't.

A few kisses meant nothing.

She was the one who had put me in this house. So it wasn't like I was to blame for moving in with the lad. The only thing I'd done wrong was accidentally hit him with a truth spell.

"This light makes you look like a magickal wood nymph."

Who even said things like that? A man who spent his time among the trees, that was who.

Either way, I needed to clear my head so I could give this kind widow a clear reading on what her future held for her this year. I silently begged the universe to not have her ask about her love life. I was terrified of giving one more reading that might end up being misinterpreted.

Finishing up, I hopped out of the shower, dried off, and hurriedly applied some light makeup before I put on jeans and a fitted long-sleeved T-shirt. Piling a few of my crystal necklaces around my neck, I took my hair down, brushed it out, and then half-plaited it back. By the time I'd finished, I had about ten minutes before Greta was due to arrive.

Cracking the door open, I peered out.

"Bracken?" I hissed.

"Aye, lass."

I muffled a shriek as the squirrel bounded from the roof above my head to the ground in front of my feet.

"Damn it, that's terrifying." I laughed. "Um, do you want to help me with my reading? Just to maybe channel energy or whatnot? I'm worried that I might do something wrong."

"Will I scare your client?"

"I don't know. Maybe if I just tell her you're my pet?" I looked up at the drive where I could hear a car approaching. "And, you know, you don't jump on her face or something."

"Damn it. That's my favorite way to greet people."

My lips quirked.

"Well, you know, maybe tone it down. Some people are terrified of rodents."

"Rodent? Rude." Bracken crossed his arms in front of his chest and I laughed. His mannerisms were so human-like at times.

"Luckily, I think you're adorable. Okay, that's her here. Maybe up on my shoulder?" I squealed as Bracken leapt straight from the ground to my shoulder and nestled by my neck. "Right, you need to give me some warning, buddy."

"Did you not ask me to go on your shoulder?"

"Aye, I did, I did." I pasted a smile on my face as Greta stopped her car and got out, a nervous smile on her face.

"Hi, Greta. How are you today?"

"Nervous, I'll admit it." Greta looked around and fidgeted with the strap of her handbag. "I've never done anything like this before."

"It's painless, I promise. You'll be happy for it."

Her eyes narrowed. "Is that a squirrel on your shoulder?"

"Och, yes. This is Bracken. He's my wee pet. Don't worry, he's harmless."

"I'm a fierce warrior, actually. But she doesn't need to know that."

"He's very handsome," Greta said, coming closer. "I've always liked red squirrels."

"I like her," Bracken said, and I smiled, stepping back to welcome her inside. I'd moved the chairs so we could face each other over the coffee table, and had my charts, my laptop, and my tarot cards ready. I'd also placed out some of my favorite crystals and lit a pure white candle to cleanse the space.

I motioned for Greta to sit, tucking one leg under me on my own chair to try to look more relaxed than I felt. I was deeply struggling to focus on Greta and not the way Torin's kiss had twisted my insides into knots.

Focus, Liora.

Greta perched on the edge of the armchair, fingers worrying the strap of her bag. She was in her mid-thirties, maybe, with tired eyes and hair twisted into a knot like an afterthought. There were faint shadows under her eyes and a smudge on her T-shirt that looked suspiciously like Weetabix.

Single mum energy.

"Can I get you anything? Tea? Water?" I asked.

"Oh, no, I'm fine, thank you." Her gaze flicked to the candle, the crystals, then to my laptop. "It's all ... very atmospheric."

"That's code for 'a bit woo-woo,'" I said lightly. "Don't

worry, we'll keep things grounded. This is all just to help me tune in a bit."

"And the squirrel?" she asked, eyes darting to Bracken, who'd rearranged himself like a furry scarf around my neck.

"Emotional support squirrel," I said solemnly.

"I am a fiercely powerful companion, actually," Bracken muttered in my ear. *"But sure, let's go with scarf."*

Greta huffed out a surprised laugh, some of the tension easing from her shoulders. "Right. Well, I suppose if I'm here, I may as well commit to giving this my all."

"Perfect," I said, pulling my laptop closer. "I'll just need birth details on the form, aye? Date, time, place? Can you write it down for me?"

Greta took the paper, wrote down her information, and handed it back to me.

"So what we'll do today is look at your natal chart—kind of like a soul blueprint, I'd say—and then we'll check in on the transits for this year, especially around what you want to focus on. Does that sound okay?"

Greta chewed her lip, then nodded. "That's ... what I was hoping for, actually. A bit of guidance. I, um..." She swallowed. "After I lost my husband, I've felt like I've just been drifting. I want to ask if I should do something. Take a chance. And I don't really trust myself to know if I'm being daft, or irresponsible, or—"

"Hey." I set my hand on the table between us, palm up. "First things first. You've obviously been through a lot. So we go slow, and we look at it together. You're not daft. You're allowed to want more."

Her eyes filled, just like that. She blinked rapidly, looking away. "Sorry. I promised myself I wouldn't cry."

"You're allowed that too." I offered a soft smile and moved a box of tissues across the table to her. I'd learned long ago to always keep tissues near during a reading. "But we'll start with the basics, okay? Greta, you're a Cancer Sun, Taurus Moon, Virgo Rising."

"Is that good or bad?" Greta dabbed at her eyes.

"It's very good," I assured her. "It's ... just who you are. This is the kind of chart that loves creating safety, comfort, and care—especially around home and family. Cancer Sun means your heart lives with your people. Taurus Moon loves tangible comfort, food, textiles, beautiful, practical things. And Virgo Rising is the part of you that's organized even when you feel like you're falling apart. You show up for everyone else, even when you're exhausted."

Greta let out a shaky laugh. "That sounds ... accurate. Too accurate. It's a bit creepy, actually."

"Occupational hazard," I said wryly. "Astrology is like cosmic people-watching. Now, before we dig into what's going on this year, is there anything you want to tell me about what's brought you here? That'll help me zero in on the right parts of the chart."

Greta took a breath, lifted her chin like she was bracing for a wave, then nodded. "It's tough ... grieving. And being a single mum, now." Her voice wobbled. "We, um, I, have two kids. They're eight and five. I ... uh ... I'm working nights at the supermarket now. Shelf-stacking and till training. It's honest work, but the hours are rubbish for the bairns. My mum comes by most nights. I barely see them awake except for the school run and weekends. And I'm ... tired. All the time."

My heart clenched. "I'm so sorry, Greta."

"Everyone keeps saying that," she whispered. "And I know they mean well, but I don't want people to be sorry. I want ... something that feels like a life again." She tugged at a chain around her neck that held a wedding ring. "But I have an idea. That maybe, I don't know ... could be something more. A business, maybe. My own thing."

"That's what you want to ask about?" I asked gently. "Whether you should go for it?"

"Aye." She nodded, eyes huge. "Because if I quit the supermarket and it goes wrong, it's not just me I'm hurting. It's the kids. The mortgage. Everything."

I nodded slowly, fingers hovering over the trackpad. "Okay. Then we'll look at your second house—money, income—and your tenth house—career. Also your fourth house, of home and family, because this decision impacts all of that. And we'll see what's lit up."

I clicked to pull up her chart, the familiar wheel spinning into place.

And then my entire world shifted.

For a moment, I thought it was a trick of the eyes. But it wasn't the screen that changed. It was ... everything.

The lines of Greta's chart—those neat aspects connecting planets across the wheel—shimmered. Just the faintest glimmer at first, like sunlight on a loch. I blinked and leaned closer.

The lines thickened, glowing softly.

I blinked, uncertain of what I was seeing, and sucked in a breath as the chart lifted. Off the screen. And floated gently into the air.

I gaped as silvery threads rose from the laptop, weaving themselves into the air between us, forming a delicate, three-dimensional web. They hummed with something old and powerful, a music I felt more than heard.

"Lass," Bracken whispered, tiny claws tightening on my shoulder. *"Do you see that?"*

"You see it too?" I whispered back. My heart was pounding so hard I could feel it in my fingertips.

"See it? It's like someone spilled the loom of fate all over your coffee table," he breathed. *"By the thistle, Liora, what are ye?"*

"Is everything all right?" Greta asked, glancing between us, oblivious. To her, the chart was still just a chart. She couldn't see the threads spiraling and twisting.

Focus. You're reading for a very real, very fragile person. You can panic about glowing fate spaghetti later.

"Everything's grand," I said quickly, forcing my voice steady. "I'm just … tuning in."

I reached out, hand passing through the luminous threads. A sensation like static skated over my skin—tiny sparks of insight or possibility, even.

And then images slammed into me.

Greta at her kitchen table, fabric strewn everywhere—tiny shirts, old rugby jerseys, a faded flannel shirt. Her hands moved with purpose, stitching pieces together. She was creating a quilt.

And then next, she looked to be at a summer market on the square and Greta sat behind a stall full of quilts, pillows, and textile keepsakes. A sign above her read *HeartStitch Memory Quilts* by Greta MacLeod. People approached with warm smiles and curiosity.

Next, it switched to a small studio room off her kitchen, where she worked at a sewing machine while the kids slept in the next room. Warm light cocooned Greta as she worked with a peaceful expression and light music in the background.

The images snapped back like a rubber band. I sucked in a breath.

Greta stared at me, eyes wide. "What ... did you see?" she whispered.

Careful, Liora, just give her the basics.

"I saw you doing something with your hands," I said, surprising myself. I wasn't psychic, that I knew of. I took a moment, thinking about what I was seeing, and steadied myself. "Working from home. Something creative, but practical. Using fabrics? Textiles?"

Greta's hand flew to her mouth. "The quilts," she whispered behind her fingers.

The threads above the chart pulsed, one of them—stretching from her Cancer Sun to the cusp of the tenth house—glowing brighter. My gaze snagged on it. It pulsed again, insistent.

Almost without thinking, I reached out and brushed my finger across the glowing thread.

The world surged.

This time I saw Greta in a tiny, tidy shop front off the main street, shelves lined with folded quilts and framed fabric art. Her kids were older here, doing homework at a corner table, the bell over the door chiming as a customer entered. A wave of quiet, steady abundance radiated from it. Not riches, but enough. Enough to breathe.

When I pulled my hand back, the thread quivered, then settled into place, thicker, more solid. Woven.

"What in the name of all the oaks was that?" Bracken hissed. *"You just tugged the bloody thing."*

"I didn't mean to," I whispered in my head, panic and awe warring. "I just ... touched it."

"And you changed it," he said, sounding half horrified, half impressed. *"Chartweaver."*

The word landed like a bell toll in my bones.

"Sorry?" I thought back.

"Later," Bracken said sharply. *"Human first, existential crisis second."*

Greta cleared her throat. "Liora? Are you talking to the squirrel?"

"Right. Sorry." I forced my gaze back to the screen, to the actual chart. The threads hovered like a translucent overlay now, but I made myself read the symbols I knew and tried to anchor myself in the familiar.

"Right," I said, slipping into astrologer mode. "Greta, you've got Cancer strong at the top of your chart, around your career zone, which means your work in the world is meant to be an extension of your heart. Something that nurtures others. And your second house of income is in Libra with Venus there, which loves beauty, art, things that are aesthetically pleasing but also relational. You don't do well in jobs where you're just a cog in the machine. You need personal connection. Stories."

Greta's eyes shone. "That's ... exactly how the supermarket feels. Like I'm just ... inventory."

"You're also in a massive transit right now," I continued, scanning. "We've got Jupiter moving through your ninth, expanding your horizons, and Saturn has been slogging through your seventh and into your eighth—grief, shared resources, all the heavy stuff. But"—I tapped the screen—"what's really important is that the North Node is going through your tenth house of career and purpose. This is literally the stars screaming that it's time to step into something more aligned with who you are."

"So ... that's good?" she asked.

"It's very good," I said. "Scary, but good. It means you're at a crossroads. The choices you make in the next year or so can set the tone for the next couple of decades. No pressure or anything."

Greta let out a watery laugh.

The glowing threads thrummed in agreement. One in particular tugged at me again, this time stretching between her Moon in Taurus in the eighth—grief and shared emotional resources—and her second house. When I focused on it, I saw flashes of worn baby clothes stitched into a tiny blanket. A woman smiling as she ran her fingers over the fabric.

"What is it you love doing?" I asked quietly. "The thing that keeps tugging at you?"

Greta swallowed, fingers twisting together. "What you're seeing is correct. It's sewing I love," she admitted. "My gran taught me when I was wee. I used to make doll clothes, then my own skirts. My husband, well, he was terrible at throwing things away. I've got all his shirts still. I couldn't bear to give them to the charity shop, so I started cutting them up and stitching them into a quilt. For the kids. So they could still have him with them, you know? When they're on the sofa watching telly, or in bed on a stormy night."

My eyes prickled. "That's beautiful."

"It made me feel ... close to him," she whispered. "And then my friend's mum passed and she asked if I could do the same. And then someone at the school gate saw it and asked if I'd make one from their dad's ties. It's just been word of mouth. A wee side thing. But when I'm doing it, it's the only time my brain goes quiet. I feel ... like me again. I thought..." She took a shuddering breath. "I thought maybe I could make a proper business out of it. Memory quilts. For folk who've lost someone. Or just ... keepsakes from baby clothes the kids have outgrown. I could do them from home, when the bairns are in bed. Then I'd be there for them more. But I'm worried. What if it isn't enough? Is that selfish of me to want this?"

The threads above the chart buzzed, like a hive of bees agreeing she was asking the right question.

I nearly laughed at the absurdity of it. Here I was, sitting in my borrowed house with a man I'd accidentally hexed, my squirrel familiar, and a cosmic loom hovering over my coffee table. And this woman, this brave, *exhausted* woman, thought she was the one taking irrational risks.

"You are not selfish," I said firmly. "You are human. You are a mother trying to make a life that actually works."

"But is it ... allowed?" she whispered. "Astrologically, I mean. Am I meant to do this? Or am I meant to suck it up and stay at the supermarket because it's sensible?"

The question pulsed through the air, hitting the web of threads. They flared, two distinct paths brightening. Reaching out, I brushed my hand lightly across the threads, careful not to pull on them.

On one side I saw Greta at the supermarket, ten years from now. Eyes flat, shoulders hunched, an air of defeat around her. The money was ... fine. Stable. But she was shrinking. It wasn't a job suited to what she needed to light her up.

On the other side I could see Greta with her sewing business. A quiet pride in her posture as she locked up her tiny shop one evening, the lights of the village twinkling around her.

I stared, pulse racing. The truth wasn't that one path was "safe" and the other was "dangerous." They both had risk. The difference was *which* kind of hard she chose.

As I watched, the path of the quilts flickered, some threads thin, others thicker. It wasn't a guarantee. It was a possibility.

Instinct guided my hand again. I reached for one of the thinner threads that branched from that path—the one tied to her Venus, I realized. To her willingness to be seen.

Now another image flickered. It was of Greta hiding her business, treating it like a guilty hobby versus Greta actually telling people, putting up a proper website, showing up at markets. The latter wove stronger lines of support from the community. I took a breath, then plucked that thread gently, imagining it thickening, anchoring.

The weave shifted, subtle but real.

Power thrummed through me, hot and bright. My fingers tingled.

Chartweaver.

The word echoed again, louder this time. Somewhere deep in my memory, a whisper surfaced—my gran bent over her big leather book, muttering something about a weaver that I'd half tuned out as a teenager, more interested in boys and eyeliner.

"Lass," Bracken murmured, awe in his tiny voice. *"Ye just nudged her future."*

"Is that ... bad?" I thought, panic spiking.

"It depends," he said. *"On whether you remember that threads can tangle if you yank on them."*

"Bracken, you're not helping," I hissed internally.

"Then maybe don't play with the loom while you're mid-appointment," he retorted. *"Finish the reading. We'll dissect your crisis while you're in your pajamas later."*

Fair.

I turned my attention fully back to Greta, who was gaping at me as I muttered to the squirrel on my shoulder, fingers curling into my palm under the table to stop myself from reaching for more threads.

"Greta," I said softly. "Astrology doesn't usually come with a neon sign that says quit your job. It gives us cycles and themes, windows where certain choices are supported. You, right now, are in a powerful window for building something from home that's rooted in your heart. Something that honors your grief instead of pretending it's not there. Your second house, your income, is lit up with opportunities for work that's relational and creative. Your tenth house is screaming for a career that is personal and not some faceless corporation. Your fourth house, home, is where the action wants to be. This quilting business? It aligns with all of that."

"But the risk," she whispered. "What if it fails?"

"It might," I said honestly. I didn't want to sugarcoat it. "Not because you're not capable, but because any new business has growing pains. But your chart shows that if you give it a structured go—set hours, real pricing, treat it like a job, not just a hobby—you have every chance of making it work. Especially over the next eighteen months while that North Node is in your career house. This is your jumping-off point."

Greta's eyes brimmed again. "I'm scared."

"Of course you are," I said. "That's totally normal. I would be too."

"You would?"

"But you're not just leaping without a parachute," I continued. "You can build a bridge. Could you, for example, scale back at the supermarket first? Reduce shifts as your quilt orders increase? Give yourself a timeline—say, six months where you throw everything at this business and reassess? That way you can ease into it. It's a transition."

"Yes," she said slowly. "I could ask for fewer nights. They're not desperate for staff, so ... they might let me drop some shifts." She pressed her fingers to her lips, thinking. "And I could use the time I'm currently trying to nap in the day to sew instead. At least at first."

"The chart supports that," I said. "It doesn't say the path will be effortless. But it does say that if you work with this energy—if you *choose* to step into it—you're not walking alone. You'll find allies. Your community wants what you're offering."

"That sounds ... really rewarding," she whispered.

I reached for my tarot deck, the cards familiar under my fingers. "Do you mind if we pull a couple of cards to clarify?"

She nodded quickly. "Please."

I shuffled, centering myself. "Let's ask. What does Greta

need to know about stepping into this business? What is the outcome if she commits to it with structure and heart?"

Greta's eyes widened as three cards slipped free, nudging my fingers. I laid them out.

The Empress. Three of Pentacles. Eight of Pentacles.

I exhaled a soft laugh. "The universe really is unsubtle today."

"What do they mean?" Greta asked, leaning in.

I tapped the Empress. "This is you. Nurturer, creator, mother. She's abundance, but not in a flashy way. She grows things slowly and steadily. This card is about tending to what you love and watching it flourish."

Next was the Three of Pentacles. "This is collaboration. Community. You don't build this alone. Word-of-mouth recommendations, maybe even partnering with local funeral homes or new parent groups down the line."

Greta's eyes widened. "I hadn't even thought of that."

"And the Eight of Pentacles," I said, smiling. "This is the card of the artisan. The craftsperson who hones their skill over time, building a solid reputation. It's long-term work. Not a quick fix, but something you become known for."

Greta stared at the cards, then at the chart, then back at me. "So ... you think I should do it?"

I took a breath. The threads above the chart shimmered, waiting.

"I think," I said carefully, feeling the truth anchor in my bones, "that if there was ever a time for you to give this an honest go, it's now. I think your chart shows that your soul is crying out for work that honors your love for your husband, your love for your kids, and your own need to create. And I think this quilting business of yours has the bones to support you—emotionally and financially—if you treat it like the real thing from the start."

We spent another twenty minutes going through practicalities like timing, brainstorming business names—we both liked HeartStitch Keepsakes—looking at months where the energy ramped up. I gave her some dates to circle for launching.

All the while, the threads hovered, occasionally pulsing when we landed on a timeline that aligned with them. I kept my hands firmly on the physical side of the table.

Eventually, Greta stood, tucking her notes into her bag alongside a small piece of rose quartz I pressed into her hand for courage.

"Thank you," she said, voice trembling but steadier somehow. "I ... I feel like I've been holding my breath for a year and someone just told me I'm allowed to breathe again."

"You are," I said, throat tight. "And you don't have to do it perfectly. Just ... start. One stitch at a time."

She laughed wetly, wiping her eyes. "That sounds like something my gran would've said." She glanced at Bracken, who was now grooming his tail like he hadn't just watched me manhandle fate. "And thank you ... to your friend."

"He says you're welcome," I said.

"*I like her,*" Bracken commented. "*She's got a brave heart.*"

When the door shut behind her and her car pulled away, the house fell into a thick, humming silence.

The threads above the coffee table were fading, sinking

back toward the chart, but not entirely gone. I stared at them, pulse roaring in my ears.

"Okay," I said slowly. "What the actual hell was that?"

Bracken hopped off my shoulder onto the table, tiny nose twitching as he sniffed at the remaining shimmer. *"That, lass, was you stepping into what you are. A chartweaver."*

"I've never even heard that word before," I protested. "Gran never said I was—"

Bracken gave me a look. *"Your gran also didn't tell you you'd end up sharing a house with your former friend's ex-boyfriend, but here we are. Just because you didn't get a pamphlet at birth doesn't mean it's not true."*

"Please explain," I said, crossing my arms, heart still racing. "Seriously, I'm, like, shaking."

He puffed himself up. *"There are witches who read charts like reading a map. There are witches who sense threads of fate like feeling vibrations on a web. And then there are the rare ones who can actually touch those threads and shift them a hair. Not rewrite fate entirely,"* he added quickly, as if he saw the panic rising on my face. *"That's beyond anyone. But they can ... nudge. Strengthen certain paths. Soften others. Help mend tears."*

"So, weaving. Or re-weaving, I guess," I said slowly.

"Aye." His eyes gleamed. *"Chartweavers. They see the pattern in the chart and the threads of what could be, not just what is."*

My stomach dropped. I stared at the empty chair where Greta had sat. "So when I told her to take the chance—"

"You didn't hypnotize the woman," Bracken said firmly. *"You didn't force her hand. You simply strengthened the*

thread of a choice she already wanted to make. You could see that path in her chart. You didn't conjure it out of nowhere, Liora. You listened. You guided."

"But what if I'm wrong?" I whispered. "What if I encourage someone down a path that ends badly? What if I weave something that tangles?"

"Then you'll learn," he said bluntly. *"And you'll be more careful next time. Power without humility is dangerous. Power with your level of overthinking? Likely manageable."*

"That doesn't make me feel better," I muttered.

He patted my hand with a tiny paw. *"Listen. You already meddled with fate the minute you flung that truth spell at Torin's face."*

"Wow, thank you for the reminder."

"You're welcome. My point is that you've always been messing with threads, lass. You just didn't see them. Now you can. Which means you can be more mindful. More deliberate. That's a good thing."

I blew out a breath, mind spinning. "Gran," I murmured. "She must've known something. She had to. She kept saying my chart work was different."

"You need to spend more time with her books," Bracken said simply. *"And I know just the right one."*

"You do?" I gaped at the squirrel.

"Aye. You only had to ask."

"Damn it, Bracken. Can you show me the book with the information that I'd dearly like to know so I don't have a meltdown?"

"Humans are so dramatic."

"Och, please. I've watched you fling yourself at a bird feeder and run away in a huff when you couldn't reach it."

"Wasn't me." Bracken shook his head.

"Lies." I laughed at the squirrel as he ran his little paws over a stack of books until he found the one he wanted.

"This one."

"How do you know?" I asked, looking at where his tiny paws rested on a book in the middle.

"I don't know. How did you know that you liked shoving your tongue down Torin's throat?"

"So rude." I glared at him and hauled the book onto the low table, the spine creaking as I opened it. The pages fell open naturally, but I couldn't help but wonder if there wasn't something more at play here.

I frowned. The top of the page was headed with a word in Gran's looping script.

Chartweavers.

My pulse thudded.

I bent closer, eyes scanning the text.

"Some magickals read the stars. Some feel the pull of the tides of fate but cannot grasp them. The rarest of all are those who can see the threads and place their fingers upon the loom. Chartweavers are born, not made, though they may sleep for years before their gift awakens. They are keepers of possibility, not dictators of destiny. Their task is not to force a future, but to mend what is torn, strengthen what is weak, and illuminate paths for those who stand at the crossroads."

My throat tightened as if someone had slipped a hand around it.

"Great care must be taken. Every weave has conse-quence. A gentle touch is required. The weaver must never forget the sovereignty of the soul before them. Consent, intention, and ethics are their safeguards."

I swallowed hard, eyes blurring. On the next page, a diagram of a chart much like the one on my laptop was drawn by hand, with threads sketched between points and notes in the margins.

My name was written, a question mark and a heart next to it, on one of the pages.

Tears stung my eyes.

"She knew," I whispered. "She knew and she didn't tell me."

"Maybe she didn't want to overload you," Bracken said gently. *"You were busy trying to survive algebra and bad haircuts. She might've been waiting for the right time."*

"The right time being ... after she was gone and I accidentally wove someone's career path?" I sniffed.

"Witches are dramatic like that."

I huffed a wet laugh, brushing at my cheeks. I read on.

"The chartweaver will often awaken fully in moments of crisis or deep service—when heart, chart, and need align. When this happens, the threads will reveal themselves. The weaver should ground, breathe, and remember. You are a guide, not a god. Speak truth. Offer choice. Weave only where the soul already leans."

Relief loosened something in my chest. That was what had happened with Greta. I hadn't conjured a path she didn't already want. I'd just ... given it a little cosmic scaffolding.

Still terrifying. But slightly less so.

A clock chimed faintly from somewhere in the house. I jumped.

"Shite." I glanced at the time on my phone. "I really have to go."

"I'll stay here and keep an eye on your tree man."

"He's not my—" I stopped. "Never mind. There's no use arguing."

I walked toward the front door, my mind buzzing with charts and threads and the image of Greta's future shop. Outside, the autumn light slanted golden across the loch, and for the first time since I'd arrived in Loren Brae, I felt the strange, dizzy sensation that maybe, just maybe, I was exactly where I was meant to be.

Even if I was a chartweaver with zero idea what I was doing.

One stitch at a time, I thought, echoing my own advice to Greta as I grabbed my coat and headed out.

One stitch at a time.

CHAPTER THIRTEEN

LIORA

I'd all but drifted through my shift on Saturday, my brain whirling with thoughts about being a chartweaver, and by the time Torin had arrived to drive me home, I was exhausted. He hadn't questioned me when I'd begged off having a nightcap with him, insisting I was tired, and I'd fallen into bed and slept straight through the night in a blissful dreamless sleep.

Apparently, that was exactly what I'd needed, because when I woke up Sunday morning, the fog had cleared.

The threads, the glowing web, the truth spell—they were still there in the back of my mind, sure, but they weren't pressing down on me like a weight. More like a new, slightly daunting tab open in my brain browser that I could click into later.

But one thought rose to the top.

I'd given a reading, and it had gone really, really well. In a way that it never had before. And I could be proud of myself for it. Even if I'd accidentally meddled with fate a bit, or more than a bit. I still wasn't quite sure on all that. But before I could let guilt swamp me for inadvertently touching the threads of someone else's fate, I shook it off.

Right now, I had one more lunch shift to get through and then I could get to the relaxation portion of my weekend.

I padded into the kitchen to find Torin already there, hair damp from a shower, wearing a dark T-shirt and jeans.

"Morning," I said, voice croaky.

He glanced up, and that slow, warm smile lit his face. "Morning, wood nymph."

Heat shot to my cheeks. "We're not keeping that nickname."

"Aye, we are." He looked at my face and then grabbed a mug and poured a cup of coffee from the pot. "You sleep all right?"

"Like the dead." I took a blessed sip. "Eight beautiful hours of unconsciousness. Highly recommend."

He studied me, eyes warm. "You look good. Rested. Not as stressed as when you first arrived."

"I guess that's progress," I said dryly.

"It is."

I leaned back against the counter, making myself focus. "Right, so. Today I've just got the lunch shift at The Tipsy Thistle. I'll be done and back by three or so."

His jaw tightened almost imperceptibly. "I'll pick you up, then."

I shook my head. "No, it's all right. It's broad daylight.

Please. You can't follow me around all over Loren Brae. What about when you're at work and I go out? This isn't sustainable, Torin."

His brows lowered. "Liora."

I held up a hand. "I know, I know. Kelpies. Danger. Blah, blah, blah. But I'll be driving on main roads in the middle of the day, not taking a scenic midnight detour along the loch. I promise I won't go monster hunting on my break."

He exhaled, running a hand through his hair. "You're sure?"

I softened, pushing off the counter and stepping into his space. "I'm sure. I appreciate your concern, truly. But I'll be back mid-afternoon, and I need you not to hover. Go... I don't know. Chop some wood. Talk to the trees. Whatever it is you do when I'm not here."

His eyes darkened, flicking to my mouth, then back up. "You're cheeky this morning."

"Rested," I corrected. "And I promise to text you when I get there and when I leave, all right? That way you can track my movements like a paranoid boyfriend and everything."

He huffed out a laugh. "I'm not paranoid." I noted he didn't say anything about the boyfriend idea though.

"You absolutely are," I said, but gently, because I couldn't be annoyed at him for caring.

I finished my coffee, grabbed my bag, and tried not to think about how much I already liked that he worried about me. That was weird, right? I shouldn't like that so much. It felt like the lines were blurring between us already.

The Tipsy Thistle was buzzing for a Sunday. Locals in

for roast lunches, a couple of tourists, and the usual mix of regulars at the bar discussing football like the fate of the world hinged on it.

But for the first time since I'd started there, everything felt ... easy.

I breezed through my tables, scribbling orders, topping up drinks, smiling and chatting. My brain, instead of spinning in eight different anxious directions, hummed along. Maybe being a chartweaver had cracked something open in me, but whatever it was, I felt more ... anchored, like I'd found a groove that actually fit.

During a lull, I ducked behind the bar to check my phone. A new message pinged through from Sophie.

Hi friend! Girls' dinner at the castle tonight – just the Order. 7p.m. You free?

MY HEART DID a delighted little flip. Friends. I had dinner plans with actual new friends at an actual castle.

Omg yes. Wouldn't miss it. What should I bring?

HER REPLY CAME BACK ALMOST INSTANTLY.

Just yourself and your appetite.

I GRINNED AT MY PHONE.

"Someone's happy," Graham observed, sliding past me with a tray of empty pint glasses.

"Girls' night," I said. "Apparently I'm going to the castle for dinner."

He arched a brow. "Is Agnes going?"

"Why do you care?" I asked and he glowered at me.

"I just haven't seen her all weekend. Usually she stops in."

"Maybe she's been busy," I said, shrugging, and went to take a Coke to a table.

I was clearing plates from a table of four when a familiar golden blur trotted in through the front door, followed by the click of sensible boots and the soft tap of a cane.

Mitch.

Zara followed behind him, her dark hair pulled back, the same self-possessed energy she'd had since we were teenagers. Mitch led her confidently through the crowd, tail wagging like a metronome.

I dumped the plates on a nearby tray station. "Hi, Z!"

Her head snapped up, her face lighting in my direction. "L?"

"Right here," I said, reaching her and gently catching her forearms. "Hi."

She broke into a huge grin and leaned forward, bumping her forehead against mine in an awkward hug. "There's my dram of chaos."

Warmth flooded my chest. "I'm sorry I haven't seen you much this week."

"It's okay, I know you've been settling in." Mitch sat at her feet, grinning up at me with his harness on.

"Here, come sit." I helped Z to a table and Mitch lay down next to her. "I'll bring him some water shortly. Do you want a roast lunch, or something light, like a Caesar salad or chicken soup?"

"Soup and salad suits me just fine." Zara bent and took Mitch's harness off, and he bounced up to give me a kiss.

"Hey, handsome. You keeping my sister out of trouble?"

He licked my cheek in answer and I gave him a quick cuddle before Zara re-harnessed him and he settled at her feet.

"So, Liora, what's going on? I can't believe I haven't heard from you. Is it awful living with Torin? I'm so sorry that I didn't realize who the landlord was. Tell me, quick, is it bad?"

My stomach did a guilty flip. I really should have filled Zara in on everything that was going on. "Life is ... good," I hedged. "But it's not actually bad at the house. Torin is a good landlord. And now that I've got the job here, I'm quite busy. I'll give you the full download later, I promise."

Guilt pricked sharp and hot under my ribs. I hadn't told her about the chartweaver thing. I hadn't really told her about Torin and me, beyond a few short texts promising her that everything was fine.

I made a mental note to tell Zara everything. Soon. She deserved to know what was going on. I'd never hidden anything like this from her before.

"Good," Zara said. "Because if you dash off to your magickal castle friends and forget all about me, I'll tell Mum."

I laughed. "I would never risk Mum's wrath."

"She can be terrifying," Zara agreed.

She wasn't really. She hadn't exactly abandoned us when she left for London, but she had certainly made a new life for herself. She was … happy. Just not particularly maternal. We heard from her every few months during her *check-ins* but that was about it. I wondered if she might come for Christmas now that I was in Loren Brae.

"I have to get back to work," I said reluctantly. "But I'll swing by to chat when I can."

"No problem, I'm just happy to not be making food for myself today." Zara settled back, comfortable with spending time in her own company, and I dove back into work.

The rest of the shift flew by in a whirl of orders and plates and the warm comfort of knowing my sister was nearby. Between tables, I'd catch glimpses of her laughing with Graham, Mitch sprawled under the table like he owned the place. Stopping by to give her a quick hug before she left, I once again promised her I'd stop by that week for a proper hang out. She left, happy enough, but guilt still tugged low in my gut.

By the time two o'clock rolled around and my shift was ending, I was pleasantly tired and buzzing with the pride of a solid weekend worked.

I said my goodbyes, collected my tips, and slid into my wee car, sending Torin a quick text.

Leaving the pub now. No Kelpies
spotted. Yet.

His reply came less than a minute later.

Good. Come home.

Ridiculous how two words on a screen could make my
stomach do somersaults. Home. With Torin.

The buildings of Loren Brae were bathed in late-after-
noon light, the leaves gilded, the loch beyond glinting like
someone had spilled a box of glitter across the surface of the
water.

Turning the music up, just so I could ignore a Kelpie's
scream if one happened to burst out of the gilded water, I
sang at the top of my lungs all the way home until I turned
the car into the drive and promptly forgot how to breathe. I
parked the car quickly and turned the engine off, cracking
open the door, because I dearly needed the icy air to bring
me back to life.

Torin was in the clearing by the side of the house, split-
ting logs.

Shirtless.

Sweat slicked his chest and shoulders, muscles flexing as
he swung the axe in a clean arc. The wood cracked with a
satisfying thud, falling neatly to either side of the chopping

block. His jeans rode low on his hips, his muscles rippled, and the whole scene looked like one of those thirst-trap lumberjack calendars come enticingly, beautifully, to life.

"Okay," I muttered to myself. "You are a mature, composed adult. You are not going to climb him like a tree."

Bracken dropped onto the bonnet of my car with a thump, making me jump. He peered through the windscreen at me, whiskers twitching.

"Careful there, lass," he said. *"Your eyes are about to fall out of your head."*

I squeaked and slapped a hand to my chest. "You can't just appear like that."

"Tell that to your thoughts." He snorted. *"They just appeared straight in the gutter."*

"Shut up," I hissed, grabbing my bag.

As I climbed out of the car, Torin straightened, wiping the back of his wrist across his forehead. He spotted me and smiled, slow and wicked.

"Welcome home," he called.

My brain short-circuited. "Hi," I managed, hoping I didn't sound as breathless as I felt.

He set the axe down, leaning on it with one hand. "Shift go all right?"

"Fine," I said, then cleared my throat. "Good. Busy. Z came by with Mitch to say hello. I only broke one glass, so that's like a personal record."

He chuckled, his gaze sweeping over me in a way that made my skin tingle. "Good." He nodded, then straightened fully, the movement making every muscle in his torso shift and flex like some cruel, deliberate show. "You're star-ing, Liora."

"I am not," I lied, badly.

His mouth curved. "You are. I'm not complaining, mind you."

Heat pooled low in my belly. I dropped my gaze, suddenly very interested in the state of my trainers. "It's your fault for being ... all ... that."

"All what?" he asked, feigning innocence as he walked toward me, slow and unhurried, like he had all the time in the world to ruin me.

"Torin," I warned.

He stopped directly in front of me, close enough that I could see a bead of sweat slide from his collarbone down the center of his chest. My imagination happily followed its path.

"I asked you a question, wood nymph," he murmured. "What am I?"

"Annoying," I said weakly. "And ... obscenely fit."

His smile turned smug. "There it is."

"Ugh," Bracken groaned from somewhere up in the nearest tree. *"Get a room."*

"Go away," I hissed under my breath.

"I live here," he chittered back. *"I'm trapped in a forest romance."*

Torin's lips twitched. "I'm assuming you're talking to Bracken and not me?"

"He doesn't like being third wheel to my hormones," I muttered.

Torin's eyes darkened, his gaze dropping briefly to my

mouth before meeting my eyes again. "Are your hormones doing something right now, Liora?"

"Yes," I blurted. "They are doing many things. All of them inappropriate to discuss while the squirrel is listening."

"Thank the goddess," Bracken murmured.

Torin laughed, delighted. "Good to know."

He leaned in, not quite touching me, the heat of his body washing over me like a physical thing. "For what it's worth, every time you walk by in those tight jeans, my brain turns to sawdust. So we're even."

Something in my chest fluttered, wild and reckless. I swallowed. "We should probably ... go inside. I need to get ready. The girls invited me to dinner at the castle."

"Fancy," he said, still too close. It was becoming increasingly hard to breathe.

"Yeah. Sophie says it's for the Order. Witchy girls' night."

His expression stilled. "Is that a good thing? Are you excited?" We still hadn't talked too much more about the Order, after I'd told Torin I needed more time to learn about it and absorb just what my role was going to be.

"Terrified," I admitted. "And excited. It's been a while since I had proper friends in my life."

He studied my face, something flickering in his eyes. "They'd be daft not to love you."

I blinked rapidly, emotion catching me off guard. "Stop saying nice things. I'm still trying to be mad at you for weaponizing your torso."

He opened his mouth, probably to say something else infuriating and sweet, when the air ... changed.

It was subtle at first. A prickle on the back of my neck that sent the hairs on my arms lifting. The breeze stilled. The birdsong that usually filled the clearing quieted, like the forest was holding its breath.

"Do you feel that?" I whispered.

Torin's muscles tensed under my hands. I realized I had, at some point, grabbed his forearms. "Aye," he murmured. "Something's ... different."

Bracken scrambled down the tree in a flurry of claws and bark, landing on a lower branch, tail puffed. *What the—*"

The light in the clearing shifted, brightening, going almost pearlescent. A soft glow coalesced at the edge of the trees, like fog gathering in one spot, swirling tighter and tighter.

My heart pounded. "Torin..."

He slid an arm around my waist, pulling me against him instinctively. I clung to him, eyes wide, as the glow elongated, took shape.

A horse stepped out of the trees.

Except it wasn't a horse.

It was ... impossibly, undeniably ... a unicorn.

Its coat was a luminous white, not just pale but radiant, like moonlight made flesh. A spiraled horn, long and slender, rose from its forehead, shimmering with faint iridescent light. Its mane and tail flowed like silk, each movement slow and graceful, and its eyes—luminous, deep, ancient— took us in with unnerving intelligence.

"Oh my God," I breathed.

"Holy shite," Torin whispered, his arm tightening around me. "Is that—"

The unicorn's hooves made no sound as it pranced lightly into the clearing, the grass seeming to brighten under its steps. It came to a halt a few feet from us, head held high.

Then, slowly, it lowered its head.

Bowed.

Once.

A simple, graceful nod that felt, somehow, like ... acknowledgment.

My throat went tight. I had the wild, irrational sensation that it could see straight through me—threads and all. It felt like standing in front of something pure. Something old and powerful and utterly uninterested in human nonsense, except that, for this one brief moment, it had decided we were worth a look.

Heat flooded my eyes. I gripped Torin's hand where it rested on my hip.

"Are we hallucinating?" he asked hoarsely.

"If we are, we're having the same hallucination," I whispered.

The unicorn held our gaze for another heartbeat, then gave the tiniest toss of its head, mane rippling like water. It turned, hooves barely kissing the ground, and trotted back toward the trees.

As it reached the shadow of the branches, its body began to glow brighter, edges blurring, until it dissolved back into mist and light and then—nothing. Just the ordinary green of the forest, the faint rustle of leaves, and the birdsong returned.

"*Okay,*" Bracken said finally, sounding slightly hysterical. "*Okay. All right. No, that's fine. That's ... that's just a unicorn. It's only the rarest bloody magickal creature in existence. No big deal. Totally normal Sunday."*

I exhaled a shaky laugh that came out half-sob. "Did that ... just happen?"

Torin turned to me, his face alight in a way I'd never seen before. With pure, childlike wonder.

"Liora," he said, voice thick. "We just saw a unicorn."

"We did," I said, my own chest too tight to contain it all. Awe, joy, terror, excitement—they all tangled together in one glorious mess.

His free hand came up to cradle my cheek, thumb brushing my skin. "I knew there was magick here, but ... that ..." He shook his head, laughing in disbelief. "That was ... beautiful."

"It chose to show itself," Bracken babbled from his branch, pacing. *"They don't do that. Not to just anyone. I need to sit down."*

I leaned into Torin, resting my forehead against his chest, trying to steady my breathing. "What does it mean?" I whispered. "Why would a unicorn just ... appear? And bow?"

"Maybe it was saying hello," Torin said softly, pressing a kiss to the top of my head. "Maybe it was ... blessing the place. Or you."

"Us," I corrected automatically. "You saw it too."

What did it mean that it appeared to both of us? Was it giving us its blessing? The way it had nodded? Because how right did it feel to be in Torin's arms in that moment?

We stood there for a long moment, clinging to each other in the quiet, the afterglow of impossible magick humming in the air.

I laughed, a little hysterical, and tightened my arms around Torin just once more before pulling back.

"I have to get ready for dinner," I said, still breathless. "And at some point, I need to process the fact that we were just casually visited by a top-tier magickal creature in the front garden."

"Go," he said, brushing a strand of hair from my face. "I'll ... finish this." He gestured vaguely at the wood pile, like his brain hadn't quite rebooted either. "We can freak out properly later."

"Deal," I said.

As I headed for the house, my legs a little wobbly, I glanced back once more at the edge of the trees.

Nothing but shadows and light and ordinary birdsong.

But I could feel it. The forest was watching.

It didn't feel like a threat, though. It felt comforting. *Affirming. As if to affirm I'm here for a reason.*

And now I'd have to spend the rest of my life peering into the woods hoping, once more, to glimpse the beauty I was just shown.

CHAPTER FOURTEEN

LIORA

I didn't even bother arguing with Torin this time. Instead, I let him drop me off at the castle and promised I'd text him or get a ride home with one of the girls as needed. I wasn't sure how long he was going to keep this up for, but I didn't have the heart to argue with him after the experience we'd shared today.

My brain was still playing unicorn re-runs on a loop.

A freaking unicorn. In the garden. Bowing.

Sure, why not. *Totally normal Sunday*, as Bracken said.

I was still buzzing with excitement when I rounded the castle, unsure of what door to enter, to find absolute chaos on the lawn.

There I found Sophie bouncing up and down, squealing at a pitch that could shatter glass, currently wrapped around a tall, lean man with dark-rimmed glasses and California written all over him. His suitcase lay abandoned at his feet, and he was hugging her back with a fondly exasperated expression, as if this wasn't the first time she'd assaulted him with her entire body weight.

Beside them, an older woman with a floral headband, a bright pink jumper, and paint-splattered jeans, was laughing, arms spread wide as five Scottie dogs zoomed frantic circles around her legs like wee hairy satellites. Sir Buster raced around the outside of them, having an absolute fit, which they completely ignored, while Lady Lola sat close by, seemingly uninterested in the new arrivals.

Lachlan, Sophie's boyfriend that I'd only met briefly in passing, stood behind them, arms folded, wearing a smug expression.

My heart did a little flip.

"Sophie?" I asked, stepping shyly forward. "Did the party start already?"

Sophie twisted so fast she nearly knocked the man over. "Liora!"

She barreled toward me, hair flying, her face lit up.

I caught her in a hug, laughing. "Someone's excited."

"Of course I'm excited!" she said, pulling back just enough to grab my shoulders and shake me a little. "Look who Lachlan brought me for Christmas. Early. Like a surprise package of emotional support humans. This is my second mom, Lottie, and my bestie, Matthew."

"Oh, that's awesome," I said, waving at the new arrivals. "Welcome."

"He's here for the holidays. And Lottie too. They're staying here. In Loren Brae. For two months!"

She sounded so giddy I half expected her to start tap dancing.

Matthew sauntered over, adjusting his glasses and eyeing the castle. "I see you've cleaned her up a bit since the last time I was here."

"When I'm not busy trying to protect Loren Brae," Sophie said cheerfully. "Matthew, this is Liora. She's an astrologer and just joined the Order earlier this week."

"Hi, nice to meet you." I shook Matthew's hand and found his eyes to be kind and his smile genuine. I was surprised he knew about the Order, but it seemed that it wasn't as much a secret as I'd first thought.

"I'm Matthew. I teach history and make poor romantic decisions in foreign countries."

I laughed, already liking him.

"Believe it or not, that's the most succinct intro he's ever given," Sophie said.

Lottie trotted up behind him, five Scotties trooping along like a tiny army. "Oh, introduce me," she said, eyes sparkling. "I need to know which one is the star witch."

Lottie clasped my hands, her rings cool against my skin. Up close, I could see faint paint smudges on her fingers and a streak of something teal in her hair.

"Lovely to meet you, dear. Don't mind if I'm a bit short tonight, we've only just arrived and it was a long flight."

"On a private plane." Matthew rolled his eyes and looked fondly at Lottie. "Where it was hard to tell who was snoring more loudly, you or the dogs."

"Oh hush." Lottie swatted his arm. "I do not snore."

"Mmmhm, must have been the dogs then."

I loved these two.

"And speaking of dogs…" Her voice brightened as she looked down at the Scotties. "This is my chaotic crew."

The dogs all stared at me.

"Hi," I said weakly. "I don't have any treats, sorry."

One of them trotted forward and sniffed my ankle, then sneezed. Within seconds I was surrounded by scruffy, enthusiastic Scottie affection.

"You've been accepted," Lottie declared. "They only do that to people they deem worthy. Or people who smell like food. Which, in this crowd, is most of us."

"Speaking of food," Sophie said, practically bouncing. "We need to get inside. The girls are already in Grasshopper."

She linked her arm through mine and started hauling me toward the castle doors. "Lottie and Matthew are joining us tonight, by the way. I told them it was 'girls' dinner,' but Matthew is an honorary girl, and Lottie obviously counts."

"I have always counted," Lottie agreed serenely, following with her Scottie parade. "Also, I brought wine."

Matthew sighed happily. "And I brought emotional baggage and the desperate desire for a life change. Should fit right in."

"Oh good," I said faintly. "Because I was worried we might not have enough of that already."

The restaurant was glowing.

The castle's restaurant had been transformed into a witch's version of a Sunday night dinner. A long table was set near the big windows, candles flickering in mismatched holders, greenery twined down the center, and what felt like a hundred tiny fairy lights draped along the stone walls. Did they put all this on for just us? I was in awe but then remembered Brice and how quickly he managed to get work done.

A group of women surrounded the table and all beamed at me.

"Matthew!" Lia cried and rounded the table. There were a few hugs and then Sophie clapped her hands.

"Right, everyone. I have three introductions to make tonight, instead of just Liora." Sophie waved at me. "This is Matthew, my bestie from home whom some of you already know, along with the best second mom in the world, Lottie."

Lottie bowed and the table clapped.

"And Liora, an astrologer, and our newest member of the Order." Sophie waved to me and I smiled at everyone. "Okay, let's do this quickly. Pay attention, Lottie. You know Agnes."

Agnes waved from her end of the table, curls in a messy halo, paint-smudged hands wrapped around a wine glass.

"Next to her is Shona." A woman sat with pink cheeks, blond hair in a messy braid, a small posy of winter greenery tied with twine at her plate. Lia moved around the table with a dish towel slung over one shoulder, hands in perpetual motion as she set out little dishes of olives and something that smelled cheesy and sinful.

"Next to her is Orla, the one in her usual builder chic, canvas overalls and boots." A tiny woman with a wide smile waved.

"Next to her is our fashionista, Willow." The woman next to Orla wore a leather shirt dress, cinched at the waist with a wide belt, and huge doorknocker earrings.

"After that, we have Kaia, our lovely metalsmith, and next to her is Faelan, our vet."

I waved at Kaia and Faelan.

"That's everyone. Please, talk among yourselves while I find Lachlan and thank him for this gift."

"Ugh, please, thank him later. You won't get back in time for dinner," Matthew groaned.

"I could be quick," Sophie argued.

"Nope, not gonna happen. I know how you two get around each other."

"Sit," Lia ordered. "Eat. Tell us everything about California and men who don't deserve you."

"Gladly," Matthew exclaimed, sliding into a chair and pulling Sophie down with him, seemingly to keep her from absconding with Lachlan.

In fast order, Brice appeared and slung pizzas across the table, along with heaping bowls of pasta, and baskets of crusty bread. The smell of garlic and rosemary filled the room, and collectively the table all sighed with appreciation.

Lia plopped down in her chair and sighed, happy to be done with cooking.

"Seriously, guys, go on and eat." Lia smiled at me. "And we'll drill Liora on if any of her powers have come out yet."

I blanched and then took a healthy gulp of my wine.

"Oh, something's happened, hasn't it?" Orla, the wee builder, asked, studying my face. "You look stressed."

"I mean, it's not the worst thing. It's just ... I can't really explain it." I glanced to Matthew and Lottie, not sure if I should continue.

"Go on, they know everything. This is a group you can

be totally open with. Even when it's annoying." Sophie gave Matthew a look and he laughed.

"Don't act like you aren't all up in my life too, lady."

"Well, so, I don't know how to say this." I took a bite of my pizza and sighed in happiness as red sauce and warm cheese filled my mouth. I chewed for a moment, thinking it through. "Basically, I gave a reading, an astrology reading like I normally do. But nothing was normal about it. Not even in the slightest. It was like, I don't know, it took life? And in it, I learned that I'm a chartweaver."

The table fell completely silent as everyone stilled and looked curiously at me.

Lia leaned back in her chair, studying me with those sharp brown eyes. "So." She dragged out the word. "Chartweaver, huh?"

I took a breath. "Apparently."

"Um, please explain," Willow said, eyes bright, a smile hovering on her lips.

I laughed, nerves easing. "Okay, but honestly, I'm still trying to figure it out myself. I'll do my best to explain."

I ran my fingers along the edge of my wine glass, grounding myself. "Yesterday I did a reading for a woman named Greta. Widow, two young kids, just dealing with some stuff. I pulled up her chart and ... something happened."

"Awww, Greta," Shona interjected, holding her hand to her heart. "How is she? I spent some time with her last year and was able to help her process some of her grief."

"She's good, I think. Or will be," I said, trying to think of how to protect Greta's confidentiality.

"What kind of something?" Kaia asked, bringing us back to my explanation.

"The chart..." I searched for the right words. "Lifted. Off the laptop. The aspect lines became actual threads hanging in the air. Glowing. And when I focused on them, I could see ... paths. Different versions of her life depending on what she chose. And when I..." I hesitated, feeling exposed. "When I touched one of them, it shifted. Just a bit. Like I strengthened a path she already wanted to take."

Silence fell, dense and electric.

Then Agnes let out a low whistle. "Bloody hell."

"That's ... a huge responsibility," Faelan said, brow furrowing. "My mother used to tell stories about weavers."

Lottie's eyes were wide. "A chartweaver! How exciting. Arthur used to talk about them too. He said they were like ... cosmic editors. Helping people revise their lives one line at a time."

"That is absolutely going on my business card," I quipped, and the table laughed, easing some of my tension. But seriously though, how were they not freaking out that I could change people's fates?

Matthew leaned forward, propping his chin on his hand. "So you see someone's chart, and instead of saying, 'You will probably ruin your life in March,' you can ... tweak it?"

"I can't rewrite fate," I said quickly. "Gran's book"—I glanced around—"my grandmother left me a grimoire. There's a chapter on chartweavers. It says we're meant to work with what's already there. Like, strengthen threads that align with the soul's path. Not just yank on things because we feel like it."

"Boring," Matthew said. "I was hoping you could erase my last three relationships."

"Even if I could, I wouldn't," I told him. "They're data. Painful data, sure. But they got you here."

He sighed. "You sound like my therapist."

"Thank you, I think." I laughed.

Sophie reached across the table and squeezed my hand. "You okay?" she asked quietly. "It's a lot."

"It is," I admitted. "But it also felt right. When I helped Greta choose her path, it wasn't about, like, playing god, or anything like that. It was about giving her permission to pursue the life she already secretly desired, I guess? The chart was already screaming it at her. I just ... amplified the volume. And my gran"—my voice wobbled—"she knew. There are notes in the book. She wrote my name next to the chapter."

Shona's eyes softened. "That must be nice. To feel like she's still guiding you."

"It is," I said, swallowing past the lump in my throat.

"Speaking of your gran," Sophie piped in. "Where's your brooch?"

"Och, it's in my handbag. Why?" I leaned back to unhook the bag I'd hung on the back of my chair.

"Just a hunch," Sophie murmured.

I fumbled for the brooch that I kept in its pouch in my handbag. Taking it out, I turned it over, and gasped.

Inside the design, where the two dragons twisted together around the stars and the moon, nestled an opal. It glowed faintly, catching the light in a way that made my heart jump.

"Oh," I breathed, pointing at the opal. "That ... that wasn't there yesterday. I swear it wasn't."

"It wasn't," Sophie confirmed. "I remember when you showed me the piece."

Lottie reached out, not touching, just hovering her fingers over it. "Arthur always said the old magick has ways of marking progress. Maybe helping Greta ... was a test."

"Congratulations," Orla said, grinning. "You passed your first challenge."

"I did?" I asked, surprised. Pleasure flooded me. Was I actually going to be a helpful member on this team of women? "No way, that's awesome. I thought it might be something crazy like stab a Kelpie with my brooch pin."

"It might still be," Faelan said, her tone serious. "They almost killed my partner, Luch."

"They've done some serious damage," Orla agreed, leaning forward. "It would be wise to not underestimate them."

"But this brings us one step forward." Sophie tapped my brooch. "So, congrats are in order."

"Thank you," I said, and sat back, amazed that I was sitting here, having this discussion about magick with these women. Apart from Zara, I'd never felt as though I'd ever really clicked with many women. Sure, I'd had girlfriends from school and hadn't struggled to make friends necessarily, but these women were embracing me with open arms, warm smiles and ... genuine acceptance. *It feels divine.* And again, I felt as though I was where I was meant to be.

Matthew's gaze had gone thoughtful. "So," he said slowly. "Hypothetically, if one were, say, an exhausted academic, could one ask a chartweaver for a reading?"

"Hypothetically, one could," I said.

"And would said chartweaver tell one if uprooting their life and moving to the arse-end of nowhere is a terrible idea?"

Sophie squealed.

"Depends on your chart," I said. "But I could tell you what themes are up for you, sure. What your soul's leaning toward."

He drummed his fingers on the table. "Hmm. Intriguing. I might need that. I'm...not in love with my life at the moment. Or my department."

Lottie smiled softly at him. "You loved it once."

"I did," he agreed. "I also loved a man who left me for an archaeologist with better calves, so clearly my judgment is evolving."

"You'd be welcome here," Sophie said quietly. "For as long as you'd like."

He looked at her, eyes warm. "I know. That's the problem. It's starting to feel more tempting than terrifying."

I caught the threads around him in the corner of my vision—just a faint shimmer, nothing like with Greta. A possibility.

Well, *that* was new.

I wondered if this was what Zara could see, and we'd always assumed it was just auras. Was she seeing people's threads as well? But the harder I tried to look at the threads around Matthew, the more they disappeared into nothingness. No, I would need a proper focused reading to actually see his chart, that was for sure.

"Whenever you're ready," I told him. "We can look at it. And see what options are available to you." Honestly, I was dying to give another reading, just for being able to get a chance to see the threads again.

"Deal," he said.

Before I could say anything else, a soft, plaintive cooing sound echoed through the room.

We all froze.

"Please tell me that was a pigeon," Willow whispered.

"In the dining room?" Lia snorted. "Absolutely not."

The sound came again, this time from the stone wall near the kitchen. It was longer this time, almost like a sigh.

"Clyde," Sophie muttered under her breath.

"Is that the—"

Her question got swallowed whole when a translucent figure shot out of the stone and into the room with a loud, echoing "Mooooo!"

Several things happened at once.

I yelped.

Shona squeaked and grabbed Orla's arm.

Lottie's dogs—all five—went absolutely ballistic, exploding into frantic barks and scrabbling under chairs as if they'd personally been offended by the afterlife.

Matthew clutched his chest. "Oh my God—"

"Breathe, professor, you're fine," Kaia said, though her own eyes were huge.

Clyde hovered above the table, tossing his head joyfully, seemingly delighted to have interrupted the dinner.

"Damn it, Clyde," Lia moaned, crossing her legs.

"He—" Sophie leaned toward me.

"Yes, yes, he made me pee my pants once, all right?" Lia glared at Sophie, as the table burst out laughing.

Clyde threw his head back and bellowed, and the candles flickered.

"Oh, he's in a *mood* tonight," Sophie said, pressing a hand to her racing heart. "All right, Clyde, we hear you, buddy."

Clyde tilted his head, studying me for another long, unnerving second. Then, abruptly, he swooped downward in a lurching, too-fast movement that sent everyone flinching back from the table.

Lottie's Scotties lost their minds, barking and lunging at thin air, nails skittering on the stone floor.

"Clyde!" Agnes hissed. "Enough with the jump-scare routine!"

He let out one last satisfied "Moooo," more pleased with himself this time, then shot upward toward the ceiling and disappeared straight back into the stone with a faint ripple, like someone had dropped a pebble into a pond.

For a moment, all any of us could do was stare.

"Well," Lia said finally, dropping into her chair. "I honestly don't think I'll ever get used to that."

"I think I just lost three years of my life," Matthew said faintly. "Do you all just ... live like this?"

"More or less," Orla said, reaching down to ruffle one of the Scotties, who was still growling at the wall. "He's mostly harmless. Just dramatic."

"Ghosts," I muttered, trying to get my heart rate back under control. "Unicorns. Chartweaving. Sure. Why not? Add jump scare ghost coo to the list."

"Wait. Unicorns?" Faelan asked and the entire table rounded on me.

"Um." My eyes widened as everyone suddenly looked extremely interested in what I was about to say next.

"Are you dating someone, Liora?" Willow leaned forward, interest on her face.

What in the world did that have to do with unicorns?

"Um, no. Yes. Kind of." I blew out a breath. "It's complicated."

"Ah, and was Mr. Complicated there when the unicorn arrived?"

"Wait, an actual unicorn?" Lottie turned and beamed at the table, her face lighting up. "Are they really real?"

"This one sure was," I said.

"That's incredible," Lottie breathed. "Och, you'll have to describe it for me so I can paint it."

"Um, sure."

"So? Was he with you?" Sophie leaned forward.

"I mean, yeah, we were both in the yard. It's his house."

"Och, lass." Orla pursed her lips in a soft smile. "Good luck to you then, on your complicated situation. Because you're going to have to get that sorted out at some point."

"Wait, why? What does this mean?" I turned to Sophie. "Explain."

"I can't." Sophie held up her hands. "It's just going to have to be something you figure out."

"But it's not dangerous ... is it? You wouldn't keep that from me?" I asked, annoyed.

"Dangerous to your heart only. Don't worry. It's a good thing. We've all seen the unicorn at some point."

"I want to see a unicorn," Matthew complained.

"Well, Matthew. You never know. If you move here for real, you just might," Sophie said.

CHAPTER FIFTEEN

LIORA

Lachlan's truck rumbled away down the lane, headlights cutting briefly across the trees before disappearing. The moment they were gone, the quiet settled over the house, the moonlight glinting over the loch. I took a moment to stare out at the silvery surface and wonder if we really could contain the Kelpies or if they would continue to terrorize Loren Brae.

Not that I'd had much terror from them, but based on what some of the women said tonight, that was a blessing. They sounded incredibly dangerous and horrifying. Maybe it was best that Torin was keeping tabs on me. That being said, did I really want to put him in harm's way? I realized that I was coming to care for him, more than was probably wise, which meant I'd be devastated if he got hurt trying to help me.

I took a breath and pushed open the front door.

The picture that greeted me had a smile blooming on my face.

Torin and Bracken sat together by the fire, while Torin read sports news to Bracken from his phone.

He sat on the floor in front of the hearth, long legs stretched out, back resting against the couch. He wore a soft grey thermal shirt, sleeves pushed up to his forearms, and I couldn't help but swallow, hard, as his muscles bunched as he gestured to the squirrel splooted out next to him, seemingly listening adamantly.

They looked absurdly domestic.

Bracken perked up first, chittering loudly when he saw me.

"Finally! I was about to call the woodland authorities. Do you know how boring your lumberjack is when you're not here?"

Torin lifted his head at the sound, concern crossing his face when he saw me. "Hey," he said, voice warm and low. "You didn't text me."

"Och, sorry. Lachlan offered to give me a ride home."

The concern cleared and he stood, crossing to the kitchen.

"Can I get you a glass of wine? Cup of tea?"

"Wine, please," I said, shutting the door behind me and taking my coat off. Hanging it up with my handbag, I then walked across the room to sit down on the couch. "Looks like you two had ... a bonding experience?"

Torin's eyes crinkled. "He chucked an acorn at my head when I was going inside, so I took that to mean he wanted to come in."

"Demanding wee one, isn't he?" I gave Bracken a look.

Bracken flicked his tail proudly, then scampered up the arm of the couch to perch near me. I stroked his head as Torin brought two glasses of wine over and settled next to me.

"You look relaxed," Torin said, studying me. "Happy."

"I am," I said, nodding a little, as I took the glass he offered. "It was a really good night."

"Do you want to tell me about it?" Torin's eyes never left my face, his attention one hundred percent zoned in on me, and I realized just how nice it was to have someone give you their undivided attention.

I curled into the corner cushion as he shifted to face me, one arm draped over his bent knee, firelight gilding his cheekbones and the strong lines of his throat. Bracken hopped down and nestled in a little hollow beside me, curling his tail around himself like he was settling in for story time.

Torin glanced down at Bracken and smirked. "He's gotten comfortable."

"Surprisingly so. I've never had a pet before."

"I'm not a pet." Bracken popped his head up, chittering furiously at me.

"Sorry, you're right. You're not a pet. Still, I enjoy your companionship." I stroked a finger down the wee man's soft fur, and he settled back down, making grumpy noises before he closed his eyes.

"Never had a pet? Really?" Torin tilted his head at me. "How come?"

"Honestly? I don't know. I guess maybe because Zara's

always had a guide dog, so it was best to keep the house a single animal household."

"But you haven't lived with her for a long time, aye?"

"Yeah, but then I mostly had roommates. I've never really lived alone. Bringing an animal into a roommate situation can sometimes not go well. How about you? I'm surprised you don't have a dog out here. You seem like a dog type."

"Och, I am. I desperately want one. I had the best dog growing up. Taco was his name."

"You named your dog Taco?" I burst out laughing as Torin shrugged one shoulder, a shy grin on his face.

"That's what you get when you let your kid name the dog. He was my best friend for ages. Losing him was rough, and, aye, well. Haven't had the heart to get another. I'm not home much, either. Not sure it's fair to the dog."

Och, this man was crying out for companionship. No wonder he'd allowed me in so easily. My heart softened.

"Go on then. How was the castle?"

"Wild," I admitted. "Hilarious. But, kind of emotional, too, I guess. But in a good way."

"As opposed to the bad way you usually get?" he teased lightly.

I winced. "Yeah, actually. Which is something I wanted to talk to you about."

He blinked, sensing the tone shift. He sat up straighter, face softening. "All right. I'm listening."

I drew in a breath. *Here goes nothing.*

"I feel like I've spent my whole life ... messing up," I said quietly. "Missing red flags. Putting my faith in people I shouldn't. Believing in the best-case scenario because...

because that's what I want to be real. What I *wish* was real."

Torin's brow furrowed slightly.

"And tonight," I continued, voice shaky, "I was surrounded by this incredible group of women—strong magickal women—and they looked at me like I belonged there. Like I wasn't the charity case or the disaster waiting to happen. Like I was … one of them."

Torin opened his mouth, but I held up a hand.

"I know I ramble," I said, needing to get this out. "I know I jump into things too fast. And tonight, being with them … it felt like being seen in a way I'm not used to. They treated me like family." My throat tightened. "Like I wasn't the screwup sister. Or the friend who needs saving. Or the weird girl with the tarot cards and wonky astrology readings. Och, I don't know, like I was someone valuable."

"You *are* valuable." Torin's eyes softened, something tender flickering in the depths there.

"But I don't feel that way most of the time," I whispered. "I hate that I screwed up like, ten minutes after moving into Loren Brae. I'm messy, Torin. And too trusting. The one who believes in people even when I shouldn't. Zara always says I 'love too loudly.' I think she means it in a nice way, but sometimes it feels like a criticism."

Torin leaned forward, forearm resting on his knee. The firelight painted amber shadows across his jaw. "Liora. Look at me."

I did.

And the world narrowed to just us.

"You're not naïve," he said, voice low but certain. "You're hopeful. There's a difference."

I swallowed.

"You see the world through possibility. People like you ... you open doors for others without asking them to knock first. That's a rare thing. A precious thing."

I blinked back sudden tears.

"Hope is brave. Not stupid."

My chest tightened painfully. "But I keep getting hurt. I keep screwing up, Torin. Look at you. Five minutes into my new life and I hexed you with a truth spell."

He nodded. "Aye. Be that as it may, it doesn't change that a hopeful heart is a special thing. But that doesn't mean you should change. Or shrink yourself." His gaze deepened. "It means you need people around you who actually see you for what and who you are. People who protect your softness instead of making fun of it."

"That's ... a lot." I let out a shaky breath.

"It's true," he said simply.

Bracken nudged my hand gently, chittering in agreement.

"Tree man is correct."

Torin glanced at the squirrel's noise, amused. "He sounds like he agrees with me."

"He does. Which is incredibly sweet, of both of you." I needed time to let his words settle into me. I knew I'd be replaying them in my head for a while. I tucked my hair behind my ear and shifted the conversation because I wasn't sure how much more sweet truths I could take at the moment before I dissolved in a puddle of need and vulnerability at Torin's feet. "Speaking of ... seeing. There's something else I have to tell you about. Something, um, strange happened for me."

His expression sharpened. "What happened?"

"I'm—" I exhaled. "A chartweaver."

Torin blinked once. Twice. "A what?"

So I told him.

Everything.

The glowing threads rising off the chart. Seeing future paths. Touching them and shifting their strength. The brooch gaining a new stone. My gran's notes. The women's reactions.

I expected him to look confused or skeptical.

But instead ... he looked *awed*.

"You can see ... our fates?" he murmured.

"Yes."

"And help people choose the right one?"

"In a way, yes."

"And you helped that woman yesterday?"

"Greta," I said. "Widow. Two kids. She's been drowning. But I saw her path so clearly. She just needed someone to help her trust it. So, aye, I think I helped her."

Torin blew out a slow breath, running a hand through his hair. "Liora ... that's incredible."

"I'm terrified," I whispered.

He shook his head. "You're made for this. If anyone should be guiding people, it's someone who sees the good in them by default."

I stared at him, undone. "You really think that?"

"I don't think it," he said steadily. "I *know* it."

Something seemed to unlock in me, loosen, and shift. Like I'd been holding on to this idea of myself for so long that I'd just assumed it to be true. And now, this incredible man was sitting across from me, telling me the kind of truths that I desperately needed to hear.

Bracken nudged my elbow again. I stroked his fur absentmindedly, blinking rapidly.

"It seems like you belong with those women and in the Order. In Loren Brae. This power, it only showed up once you were here, right?"

"Aye."

"Then don't you think it's a sign? A good one?"

I took a sip of my wine, trying to steady myself. "I just ... don't want to screw it up."

"You won't."

"How do you know? I literally put a truth spell on your head."

"I mean, you didn't direct it at me. From my understanding, I interrupted it, didn't I?"

I shrugged one shoulder, noncommittal, and he laughed.

"You can't fully take the blame on that one, darling."

My insides did a funny thing when he called me *darling* in that tone.

"What about Avery?" I asked softly, hating that I needed to go there. I didn't want to ruin this sweet moment, but it was clear that Torin had invaded my mind, and possibly my heart. If I were to think about truly giving this a go, I needed to clear up the past. "I ... haven't wanted to bring it up. But I think I should understand what happened with you two. Really understand. Because I've carried that guilt for years."

His jaw tightened slightly. He shifted closer, his knee brushing mine, and I met his gaze.

"I've always been a steady as you go kind of lad," he began. "It's my nature."

"Taurus, through and through." I smiled at him and gestured with my wine glass for him to continue.

"I guess when I care for someone—my mum, my mates ... I'm there. Always. I show up. I like to make sure people are safe. I like to help to ... I don't know, keep their worlds running. Whatever."

Classic for his chart. His Cancer Moon made him a natural nurturer.

"Avery liked that about me at first," he said. "Said it made her feel secure. But over time..." He shook his head. "She grew restless. She had an agenda, you see? And I didn't follow it closely enough. She had our whole lives mapped out while I was still just getting to know her."

My breath caught. So there had been issues outside of my reading that had caused them to break.

"You had a tricky chart alignment," I said, looking at him over my wine glass. "It was what I was trying to explain to her. It's not impossible, no partnership is impossible. But some take a hell of a lot more work than others."

"I did try," Torin continued. "I did work hard at that relationship. But she wanted the kind of man who would fall neatly in line with her plans." His mouth curved wryly. "That's not me."

"No," I said softly. "It's not."

"And I'm not sorry about that," he said. "What hurt wasn't that she left. I think we both knew it was coming. What hurt..." His throat bobbed. "Was her telling people I cheated on her. That I broke her heart and that I was untrustworthy."

"I know." I did, because I'd been blasted with the same rumor.

"She said it to justify leaving. And once she said it, she had to keep going." He shrugged one shoulder. "People believed her."

"People shouldn't have. It wasn't fair," I insisted.

"Life isn't fair. But I've always been a man of my word. I take pride in that. And suddenly I was … branded a cheat." He looked down at his hands. "I retreated after that. Work, the woods, my mum. Few close friends. Kept my circle small. Easier that way."

I'd done the same. In the form of running to Glasgow and starting my life over.

"And now?" I whispered.

He lifted his gaze to mine. "And now … you're here."

My heart thudded.

"You're nothing like her," he said gently. "You're warm, open, funny as hell. You feel everything. You believe in good, everywhere you go. You're constantly talking to yourself or drifting away mid-conversation. You leave crystals and flowers and earrings all over the place. It was like I was living in black and white, and you've brought a box of crayons to color in my empty spaces."

My eyes filled. It was probably the nicest thing anyone had ever said to me.

And I knew it was the truth as he literally couldn't lie. This man was knocking me sideways, but it also felt so right to be with him.

"Don't cry," Torin said, panic filling his voice. "I didn't mean to make you cry."

"No, it's a good cry. I promise." I dashed the back of my

hand across my cheek. "You don't need to apologize for anything you've said."

Torin tilted his head at me. "And that's another thing … you don't demand I be anything I'm not."

A soft, trembling laugh escaped me. "I think you're probably giving me too much praise, Torin. I don't know what I'm doing half the time."

"That's fine," he murmured. "I do."

His hand moved—slowly, deliberately—just enough to brush my knee.

A spark shot through me.

Bracken jumped up, shooting a look between us, and scampered off the couch and down the hallway.

"Can he get outside?"

"Back door is cracked just a smidge for him," Torin promised. I smiled. It was these little things that Torin did, always looking out for others, that was making it impossible for me not to want to climb on his lap and not think about what would come tomorrow.

"I don't want to be naïve," I whispered. "I don't want to be the fool who trusts too easily."

"You're not naïve," he said, voice low and certain. "You're brave. You walk into the world without armor. I respect that more than you know."

My breath hitched.

He continued softly, "And I'm not going to hurt you, Liora. Not intentionally. Not ever."

I swallowed hard. "You can't promise that."

"No," he agreed. "But I can promise I'll try my damned hardest."

He paused.

"And that when I feel something, I won't run from it."

My entire body went still.

"You feel something?" I whispered.

He moved closer.

Firelight danced across his features, making his eyes look darker and more dangerous.

"I do," he said. "More than I should. More than I expected."

I exhaled shakily.

Torin took a slow breath. "Tell me what you're afraid of."

I tore my gaze from his and stared into the flames. "I'm afraid ... that I'll mess this up."

"You won't."

"I'm afraid I'll fall too fast."

"So do I."

I looked at him.

He held my gaze, unflinching.

"I'm afraid," I whispered, "I'm not enough."

Torin reached up, fingers brushing my jaw.

"Liora," he said, voice roughening. "You are more than enough. You're more than I deserve."

Emotion clawed up my throat. That wasn't remotely true, but since he couldn't lie, it was clear he believed it.

"And I'm afraid," I whispered, "that if I let myself hope that this could be real, the moment that I do? It will all fall apart."

He shifted, kneeling on the rug before me, sliding between my thighs as if it was the most natural thing in the world.

"I won't leave," he said softly, looking up at me. He

took the wine glass from my hand and put it on the table behind him. Nerves hummed, hot and low, and I shifted, opening my legs further. "Not unless you tell me to. I'm here. Choosing you."

My breath caught. "You can't know that yet."

"I do." His hands slid up my thighs and then back down, absently stroking, while desire came to life under his touch. "I don't know where this will go, Liora. I can't presume to know what next year will look like. But I know what I want in the now. And how I can see a future with you."

A tremor ran through me. "Torin..."

He leaned closer, his hands continuing to stroke my legs. A fine tremble began to work its way through my body.

"I bet you could see it too, if you let yourself look."

"Bad idea," I said, shifting and widening my legs even more. I desperately wanted this man's hands on me. "I'm too emotionally attached to the outcome to look."

"Tell me," he whispered, leaning forward, his gaze desperate. "Tell me you want this too."

I closed my eyes.

"I want this," I breathed. "I want you."

He exhaled like he'd been holding it for hours.

"Good," he murmured.

Then his mouth found mine.

The kiss wasn't tentative.

It demanded. Everything.

His hand slid into my hair, tilting my face up. My fingers dug into his shoulders, pulling him closer until the world narrowed to heat and heartbeat and want. His lips were warm and firm, coaxing mine open, tasting like wine and something sweeter—like he was letting himself hope, too.

I made a soft, helpless sound against his mouth, arching my hips against him, and he broke the kiss, smiling wickedly at me.

"You did that the other night too, didn't ye, lass?" Torin trailed a finger across the snap of my jeans. "At the pub. When I had you pressed against the wall. You remember? You rocked into me. Needing more."

"I..." I dropped my head back when he unsnapped my jeans and tugged them down, along with my pants, leaving me exposed to his face. It was such a shocking move, to go from kissing all week to suddenly being half naked in front of him, that I struggled to sit up a bit. "Torin!"

"I won't touch if you don't want me to." Torin stopped where he was pulling my jeans off around my ankles and sat back on his knees, waiting for permission.

My entire body thrummed with need. It seemed to always do so, around him. It had probably been the shirtless wood chopping that had tipped the decision in my head, I just hadn't admitted it to myself yet. But, bloody hell, did I want this man.

"Och, I mean, go ahead. If you're so inclined, that is." I sniffed, awkwardly, and mentally died a bit inside at my words.

If you're so inclined. *Bloody hell, Liora.* Who even said things like that?

But then I couldn't think anymore as his mouth found me and he devoured me like a man who had been desperate for a taste.

It was so starkly shocking. One moment he was lightly stroking my legs, and the next he'd opened me, delving deeply with his tongue, the friction and heat hitting me just right. I arched my back, falling backward on the cushion, as his mouth took over and all I could do was feel.

This man was made for loving.

That's all I could think about as he dedicated his entire focus on my pleasure. If I moaned, he paused, repeating where he licked. If I squealed, he paused and then sucked harder, in the exact spot that I needed. As pleasure built inside me, low and hot, rising to a crest, I began to moan and rock against his face.

"Please, Torin. Please. I need..." I trailed off as he lapped across me, sending a shockwave of desire through me, and then slid a finger deep inside of me.

"Please what?" Torin asked, as mildly as if I was asking for more sugar in my tea.

"It's ... och, aye. There, there, there," I shrieked and threw my head back as he curled his finger upward, and licked deeply against me, his tongue swirling in just the right way until my orgasm hit, and I dissolved in a puddle, my entire body shaking with the release. Pulling back, Torin grinned up at me, a satisfied look on his face.

"I've been dying to do that since the moment I saw you in my house."

"*What*? But you were raging at me."

"I can still be mad and want you to ride my face, Liora."

"You can't say things like that." I laughed, putting my hands to my face. My body throbbed where his mouth had been, and I realized that I desperately wanted more.

And I wanted to be the one in control.

I wanted to bring that same release to him, that same pleasure he'd just given me to his handsome face.

"Up." I pointed at him, tapping the couch. "My turn."

"You don't have to," Torin said, smiling softly. "This was entirely my pleasure."

"Och, no, I do. Trust me, I really do." I surprised Torin by launching myself up and dragging him until he was seated in front of me and I was standing. Whipping off my jumper and bra, I bent over and he quickly helped me slide his joggers down.

"Bloody hell, Liora. You're gorgeous." I stopped and looked up to see Torin gazing at me, reverence on his face. I honestly couldn't remember a time that any lover of mine had looked at me that way. It was like I was giving him the most perfect gift in the world.

Naked adoration filled his eyes and I couldn't even explain how that made me feel, to be looked at with pure joy and lust and need ... it just did something to me that made me toss every last inhibition I had to the wind. I didn't need the future planned out. I didn't even need the rest of this week to be planned out. Maybe that was something that I finally just needed to accept about myself. That I was more than comfortable drifting, flowing with the vibes in the moment, because at the end of the day, I could rely on myself to handle any problems that arose. Thus far, I had a one hundred percent success rate with surviving any messes that I landed myself in, and frankly, some of them? Well, they'd been a whole hell of a lot of fun.

Decided, I straddled Torin on the couch and gripped him with my hand, watching as his eyes went dark and almost feral. Stroking him lightly, my hand tight around his girth, I smiled as he moaned slightly.

"I'd like you to take your jumper off for me so I can ogle those abs that made me forget how to speak in coherent sentences earlier today."

Torin hastily obliged, tossing the jumper behind him without looking, and I swallowed a laugh as it landed on top of the dining room table.

"I have the coil," I said, and Torin tilted his head, understanding dawning.

"And I've been tested. It's been over a year since I've dated anyone, Liora."

"More for me." It was shocking to admit it, and to realize just how much I'd missed a man's touch on my body. "But I'm clear as well."

I'd never much minded being single. I loved people, even if they didn't quite know what to do with me, but the downside of being single was the lack of physical touch. *I'm a cuddler.* As Torin's hands stroked up my thighs and gripped my hips, I arched back, angling myself over him so he could slide deeply inside me.

We both groaned at the same time, shocked at the feel, hard to soft, my body slick with need for him.

"Liora." Torin said my name like a prayer. He slid his hands up my sides to cup my breasts, thumbing my nipples as I arched back, the movement sliding him deeper inside of me. Already I was starting to contract around him, my body languid and ready for more pleasure, desire building to a crest inside me once more. Sliding his hand farther up, Torin cupped it around the back of my neck, pulling my head forward until his mouth caught mine in a searing kiss.

Our tongues tangled as I rocked against him, pleasure building, loving the feel of him everywhere.

He was just so hard.

So *masculine.*

His body felt like it was made from marble, a creation worthy of Michelangelo. The firelight flickered across the dips and curves of his chest, and I wanted to touch him everywhere. We both were hungry, our hands trailing across each other's body, squeezing and stroking, exploring new territories together as I picked up my pace, riding him closer to the finish.

"Bloody hell. My gorgeous wood nymph. I want to devour you," Torin gasped against my mouth, nipping at my bottom lip, before bending his head to suckle at my breast as his fingers dug into my bum. He controlled my pace, forcing me to slow it down, to rock more gently against him. "Easy there, darling. You'll finish me too soon and I need this to last."

"You do?" I gasped, my orgasm desperately close.

"Och, aye. I want to savor this moment. Our first time together." Torin leaned back, his smile lazy and languid, and slid a thumb down my stomach until he found me, wet and sensitive, and circled his thumb over me. I gasped, arching back, the combination of his hard cock inside me and the lazy circles he was torturing me with, bringing me right to the edge.

"Torin," I keened, rocking against his hand, needing more.

"That's a good lass. Break for me, darling."

And I did, pleasure cresting up and over, coming undone as I clenched around him. Torin threw his head back and groaned, arching up into me, spearing me with his cock as I shattered around him, rocking fast until he, too, finally broke.

It was a joy to watch him come apart for me, his body seizing up as he poured himself into me, gripping my hips and holding me still as he finished.

His eyes looked unseeing for a moment, bliss poured across his face, and then he blinked up at me and gave one of the sexiest grins I'd ever seen in my life.

"I'd like to do that again. About seventeen more times. Tonight, if we can fit it in."

"Easy there, tiger. A lady has to get her beauty sleep, you know?" I gasped as Torin stood, lifting me with him, and hitched my legs around his waist. "Torin!"

His strength, quite literally, took my breath away.

Firelight painted our shadows on the wall—two shapes leaning into each other, dissolving into one.

His hands held my thighs, keeping me close around him, and he bent his forehead to mine.

"You undo me, Liora."

I let out a small breath, my heart melting at his words.

"Torin, I don't know what to say…"

"Then say nothing." Torin pressed a gentle kiss against my lips as he walked me across the room and toward his bedroom.

Maybe he was right. Sometimes moments were all you needed when words failed you altogether. Sighing, I wrapped my arms around his shoulders and buried my face in his neck, allowing myself to be carried into a new thread of my future.

CHAPTER SIXTEEN

TORIN

If anyone had told me a month ago that I'd wake up with a witch drooling on my chest and a squirrel staring at me like he was judging my life choices, I'd have called them daft.

Yet here we were.

Monday morning. Liora was sprawled half on top of me, hair everywhere, hand fisted in my T-shirt like she'd tried to wrestle me in her sleep and lost. Her cheek was pressed over my heart, lips parted, and she was making the cutest little snoring sound.

Bracken sat in a nest of towels on the nightstand, tiny paws tucked under his chest, while Liora snored quietly. He'd joined us later in the evening, and we'd put together a small nest for him to cozy into for the night.

Liora made a sleepy sound and burrowed closer, one

bare thigh sliding over my hip. Every cell in my body woke up with her.

Right. Probably best not to think too hard about last night or I'd end up keeping her in bed all day and we'd both be useless.

I smoothed my hand down her back, thumb brushing over the dip of her spine. She shivered and blinked up at me, eyes hazy. For a second, she just stared, like she was trying to remember who I was.

Then she smiled.

My heart seemed to shiver in my chest and I swallowed thickly. *Oh, I was done for.*

"Hi," she rasped.

"Morning, wood nymph."

She groaned and buried her face in my chest. "We've talked about this. We're not keeping that nickname."

"Aye, we are." I kissed the top of her head. "How's your body?"

"That's a very forward question," she mumbled.

Heat crawled up my neck. "I meant—och, you know what I meant. Are you sore? Too much?"

She shifted experimentally, winced a little, then grinned. "In a good way. Like I did a very enthusiastic yoga class. With ... added benefits."

My chest did something suspiciously like swelling.

Truth spell or not, there was no way I could hide what came out next. "I like you in my bed."

Her head popped up, eyes wide. Then she laughed. "I like me in your bed, too."

Bracken chittered loudly and jumped to the floor, scampering out of the room as if he'd seen far more than he wanted.

"Your familiar doesn't approve," I said dryly.

"He can lodge a formal complaint later," she said. "I'm busy."

She kissed me—soft and sweet, and if we weren't careful we were going to be late for … well, for life.

"I've got work." Reluctantly, I pulled back.

She sighed dramatically. "Responsibilities. How rude."

Real life. Except none of this felt like the life I'd had before. Everything had color now. Liora had done that. Bringing laughter and crystals and flowers and, well, joy into my house.

I cleared my throat, I really needed to calm down. It had been just over a *week* since she'd arrived. "Come on then. I'll make breakfast."

"You're very bossy," she muttered, rolling out of bed and nearly tripping on my socks.

I watched her pad toward the bathroom, hair wild, my T-shirt riding up on the smooth curve of her generous bum.

Steadfast Taurus, my arse. I was a goner.

The week slid into a rhythm so smoothly it scared me.

Mornings, she'd pad around the kitchen half asleep while I made tea and eggs, Bracken perched on a cabinet like quality control. Liora would ramble about her dreams, or things she'd read about in her gran's book, or some podcast she'd half-listened to about emotional wounds and inner children.

I could listen to her talk about anything. Her voice was

soothing and melodic, and the noise of her filled the empty spaces in my heart.

Evenings, she'd curl up on the couch with her laptop and notes, asking my opinion on things I knew nothing about ... like if the Kelpies were made of water, would they freeze in winter and go dormant?

I still worried, desperately, about the Kelpies, but I wasn't sure who I could talk to about my concerns. Maybe I could catch Graham on a slower day and have a quiet chat, because Liora had told me that he knew what was going on in Loren Brae. I supposed most people did, even if it wasn't a very public topic of conversation.

I'd just come to realize that my conversation skills, in general, had grown rusty. I'd been spending too much time with my trees, and not with my community. Something that Liora seemed hell-bent on changing.

"Do you think we should have a party?" she asked one night, chewing on the end of a pen while she scribbled in a notebook.

I almost choked.

"A party ... for what?"

"I don't know. Just to, you know, hang out with people?"

I looked at her, askance, and she burst out laughing when she glanced up at me.

"Right, I'll need to ease you into that idea."

Little did she know that I'd give her anything she wanted, she only had to ask.

We had small moments like that all week, and each one lodged under my skin.

Wednesday morning, I came inside, logs in my arms to

stack by the fire, and found her at the kitchen table, frowning at her laptop. Her hair was in a messy bun and she tapped a pen against her teeth.

"What's wrong?" I asked, setting the basket down.

She chewed on her thumbnail. "Greta just emailed. She got her first order. From someone she doesn't even know. I'm so proud I could pop."

"So what's the problem?"

She stared at the screen. "Now I'm terrified I saw the wrong path. What if it all goes wrong? What if her business fails and her kids resent me and she ends up destitute and it's all my fault?"

I walked over, gently tipped her chin up. "Liora. You saw possibility, not a guarantee. You nudged her toward what she already wanted. The rest is up to her. That's how this works."

"Is it?" she whispered. "What if I've taken on too much?"

I thought about how earnest she was, how she rooted for everyone to win, always. The way she'd talked about destiny like something that could be mended.

"You're not in charge of everything," I said. "Just your part. And your part, as far as I can tell, is giving people courage. They decide what to do with it."

She breathed out slowly, shoulders relaxing. "You're annoyingly good at this."

"At what?"

"These talks," she said. "The way you reframe things. It helps."

I shrugged, embarrassed. "Just telling you what I see."

"Do you think Greta's business will work?" she asked, worry clouding her gorgeous face again.

"You already know it will," I said, confident that her magick was strong. Hell, it was strong enough to force me into a truth spell. Which, admittedly, was still decidedly annoying when working with customers, but I also was getting used to navigating it. At the end of the day, the spell hadn't been horribly disruptive to my life. "You saw it."

"Aye, but it does help to hear you say it," she admitted. "It makes me feel less like I'm playing cosmic Jenga with people's lives."

"You're not," I said firmly. "You're just helping them see what's already there."

She smiled shyly at that, and I realized just how much I wanted to make her feel good—all the time, not just in bed. It was like watching a flower bloom slowly, and I wanted to gently water her, so she could show the world her beauty.

On Thursday, I took her into the forest with me.

It had been my idea. I wanted to share my world with her so she could get a sense of what my everyday life was like. The solitude. Inviting her into that felt like handing her the key to the last locked room in my house. I'd never really done that with a partner before.

"Will there be mud?" she asked that morning, standing in the hallway in jeans and a chunky jumper, hair braided back from her face. Bracken was perched on her shoulder like a tiny, judgmental parrot.

"Aye."

"Will there be bugs?"

"Might be. But also it's heading into winter, so far less of them, I'm sure." I bit back a smile.

"Will there be murdering?" She eyed the chainsaw in my hand.

"None on the agenda today," I said. "Just clearing up fallen trees on a path, darling."

"Good. I don't think I'd feel good about you taking down a healthy tree," Liora said.

"I try not to. But those we take for cabinetry or firewood, we're constantly replanting. I suppose I do things a little differently than some. I keep my land as a thriving ecosystem, and it's a give and take, really."

She pursed her lips, taking in my words, then nodded. "Then I approve."

"Good to know I've got your permission," I muttered, but my mouth twitched.

We hiked up the slope behind the house, the air was sharp and clean outside, the sunlight faded and soft as it crept toward winter. Frost clung to the edges of leaves and the ground was firm under our boots. Bracken hopped from her shoulder to mine and back again, chittering like he was running field commentary.

"Is he narrating our walk?" I asked, amused, but also enjoying having the wee man come along with us.

He chattered energetically.

"He says you walk heavy but have a nice aura," she translated.

"I walk heavy? Is he calling me fat?" I gasped and pretended to be offended.

"Och, please, like you have an ounce of fat on you." I glanced over to see Liora's cheeks pinken.

"Do you like thinking about my body, Liora?" I asked, knowing she got flustered when I was explicit with her.

"Me? I hardly think of it." Liora put her nose in the air.

"Oh really? Not at all? Not even when I lift you over my shoulder and throw you down on the bed."

Liora tripped on a root, and I caught her arm and laughed as she waved a hand in front of her face. "Damn it, Torin."

"I'd say that I'm sorry, but I can't, since I can't lie. I love how much you enjoy my body."

Liora whirled on me, her lips rounding in an O.

"You can't say … I mean I do … but—"

"But what? It's true, isn't it? You seem to love touching me … everywhere." I looked down, pointedly, at where her hands were absentmindedly stroking my abs.

"Oh my God." Liora whirled and stomped up the path. I took a moment to admire the view, and then followed, wisely keeping my laughter inside.

We reached a stand of pines marked with orange tape. The forester in me clocked the signs automatically—the thinning needles, the fungus at the roots, the slight lean toward the path where tourists loved to wander in summer.

"They're beautiful," Liora said softly, laying a hand on one of the trunks. "But sad."

"Aye," I said. "They're done. Might take a year or two, but the next big storm will finish the job if we don't. Better to bring them down controlled than let the wind do it."

She nodded, serious now. "Like letting go of something before it falls on your head."

I huffed a laugh. "Something like that." I put my chainsaw down to assess the situation. I didn't have to take them all down, just the worst one, and hopefully the others would stand a chance. Gesturing Liora over, I showed her what I'd be doing—where I'd cut, how the tree would fall, and where she needed to stand to be safe.

"I mean it," I said, catching her gaze. "If I tell you to move, you move. No arguing, no questions. You go where I point and you stay there. Aye?"

"Aye," she said, sobering. "No heroics. I promise."

Bracken chittered sharply at her shoulder.

"He understands to stay clear."

I started the saw, the familiar roar vibrating through my bones, and fell into the rhythm I knew best. Woodchips flew, sharp and resin-scented. The tree shuddered, groaned, then began its slow, inevitable fall.

I stepped back, guiding it with the cut, heart steady.

It hit the ground with a heavy thud that echoed through my ribs.

When I turned, Liora stood exactly where I'd put her, eyes huge, mouth hanging open.

"That was..." She shook her head. "Weirdly hot."

My mouth twitched. "It's just tree work, lass."

"Aye, but you're so competent," she said earnestly. "It does things to me."

Heat shot straight to my gut. "Don't say things like that while I'm holding power tools."

She laughed, delighted, and moved in to help me limb the branches once I killed the saw. She wasn't very efficient —kept stopping to talk to the trees, or apologize to them, or inspect a patch of moss as if it held the secrets of the universe—but she was willing, and she listened when I corrected her grip or her stance.

At one point, I glanced up to find her standing with her hands on her hips, breath puffing in white clouds, hair escaping her braid, Bracken perched on the felled trunk beside her like a foreman. The sunlight slanted through the trees, catching the copper strands in her hair, the curve of her smile.

Something inside me settled with a click.

This. *This* was what I wanted.

Not just the kisses. Not just the nights. This—her in my world, my house, *hell*, my life.

She caught me staring. "What?"

The truth spell punched my shoulder and I sighed. "Everything."

Her gaze softened. "You okay?"

I set down the branch I was stripping. "Aye. Just ... glad you're here."

Her smile then was small and staggering. "Me too."

We'd had small moments like that all week, and each one seemed to dig deeper into my heart.

That night we stood outside after dark, looking out over the loch. The unicorn hadn't shown itself again, but every time I glanced at the tree line, I half expected to see a flash of white.

"You think it'll come back?" she asked quietly.

"I hope so," I admitted.

She slipped her hand into mine. "It felt like ... approval."

"Aye," I said. "Like it was saying we're on the right track."

"Us?" she asked, glancing up.

"This place," I said quickly. "The village. The Order."

The truth spell warmed against my tongue. "And maybe us, aye."

She squeezed my fingers and went inside.

Later, I found her sitting cross-legged on the rug in front of the fire, her gran's brooch in her palm. The opal glittered softly in the firelight.

"You all right?" I asked, dropping down beside her.

She nodded, eyes on the brooch. "Just ... trying to feel into what's next."

I looked at the tiny brooch and up at the tense line on her forehead. There were challenges yet to come. Trials she hadn't faced.

The thought made my shoulders tense.

"Whatever it is," I said, "we'll handle it."

She glanced at me. "We?"

"Aye."

She studied my face for a long moment, as if testing the shape of that word.

Then she leaned into me, resting her head on my shoulder.

"You know," she said softly, "for a man who likes trees more than people, you're very good at this whole relationship thing."

I snorted. "Don't tell anyone. I'll lose my reputation."

She laughed, the sound soft and content, and turned her face into my neck.

When I'd been with Avery, I'd never felt she was happy with our relationship. That whatever I did or said had never been enough. And yet, Liora had just given me words I'd never expected to hear.

I wrapped an arm around her, breathing in the scent of her shampoo and something that was becoming like home to me.

Nearly two weeks ago, my life had been quiet. Predictable. Fine.

Now I had a witch in my arms, a squirrel in my curtains, a unicorn at the forest edge, and a brooch on my coffee table that, apparently, was magick.

And I'd never felt more certain of anything than I did of this simple truth ...

I didn't want any of it without her.

CHAPTER SEVENTEEN

LIORA

How the hell was I supposed to focus on giving a proper reading when my brain was still replaying Torin's mouth on mine like it was on a cursed loop?

I trudged up the path to the castle with my laptop bag bumping against my hip, trying very hard not to think about the fact that I now knew exactly what Torin sounded like when he lost control a little.

And it was excellent.

To say I was primed and ready to go once we got back from the forest was an understatement. Seeing him in his element ... seeing his strength in action ... I was practically frothing. *Definitely drooling.* It was no surprise he could carry me around the house as if I weighed nothing. *And good God, the man in bed?*

But it was also the words he spoke into my insecurity that had my heart thumping madly.

"You're not in charge of everything. Just your part. And your part, as far as I can tell, is giving people courage. They decide what to do with it."

He was so affirming, so good with words … just like he was so good with his hands.

"Focus," I muttered to myself as MacAlpine Castle loomed overhead, all turrets and stone and lovely in the soft afternoon light. "This is for Matthew, who seems like a perfectly lovely person. No thinking about your sex life while you're poking around in his soul chart."

A text pinged on my phone, and seeing it was from Zara asking when we could hang out, I put my phone on silent. Guilt tugged low in my stomach. She'd been asking to get together for a while now, and I kept blowing her off, happy in my little cocoon of bliss and not wanting anyone to burst it for me. Tossing my phone back in my handbag, I rang the bell at the castle doors.

The autumn air bit at my cheeks and Matthew beamed at me as he swept the doors open and laughed as I gaped up at the vaulted ceilings over my head.

"Impressive, isn't it?"

"Mind-blowing," I agreed, giving him a quick hug. He looked dashing today, in a tweed suitcoat, a Ramones T-shirt, and fitted dark denim jeans.

"I've got a fire going in the library for us. It's just, ugh, it's the best. One of my favorite rooms, not just in this castle, but in the world. I would live there if I could."

"Sounds dreamy," I said, beaming at him, and following

him down a stone corridor lined with the kind of fancy portraits that implied a once noble family had lived here.

At two arched wooden doors, Matthew paused and swept the doors open.

I sighed.

The library was straight out of a fantasy film. Floor-to-ceiling shelves lined in dark wood, a rolling ladder, a stone fireplace with a cheerful fire going, wingback chairs, green glass lamps casting pools of soft light. There was an honest-to-goodness-actual mural on the ceiling. The afternoon sky outside the tall windows was pewter-grey, but in here everything was cozy and welcoming.

Sir Buster stood in the middle of the rug, vibrating with disapproval, growling low the second he saw me.

"Good day to you too, sir," I said.

His growl tapered off into a grumble.

Matthew turned to me and grinned and then paused, narrowing his eyes. "My God, you're glowing."

"I am not glowing," I protested. "Am I?"

"You are absolutely glowing," he insisted. "Someone's been complicating things further with Mr. Complicated."

I sputtered. "I ... how did—"

"You have the look of someone who has been thoroughly *appreciated*." Matthew arched a brow and heat flooded my face.

Sir Buster growled and then pawed at my foot.

"We are not discussing my ... appreciation ... in front of the dog."

"We absolutely are," Matthew said serenely. "Sir Buster *loves* romance."

Sir Buster huffed when I bent to pick him up.

"Somehow, I highly doubt that."

Tucking Sir Buster in the crook of my arm, I dropped my bag by the nearest armchair and blew out a breath. "Right. I am officially compartmentalizing my love life now. This is about you. And your chart. And your huge life question that you want to ask."

"Fine. But you'll have to give me details later. I may be doomed to live vicariously through others."

I totally understood Sophie's joy at seeing her best friend now. He had an easy manner about him that made him already feel like a close friend. But today was about him and his needs. Not mine. *And how I was thoroughly "appreciated" last night.*

"I guess we'll see what your chart says."

We settled into opposite chairs, a low table between us. I'd brought my laptop, tarot deck, a couple of crystals because I liked to create an atmosphere and they helped my energy. The fire crackled in the hearth, and Sir Buster bounded down from my lap and settled himself at a wee bed next to where Lady Lola napped peacefully.

Matthew poured us both a cup of tea, and turned to me, studying my face as I pulled my laptop out and opened it.

"You look nervous."

"I'm not nervous," I said and then paused, lifting my eyes to the mural on the ceiling above me. "Okay, I'm a little nervous. I have been trying to read up on being a chartweaver, I don't want to accidentally tangle your entire life."

Matthew blinked. "Yes, that wouldn't be ideal."

"Sorry." I took a breath. "I'll explain as we go. But I

want you to know, I won't shift anything without your explicit consent, all right? You have full veto power here."

Something in his shoulders relaxed. "I trust you," he said simply.

My throat tightened. "Thank you."

"We can be terrified together," he added. "You, of your loom of destiny. Me, of the possibility of moving my entire life across the ocean."

"Right." I clicked open my astrology software. "Let's start with the basics. You wrote your birth details down?"

He slid a folded paper across the table with a flourish. "Date, time, location. I even triple-checked the time with my mother. She was very excited you're looking at my chart. She thinks I need 'cosmic guidance' to stop me from dating men who own more leather bracelets than books."

I snorted. "Your mother sounds wise."

"Oh, she is," he said. "Terrifying, but wise."

I typed in his details, hit enter, and the familiar wheel spun into place.

I leaned in.

"Okay," I said slowly. "Interesting."

"Is interesting good?" Matthew asked. "Or is it astrologer code for 'oh honey, you're a mess'?"

"It's good," I assured him. "Matthew, you are a Sagittarius Sun, Libra Moon, Virgo Rising."

He considered that. "So, I'm a cosmic mess?"

I laughed. "Not quite. Sagittarius Sun means you are a seeker. Truth, knowledge, experiences—you're not meant to sit still and accept what you're told. You're built to explore, to teach, to tell stories about what you've seen.

That's the professor in you. The guy who takes off on sabbatical to dig in the dirt and call it fun."

"Guilty," he said. "And the moon?"

"Libra Moon is your heart," I said. "You crave connection. Partnership. Balance. You feel best when you're in harmonious relationships. You're the friend who remembers everyone's birthday and texts people back in actual paragraphs."

"I feel attacked." He put a hand to his chest, faking outrage.

"Virgo Rising," I went on, "means the way you move through the world is practical, observant, maybe just a touch perfectionistic. People see you as put-together, reliable, kind of quietly competent. You notice the little things."

He smiled, but his fingers twitched slightly on the mug. "So far so good. And what about ... now?"

I glanced at him. "Meaning, what the hell you're meant to do with your life choices?"

"Yes, that."

I studied the chart again, moving to his transits.

"Okay," I murmured, watching the outer planets line up. "We've got Saturn having just marched its heavy boots through your sixth and seventh houses these last couple of years—work, health, relationships. I'd wager work has felt like a grind and your love life ..." I quirked a brow. "I mean, that doesn't sound like it went all that well."

He winced. "That it did not."

"Pluto," I went on, "is finishing up tearing through your fifth house of joy and romance. Which would explain why what used to light you up stopped working the way it did. And why love felt … intense. Transformative. Maybe a bit obsessive at times."

He made a face. "I hate how called out I feel."

"That's Pluto's whole brand." I glanced at the current positions. "But here's the big thing. See here?" I pointed to the little glyph for the lunar North Node, inching its way across his fourth house. "This is your North Node transit through your house of home, roots, and belonging. When this happens, life tends to shove you toward a new sense of home. Often literally."

He sucked in a breath. "As in … Scotland literally?"

I shrugged, a smile tugging at my lips. "It's not like the chart draws a wee picture of a loch and a castle. But … aye. It suggests a shift of base. Moving closer to chosen family. Building a new foundation."

"And here I am," he said quietly, glancing around the library. "In a castle in the Highlands, wondering if I could live here."

"Exactly," I said. I watched his face carefully. "What are you feeling, underneath the jokes?"

He took a long breath, staring into the fire for a moment. Sir Buster had fallen asleep and looked the most at peace I'd ever seen him.

"Lost," he admitted. "When I left California, I told myself it was temporary. A sabbatical from the sabbatical. I'd write and drink too much tea and try to get Sophie to buy some new clothes. But every day I wake up here and it feels … right. More 'home' than home has felt in a long time."

I nodded, letting him talk.

"I love my work," he went on. "Teaching, researching,

all of it. But the politics at the university, the pressure to publish, the constant hustle … it's been wearing on me for years." His mouth twisted. "It's not just my ex. It's the accumulation of everything. My life there feels brittle. This" —he gestured around the room—"feels like possibility."

The threads. I could feel them humming already, just beneath the surface of reality, like a kettle about to boil.

"And you want to know if you're being impulsive," I said softly. "Or if you're meant to stay. Or go."

"Yes." His eyes met mine, vulnerable behind his glasses. "I don't want to blow up my life on a whim. But I also don't want to cling to something that's already dead because I'm afraid of change."

I took a breath, steadying myself. "Okay. Then let's ask the chart."

I clicked to overlay the current transits on his natal chart. The wheel realigned, symbols shifting, and—

There it was.

That shimmer.

My breath stuttered. It started as a faint glimmer along the aspect lines—Mercury trine Jupiter, Saturn nudging his Midheaven, the Node crossing the IC—and then, as I watched, the lines lifted.

Silver-gold threads rose gently from the laptop screen, weaving themselves into the air between us. They arched and looped, delicate and bright, forming a three-dimensional web that pulsed faintly with light.

Matthew's eyes went huge behind his glasses. "Oh," he whispered. "Oh, wow."

"You can see them?" I almost dropped my laptop as I whirled to Matthew.

"Faintly, I can." His eyes were huge in his face.

He could see them. *Of course* he could. Matthew's chart practically shouted "open to woo."

I reached out slowly, remembering Gran's admonition on the crackling pages. *Guide, don't dictate. Weave where the soul already leans.*

As my fingertips brushed the nearest strand, a ripple of sensation shot up my arm. Not painful, exactly, more like the zing of static electricity.

Images flooded my mind.

California first.

Matthew in his apartment, alone at a small table piled with notebooks. His shoulders were hunched, blue light from his laptop washing his face. Outside, horns sounded from traffic. He went to campus, out to dinners, smiled at colleagues, but there was a shadow behind his eyes. There were good moments—students who got excited about his lectures, the satisfaction of finishing a chapter. But everything felt ... strained.

I ran my hand along another thread as Matthew stayed silent, watching me.

Loren Brae.

Matthew sitting in this very library, laptop open, sunlight slanting across the table. He was laughing at something Lottie said, gesturing wildly with a pen. A noticeboard in the village showed a flyer with Local History Talk at MacAlpine Castle written across it. Matthew helping Lachlan and Sophie set up museum displays in one of the castle's unused wings. Long walks in the hills with his breath fogging the air.

And then, softer, fuzzier, but there—a hand in his.

Someone walking beside him, their face just out of focus, but the feeling of companionship was clear. Warmth. Love, built slowly and honestly, nothing like the fast-burning brittle relationships he'd had before.

The threads carrying that latter image pulsed brighter.

"Liora?" Matthew's voice was soft, reverent. "What do you see?"

I swallowed, heart pounding. "Two main paths," I said. "One where you go back to LA, slide back into the old life. It's not ... terrible. But there's just this ... heaviness there. I don't know. Maybe not heaviness, but it's strained. Tired, I guess? Everything feels like pushing a boulder uphill."

His mouth tightened.

"And another," I said gently, "where you stay here in Loren Brae. You cobble together a new kind of career—teaching part-time, consulting on projects, or maybe even starting your own thing. You're surrounded by people who love you. And ... well, there might be someone here for you. A partner. Someone who sees you for you."

He closed his eyes briefly, a line forming across his brow, as he opened them back up and looked at me.

"What if I'm romanticizing that second path?" Matthew asked. "What if I'm projecting because Sophie's happy and everything feels like a Hallmark Christmas film and I've eaten too many of Hilda's cookies?"

"That's fair," I said. The threads shimmered, waiting. "But your chart backs it up. Look—your North Node is in the fourth house. Your soul's growth is tied to home and chosen family. You were never meant to be the eternal bachelor professor in the city high-rise. And right now, transiting North Node is conjunct with that natal placement.

It's like a cosmic highlighter saying 'hey, over here, this way.'"

He leaned forward slightly, eyes following my hand as I gestured to the glowing web. "And the moving?"

"Ninth house," I said. "Long-distance travel. That's being activated too. But instead of the usual Sagittarius story of *I will roam forever and never settle*, your chart wants adventure that leads to belonging. Not endless running."

He huffed out a shaky laugh. "I do run a lot."

"That tracks, too."

"Rude but true."

I gave him a small smile and waited.

"So this partner? Does it really seem to say I'll find love here? Or am I really a lost cause?"

I smiled, feeling the softness of it all the way through me. "We always have the potential for love. But in your case..." I pointed to his Libra Moon. "Your moon wants partnership. It's wired for it. And transiting Jupiter—the planet of expansion and luck—is moving into your seventh house over the next year. That's relationships. What you learn from them, what you attract. It doesn't promise a ring and a mortgage, but it does suggest that if you show up and open up, the potential for something real is extraordinarily strong. Especially if you're in a place where you feel more like yourself."

He looked at the threads again—the California path, fine and tight, and the Loren Brae path, brighter and wider.

"Can you..." He hesitated, swallowing. "Would it be possible for you to ... nudge it? Just a little? The Loren Brae one."

I held his gaze. "I can," I said slowly, swallowing down my nerves. "But only if you're already choosing it. I won't override your free will and I can't force what isn't yours."

"I know," he said. "I'm not asking you to decide for me. I think ... I've already decided. That's the terrifying part. I want to be here. With Soph and Lachlan. With all of you. I want to try a life that isn't built solely around my job title. But a part of me still clings to the old story. The safe story. If you can help me ... commit, I suppose. It would be comforting. To know the universe is backing me up, even a little."

I felt that right down to my bones.

"All right," I whispered. "Then yes. I can try."

The threads brightened, as if they'd heard.

"Before I do," I added, "a couple of ground rules. One, this doesn't erase hard things. If you stay, there will still be moments of homesickness, financial stress, all of that. Two, you still have to do the practical bits. Talk to your university. Sort out visas. Figure out how many cardigans you need for Scottish winters. Three, if at any point your gut says no, you listen to that over me, over the chart, over everything. Deal?"

"Deal," he said immediately, a corner of his mouth twitching upward.

"And four," I added, because Gran's words rang in my head, "I am not a vending machine of destiny, okay? This is a co-creation. You and me and the stars. And possibly Sir Buster, who I suspect is some sort of minor god."

We both glanced over. Sir Buster rolled onto his back with a groan, four little legs in the air.

Matthew smiled, eyes suspiciously bright. "Understood."

I took another breath, centering myself. "All right then. Let's see what the loom has in store."

I reached for the golden thread that represented Loren Brae—thicker than the California one now, but still delicate. As my fingers brushed it, heat flared in my palm. Images spilled through me again, faster this time.

Matthew at the village pub, arguing animatedly with Agnes about the ethics of museums and stolen artifacts, everyone around them tossing in opinions. Matthew in a small, bright kitchen, books crammed on every surface, a mug of tea steaming by his elbow as he typed. Matthew laughing in the snow with the Scotties, Sophie pelting him with a snowball and immediately denying it. Matthew standing at the front of a wee community hall, giving a talk about local legends to a packed audience, eyes alight.

And then—oh.

There.

A studio somewhere in the village, light pouring in, canvases leaning against the wall. A person stood with their back to me, hands stained with paint or clay or something equally messy, listening as Matthew talked about some old artifact he was helping them reference. I couldn't see their face, but I felt the warmth between them. The ease. The way their laughter curled around him. Threads of color linked them, cocooning them in soft golds.

It was blurry. Unformed. Not set. But it was there.

My heart squeezed.

Gently, carefully, I tugged that thread, pulling it forward, tightening the weave.

The thread glowed brighter. The whole web shifted subtly, the California path still present but now distinctly less dominant, like the memory of an old road you no longer use.

Energy shot up through my arm, leaving my fingertips tingling, my chest buzzing. It was a softer feeling this time than with Greta. Less like shoving something into place and more like saying yes to a door that was already half open.

I let go.

The shimmer dimmed, the threads slowly lowering back toward the chart. My inner vision still held the echo of them, like the afterimage of fairy lights when you close your eyes.

For a moment, neither of us spoke.

Then Matthew let out a shuddering breath. "I felt that," he said softly. "I don't know what you did, exactly, but I felt something ... click. Like the moment you finally choose a flight and hit 'confirm' after weeks of stalking the prices."

I laughed weakly. "A good feeling, then."

He scrubbed a hand over his face, then looked at me, eyes shining. "So? What now, oh Weaver of Charts?"

"Now," I said, forcing myself back into practical mode, "we talk about timing. Saturn's moving into your ninth in a way that supports serious study and long-term relocation. Over the next year, you'll have windows—points where starting the paperwork, having certain conversations, will flow more easily. I'll give you dates. But the headline is that you need to take your time with this choice. Don't rush it. You are meant to be deliberate."

We spent the next half hour going over details. I flagged

a few months where opportunities were likely—unexpected offers, potential job opportunities and so on. I pointed out when Jupiter would exactly trine his natal Sun—prime time for saying yes to something big. We talked about practicalities of subletting his apartment, what it would look like to go part-time at the university before maybe cutting ties altogether.

Some of it was silly—arguing about which Scottish knitwear brand would become his new personality—and some of it was far more serious.

At one point, he went quiet.

"What if I move here and … nothing magickal happens? What if I'm just sad in a different time zone?"

I reached across the table and took his hand. "Then you'll be sad with us," I said simply. "We'll feed you carbs and drag you to the pub and make you watch terrible Christmas films and help you write your book. Nothing in life is a guarantee. But at least here…you won't be alone."

His eyes filled. "Damn it. I'm surprised I'm this emotional. You're very annoying, you know."

"I know," I said gently.

He squeezed my hand. "Thank you."

We finished with a couple of tarot cards—The Fool, naturally, for the leap, and the Six of Cups for the sweetness of returning to something that feels like home even if it's new. Last, he pulled the Ten of Pentacles showing a family, chosen and built, over time.

Matthew stared at them, then nodded once, decisively. "All right," he said. "I'm doing it."

My heart leapt. "You are?"

"I am," he said. "I'll start working on the logistics. And

I'll talk to Sophie and Lachlan about timing and whether they're prepared to put up with me long-term."

I snorted. "They'll be ecstatic."

He stood up abruptly, came around the table, and hauled me into a hug that nearly cracked my ribs.

"Thank you," he whispered into my hair. "For this. For helping me to see what I needed to see and have clearly been avoiding."

Tears pricked my eyes. I could understand that sentiment. "Anytime," I said. "That's what I'm here for, apparently. Seeing threads, I guess. And nudging the brave ones."

He let me go, sniffed loudly, and reached for his mug like nothing had happened. Sir Buster got up, shook himself, and came over to bump his head against my shin in what I chose to interpret as grudging approval.

"See?" I told the dog. "He's staying. You get another human to boss around."

Sir Buster grunted, clearly satisfied.

As I packed up my things, Matthew flopped back into his armchair, staring at the ceiling with a dazed smile.

"I'm going to live in Scotland," he said, as if testing the words. "I'm going to live in Scotland and fall in love again and probably adopt a dog and develop an addiction to oatcakes."

"Correct," I said. "The stars have spoken. Also your heart."

He lowered his gaze to me. "And you? How are you doing, Chartweaver? You're still new to the area, aren't you? Too new to have a situationship with Mr. Complicated?"

I thought of my brooch with the new opal, of the threads in Matthew's chart, of Torin's hands on my skin.

"I'm..." I blew out a breath. "Overwhelmed and terrified. But also excited. All at once."

"Good," he said. "Excellent. Means you're alive."

Giving him a hug, I left him staring at the fire, arms crossed over his chest.

On my way out, I passed Sophie in the corridor, wringing her hands.

"How did it go?"

"Well, really well, I think."

"Is he moving here?" Sophie demanded and I just laughed, shrugging a shoulder.

"I can't say. That's for him to talk about it, if he chooses to."

"Damn it." Sophie stomped a foot.

"You're so nosey," Matthew drawled, coming out of the door of the library with the dogs at his feet.

"You're my best friend. You're not allowed to keep secrets from me," Sophie complained, putting her hands on her hips.

"Fine, drama queen. Think this old pile of bricks can fit my wardrobe?"

Sophie screamed and launched herself at Matthew, throwing her arms around his neck. The dogs went ballistic, barking as they raced in circles, and Hilda came running down the hallway.

"What's going on?"

"Matthew's going to move here!" Sophie cried.

Hilda joined the hug and the three bounced in a circle in the hallway.

A bellow filled the hallway, causing me to duck my

head, just before Clyde jumped out of a wall at the end of the corridor and barreled toward us.

"Clyde, no!" Sophie shrieked and then he trampled right over the three of them, mooing with joy.

"Damn it, he's icy," Matthew complained, rubbing his hands up and down his arms.

"He just wants to be part of the fun," Sophie sighed.

A wailing "moo" of agreement came through the walls, and we all laughed.

I laughed all the way down the path toward my car, happy that once again, I was able to give a meaningful reading that actually helped people. It was beginning to look like returning to Loren Brae was exactly the decision I needed to make to really step into my powers.

CHAPTER EIGHTEEN

LIORA

Another week flew by, and when I saw the text message from my sister—an invite for tea after my shift on Sunday—guilt assuaged me. I'd been neglecting her, caught up with Torin and my new chartweaving powers, and hadn't responded to many of her messages. I was being a bad sister, and I knew it, but for some reason I just wanted to keep what Torin and I had to myself. I knew that as soon as I put it under Zara's microscope, she'd show me all the cracks.

By the time I reached Zara's flat, my stomach was doing somersaults that had nothing to do with the half-eaten bacon roll I'd inhaled on the walk over.

"This is fine," I muttered to myself as I juggled a bakery box and my handbag. "Just a wee sister chat. Tea. Cake. Maybe a light scolding."

I knocked and the door swung open.

"You're late," Zara said.

That was the first bad sign.

Normally she opened with "Hi," or "Mitch, who's here?" Today, her brown eyes were narrowed, her dark hair scraped back into a tight plait and her mouth was a tight line.

"I know, I know. I'm sorry," I said. "But I brought sweets."

"Then, of course, you may enter."

I shouldered past her into the flat and dropped the box on the counter. Warmth and the familiar scent of her spicy perfume wrapped around me. Mitch's claws skittered on the floor as he bounded in from the lounge, tail going like a metronome set to rave.

"Hi, handsome boy," I crooned, crouching to greet him. "Free for cuddles or on duty?"

"He's off," Zara said shortly. "I asked him to stand down."

Mitch licked my hands, and I took my time petting him, while Zara just let the silence draw out as she walked to the kitchen counter.

I stood and shrugged off my coat, hanging it on the peg in exactly the place Zara preferred. Everything in her flat had a place. It made it easier for her to move around and also made it much easier for her to notice when something was off.

Like, say, her little sister's entire vibe.

"Tea?" she asked, already reaching for the kettle.

"Please." I sat at one of the chairs at the wee dining

table, suddenly feeling twelve again, waiting for a telling-off about forgetting to put my shoes away.

Silence stretched thin between us as she filled the kettle, measured water with her usual precise efficiency, took down the sage-green mugs, put the teabags in. The normal sounds —running water, clink of a spoon against the mug, Mitch snuffling at my knee—should have been comforting.

They weren't.

"So." Zara's voice cut through the quiet while the kettle hummed. "How's life?"

The tone said everything that I needed to know.

"Grand," I said, too brightly. How was I even going to get started downloading her on everything when she was in a mood like this? "Busy. You know. Work. Life, all that. You?"

Her head tipped slightly, her brows drawing together. "Do you think I'm an idiot, Liora?"

I winced. "Why do you sound like you're about to fire me from being your sister?"

"I'm considering it," she said flatly.

"Is this about me not popping by last week?" I asked. "I'm sorry I've just—"

"Been sleeping with Torin and afraid to tell me about it?"

I choked on absolutely nothing. "Wow. Straight to it, then."

Mitch whined and walked across the room to lean against her leg. "Am I wrong?"

"No," I muttered.

Zara turned off the kettle with a decisive click. "How long, Liora?"

"How long what?"

"How long have you and Torin been … involved?" She said the last word like it tasted bad.

"Not that long," I hedged. "Just a couple of … weeks?"

"So basically you moved in and jumped him."

Anger flared hot under my ribs, surprising me. "Why are you mad about this? Because it's Torin? Because of what happened with Avery? Because you think I'm incapable of separating my libido from my poor life choices?"

Zara set the mugs down with a soft thud and leaned her hands on the counter, facing me fully.

"Because you usually tell me everything," she said quietly. "And this time, you didn't."

The words landed like a stone in my stomach.

I looked away, suddenly fascinated by a pigeon on a branch outside her window. "I was going to. It's just … complicated."

"Och, is it?" She let out a humorless laugh. "You, living in the house of the man your ex-friend accused you of trying to steal, while half the town still thinks you're a homewrecker, and now you're actually sleeping with him? Can't imagine why that would be complicated."

I flinched. "That's unfair."

"Is it?" she pressed. "Or is it me saying out loud the things you're desperately trying not to think?"

Mitch returned to me and put his head on my knee. His warm brown eyes looked lovingly up at me and I stroked his soft ears automatically, my throat tight. "It's not like that, Z. It's not some … revenge fling or proof the gossip was right. We've been talking. A lot. We're actually … connecting. And honestly?" I swallowed. "I like him. Like, this actually feels good. It's ... real."

Her mouth trembled almost imperceptibly. "And you didn't think that maybe your sister might want to know before she finds out when someone mentions they saw you snogging him in a pub alley?"

Heat flooded my face. "Who saw?"

"Quite a few people, apparently," she said tersely. "Lachlan mentioned it to Sophie, Sophie mentioned it to Faelan, Faelan mentioned it to me because she thought surely I knew. Imagine my surprise when I didn't."

I winced. "It wasn't— We were just—"

"Liora." Her voice cut through my flailing. "This isn't about you kissing someone. You're allowed to have a love life. I am not the celibacy police."

"Could've fooled me," I muttered.

"It's about the secrets," she said bluntly. "You moved back here because things were spiraling. You lost your flat, your reputation was in tatters, you were ready to give up astrology altogether. You cried on the phone to me in that grim hotel room and said you needed help. I found you a place to live. I even paid your first month's rent." Her fingers curled against the counter, knuckles white. "And then you promptly got yourself entangled in a situation that could blow up in your face in a dozen different ways, and you didn't think to tell me?"

"Because I knew you'd react like this," I shot back. "Like I'm some daft child who needs to come ask your permission before I kiss someone."

This time, she recoiled like I'd slapped her.

"That's not fair," she said, low. "You don't need my

permission. I've only asked you for honesty. There's a difference."

For a moment, I wanted to cave. To apologize and promise to do better, to fold myself back into the familiar shape of the sister who was always screwing up. It would be so easy. We'd done this dance a hundred times.

But something stiffened inside me. Maybe it was the way Sophie and the others had looked at me around that dinner table, like I was someone capable. Maybe it was the threads I'd seen glowing above Matthew's chart, trusting my hands. Maybe it was Torin's voice in my ear, telling me I wasn't naïve, I was hopeful, and that I deserved people who protected that softness instead of shaming it.

"I'm allowed to have things that are mine," I said, surprising myself with the steadiness of my tone. "That aren't run through the Zara Filter first."

Zara's nostrils flared. "The Zara Filter?"

"Aye," I said. "Where every choice I make gets assessed for risk and stupidity, and then you let me know how much I've disappointed you."

"That's not—" She broke off, visibly reining herself in. "I worry. *Of course* I worry. Because you leap. You always have. Headfirst, no looking. And I've … spent a lot of years digging you out of messes."

"I've never asked you to," I said quietly.

The second the words left my mouth, regret punched me in the chest. That wasn't true and we both knew it. I'd asked for her help more times than I could count. I'd cried on her sofa, raided her tea cupboard, let her pay deposits I couldn't afford.

But I was so tired of feeling like a walking cautionary tale in her eyes.

Her jaw clenched. "You have. But I don't care, Liora. Don't you see? That's what being a big sister means. I'm the one who sees the cliff before you cheerfully walk off it."

"Oh, come on," I snapped, frustration spiking. "I'm not that bad."

Zara lifted a hand and began counting off on her fingers. "The time you moved in with a man after three weeks because your synastry was off the charts and he turned out to be a kleptomaniac. The time you started that MLM candle business because Mercury was in your second house and thought it meant start a company rather than don't sign contracts with pyramid schemes. The viral *WitchTok* reading that got you booted from your flat. The Avery incident. Do I need to keep going?"

I flinched with each example, even the ones I could laugh about on a good day. *But why was she so insistent to remember every failure? Is she also aware of the times I've succeeded?*

"Okay," I said tightly. "I get it. I'm the common denominator in my disasters."

"That's not what I said," she protested.

"It's what you meant," I fired back.

Silence crackled between us, as sharp as broken glass.

Mitch whined again and returned to Zara to put his paw on her foot. She reached down to stroke his head, her fingers trembling.

"Fine," she said after a moment, voice brittle. "You're seeing Torin. You're an adult. You can sleep with whomever you want. I may think it's a catastrophically bad idea, but I can't stop you." She inhaled slowly. "What I do need to talk to you about is the magick."

Every muscle in my body tensed. "What about it?"

"Don't do that," she said sharply. "Don't play dumb. I can feel you humming, Liora. Your aura is a mess of new colors. There's something different about you and it is not just post-sex glow. Something happened."

I stared at the knotted grain of the wood table in front of me, wishing I could sink into it.

"Okay," I said finally. "Fine. Two things. Maybe three."

"Start with the worst one," she said without missing a beat.

I let out a slightly hysterical laugh. "That's subjective."

"Liora."

"Right, right." I chewed my lip. "I ... may have accidentally hit Torin with a truth spell."

She went very, very still.

"Explain," she said, voice dangerously calm.

"Och, don't use that tone, it makes me feel like a naughty ten-year-old," I muttered. "It was the first night, when I got to the house. I found spells in Gran's book and just thought I'd test one out. I thought I was alone. And Torin walked in." I fluttered my hands. "Boom. Truth spell right to the face."

Zara slapped a hand over her mouth like she was physically holding in a scream.

"It was an accident," I rushed on. "I didn't mean to. And we've been managing it. Mostly. He has to answer truthfully if I ask him something direct, but he can sort of ... work around it if I don't phrase things too pointedly, and he's getting better at pausing before he speaks, and—"

"Liora." Her voice shook. "You took away a man's ability to choose what he shares. You say it like you spilled tea on his shirt."

Guilt washed over me, hot and sour. "I know. I know. I felt awful. But what was I meant to do? There's no easy reversal, not until we figure out exactly what I did. And I've spoken to Sophie and Agnes and they're helping me look into it. It's not like I've just shrugged and gone, well, that's his problem now."

"Oh God," Zara whispered, pressing her thumb and forefinger to her eyes. "This is why you didn't tell me. Because you knew I would lose my mind."

"I knew you'd make that face," I said weakly.

"This isn't about my face, Liora." She dropped her hand. "Consent matters. In magick and everything else. How can he trust you? How can you trust that what he says is fully his, and not coerced?"

"It's not like that," I protested, sickness churning. "I'm not interrogating him. I'm not using it to ... to catch him out or anything. Half the time it's just him blurting some grumpy compliment and then glaring at me because he didn't expect to say it out loud."

"That's not the point," she said. "The point is that his free will was compromised and you're living in his house and sleeping with him."

The way she said it made my skin prickle with shame.

"I told him," I said, my voice small. "He knows. I explained. He chose to keep me there. If he wanted me gone, trust me, I'd be gone."

"He might also be lonely and terrible at boundaries," she shot back. "Doesn't mean this is healthy."

I bristled. "You don't even know him. You knew him years ago through Avery's lens."

"And you're seeing him clearly through the lens of a spell you cast on him," she said ruthlessly. "You don't see why that might concern me?"

"Of course, it's a concern," I snapped. "I'm not a sociopath. That's why I'm working to undo it. And in the meantime, we're trying to be careful with each other. Honest."

Zara let out a harsh breath. "And the other thing?"

"The ... other thing," I repeated.

"The thing that has your aura looking like a Jackson Pollock painting," she said. "The thing that has every plant I pass whispering that you're different. Don't insult my intelligence. What happened?"

I swallowed hard.

"Liora," Zara said quietly. "Please. I know I give you a hard time. I know I can be overbearing. But I'm scared. I can feel something big shifting around you and I'm stumbling in the dark. Literally and figuratively. Just ... let me in."

The plea in her voice undid me. My eyes burned.

"I'm a chartweaver," I blurted.

The word seemed to hang in the little kitchen, heavy and strange.

I couldn't handle the silence, so I rushed on.

"I—" I licked dry lips. "I'm a chartweaver. It started with Greta's reading. Her chart sort of ... lifted. Threads everywhere. And I could see paths, Z. Actual paths. What would happen if she stayed at the supermarket, what would happen if she started this quilting business from home.

And when I touched the threads, they changed. Just a bit. Got stronger. Then with Matthew, it happened again. His paths, California and Loren Brae. I ... nudged the Loren Brae one. With his permission, of course." I shrugged helplessly. "And then I found Gran's notes. She'd written about chartweavers. There was a wee heart next to a line that might have been about me. It was like she'd known."

The words spilled out of me in a rush, tumbling into the space between us.

Zara just stared, breathing hard.

"I was going to tell you," I added quickly. "I wanted to have more information first. To not come running to you with half-formed panic. I thought—I don't know what I thought. That I could figure it out on my own, maybe. Just for once."

Her laugh was wet and disbelieving. "You thought you could keep something this big from me?"

Heat rushed to my face. "It's not about you, Z. Not everything is about you."

"It's not about me," she retorted. "It's about the fact that my little sister can now literally put her hands on fate. That she's weaving people's futures without training. Without safeguards. Without telling the one person who has spent years trying to help her not accidentally set her life on fire every six months."

"I'm not weaving willy-nilly," I protested. "I'm careful. I've got Bracken to help too. I only touch threads when the person clearly wants that path. When their chart backs it up. When my gut says it's aligned."

"You're trusting a squirrel's risk assessment?" Zara crossed her arms over her chest.

She had a point.

"I am being careful," I insisted, my own temper flaring now that the initial shame had subsided. "And, actually, it's been good. Greta finally has the courage to start the business she's dreamed of. Matthew's going to stay here and build a life that actually fits him. I'm not forcing anything. I'm supporting what's already there."

Zara's hands clenched into fists on the counter. "You don't see it, do you?"

"See what?" I demanded.

"How powerful this is," she said hoarsely. "How dangerous. Not just to them. To you."

I opened my mouth to argue, but she barreled on.

"You give big readings, Liora. Big pronouncements. You always have. 'This relationship is doomed.' 'You're destined for more than one great love.' 'This is the year you should leave your job.' And sometimes, aye, there's truth in it. But words have weight. People hear you and they change their lives. Now, those words are tethered to actual threads. You nudge a strand and someone moves across the world. Ends a marriage. Starts a business that might bankrupt them or make them thrive." Her voice broke. "And when it all goes wrong, because sometimes it will—you know it will —you'll blame yourself. You'll drown in it. I will be the one picking you up again."

Tears stung my eyes. "So your solution is what? That I never use it? That I shut it down and pretend I'm just a normal witch with a dodgy *WitchTok* history?"

Her jaw set. "My solution is that you slow down. That you stop reading for random people until we understand what this is. That you tell everyone in the Order about it so they can help. That you bring me in instead of treating me like the enemy."

"I already told the Order," I said, stung. "At dinner. They know. They're thrilled, actually. Agnes thinks Gran must have been waiting for someone like me for generations."

Zara flinched like I'd stabbed her.

"You told them," she repeated, voice flat. "Before you told me."

Guilt twisted in my gut. "It just came out," I said weakly. "We were talking about the brooch and the new stone and—"

She covered her mouth with her hand, shoulders shaking.

"Z..." I stood and walked over to her, putting my hand on her shoulder.

She flinched away as if my touch burned.

"Don't," she said, voice raw. "Just ... don't."

The ache in my chest sharpened into anger.

"I'm allowed to have my own relationships," I said. "My own support system. It doesn't have to be you and only you."

"That's not what this is about," she said, chin coming up. Her cheeks were wet. "You can have as many friends as you like. Hell, I'm glad you do. But you shut me out of two of the biggest things that have ever happened to you. One, the man you're falling in love with. Two, the power that could make or break you. And you only told me because you got cornered in my kitchen."

"I was going to tell you," I repeated, the words feeling feeble even to my own ears.

"When?" she demanded. "After you rewove half the village? After Torin's spell backfires in some horrific way?"

"That's not how any of this works," I snapped. "You're catastrophizing."

"And you're minimizing," she shot back. "As usual."

I stopped, caught, fury working its way through me. "You know what? I didn't come here to be told, again, that I'm the problem in every scenario. That if something goes wrong, it's because I leapt without thinking. I know that's how you see me. The common denominator. The screwup. The one you have to rescue."

"That's not—"

"It is," I insisted, tears spilling over now. "You might wrap it in concern but underneath, there's always this ... this tone. Like you're just waiting for me to botch it again so you get to be the sensible one."

"Someone has to be," she said quietly. "It was never Mum. I've always had to be. Not being able to see doesn't lend itself toward a lot of frivolity."

The silence that followed was thick and painful.

Mitch whined again, shifting between us, tail drooping as if he'd absorb the tension if he could.

"Maybe," I said, my voice shaking, "I don't want to be the one you have to manage anymore. Maybe I want to figure out who I am without your commentary."

Her chin lifted, the muscle in her jaw ticking. "And maybe I'm tired of feeling like the only thing standing between you and your next disaster."

We stared at each other—me seeing my sister, rigid and wounded, her eyes shining with tears, her seeing me in whatever way she saw auras and energy and only a big sister could.

"I thought you'd be happy for me," I whispered. "About the chartweaving. About Torin. About ... anything."

"I'm worried for you," she shot back. "There's a difference."

"I think I should go," I said, heart pounding.

"Maybe you should," she replied, voice like ice.

The words slashed across my chest.

I grabbed my bag and coat with shaking hands. Mitch moved toward me, uncertain, and I bent to press a kiss to the top of his head.

"Love you, Mitch," I whispered.

His tail thumped weakly.

"Liora," Zara said.

For a hopeful second, I thought she might soften. That we'd hug it out, promise to talk later, do what we always did.

But she only tilted her head, her expression closed.

"Until you're ready to be honest with me," she said quietly, "I don't know what to do with you."

The words hit harder than any shouted accusation.

I swallowed the lump in my throat, pulled my coat on, and opened the door.

"Fine," I said, without looking back. "Then maybe we take a break from each other. Since I'm so much work."

"Don't twist my words," she said sharply.

"I don't have to," I replied. "They're already tangled."

I stepped outside.

"Liora." Her voice followed me, thin and strained.

I hesitated, hand on the knob.

But whatever she was going to say, she didn't.

The silence between us yawned wide.

"Be well, Z," I said, and closed the door gently behind me.

The cold air outside slapped my cheeks as I stepped onto the street. Automatically, my eyes were drawn to the loch where icy wind kicked up waves, and the circle of trees on the island shifted in the wind.

For the first time since I'd come back to Loren Brae, I didn't feel like I had a home base. No sofa to collapse on with tea and Zara's dry commentary.

Unsettled, and questioning myself all over again, I headed home.

Not home.

To Torin's house.

Because I didn't really have a home I could call my own. And right now, when I felt so untethered, so ... alone, I feared I'd just lost my safest place. *My person.* My sister who I'd always relied on.

"And maybe I'm tired of feeling like the only thing standing between you and your next disaster."

My sister who was tired of me ... of seeing me fail.

And the scary thing was I wasn't sure her intuition wouldn't be proven right.

CHAPTER NINETEEN

TORIN

B y the end of the week, I'd talked to more trees than
people.

Didn't matter much, all things considered—trees were
better listeners, and they didn't look at you with wide blue
eyes and say "I'm fine" in a voice that very clearly meant "I
am absolutely not fine, but I'm also not going to tell you
why, so good luck with that."

But it was getting to me.

The week after Liora's row with Zara—I didn't know
the details, only that she'd come home tight-jawed and
quiet—felt like someone had swapped my bright, humming
housemate for a ghost that still left crystals everywhere.

She still slept in my bed, mostly. She still laughed at
Bracken's antics and read through her gran's books. But
there was a new distance there. She was guarding herself,

holding back somehow, and I didn't really know how to reach her.

She didn't tuck herself under my arm when we watched telly. She didn't reach for my hand in the kitchen.

And in bed...

Where last week she'd curled into me like I was the world's largest, warmest hot water bottle, she now lay on her side facing away, breathing steady, a whole inch of mattress between us that may as well have been the Atlantic.

An inch was a chasm when until a few days ago we couldn't keep our hands off each other.

"Everything all right, darling?" I asked one morning, brushing my knuckles over her shoulder as she sat at the table surrounded by charts and notes, laptop open, her gran's book propped beside it.

"I'm fine," she'd said too brightly, shrugging off my hand. "Just lots to think about. Don't worry."

Unfortunately for both of us, that was impossible not to do. Not with her.

"Lass," I'd tried again. "Talk to me. Something's bothering you."

"I just need to figure things out on my own," she'd said, jaw tightening. "Please, Torin. I promise I'll talk when I'm ready."

And that was that.

I couldn't push. Not when she looked at me like she was balancing on a tightrope and I'd be the one to knock her off.

So I did what I always did when my world didn't make sense.

I went to the woods.

To distract myself, I cleared half a kilometer of trail, took down a dead ash threatening to fall across the path, and gave three separate lectures to customers about paying better attention to the trees where their branches hung over their roofs.

Bracken often followed me, chittering away, and I talked to him too, even though I couldn't understand anything he said back to me.

The truth was, I was worried. I could feel Liora pulling back and it was triggering every protective instinct I had. I wanted to fix it. To shore up whatever crack had appeared. But this wasn't like a broken fence post I could replace. This was Liora, and she'd asked for space without quite saying the word.

So I was respecting that.

Mostly.

Which was why, when Friday morning rolled around and I reached for my keys and she told me that I didn't need to pick her up from the pub after her shift, that Graham would drop her home or she'd walk, I said, looking her square in the eye, "That isn't going to happen."

She groaned. "Torin."

"Liora." I folded my arms. "There are Kelpies in the loch and you've barely talked to me all week. I know you're not going to be paying attention to whatever's out there. You think I'm letting you walk home alone on a Friday in the dark? Not a chance. I'll come in for trivia and bring you home. I'm not taking no for an answer."

Her mouth quirked despite her exasperation. "You're

very bossy for a man who spends most of his time with trees."

"Trees respect routine," I said. "You might try it sometime."

She threw a cushion at my head.

So that was how I ended up at The Tipsy Thistle on Friday night, walking into the hum of voices and clink of glasses, the smell of chips and beer wrapping around me like something familiar.

The pub was packed. Trivia nights always were. You could be promised a good show when Agnes and Graham argued over obscure questions, which ended up making half the village shout at each other over whether a wombat's poo was square or round.

For the record, it was square. Agnes had proved this once with a very graphic demonstration involving sugar cubes and a diagram on the back of a coaster. I still wasn't over it.

I spotted Liora straightaway, my gaze drawn to her like a heat-seeking missile.

She was at the far end of the bar, a notebook tucked under one arm, balancing a tray of pints with more grace than she claimed to have. Her hair was in some kind of messy knot with bits falling out around her face, her cheeks flushed, eyes sparkly as she laughed at something a regular said.

She looked ... happy, damn it.

Which should've eased the tightness in my chest but somehow made it worse, because now I had no idea if I was part of the reason she was unhappy and something she'd decided to keep at arms' length.

"There's a lad who needs a pint," Graham said, following my gaze to Liora.

"Och, Irn-Bru for me, mate. Driving."

"Nae bother."

"Hiya, Torin," Agnes said, turning from her stool to smile at me. "You want to join our team?"

Agnes was looking lovely in a pretty scoop-necked jumper, auburn curls framing her face.

"You're late," Graham said, bringing me my drink. "First round of trivia starts in ten."

"I was lecturing people about responsible shrubbery care," I said, reaching for the can.

"That's the saddest sentence I've heard all week," Agnes observed, then elbowed Graham when he leaned on the bar too close to her. "Excuse me, but have you heard of personal space?"

"Personal space is a construct," Graham said cheerfully, unbothered. "We're team-mates tonight, darling. You cannae push away the brains of the operation."

She snorted. "If we were relying on your brains, we'd list Finland as a kind of fish."

"Is it not?"

She rolled her eyes so hard I worried she'd detach a retina. But there was warmth there too, a fondness that made Graham stand a bit taller. He reminded me of a plant shifting upward when the sun shone on it.

It was clear he was hopelessly in love with her. Everyone knew it except, apparently, Agnes.

"You two need a room or another teammate?" I asked.

"Liora promised to be on our team if she ever puts

down her tray," Graham said, scanning the room. "Oi, sunshine!"

"Sorry," Liora said, tucking a stray strand of hair behind her ear, as she hurried back over. "I'm really not sure how I'm meant to be of much help when I'm working."

"It'll be fine, I promise," Graham said. "We need all the help we can get. Agnes keeps answering every question with Outlander."

"Oh sod off! There was *one* question about television ages ago," Agnes said, her mouth dropping open. "And I'll have you know that I was correct."

Liora laughed, the sound tripping up my spine. "Okay, okay. As long as I can still serve my tables."

"You can sneak a look at their answers too," Graham said and Liora shook her head, the smile still hovering on her lips. It was nice to see. I didn't even care that it wasn't from something I had said. I was just happy to see her marginally more relaxed than she had been all week.

"We need a team name," Agnes said, tapping the paper with her pen.

"I'm telling you, Quiztopher Columbus is a solid name," Graham said. "It's topical."

"It's offensive," Agnes retorted. "We are not naming our team after a colonizer, you arse."

"Fine. Agnes and Her Useless Menfolk," he offered.

"That has a nice ring," I said, and Agnes laughed.

"I'm keeping that one for my autobiography," she muttered.

Liora laughed, her gaze bouncing between the three of us. "Right. Let me just see if any of my tables need anything else before we start."

As she turned, I couldn't resist letting my hand drift down the center of her back—just a light touch at her waist as had become habit.

She went still for half a second, like she always did when I touched her, and the door to the pub opened. The air in the room seemed to shift and somehow I knew before turning.

Avery stood in the doorway like she owned the place.

She looked ... exactly the same and completely different.

Her hair was in a sleek bob now instead of long waves, her lipstick a sharp, glossy red. She wore a camel coat over a fitted dress, and heels that definitely weren't designed for cobblestones. She'd always had a way of looking like she'd stepped out of a magazine, even in a town where wellies were considered formal wear.

Her gaze swept the room and, for one blissful second, I thought maybe she hadn't seen me.

Then her eyes landed on our wee huddle by the bar.

On me.

On my hand, which was currently resting on the small of Liora's back.

Everything in her expression sharpened.

"Oh," she said, loud enough to cut through the hum. "Well. Isn't this cozy?"

Conversations faltered. Heads turned. You could feel the pub's attention swivel, the way a forest goes quiet when a predator appears.

Liora's back tensed under my palm. She went rigid and then turned.

"Evening, Avery," I said, praying she wouldn't make a

scene, but already getting an idea of where this was heading. "What are you doing here?"

"I'm back to visit my auntie. But the real question should be what are *you* doing here?" she demanded. "You hate trivia."

"I do not hate trivia," I said, truth spell dragging the words into something more honest. "I hate *losing* at trivia."

"Same, mate," Graham muttered.

Avery stalked closer, heels clicking on the worn floorboards. "So, it seems you two couldn't keep away from each other after all."

"Avery." Agnes's voice held a warning. "Don't start."

"Oh, I'm late to the starting, apparently," Avery said sharply. She looked me up and down, then Liora. "You couldn't help yourself, could you? Either of you. Full circle. Poetic."

I felt every eye in the place on us. Old memories stirred—the whispers from years ago. Did he? Didn't he?

All I wanted to do was protect Liora from Avery. I didn't have to look at her face to know she was already pulling further into herself to hide from Avery's words.

"We never cheated," I said, the truth spell making my voice come out rough and uncompromising. "*Never* have I lied to you, Avery. And if you were even an ounce of the woman I once thought you were, you'd admit that."

Avery's laugh was brittle. "Right. Of course. Like I didn't see the way you looked at her?" She shifted her gaze to Liora. "And you just happened to show me the reading where your chart aligned perfectly with his for what? Just out of the goodness of your heart, right?"

"I didn't—" Liora started and I turned to see the color draining from her face.

"You did," Avery cut in, sweet as vinegar. She tilted her head. "What do they call you on *WitchTok*? The Heartbreak Witch?"

A ripple went through the crowd. Someone at a nearby table muttered, "Oh shite," under their breath.

Liora flinched like she'd been slapped.

Graham leaned forward. "Okay, that's enough. You don't get to come in here and start slagging off my staff."

"Your staff?" Avery arched a brow. "Is that what we're calling her now?"

"Aye. That's exactly what we're calling her," he said, steady. "She pulls her weight, she's kind to my customers, and she doesn't talk rubbish about people in the middle of my establishment. You want a drink, you queue like everyone else. You want to fight, take it outside and not in my pub."

There was a murmur of agreement. Agnes stood, small frame radiating a surprising amount of menace.

"Avery, sit down or go home," she said. "It's trivia night, not drama club."

For a second, Avery looked around, clearly expecting more support than she was getting. Some people glanced away while others met her eyes evenly. Time had moved on. A spark of hope filled me. Perhaps people had made up their own minds about me, about Liora.

That didn't seem to fit whatever script she'd rehearsed in her head.

Her gaze landed back on me, then on my hand still at

Liora's back. I forced myself to take it away, fingers curling into a fist at my side.

"I knew it. I *knew* you fancied her," she said quietly, almost to herself. Then louder, for the room, "You two deserve each other."

With that, she spun on her heel and stalked back out, coat flaring behind her.

The door slammed.

Silence hovered for a beat, then someone coughed. Glasses clinked. The pub's hum crept back in, tentative at first, then louder as people retreated into their own conversations, attention shifting back to pints and answer sheets.

"All right, the lot of you." Graham raised his voice and the entirety of the pub swiveled to look at him. "If any of you think, for a minute, that this upstanding lad who has worked fairly and honestly in this community for years would cheat and lie, you're welcome to leave my establishment. And while I haven't known Liora as long as I've known Torin, I can tell you she's a great employee and has a good heart. Don't leave here tonight spinning such nonsense that it comes back my way again, understood?"

I breathed a sigh of relief as everyone cheered in response.

But I could still feel the aftershock.

Liora stood very still, eyes fixed on the floor.

"Hey," I said softly. "You okay?"

"Fine," she said, voice thin.

Lie.

"I'm sorry," I said. "I didn't know she was back."

"Of course she's back," Liora murmured, more to herself than to me. "Why wouldn't she be?" She took a breath, pasted on a brittle smile. "I've got tables. I should … I should work. Trivia, remember? People need drinks."

"Liora—"

"Later," she said, ducking away before I could stop her.

She moved through the crowd on autopilot, smile in place, tray steady. If you didn't know her, you might've thought she was fine. Happy, even.

I knew better.

Trivia blurred. I couldn't tell you a single question Graham asked. Apparently we came second by one point. Agnes blamed Graham. Graham blamed me.

Through it all, I kept an eye on Liora.

She moved faster than usual, like if she slowed down for even a second, the feelings would catch her. Her laugh was a decibel too high, her smile flashing on and off like a faulty fairy light. When last orders were called and the crowd started to thin, she disappeared into the back for a suspiciously long time.

I waited by the door, jacket on, keys in hand, until she finally emerged in her own coat, hair twisted up haphazardly, eyes rimmed a little red.

"I can walk," she said before I could open my mouth.

"I know," I said. "I'm still driving you."

She hesitated, then sighed. "Fine. But I'm not in the mood for a post-game analysis."

"Noted," I said quietly, opening the truck door for her.

The drive home was thick with silence. The kind that had weight.

Rain dabbled the windscreen and the wipers thumped in a steady rhythm. The loch was a dark stretch to our right, the lights of Loren Brae fading behind us.

"You want music?" I asked eventually.

"No."

Right.

We were almost at the turn-off to the house when she spoke.

"She's right, you know," Liora said softly.

My hands tightened on the wheel. "About what?"

"About me." She stared out the window. "The Heartbreak Witch. I ruin things. I ruined your relationship with her. I should have known better about showing her how our charts lined up. I should have known her well enough to know that she wouldn't have handled that well. And who knows? Maybe I've ruined Greta too, and probably now Matthew. I drag people into my mess and I make everything worse, and then I run away and someone else has to clean it up."

"Liora." My chest ached. "That's not—"

"It is," she said sharply. "You don't see it because you're … *you*. Steady. Kind. But that doesn't change the facts."

"Facts?" I pulled into the drive, parked, turned off the engine, and turned to face her. "Here are the facts as I know them. You gave Avery a reading. She reacted badly because it confirmed things she didn't want to face. She lied about me to cover her own arse. That's not on you."

"That reading blew up your life." Her voice cracked. "You just said yourself people still remember. And tonight" —she let out a brittle laugh—"proves they're not going to forget anytime soon."

"Most people in there didn't give her the time of day," I pointed out. "Did you not notice that?"

"I noticed that the second she said 'Heartbreak Witch,'

every head turned," Liora whispered. "I noticed that the thing I'm most ashamed of is now a fun label strangers get to throw around."

She scrubbed her hands over her face. "And Zara—"

She stopped dead.

I waited.

"And Zara?" I asked gently.

She shook her head, jaw tightening. "It doesn't matter."

"It matters to you," I said. "So it matters to me."

She hesitated, then blew out a breath. "As you know, we had a fight."

I stayed quiet.

"She thinks I should have told her about you," Liora said, the words coming out rushed now. "And the truth spell. And being a chartweaver. And she's right. I should have. She's my sister, she's always been there for me, and I just ... didn't tell her. I kept it all to myself because I was happy and scared it would disappear if I said it out loud."

"That's understandable," I said, not moving though I wanted to gather her into my arms.

"She doesn't see it that way," Liora said, voice going wobbly. "She thinks I'm reckless. That I jump into things without thinking. That I don't learn. That I'm always the one causing chaos and then expecting her to fix it. And she's not wrong."

"Liora—"

"I didn't tell her about you because I knew she'd have concerns." Her mouth twisted around the word. "She'd tell me to slow down. To think. To remember what happened last time. And I didn't want to hear it because I wanted this.

You. Without the lecture. Without the reminder that I'm the screwup."

There it was. The raw thing at the center of her.

"You're not a screwup," I said, feeling the truth of it settle deep.

She huffed out a laugh that wasn't amused. "Funny how the common thread in every disaster of my life is me."

"That doesn't make you the disaster," I said.

"It might."

I wanted to argue until she believed me, but the truth spell hummed under my skin, keeping me honest. I couldn't say it would all be fine when I didn't know that.

"What are you saying?" I asked quietly.

She stared straight ahead, breaths coming shallow. "I'm saying that I think I need some space."

The words landed like a physical blow.

"From ... me?" I managed.

"I don't know," she said quickly. "Yes, I guess. I need to get my head on straight. I need to figure out what being a chartweaver actually means. I need to fix things with my sister. I need to help the Order. And I can't do any of that if I'm ..." She gestured between us, fingers shaking. "If I'm falling apart every time you look at me like that."

"Like what?" I asked, hoarse.

"Like I'm good," she whispered. "Like I'm worth choosing."

"Because you are," I said simply.

She squeezed her eyes shut, a tear slipping free. "See? *That.* That's exactly the problem. I want to believe you so badly that I'm afraid I'll hand you my whole heart and then watch you get dragged through the mud again because of me. And I can't—*I won't*—do that to you."

I swallowed hard. "You don't get to decide what I can handle."

"Maybe not," she said. "But I get to decide what I bring into your life. And right now that's ... a lot of chaos."

Silence pressed in on us. The truck felt too small, the night outside too big.

"What does space look like?" I asked because I needed specifics.

She drew a shaky breath. "I'd like to ... sleep in my bed for a bit," she said, voice barely above a whisper. "No kissing, no ... you know." She waved a hand in the general direction of my lap and turned bright red. "We can still live here. Still be ... friendly. I'm not saying we never talk again. I just ... I need to take the pressure off. On us. On what this is. Maybe we just moved too fast."

I stared at her, every instinct in me roaring to not let this happen.

I wanted to say it. To refuse. To tell her that once I'd set my sights, that was it, and she'd just have to deal with being cherished for the rest of her life.

But the truth spell throbbed in my chest like a warning.

If I said I was fine with this, I'd be lying. If I said I didn't mind, I'd be lying.

So I didn't.

"I hate this," I said honestly. My voice came out rougher than I meant it to. "Every part of me hates this. I don't want distance. I don't want separate beds. I want you next to me, stealing the covers and poking me in the ribs when I snore."

Her shoulders shook.

"But," I forced out, "if space is what you need to feel safe, then I'll give it to you. I'll try, at least."

Her eyes flew to mine, searching. "You will?"

"Aye." I swallowed. "I'm not going anywhere, Liora. You want to slow down? Fine. We'll slow down. You want to sort things with your sister first? I'll cheer from the sidelines. You want to spend your nights talking to your squirrel instead of me? I'll try not to be jealous."

A tiny, broken laugh escaped her.

"But know this," I continued, because the truth spell was buzzing and I couldn't not say it. "I'm not switching off how I feel. I can't. I've locked on, and that's not something I do lightly. I'll respect your boundaries. I'll give you the space you're asking for. But I'm still here. Still choosing you. Even if I have to do it from the other side of the bloody house."

We sat there for a long moment, breathing the same air, not quite touching.

Finally she reached for the door handle. "Thank you," she said quietly. "For understanding."

"I don't," I admitted. "But I'm trying."

She paused, hand on the handle. "Please don't be angry."

"I'm not angry," I said, surprised to realize it was true. "I'm worried. And gutted, if I'm honest. But I'm not angry at you."

I was angry at those who had subjected this beautiful woman's gentle heart to viciousness. Who used words to harm rather than build up. Who were so bloody short-sighted and heartless that they'd speak without considering the consequences.

She nodded once, then slipped out of the truck.

I watched her walk up the path, shoulders hunched. Bracken darted out of a bush to run beside her, chittering anxiously. She paused at the front door, glancing back at the truck, then shook her head and went inside.

By the time I locked up and followed, she'd already vanished down the hall.

Her bedroom door was closed. Mine—*ours*—stood open, bed half-made, the dent on her side of the mattress still there.

I stood there for a long time, staring at that empty space.

The house felt different. Less bright, somehow, even though all the lights were on.

I could hear her moving around in the spare room—the creak of the bed, the rustle of sheets, Bracken's muted chittering.

"I'm not going anywhere, darling," I said quietly, to the empty hallway, to the sleeping trees beyond the walls, to whatever magick was listening.

It didn't change the fact that Liora was hiding behind a door she'd firmly closed in my face.

And I had absolutely no idea how to open it without breaking something fragile on the other side.

CHAPTER TWENTY

LIORA

Will you snap out of it?

How long could I sulk for? It just wasn't in my nature to linger in this sodden state of sadness for so long.

By Sunday afternoon, even I was sick of myself.

I'd spent most of Saturday night hiding behind astrology charts and cleaning my bathroom so intensely with the hope that maybe I could scour out the image of Torin's face when I'd asked for space.

Kicked puppy didn't even begin to cover it.

So when my phone buzzed before my lunch shift on Sunday with a message from Agnes, I nearly kissed it.

Come by my shop after your shift today. Bring your laptop. And Bracken! Tell him to come too.

I STARED AT THE MESSAGE, chewing my lip.

Is this a social call or a professional consultation?

HER REPLY CAME BACK ALMOST INSTANTLY.

Yes.

I HUFFED out a laugh in spite of myself.

"Looks like we've been summoned," I told Bracken, who was currently flopped on the arm of the couch like a tiny, judgmental fur stole.

"Is there food?"

"Likely just biscuits."

He flicked his tail. *"I accept."*

"But how will you get there? I can't take you to my shift."

"Och, lass. Plenty of time for me to run into town while

you're at work. I know where the bookshop is. I'll see you there."

It looked like I wasn't getting out of this one. Which was probably good for me, because otherwise I'd just come home and question my life choices, holed up in my bedroom all afternoon. Hastily agreeing, I grabbed my laptop, popped it in my bag, and then drove to work. Torin seemed fine with me driving during the day, and it was a welcome relief instead of having to ride next to him and worry over any awkwardness I'd created by asking for space.

My shift was busy, but normal, and despite how much I listened, I didn't hear one person whisper about me and Torin or bring up Avery's name at all.

It seemed that Graham's shout to the crowd had done its job.

Maybe, just maybe, people believed the truth because they knew Torin ... and they were beginning to know me again too.

I still couldn't believe that Avery had shown up. Out of nowhere. She'd walked right in and dropped a bomb on my head in the middle of an already tricky week. That was how the universe worked, though, wasn't it? And typically, these things came in threes. Which only introduced a whole different worry to consume my thoughts during work. By the time my shift was over, I was pretty much done peopling for the weekend and looking forward to some quiet time with Agnes.

Crossing the street from the pub to Bonnie Books, I glanced down the road toward my sister's flat.

I should just go talk to her.

This was stupid. She was entitled to her feelings. I'd

changed our pattern on her, hadn't I? She was used to being the one who looked after me. And I'd taken that from her. If the situation had been reversed, I would have probably felt much the same. Resolved to stop by after hanging with Agnes, I opened the door to Bonnie Books and laughed as Bracken darted between my feet.

"Oh hi, I didn't see you."

"A crow followed me. His name is Murdoch. He says he's worried today."

"Och, really? Why?" My eyes darted out the window to the loch.

"Says he feels it in his feathers."

Not sure what to do with that, I walked inside.

It was a cheerful shop, and had only grown more cozy since the last time I'd seen it. It smelled like paper, woodsmoke, and the faintest hint of cinnamon. A fire crackled in the fireplace, and bookshelves were set up in little areas around the room, with chairs that invited you to nestle in and relax. Pretty rugs were thrown over the wood floors, and the arched windows gave a view of the pub and the loch stretching out behind it.

The wee bell over the door chimed as I stepped in, the crisp autumn air giving way to warmth and lamplight.

"Liora?"

"Aye," I said, pulling the door shut behind me.

"Just throw the lock behind you!" Agnes called. "Then come on back."

I wove my way through the stacks, Bracken scampering along beside me.

Agnes was in the nook at the back, where she kept a mismatched cluster of armchairs and a low coffee table for book clubs and gossip. In the middle, a squat teapot had been placed with a platter of biscuits next to it.

She was curled into one of the armchairs, legs tucked under her, wearing paint-splattered trousers, auburn curls escaping a flower clip in her hair. A book lay open, face-down, on the arm of the chair beside her.

She looked up as I approached, sharp gaze scanning my face.

"Right," she said. "You look like you've been run over by a herd of disgruntled coos."

"Good to see you too," I said weakly, shrugging out of my coat.

"Sit," she ordered, pouring tea. "And tell me why Torin's been moping around the town like someone stole his favorite axe."

Heat rushed to my face. "He hasn't."

"Oh, he has," she said dryly. "We're not blind, Liora."

"I don't know what to say."

"And while I do find watching men sulk vaguely entertaining, I'm more concerned about you. Something's off. So." She handed me a mug. "Spill."

I took the tea, wrapping my hands around the warmth, and sank into the opposite chair.

Bracken hopped down to the table and immediately began investigating the biscuits.

"Those are comfort food," Agnes told him. "For Liora. You can have crumbs if she says it's okay. Also, nice to meet you."

"Tell her I prefer seeds or something of that sort." Bracken chittered, and I smiled.

"He says he prefers seeds."

"I'll see what I have in back in a bit."

"So." Agnes gave me an encouraging smile. "Talk to me. What's going on?"

"I hurt my sister's feelings. And she wasn't entirely wrong to be worried about me. And then I kind of froze Torin out all week, which is why he's been moping about, and then Friday night I told him I needed space," I admitted, the words tumbling out before I could stop them. "And now everything is murky and muddy and I don't know what to do."

"Let's unpack that a bit more slowly," she suggested.

I let out a shaky breath. "Zara and I had a big fight."

Her brows went up. "But you two are like"—she pressed her hands together—"super close."

"Maybe too close," I muttered. "She's furious with me. And she's right."

"About?"

I stared into my tea. "Not telling her things. Like that I was hooking up with Torin. And about a truth spell I screwed up. Or even not telling her about me being a chartweaver."

Agnes whistled softly. "Right. So. Those are not minor omissions."

"I know." My throat tightened. "I should have told her. She's my sister. We tell each other everything. But I was afraid if I said it out loud it would all ... evaporate. Or she'd give me The Talk."

"The Talk?"

"About how I rush into things. How I don't think. How I blow up my life and then expect everyone else to help me pick up the pieces."

"Is that what you expect?" Agnes asked quietly.

I swallowed. "It's what she thinks I do."

"And what do you think you do?"

I stared at her, caught.

Because the ugly truth was, a part of me agreed. There were times where my optimism just failed me completely and I was convinced I was the absolute screwup who left a trail of messes across Scotland like glitter, clinging to everyone unfortunate enough to know me.

"I guess I am messy. Maybe that's just my lot in life."

Agnes tapped her fingers against her mug, thoughtful. "I think you're giving yourself too much credit, darling."

I blinked. "Sorry?"

"Other people are not puppets," she said. "They make their own choices. Avery chose to weaponize your reading instead of taking responsibility for the cracks in her relationship. That's on her. Not you. The trolls on TikTok are just shitty people."

"But I'm the common denominator," I protested.

"You're the common witness," she corrected. "There's a difference. Look, I'm not saying you don't contribute to the chaos. You probably do." Her mouth curved. "But you also care deeply about other people and want to help."

Tears pricked my eyes. "Zara doesn't see it that way."

"Zara is scared," Agnes said simply. "She's watched you get battered by life more than once. You come back, you're happy, things are finally going right—new power, new place in the Order, new fella—and from her point of view, it probably looks like you're standing in the middle of a lightning storm holding up a metal rod. She's bracing for the strike."

"That's a poetic way to say she thinks I'm an eejit," I muttered.

"She thinks you're vulnerable," Agnes corrected. "Sometimes fear for someone comes out sideways as control or as criticism. It doesn't mean she doesn't love you. It means she loves you so much she'd rather push you away than watch you get hurt again."

I took a shaky sip of tea, letting her words sink in.

"And Torin?" I asked, voice small.

"Torin," she said slowly, "is a walking tree with feelings. Deep ones. He's been half in love with you since before you left, whether he admitted it or not. Now that you're back, there's finally a chance to see what that could be, and he's all in. And then Avery shows up, the old wounds get poked, your sister's upset with you, and you ask him for space." She lifted a brow. "Of course he looks like a kicked puppy. His worst fear is probably losing something he's finally let himself want."

Guilt twisted in my gut. "I didn't mean to hurt him."

"I know." Her gaze softened. "And for what it's worth, I don't think asking for space was wrong. Boundaries are not punishment."

"So why does it feel like I've ripped his heart out and thrown it in the loch?"

"Because you care about him," Agnes said simply. "And because you're used to seeing yourself as the villain in everyone else's story. Try reframing."

"Reframing," I repeated faintly.

Bracken held up his paws and made a little square motion like he was framing a picture. Despite myself, I chuckled.

"Aye. Instead of 'I've ruined everything,' try 'I'm allowed to take a breath while I figure out how to show up fully for the people I love.'" She lifted a shoulder. "And maybe, when you're ready, you sit Zara down and say to her that you're not shutting her out because you don't trust her. It's just that you're trying to learn your own voice too. And you sit Torin down and tell him that you're terrified but trying and ask him to be patient. Knowing him, he'll build you a log cabin with his bare hands as a gesture of support."

A watery laugh escaped me. "He would, wouldn't he?"

"He would," she agreed. "He also looks like he might cry if I tell him one more time that you're fine. So do me a solid and talk to him sooner rather than later, hmm?"

"I will," I said, resolve filling me. I was glad I'd decided to accept her invitation. This was the kind of stern but loving talking to that I needed to get my head on straight.

"Right," Agnes said, turning back to me. "That's enough emotional excavation for the moment. I did actually invite you here for a reason."

"Giving out free therapy wasn't the reason?"

"That's just a bonus." She leaned forward, eyes gleaming. "I want a reading."

I blinked. "From ... me?"

"No, from the squirrel," she said. "Of course from you. You're the chartweaver. I want to see what the threads say."

A mix of pride and panic fluttered in my chest. "Are you sure? Chartweaving isn't exactly ... simple."

"Nothing worth doing is simple," she said calmly. "And if you're going to be meddling with fate, better you practice on someone who knows what they're in for."

"What do you mean by that?" I asked, tilting my head at her.

For a moment, Agnes's eyes grew sad as she looked across the room, and out the front window.

"I already know a lot of my fate. This will be a good test to see if you see the same."

"But how?" I asked, but Agnes just shook her head.

"Best not to get into it. Plus, I want to see what you see without any information leading you one way or the other."

"That's fair," I said, bending over and pulling my laptop from my bag. "All right. Birth details, then. I don't suppose you know your exact time?"

"Of course I do." She rattled off the date, time, and place. "You can't live around all these witches and not know some of your astrology."

The chart wheel spun onto the screen, familiar and yet … not. Because even before the threads rose, even before the magick, I could feel the density of it.

As I stared, the now-familiar shimmer started.

Lines glowed, lifting off the screen, weaving themselves into a silvery web between us. Bracken scampered up to my shoulder.

"Here we go," he whispered.

Agnes squinted. "I can't see what you're seeing, can I?"

"No," I said softly. "Maybe. I don't know. You might feel it. Matthew could see it faintly. Greta couldn't at all."

The threads vibrated gently, like a harp string plucked in a distant room. I reached out, letting my fingers hover just above them, grounding myself in the way Gran's book had advised to—breathe, anchor, remember you're a guide, *not* a god.

"Okay," I said, slipping into the comfort of astrologer mode. "Agnes, you're a Virgo Sun, Capricorn Rising, Pisces Moon."

"Right, that doesn't sound too bad, does it?"

"It's not," I agreed. "Virgo Sun means you're here to be of service, to refine, to analyze, to make things better than you found them. You're detail-oriented, practical in your own way, but you also hold ridiculous amounts of information in your head."

"And the Capricorn?"

"Cap Rising is how you move through the world. Serious and responsible. People look at you and think, 'She knows what she's doing, I'll follow her into battle.'"

"Och, aye? That's a fine compliment." Agnes patted her own shoulder.

"And then," I continued, smiling, "Pisces Moon. All squishy feelings and intuition and art. That's your inner world. The creative. The historian who doesn't just catalog facts but feels the stories behind them."

Her lips twitched. "Truth."

"That mix—earth and water—makes you this fascinating blend of practical and dreamy. You build containers for other people's feelings. Book clubs. This shop. The Order."

She shifted, looking oddly uncomfortable. "All right. Don't get too complimentary. I'll break out in hives."

I laughed, then sobered as one of the threads pulsed more brightly. It ran from her Moon in Pisces in the third house—communication, stories—to her seventh house of partnership, where Venus was snuggled up close to Saturn.

"Ah," I murmured. "Here we are."

"What?"

"You've got Venus and Saturn conjunct in your seventh house," I said. "Partnership is ... serious business for you. You don't do casual. When you commit, you commit."

"No half measures," she said quietly.

"Exactly. Saturn there can mean ... delays. Lessons. Sometimes relationships that feel fated but blocked, or that require a lot of work. Venus wants warmth and affection and romance, and Saturn wants structure and long-term commitment. Put them together and you get soulmate energy, but with obstacles."

She swallowed. "That sounds ... about right."

The thread connecting those points shimmered gold and charcoal by turns, like it couldn't decide whether to be a blessing or a burden.

Curiosity tugged at me. I let my fingers brush it—just lightly, a feather touch.

Images flickered.

Agnes in this very shop, closing up, the light from the street spilling across the worn wood floors.

A man leaning in the doorway, watching her. Tall. Broad-shouldered. Tattoo peeking from under a rolled-up sleeve.

Graham.

Of course.

He stepped in, took a mug from her hands, their fingers brushing. The air between them hummed with something old and familiar and electrifying.

Another flash. Agnes and Graham at the loch's edge, arguing fiercely, faces inches apart, rain pouring down. The kind of fight you only have with someone you love enough to be that honest with.

Another. Agnes alone in her pottery studio, working late, clay up to her elbows, an ache in her chest like something was missing.

My heart squeezed.

The thread pulsed harder, drawing my attention down its length. And there—like a knot in the weave—was something else.

A darker strand twined around the gold, barbed and glinting.

I focused—and saw, just for a second, the reason.

Oh.

Oh no.

My breath caught.

That—

That changed everything.

"Lass?" Bracken's voice was sharp. *"Don't pull that."*

I hadn't realized my fingers had curled, tugging at the knot. The threads shivered, the entire web ringing with a low, warning hum.

"Shite," I whispered, snatching my hand back like I'd been burned.

"What?" Agnes demanded, eyes narrowed. "What did you see?"

"I..." My heart hammered. How was I supposed to tell her that she and Graham were written into each other's stars and yet ...

"Liora." Agnes's voice softened. "Whatever it is, I can handle—"

A sharp thump sounded from the front of the shop.

We both froze.

Another thump. This time accompanied by a high, urgent whine.

Bracken shot to the edge of the table, fur puffed. *Something's wrong.*

My stomach dropped. I knew that sound.

We bolted from the reading nook, weaving through the shelves. My heart was already racing before we rounded the last stack and saw him.

Mitch.

Zara's golden retriever was on his hind legs, paws scrabbling desperately at the front window, nails squeaking against the glass. His harness hung crooked, the lead trailing uselessly behind him. His eyes were wild, foam flecking his mouth as he barked, frantic, at the sight of us.

"Mitch?" I breathed, horror slicing through me.

Because Mitch never went anywhere without Zara.

Ever.

And if he was here alone...

Something was very, very wrong.

CHAPTER TWENTY-ONE

LIORA

We followed Mitch at a run, the dog far faster than us, but stopping to turn around every so often to make sure we were coming.

A shriek split the sky, and ice filled my veins.

"We need backup!" Agnes shouted behind me, veering off to bang on the front window of the pub.

I barely clocked the startled shouts from inside The Tipsy Thistle as I tore after Mitch. The golden retriever was a streak of pale fur in the gathering dusk, barreling down the cobbled lane toward the loch. My lungs burned, the cold air slicing down my throat, and my boots skidded on damp leaves as the pavement gave way to the rougher track that edged the water.

"Mitch!" I yelled. "Slow down, buddy, come on—"

He didn't slow. If anything, he pushed harder, nails

digging into mud as he veered off the main path toward the trees that lined the shore.

The loch spread out beside us, a black mirror under a bruise-colored sky. Out toward the island, the water seethed and foamed, as if something massive was turning beneath the surface. A low, eerie whinny carried over the water, the sound somehow both horse and nightmare all at once.

Kelpies.

"Holy hell."

Behind me, pounding footsteps grew louder as people followed. Agnes reappeared at my side, breath puffing in white clouds.

"Graham's getting the others," she panted. "Keep going! Mitch, good lad, show us where!"

Mitch answered with a sharp bark and plunged into a stand of trees where the ground dipped away more steeply than I'd realized. I skidded to a halt at the edge of a narrow gully that slashed down toward the loch like a wound, its sides slick with moss and loose rock.

Mitch stood halfway down the slope, paws braced, barking frantically at a crumpled shape in the shadows below.

"Zara," I breathed.

My sister lay twisted near the bottom of the gully, one leg at a wrong, horrible angle, her dark hair fanned around her head. Her cane lay higher up the slope, wedged against a root, useless.

"Z!" My voice came out strangled.

"Liora, don't—" Agnes started, but there was no stopping me.

I went after my sister.

My boots lost traction almost immediately. I half slid, half fell, branches whipping at my arms as I careened down the steep incline. Something sharp raked my calf, another jabbed into my hip, and then I hit a patch of wet leaves and went down hard on my backside.

"Oof—bloody hell—" I tumbled the last few feet and landed in an inelegant heap next to Zara, breath knocked clean out of me, head stinging in pain.

For a moment, everything was just pain and the taste of mud in my mouth.

Then I heard her.

"L?" Zara's voice was thin and tight with pain. "Is that you?"

I spat out a leaf and dragged myself up onto my elbows. "Aye, it's me. You've picked a shite spot for a nap, by the way."

"Your commentary is not appreciated," she whispered, but a faint ghost of a smile brushed her lips. Her face was pale, a sheen of sweat on her forehead.

I swallowed hard as my gaze went to her leg. Even without medical training, I could see the break. Her shin bowed at an angle legs were not meant to bow.

"Oh God." My words came out garbled.

"Don't you dare faint," Zara hissed. "I need you lucid."

"I'm fine," I lied. "You, on the other hand ... What happened? Did you fall? Were you pushed? Magickly yeeted?"

"Pulled," she gritted out. "Something ... tugged. In my head. Like a rope around my thoughts."

Another screech ripped across the water, closer this

time. I glanced toward the loch and my stomach turned over.

Shapes were emerging out by the island. Equine forms heaving up from the depths, slick black hides gleaming, manes like dripping ink. Water poured off them in sheets as they pawed at the surface, eyes like coals burning through the mist.

Kelpies. A whole bloody herd of them.

"Right," I whispered. "Cool cool cool. Love this for us."

A flurry of fur and anxious whines breezed between us and Mitch pressed himself against Zara's good side, whining low, trying to anchor himself to her.

"Liora." Zara's hand shot out and grabbed mine, fingers digging in. "Listen to me. I don't know how much time we have."

"Don't say it like that," I choked. "You're not dying, okay? We just have to get you up this hill and to the hospital and they'll fix your leg and—"

"L," she said sharply, and I shut up. Her blind eyes were unfocused but fierce. "I'm holding them back."

"The Kelpies?" My breath caught.

She nodded, jaw clenched. "They're in my head. I can ... see them. *Feel* them. They're angry, L. Furious. The Stone —something with the Truth Stone and the island and old bargains. I'm like a ... a dam." Her voice wavered. "But they're pushing."

Fear crawled cold fingers up my spine. "Okay," I said, trying to breathe around the panic. "Okay, okay, we've got backup coming. The pub knows we're here. Agnes is up top. The Order will be here. You don't have to do this alone."

"Too late," she whispered, breath hitching. "I'm already in it. I can ... I don't know, speak to them. Negotiate. But I can't move. And my leg—bloody hell." Tears leaked from the corners of her eyes, and it gutted me.

I squeezed her hand, my own eyes burning. "I'm here. I've got you. I'm so sorry, Z. For everything. For being a mess. For not telling you things. For being a shite sister."

Her mouth trembled. "You are a shite sister but only once in a while," she whispered. "And you're *my* shite sister. I love you, you bloody eejit."

A quiet sob broke out of me. "I love you too."

Above us, voices shouted, branches cracking as people crashed through the trees toward the rim of the gully.

"Help!" I yelled, tipping my head back. "We need something to stabilize her!"

A familiar Highland burr cut through the noise. Archie, barking orders. Sophie's sharper tone right behind him. Agnes. Lia. Shona. The whole bloody Order, by the sounds of it.

Magick prickled over my skin, a low hum building in the air like distant thunder.

"I'll hold them off," Zara muttered under her breath, eyes squeezed shut. "Just a little longer. We're trying. We're not your enemy. The Stone—yes, I know, I know—"

She wasn't talking to me.

A hand grabbed the edge of the gully above, and Sophie's face appeared, hair wild in the wind.

"Stay where you are!" she yelled. "We're working on a safe way down. Don't move."

"Wouldn't dream of it," I called back, voice wobbling, my head throbbing from where I'd cracked it on a rock on the way down.

Other faces appeared along the rim. Lia with flour on her cheek and a knife clutched in one hand like she'd run straight from the kitchen. Shona, eyes wide, chanting as she coaxed roots to twist into makeshift steps down the side of the gully. Willow, eyes closed, muttering something to herself.

Beside them, familiars and creatures crowded the edge. Gnorman and Gnora, the gnomes that I'd only been told about, but hadn't met yet, peered down with identical looks of horrified fascination. Gloam, Faelan's fox, paced restlessly, fur bristling. A sleek black crow—Kaia's— swooped close, cawing in agitation. Bracken scampered down the side of the gully, his fur puffed out.

And there, shouldering his way through the cluster, was Torin. His gaze found me instantly, something raw and wrecked in his eyes when he saw me crouched by Zara, mud-smeared and shaking.

"Liora!" His voice cracked. "Are you hurt?"

"I'm fine," I lied again, because there were bigger problems than my bruised backside and the gash in my head. "Zara's leg's broken. And she's ... holding them off. Somehow."

His jaw tightened, but he nodded once, and I wanted nothing more than to crawl into his strong arms because it was truly where I felt the safest. It was a bit of a shite time to come to that realization, but nonetheless, there it was.

"Right," Shona shouted, voice carrying over the chaos.

"We need a stabilization spell on her leg before we move her. Lia, can you—"

"I've got it," Lia called, already digging in her bag for herbs. "Shona, with me."

Zara's grip on my hand tightened so suddenly I flinched.

"Liora," she gasped. "They're pushing harder. I can't—shite, they're angry. The Stone, the island, the bargains—"

"Okay," I said, panic spiking again. "Okay, okay, what do you need from me? I'm a chartweaver, not a Kelpie whisperer, but I'm an excellent panicker, if that helps."

She actually huffed a tiny breath of laughter, then sucked it back on a groan as her leg shifted. "I need you to see," she whispered. "You can see threads. I can see intent. Together we might—*bloody hell, hold off!*—buy Loren Brae some time."

"See what?" I asked, throat dry.

"The choice," she said. "There's always one. They want to be seen. To be counted. As a part of this place. Not just monsters in the dark. If we don't acknowledge them, they'll tear it all down. The Stone is only part of it. There's something about a bargain ... that needs to change."

My brain tried to process "renegotiate magickal bargains with ancient elemental loch spirits" and promptly short-circuited.

Behind us, the Kelpies shrieked again.

I risked a glance.

They were closer now, churning toward the water at the mouth of the gully. Their long tails lashed the surface, sending up plumes of spray, and where their hooves struck, the loch boiled.

"They're coming," Agnes's voice warned from above.

"I know," Zara whispered. "Right. Enough talking."

She sucked in a breath, her fingers crushing mine, and began to chant.

The words were Gaelic. They rolled out of her in low, rhythmic waves, each phrase vibrating in my bones. My skin broke out in goose bumps, and I swear the air thickened around us.

And as the Kelpies barreled toward us, my vision shifted.

An astral map appeared before me and glowing lines flowed, the threads of all those around us, those of Loren Brae, those who had come before and those who would go ahead of us, flinging into the air in one giant astral map.

And the Kelpies' threads joined it.

The Kelpies were just as much a part of Loren Brae as anyone else was.

Their history ran deep, if not deeper, than anyone before us.

But as I gasped, and looked around, one thick glimmering thread rose above all of us, and I turned, following it as it connected from the island where the Truth Stone was buried all the way to the shore.

To one woman.

Agnes.

I sucked in a sharp breath. The thread was unlike anything I'd seen before—even with Greta, even with Matthew. It was braided and shimmering with multiple colors—deep loch blue, molten gold, and moss green. It twanged with purpose, stretching taut between the island and Agnes's small, fierce frame at the rim of the gully.

"Agnes," I shouted.

She startled, one hand flying to her chest. "What? What is it?"

I could barely drag my gaze away from the thread humming above us. Images hit me in flashes of Agnes as a wee girl, toes in the loch, Agnes as a teenager sketching the island from the shore, Agnes in her shop, facing toward the loch.

She wasn't just part of Loren Brae's story.

She was pivotal to it.

"Liora?" Zara's voice came from very far away and very close all at once, layered over the chant still pouring from her mouth. "What do you see?"

"I," I whispered, eyes locked on the thread, "think we've got a bigger problem here."

"There's more," Zara gasped, and I whipped my head back to the loch to see the surface disrupted. "They've brought friends. I can only dissuade them so long."

The water beyond the Kelpies heaved, a swell rising that had nothing to do with wind. The surface bulged, then collapsed inward, then bulged again, as if something colossal was coiling deep below.

The Kelpies tossed their heads and screamed, not in rage this time but in something like exultation.

"Oh, that's not good," Kaia shouted. "We need to get them out."

"What do we do?" Graham shouted, frustration deep in his voice.

The loch answered for him.

A massive ripple rolled outward from the island, waves slapping against the rocky shore. The air dropped a few degrees, a chill sinking straight to the marrow of my bones.

Then the water exploded.

A creature erupted from the depths with a roar that shook the trees.

It was not Nessie. It was worse.

Longer than The Tipsy Thistle and the bookshop combined, its serpentine body was armored in overlapping plates that shimmered like wet slate. A mane of water and kelp streamed from a crown of horned ridges along its skull, and its eyes glowed a furious, otherworldly teal. Great fins flared along its spine, each beat sending torrents cascading back into the loch. Its mouth opened, revealing rows upon rows of needle teeth, and the sound that tore out of it was half dragon roar ... half tidal wave.

The beast of all beasts.

The Kelpies reared around it, shrieking in wild joy, as if they'd just called their gigantic, horrifying cousin in for backup.

Beside me, Zara's chant faltered, her fingers crushing mine so hard my knuckles ground together.

"Well," I whispered, heart hammering so hard I felt a bit sick. "Bugger."

Torin's shout cracked through the chaos—raw, panicked, furious in a way I had never heard from him before.

"Liora!"

I jerked upward, heart seizing.

Torin wasn't at the top of the gully anymore.

He was moving through the trees.

No—the trees were moving for *him*.

Branches twisted aside, trunks tilted—*curved*—as if bending in a bow of recognition. Roots pulled back from the earth and vines untangled themselves from jutting stone. The thick green tangle that had hemmed us in moments ago now opened in a precise, spiraling path like a living staircase.

"Go on, lad!" Lachlan shouted after Torin.

It was impossible not to stare.

Torin descended the steep slope as if gravity had taken one look at him and decided it wasn't worth the argument. He moved quickly, his boots finding hold after hold with impossible precision. Determination made his face steely.

For a man who claimed not to be magickal, he looked like the forest's chosen son.

Torin reached us and immediately crouched by my sister. His eyes flicked to her leg and tightened.

"This'll hurt," he warned.

"Everything already fecking hurts," Zara gritted.

He slid one arm under her bum—carefully avoiding her legs the best he could—and braced the other behind her back. With a strength that made Zara gasp and bite her lip, he scooped her into his chest as if she weighed nothing at all. Lia and Shona's stabilization spell seemed to be working. For now.

"It's okay, I've got you." His eyes flew to mine, understanding passing between us. He knew.

I'd always choose for my sister to get out first in times of trouble. Just like she'd do for me, if the situation was reversed.

"I'm coming back for you," Torin promised, his words cutting through me.

I didn't say what was in my head. *If there was time.*

A deep, rumbling growl echoed down the slope behind him.

A wolf sprang neatly down the side of the gully as though the precarious cliffs were mere child's play for him. Luch, Faelan's partner, had arrived. I'd been told, in secret, from Zara, of his true identity. At the time, I couldn't quite bring myself to believe it. But here he was.

A wulver.

Taking in the sight of him, in wolf form, took my breath away.

He stood above me now, hackles raised, golden eyes blazing like torches. He descended fast, then stopped in front of me, massive body turned broadside.

"Luch?" I whispered.

He didn't growl. He didn't bare teeth. He simply looked at me—long, direct—and then nudged his shoulder into my side.

Hard.

I gasped. He nudged again. Insistent.

"Oh," I breathed. "You want me to—"

Another nudge, more forceful.

"...ride you?"

A snort of hot wolf breath hit my face.

"Right. Yes. That's a yes."

I scrambled awkwardly up, my stomach pressed against his backside and my arms looped around his neck. My fingers sank into his thick fur and I felt his muscles coil beneath me.

Behind us, the Kelpies screamed—closer now. A wave crashed against the rocks, spraying icy mist.

"Go," Torin ordered, voice low and fierce. "Get her out. Now."

The wolf didn't need to be told twice.

He surged upward, powerful legs launching us up the steep incline in impossible bounds. I clung to him, breath ripped out of me as branches whipped past and mud spattered my clothes. Glancing back, I watched as Torin clambered upward with Zara in his arms, taking the same shifting path the trees offered him—a path that revealed itself with each of his steps. The forest *was* laying down stones for its king. *Amazing.*

Above the gully rim, the world had become a battleground.

The entire Order of Caledonia stood arrayed in a defensive crescent.

Sophie was at the front, her dirk gleaming as she held it in front of her, her stance steady despite the shaking earth. Lachlan was beside her, shield up, eyes murderous. Lia muttered under her breath, the air around her humming with heat. Shona's hands were outstretched, a garden staff raised to the air, vines crawling at her command. Orla lifted a hammer made of glowing ember-metal, her eyes sharp. Willow raised glowing sheers. Kaia had a chisel in her hand and an angry look on her face.

Other men flanked them—Finlay, Thane, Ramsay, Munroe—all wide-eyed but resolute.

Familiars filled the rest of the space. The gnomes brandished tiny pickaxes. Gloam paced, tail puffed. Brice hovered at Lia's leg, ready to help. The crow perched atop Kaia's shoulder, feathers glowing faintly blue. A cat wound itself between Willow's legs, its hackles raised. Bracken raced next to Luch, never leaving my side.

And Clyde floated above them all, bellowing.

The wolf bounded to the edge of the line and stopped, lowering himself so I could slide off. My legs shook violently when my feet hit the ground. Turning, I took a step back toward the gully and Torin emerged seconds later, leaping over the rim with Zara in his arms. Agnes rushed to help, guiding him toward Faelan.

But everyone else stared at the loch.

It was impossible not to.

Because the dragon-like creature was still rising.

Its massive head reared higher, plates shining as water streamed down in sheets. Its roar rolled across the shore, rattling stones and making my bones feel hollow.

"Oh," Lia whispered. "Oh, that's not just a beast."

"No," Sophie breathed, eyes narrowed. "It's a guardian."

The water surged again.

The Kelpies threw back their heads and screamed, their voices a chorus of fury and triumph.

The enormous creature lashed its tail, sending a tidal wave surging toward the shore.

"Lock in, ladies!" Sophie shouted, lifting her dirk high.

The Order responded as one.

Shona's vines shot forward like spears. Willow's chanting grew louder. Lia flung a handful of herbs into the wind, flames roaring to life along the ground in a protective arc. Orla slammed her hammer down, sending ripples of molten magick through the earth. Faelan's hands were already around my sister's leg, her eyes closed as she went deep inside herself.

Agnes stood, frozen, her hands raised in front of her, and her thread flared in my vision again, brilliant and commanding.

The Order's combined magick met the tidal wave head-on.

Light collided with water.

And the world exploded into sound and energy.

The tidal wave broke against the magickal shield, spraying harmlessly into steam. The Kelpies shrieked in outrage as invisible forces shoved them backward, hooves skidding on churning water. The dragon-like creature roared again, the sound echoing off the cliffs—but then its massive head jerked sideways, as if something ancient and unseen had tugged on its reins.

One heartbeat.

Two.

Three.

Then—

With a final, frustrated roar that shook the air, the creature slipped backward into the depths.

The Kelpies followed, sucked into the swirl of receding currents. Their shrieks faded into the loch, swallowed whole.

The water stilled.

The loch became dark and quiet again.

The entire shoreline fell silent except for the ragged sound of our collective breathing.

Sophie lowered her dirk.

"It's done," she said softly. "For now."

"For now," Lachlan echoed grimly.

Mitch pressed against my leg, as if grounding me.

Torin turned to me, Zara still cradled in his arms as Faelan worked, horror in his expression.

"You all right?" he murmured.

I nodded but couldn't speak.

Because something deep in the loch stirred.

Something old.

And the glimmering thread above Agnes still hummed, stretched taut toward the island.

We had won tonight.

But the real reckoning had only just begun.

Something was seriously wrong.

CHAPTER TWENTY-TWO

TORIN

If anyone ever asked me what terror smelled like, I'd say wet earth and loch water and the sharp tang of magick burning the air.

We didn't celebrate on the shore.

There was no cheering, no relieved laughter. Just a stunned, shivery silence as the loch went still and the last ripples from that … thing faded into the dark.

Then Sophie dragged in a breath and clapped the flat of her dirk against her thigh.

"Right," she said, voice steady. "Retreat. Now. We regroup at the castle. Faelan, how's Zara?"

Faelan swayed on her feet but lifted her chin. "Bone's knitted enough she can be moved. I'll need more time to finish it." Her voice was hoarse, like every word scraped her throat.

"I'll take her." I tightened my grip around Zara's shoulders. She felt light in my arms, too light. My heart was still hammering so hard my hands shook.

Zara grimaced. "I can probably walk now."

"You absolutely can't," Faelan snapped. "Unless you want it to heal crooked and I have to re-break it. Don't test me, woman."

Zara's mouth flattened. "Fine."

The wolf huffed at all of us, then trotted ahead. I gave it a wide berth. A squirrel familiar was one thing, but a wolf? I wasn't about to interfere with that. Mitch stuck close to Zara's dangling hand, nose bumping her fingers every few steps as if checking she was still in one piece.

And Liora—

My gaze snagged on her. Mud streaked her jeans and jumper. A smear of blood marred her forearm. There was a cut at her temple I hadn't noticed in the chaos, and she was moving stiffly, favoring her left side.

Everything in my body ached to go to her, but first, I had to get Zara somewhere Faelan could work properly.

Archie frantically waved us towards his lorry. Hilda had the side door flung open. Archie grimaced as we neared the truck, his white hair wild, thick eyebrows drawn together in concern. Hilda hovered close to him, her hand on his shoulder.

"Put Zara in here," Archie barked. "Faelan, in with us."

I eased Zara into the back seat of the lorry, careful of her leg. Faelan climbed in after her with a soft groan, already reaching for her bag of supplies.

"We'll be getting your healing tea on for you," Hilda

said sharply, pointing at Faelan. "You'll not be taking this pain into yourself."

Faelan managed a tired smile. "Aye, ma'am."

I let my hand rest on Zara's shoulder for a beat. "You all right, Zara?"

She gave me a crooked smile. "Feels like someone played knucklebones with my tibia, but other than that? Grand." Mitch hopped in next to her and she threaded her hand into his fur.

I snorted, some of the tightness in my chest easing.

I stepped back and shut the door, banged twice on the side to let Archie know we were good, then spun around, already searching.

Liora stood a little apart from the others, arms wrapped around herself, staring at the loch.

My stomach twisted.

She looked like she was folded in on herself.

"Liora," I said, softly.

She startled like she'd forgotten anyone else existed, then turned. Her eyes were too wide, lashes clumped with tears. My heart broke open.

I didn't care that she'd asked me for space. For once, I was thinking about my needs. And what I needed was her close.

I strode over, closing the distance in half a dozen steps, and without really thinking about it, I scooped her up.

She let out a startled squeak, hands flying to my shoulders.

"Torin!"

"You're coming with me," I muttered, hoisting her against my chest like she weighed next to nothing, all soft curves and trembling muscles. "I'm not letting you walk one more bloody step after that."

Her fingers fisted in my shirt. "I can walk," she protested weakly. "You already carried one of us today."

"I've got two arms, haven't I? And if you think I'm letting you limp along behind like an afterthought after you just flung yourself down a ravine for your sister, you're dafter than I thought."

Her breath hitched. "I didn't—I mean, of course I did. It's Zara."

"Aye, it is." Emotion burned the back of my throat. I dipped my head, pressing my mouth to her damp hair for the briefest of moments. "You scared the absolute shite out of me, lass."

She went very still.

"I'm fine," she said after a beat, too quickly. "Really. You don't need to—"

Something wet landed on my arm.

Blood.

I swore under my breath. "You're bleeding."

"It's nothing," she mumbled.

"Nothing, my arse."

Bracken appeared out of nowhere, chittering furiously at me like this was somehow my fault. I ignored him.

I followed the group as we all loped up the lane toward the castle, Gloam keeping pace at our side, while a crow flew over our heads.

"I'm fine," Liora said again, quieter now.

I barely glanced down at her, just needing one of these magickal women to see to her injuries. "You're bleeding on my jumper, lass. I wouldn't call that fine. And I can feel you shaking."

"I nearly watched my sister get trampled by demon water horses and then a dragon or whatever that was tried to storm out of the loch," she said, voice wobbling. "Of course I'm shaking."

Fair point.

I cupped the side of her face, thumb brushing just under the cut at her temple. She flinched, then relaxed into it, eyes closing for a heartbeat.

"I've got you," I said quietly. "All right? I know things are … difficult. Between you and Zara. Between you and me." My chest tightened, but I forced myself to keep going. "But I'm not going anywhere. Not after tonight. Not ever, unless you kick me out yourself."

Her lashes fluttered. For a second, something like longing flashed across her face, raw and bright.

Then she swallowed it back down.

"Let's just get to the castle."

I wanted to push. To demand she look at me properly. To tell me what was breaking her apart inside.

Instead, I pressed a kiss to her forehead, gentle, unable not to touch her.

"Soon," I murmured. "We're going to talk. You and me."

She didn't answer.

But her hand cupped my wrist, fingers tightening for half a second before she let go.

It was enough to keep me breathing. Because, this woman, this brave, beautiful lass, was my heart.

I love her.

Over the last few days, all I'd thought about was her and her pain. I'd missed her laughter too, her light, but I'd also just missed being with her in silence as we walked the woods. I just needed to figure out how to convince her that I wasn't going anywhere. Picking up my pace, I followed the beleaguered crowd up the hill.

MacAlpine Castle had seen its fair share of gatherings over the years, but I doubted it had ever hosted one quite like this. The castle loomed against the now-dark sky, its stone walls glowing warm with light. It should have felt comforting, but it didn't.

It felt like we were limping back to a fortress between sieges.

Archie parked as close to the back entrance as he could manage. The moment the truck stopped, Hilda took charge.

"Right, all of you, inside," she ordered. "Don't track half the loch across my floors. Wipe your boots."

We obeyed instinctually as we followed everyone down the hall and into a large lounge.

I carried Liora straight through to a couch and looked up.

"She's hurt too. Can I lay her down? She's bleeding."

At that, the group turned, reanimating as they realized someone else was hurt, and Lia and Shona broke away, coming to hover by where I cradled Liora against my chest.

"Here," Hilda murmured, directing me toward a worn leather settee near the hearth. "Lay her down there."

I did, easing Liora onto the cushions. She grunted but didn't complain.

Faelan looked up from where she hovered over Zara on another couch.

"Do you need me?"

"No, we've got this. We'll let you know," Lia said, and Shona nudged me gently aside, to murmur quietly with Liora. I grimaced as Liora tilted her head and revealed a sharp wound at the side of her head, just above her ear. Her hair was matted and thick with blood.

"May I?" I glanced over to see a man I hadn't met yet, in hospital scrubs, come to stand by the chair.

"Where did you come from?" I asked, squinting at him.

"I'm Dr. Luch Carmichael," the man said, bending over the settee.

"Wulver," Liora whispered, her eyes going bright. "Thank you."

I glanced in confusion between the two as they shared silent communication before it dawned on me just *what* I was seeing.

Luch had been with us down in the gully.

Just not in this form.

Before my mind could even process the wildness of it all, he pushed Liora's hair gently aside and took a look.

"I'll need to clean this up to get a better look," Luch murmured. "Anywhere else?"

"I think just scrapes, a slice on my calf, and a really bruised backside," Liora admitted.

Shona left and returned with a tin. Shona's plaits were coming loose, her cheeks were flushed, and her eyes still a bit too wide from what we'd just seen on the loch.

"I've got a poultice that'll help with the scrapes," she

said, already unscrewing a tin. "And a comfrey-and-calendula salve for the deeper cuts."

"That'll help."

"And I've got a regular first aid kit if you want it," Hilda said from behind her, brandishing a large plastic box.

Luch took the first aid kit while Shona crouched at Liora's side, ordering her to roll up the sleeves of her jumper. I winced at the sight of the bruises already forming on her pale skin, and jagged pink scratches that looked painful.

Shona took one arm gently, rubbing it with a warm, damp cloth, then smoothed the cool green paste over the worst of the grazes. A fresh, earthy smell filled the air—crushed leaves and something floral.

"Oooh," Liora breathed. "That's nice."

"It'll sting less in a minute," Shona said. "You'll be scabbed now, but by morning, this should take a good bit of the ache out."

"You did good, you know," I said, leaning closer to her.

Liora's gaze dropped. "Did I?" she whispered.

I wanted to shake her. Kiss her. Wrap her in blankets and never let anything sharp touch her again.

Instead, I squeezed her shoulder gently, thumb rubbing circles into the tense muscles there.

"You did," I said quietly. "You were brave as hell."

Her shoulder trembled under my hand. For a second, I thought she might lean back into me.

Then Archie cleared his throat, the sound cutting across the room like a bell.

"All right," he said. "We need to talk about what just crawled out of our loch."

"Let's go to Grasshopper. I can't handle this much trauma without food. And neither can all of you," Lia ordered.

We reconvened in the castle's restaurant once Faelan had finished with Zara and assured everyone she'd live, provided she stayed off the leg for a few days and Luch made sure that Faelan had downed a specialty tea to help with her strength. Zara leaned back and closed her eyes on the couch, Mitch cuddled at her side.

"I'll stay here with the lass. You lot go on," Hilda said, already unfolding a throw blanket to tuck over Zara.

The rest of us filed into the restaurant, in varying states of exhaustion, shock, and mud. The big room glowed with gentle light, and the women went around lighting candles, and pulling tables together.

Archie stood at the head of the long table, his face still masked in concern. Sophie leaned against the opposite end, Lachlan at her back, arms crossed.

I took a seat halfway down, Liora beside me. I made sure our knees touched. She didn't move away, and I took that as a small miracle and didn't push for more.

"All right," Archie said again, voice grave. "Who wants to start?"

Silence stretched.

Then Zara—who I'd thought was asleep—croaked from the doorway where she'd appeared, blanket around her shoulders, and Mitch guiding her path. "I'll go," she said. "Seeing as I was daft enough to get dragged out there in the first place."

"Z—you should be resting," Liora protested, frustration crossing her face.

"I couldn't stop her," Hilda said breathlessly from behind her.

"Sit down." Lachlan stepped forward and helped Zara to a chair, while Liora all but vibrated with worry next to me.

Lia zipped into the room, bowls of soup in her hands.

"Soup first. You all need your strength." I blinked as a blur of motion zipped past me and a bowl of steaming soup appeared in front of me. What the hell had that been?

"And whisky," Lachlan added, disappearing and returning with a bottle. Another blur of motion and glasses appeared at the table.

"What is going on?" I whispered to Liora and a soft smile came to her lips.

"Brice. He's Lia's kitchen broonie."

"Right, of course. Why not?" After seeing a dragon rise out of the loch, nothing else would likely shake me at this point.

Was there anything that would ever be as terrifying?

We all tucked into the soup in silence, Lia hovering over the table, bringing out baskets of bread, plates of cheese, massive amounts of food until Munroe slung an arm around her waist and pulled her onto his lap, demanding she eat as well.

"I'm sorry. I need to feed people. It's my love language," Lia said.

"But you need strength too," Munroe said, and Lia relented, tucking into her soup as well.

"I think I need to explain. And apologize," Zara said, and the table all turned to her. She looked incredibly small, her face white with exhaustion, her eyes huge in her face. My chest tightened.

"I heard them," Zara continued, quietly. "The Kelpies. Not with my ears. In my head. Whispering. Pushing images. They've been … louder, lately. I don't think I realized just what it was at first, but I did tonight. Over the past few weeks, I started to understand what I was seeing."

Faelan's brows drew together. "Zara, why didn't you tell me? You know you could come to me."

Beside me, Liora's hand tightened on her soup spoon. Helpless not to, I reached out and traced soothing circles on her back.

"I was going to." Zara grimaced. "I went out to the loch with Mitch to see if I could get a clearer sense of what they wanted before I rang anyone. Next thing I knew, the ground's gone from under me and I'm in that bloody gully with a broken leg and the Kelpies shrieking at my back."

Sophie swore under her breath. "They pulled you."

"Aye." Zara's hand dug into the fur at the back of Mitch's neck where he'd put his head on her lap. "It wasn't an accident. Something wanted me down there. Close. I could … talk to them better." Her lips pressed into a thin line. "They're angry."

"Lovely." Orla shuddered. "Just what we need."

Zara nodded slowly. "And there was something else under them. I thought it was just the loch itself, at first. Then it started to move."

A low murmur rippled around the table.

"The dragon," Willow said.

Everyone went quiet again.

The image of that massive, scaled head rearing from the

water flickered behind my eyes. I clenched my jaw. The memory was bound to haunt my dreams.

"Aye," Zara whispered. "I didn't see it the way you lot did, not with my eyes. But I felt it. Its ... mind." She swallowed. "Old. Furious. Bound. By something."

Archie looked like someone had punched him. Hilda turned to him, a dismayed expression on her face.

"What was that thing?" Willow asked from near the far end of the table, eyes huge. "Please tell me someone knows."

All eyes turned, almost as one, to Agnes.

She stiffened. "What?" she demanded, clutching Calvin, Willow's cat, tightly against her chest.

"You're the folklore expert," Shona said gently. "If anyone would know..."

Agnes chewed the inside of her cheek for a moment, gaze slightly unfocused, as she thought about it.

"If we're going with traditional mythology," she said finally. "It's not like a Nessie derivative. What we saw tonight..."—she exhaled—"I'd say, in all honesty? Was probably a Beithir."

The word seemed to suck some of the warmth out of the room.

Sophie straightened. Archie swore under his breath. Hilda closed her eyes briefly, muttering something that sounded suspiciously like a prayer.

Liora glanced at me, eyes wide. I had no idea what a Beithir was, but the reaction alone was enough to make my skin crawl.

"A what now?" Finlay asked, echoing my thoughts.

"A Beithir," Agnes repeated, voice steadier now, slipping into lecture rhythm. "They're one of the great serpents of Scottish lore. Sometimes called lightning serpents. They're … not dragons in the fire-breathing, winged sense. More like colossal, venomous water-and-storm creatures. Born when lightning strikes the earth and doesn't release properly."

Willow blinked. "So it's a weather glitch with fangs."

"An incredibly dangerous weather glitch with fangs," Agnes corrected. "The old tales say they're the largest and most deadly of all Scottish serpents. They rarely appear, and when they do, it's usually an omen of … well, nothing good. Catastrophic storms. Great battles. Floods. That sort of thing."

My stomach dropped. "Grand."

"They aren't meant to be real," Archie said quietly. "That's just folklore."

"They aren't," Agnes agreed. "But then there are a lot of things in Loren Brae that aren't meant to be real." Agnes gestured to where two gnomes were making out in the corner.

"Gnorman!" Shona hissed, slapping a hand to her forehead. "Get your hands off Gnora. Now is *not* the time."

Despite everything, I had to bite back a laugh as the wee gnome turned and glared at the interruption.

"Och, lass. It's those near-death experiences. They just get the blood surging, don't they?" The wee gnome shocked me by growling back at her.

"Take it outside then," Shona said, rolling her eyes. Gnora giggled and sauntered off and Gnorman took chase, the two gnomes racing from the restaurant while giggling.

I had no words.

None at all.

I was still processing the dragon. *And the wulver.*

"I would have to look through some of our personal records. From the Order." Agnes sat back in her chair and closed her eyes as she thought. "But the last recorded Beithir sighting was centuries ago, and that was just in myths ... but if something—or someone—has bound one to the loch..."

"The Kelpies," Zara whispered. "They said they had a guardian."

"Aye." Agnes grimaced. "That would fit."

Kaia frowned. "Can you kill it?"

Agnes hesitated.

"The stories say the only way to truly kill a Beithir is to cut off its head and make sure the body and head are never reunited. If they touch again, it comes back to life." She spread her hands. "Which is ... not exactly practical in the middle of a loch against something the size of a bloody train."

"Right," Thane muttered, reaching over to pull Kaia's hand into his lap. "So we don't kill it. We ... what? Send it to sleep?"

"You can also lure it out. Block its path back to its home. It will die without water, right?" Orla leaned forward. "I remember a story like this."

"Aye, that's also an option, I believe." Agnes sighed, her shoulders slumping.

"Or," Lia offered dryly, "we all move to Spain."

A tiny ripple of laughter went around the room, too thin to really catch, but better than nothing.

Archie rubbed a hand over his face. "The important thing is, we know what we're dealing with now. Sort of."

"It's more than we had yesterday," Hilda said firmly. "And tonight, you lot"—she jabbed her finger toward Sophie and the others—"pushed a Beithir back into its den. That's no small feat."

"Barely," Sophie said, jaw tight. "If it had come any closer—"

"But it didn't," Hilda said. "You held the line. All of you. With very little warning and some of us injured. I'd say that's not nothing."

"What worries me," Archie said quietly, "is why now. Why is this escalating?"

The question hung heavy.

Beside me, Liora shifted and lifted her head to look at Agnes, who met her gaze and gave a subtle shake of her head.

It was imperceptible, but I caught it.

"They've made bargains," Zara said, and the table went still, caught on her words. "It isn't that the Stone is using them or forcing them into protecting the island. It was a bargain struck. I couldn't quite get a read on what's changed, but there's something else at play here. It's like they want to be recognized ... as a part of Loren Brae. Not against it? I don't know." Zara fluttered her hands in front of her face, clearly frustrated at not being able to read more of the Kelpies.

"Well, that's new," Orla said, her expression thoughtful. "Bargains made. And perhaps broken. Agnes—"

"Already making a note of it." Agnes was typing furiously into her phone.

Archie straightened, shoulders squaring. "All right. We know three things we didn't know this morning. One, the

Kelpies are organized and have a bloody serpent on call. Two, Zara can communicate with them somehow and, three, when push comes to shove, the Order can stand against them."

He jabbed a finger at us. "I saw you lot on that shore. You were bloody magnificent. Uncoordinated, but magnificent. If you can do that on the fly, imagine what you could do with a plan."

Hilda nodded, eyes fierce. "You're stronger together than any of you are apart. That's your advantage. The Kelpies are bound by duty and rage. You're bound by choice. By oaths. By love." She wrinkled her nose. "And, apparently, by a growing number of familiars."

Clyde bellowed, and we all waited a moment, but he didn't jump out of the wall.

"Phew," Lia said. "I really don't think I can take another—"

Clyde leapt down from the ceiling, crashing across the table, and raced across the restaurant as all the dogs jumped up and took chase.

"Damn it, Clyde," Lia shouted, her hand at her heart. "I will *never* get used to that. Never."

"Do you need the toilet—"

"No, thank you very much. I'm fine." Lia sniffed, shooting Munroe a glare.

"Well, I have a right to be concerned. You're sitting on my lap, aren't you?"

The whole table laughed, the tension having broken, and I eased closer to Liora, wanting her to look at me and tell me she was okay.

That *we* were okay.

Sophie pushed up from the end of the table, dirk sheathed now, expression resolute.

"Archie's right," she said. "Tonight was ... well, it was horrible. It could've been much worse. We're not going to pretend it isn't scary. Or that there isn't a very real chance of things getting worse before they get better. But we're not doing this alone. Not any of us." Her gaze found mine, then Liora's, then Zara's. "If the Kelpies think picking off one of us will make the rest fall, they've badly miscalculated."

Lachlan slid his hand into hers. "They come for one of us, they get all of us."

"Aye," Thane said quietly, Kaia's fingers twined with his. "That's how this works."

Beside me, Liora let out a breath that sounded like something loosening inside her. I took the risk and slid my hand under the table, curling my fingers around hers.

She didn't pull away.

Her grip was cool and a little shaky, but she held on.

"For better or worse," I said quietly, mostly to her but loud enough that the nearest few could hear, "I think we've found our people."

Her eyes lifted to mine, blue and deep and full of a fear that hadn't quite receded—but there was something else there too.

Hope. Just the tiniest spark of it.

"Ceud mìle fàilte, then," she whispered back. "One hundred thousand welcomes."

I squeezed her hand.

Outside the windows, the loch lay quiet under the night, pretending to be nothing more than water and reflection. Inside the castle, battered and bruised and covered in mud, we sat shoulder to shoulder around worn wooden tables—humans, witches, familiars, ghosts and all. United.

Whatever monsters waited in the depths, whatever bargains had been struck before our time, whatever lightning serpents uncoiled beneath the surface ...

We'd face them.

I was in this now, and I would do whatever I could to keep Liora, and Loren Brae, safe. And I truly believed, as I looked around this room filled with magickals, that we could do it.

Together.

CHAPTER TWENTY-THREE

LIORA

We took Zara home with us because she needed to heal and I needed to see that she was actually okay. I was pretty certain I'd taken a few years off my life after seeing her crumpled at the bottom of that ravine.

By the time we got home and Torin carried Zara in like she weighed nothing, Mitch pacing anxiously at his heels, I was bone-deep exhausted. Faelan had used her healing on Zara's leg at the castle, but she'd insisted Zara rest up for a few days to make sure the break did heal.

Quite a power, Faelan had. I had about a million questions for her at some point, particularly about her furry boyfriend, but that would have to come at another time.

"I'm fine," Zara muttered as Torin lowered her carefully onto my bed, her jaw set in that stubborn line. "Honestly, I don't need this much fussing."

"You nearly got dragged to your death by murder water horses," I snapped, too frayed to soften it. "You're allowed a bit of fussing."

Torin glanced between us, reading the tension in the room like it was printed in bold. He rested a big, warm hand briefly on my shoulder.

"I'll put the kettle on," he said gently. "Give you two a minute."

He disappeared into the kitchen. The soft clink of mugs and the hiss of the kettle filled the silence. Mitch hopped up on the bed, pressing his head into Zara's lap with a whine. She slid her fingers into his fur automatically, shoulders loosening a fraction.

I hovered near the end of the bed and then sat, hands linked so tightly in my lap my knuckles ached.

For a long beat, we just breathed together.

Her dark hair was mussed, curls escaping her plait. She had dirt on her cheekbone, a leaf stuck in the sleeve of her cardigan, but she was here. Alive. Not broken at the bottom of a gully with Kelpies bearing down.

My eyes burned.

"You scared the absolute shite out of me," I blurted, voice wobbling.

Zara's lips parted, the fight that had been coiled in her easing into something softer. "I could say the same about you, you know. Coming after me like that. I know how hard it hurt to fall down there."

I let out a somewhat hysterical laugh. "Very on-brand of me."

"Aye, it is." She sighed and leaned her head back against the pillows. "Come here then, you menace."

I scooted forward and curled into her side, sharing the same pillow as we did as teenagers gossiping about boys.

"I'm sorry," we both said at the same time.

And then, ridiculously, we both started laughing. It broke something open in my chest, all tangled with tears.

"You first," she said.

"I'm sorry I didn't tell you everything," I said in a rush. "About Torin. About the truth spell. About the whole Order thing, and the chartweaver ... situation. You're my person, Z. I should've come to you. I just"—I blew out air, trying to find words for the knot in my ribs—"I didn't want you to look at me like I'd messed it all up again," I admitted. "I thought if I said it out loud, you'd tell me I was being naïve or reckless, and I already ... I already think that about myself most days. I didn't want to hear it from you too."

Zara's face crumpled, just a little. "Oh, L," she whispered. "Is that what you think?"

"Have you met me?" I couldn't help but give a small laugh.

"In fairness, the truth spell was impressive work," she muttered.

"That is not the takeaway," I groaned, but a little snort escaped me.

She shifted, wincing slightly as she adjusted her leg. "Listen to me, you daft ray of sunshine." Her voice softened. "When I get ... sharp with you, it's not because I think you're a screwup. It's because I see you walking into storms without a coat and I want to run after you with a brolly."

"That's ... actually quite sweet," I said.

"I know. I wish you would see that more." A corner of her mouth lifted. "I *was* upset you didn't tell me about you and Torin. But underneath that? I was just worried. You just dove right in."

"I wish you could see how built he was. It might explain it, just a little?" I protested. "Ridiculous shoulders. Woodsman thighs. Very dive-in-able."

She pinched the bridge of her nose like she had a headache. "Aye, I felt how strong he was, all right? But I can also see things you can't."

"His aura," I said quietly.

"Aye." She stroked Mitch's ears, her fingers steady again. "Last time I saw him? It was dull. But since you came back?" She huffed out a breath. "Color. Proper color."

"Is that right?" I smiled, happy to know Torin's aura was shiny again.

"It's true." She tilted her head toward me. "You think I didn't notice how his voice sounded when he spoke to you tonight? How devastated he was?"

My chest squeezed. I thought of him carrying my sister up the gully, even though I could tell he didn't want to leave me. Or the way his voice had broken when he'd seen the blood on my forehead. The way he'd looked at me in the castle, worry etched into every line of him.

"I didn't tell you because I was happy," I admitted in a small voice. "And that feels like borrowed magick for me. Like something that'll be taken away as soon as I name it."

"Oh, sweetheart." Her voice went thick. She reached out and found my hand, squeezing hard. "You are allowed happy. You are not on cosmic probation."

I blinked fast.

"Also," she added dryly, "for the record? I approve."

My head snapped up. "You do?"

"Aye." She laughed. "It pains me to say it, but the man's a good one. Solid. Loyal."

"He's a Taurus," I explained.

"And he loves you."

Air evacuated my lungs. "You don't know that," I whispered, even as my heart thudded loud enough to hear.

"Liora, I can literally see emotional bonds," she said flatly. "It's like a soap opera in my head most days. That man is head over mud-splattered boots for you."

My eyes burned. "He's under a truth spell," I reminded her. "He says what he has to say."

"Does he?" she asked gently. "Or is that just a convenient excuse so you don't have to believe someone could choose you freely?"

Well. *Ouch.*

"Rude," I croaked.

"Accurate," she countered.

"I think I love him, Z."

"Well, *duh.*"

I laughed, and then sobered, realizing just how much I'd come to care for Torin in such a short time. He was also my person. He and Z were the most important people in my world.

We sat there for a moment, the quiet filling up with all the unsaid things.

"I am sorry," she said again, softer. "For making you feel judged. For being so busy trying to steer your life from the sidelines that I forgot you're the one actually living it. You don't owe me a report of every decision you make. I just ... want to be in your corner, L. Not standing over you with a clipboard."

My throat closed up. "I want you there," I managed. "You're my favorite person in the world, even when you're being a sanctimonious cow."

Zara snorted a laugh. "Likewise, you chaotic hedgehog."

I leaned forward and we fumbled our way into a hug, careful of her leg and Mitch's giant golden head wedged between us like a furry chaperone. Her arms tightened around me, and that familiar Zara scent wrapped around my nervous system like a blanket.

"I'm so glad you're okay," I whispered into her shoulder, tears finally spilling.

"I'm not going anywhere," she murmured back.

We pulled apart, both sniffing. Mitch licked a stripe up my cheek with impeccable timing.

"Ugh, thanks, buddy," I muttered, wiping my face.

"Right," Zara said, shifting back into business mode like flicking a switch. "We need to sort that truth spell, aye?"

My stomach dipped. "The one I put on Torin."

"The one he walked into," Zara amended. "But I don't like the idea of anything messing with his free will. Even if it's made him more charming."

"He was charming before," I argued automatically, then winced. "I mean—"

"I know what you mean." Zara felt around until she could grab my hand. "I know how to break the spell."

"You do?" I gasped, my words going up a notch.

"Aye, I did some research. It's a binding spell you did. The most important part of undoing it is that the original caster must unbind."

"Original caster," I repeated, relief filling me. "So ... me."

"Afraid so." Zara's mouth quirked. "You break it, you buy it, etcetera."

"That's ... fair."

"It's simple enough. Uses breath and intention. No eye of newt or toenails of exes required."

"Thank the stars," I muttered. "I don't think Avery would give us hers if I asked."

Zara snorted. "You'll stand in front of him," she said, slipping into her practical-teacher voice. "You'll own what you did. Then, if he agrees, you'll say this." She hesitated. "Do you want me to say it out loud once, and you repeat? It'll stick better."

"Yes, please," I said, palms suddenly clammy.

She cleared her throat, then spoke in a low, measured cadence, the syllables rolling rich and old.

"Words I wound, I now unbind,

By star and breath, by heart and mind.

By your consent and my regret,

I unbind this spell. Our fates reset."

Energy prickled along my arms just hearing it.

"You'll add his name," Zara continued. "And yours. Tie it specifically to the spell you were playing with that night."

I sighed. "I really am an eejit."

"A talented one," she said dryly. "Liora, listen to me."

I turned to her, waiting for whatever truth bomb she was about to drop on my head.

"This isn't about punishing you," she said. "It's about making sure whatever grows between you and that man is clean. If he tells you he loves you after this—and he will," she added, so matter-of-fact my heart tripped, "you'll know it's his choice. Not some cosmic compulsion."

Tears threatened again. "And you're ... okay with that? With me loving him?"

Her expression softened. "I want you happy," she said simply. "If that happiness comes with broad shoulders and a fondness for trees, who am I to argue?"

A watery laugh escaped me. "Z."

"Go on then." She shooed me with a little flap of her hand. "He's probably pacing holes into his floor worrying about you. I'll be fine here with Mitch and some paracetamol. If I need anything, I'll shout."

"You sure?" I hesitated.

"Yes. Now go break the spell and fix your love life, you numpty."

"Bossy," I muttered, but my heart felt lighter than it had in days.

I bent to kiss her forehead, then straightened, nerves fluttering in my chest as I padded down the hallway.

Bracken peeked his head around my bedroom door as I passed.

"You look like you're walking to either a proposal or an execution," he commented.

"Potentially both," I whispered back.

"Och, grand, I love a bit of drama," he said, scampering up to my shoulder. *"Carry on."*

Torin was in the kitchen, exactly as Zara had predicted.

He stood at the counter, hands braced, head bowed. A mug of tea sat forgotten beside him, steam long gone. The muscles in his forearms flexed, the veins standing out, and guilt punched me right in the solar plexus.

"You see the world through possibility. People like you ... you open doors for others without asking them to knock first. That's a rare thing. A precious thing."

His words came back to me, filling me with conviction that I was making the right choice in him—in choosing this life with him—and I cleared my throat as I stepped forward.

His head snapped up. Relief flooded his features so fast it made my eyes sting.

"Hey," he said quietly. "How's Zara?"

"She'll live," I said, voice soft. "Grumpy, which is how we know she's on the mend."

His mouth twitched. "Good."

Silence stretched between us, thick and full.

Bracken shifted against my neck.

"I'm just going to ... go ... not be here," he muttered, dropping to the floor and scampering toward the back door. *"If anyone needs me, I'll be climbing the bird feeder."*

I drew in a breath. "Torin, can we talk?"

He straightened fully, that steady, unwavering attention locking on me. Even with worry etched under his eyes and streaks of mud still on his jeans, he was ... beautiful. Solid.

Home.

"Aye," he said. "Please."

I walked around the island so there was nothing between us. My hands shook, so I wrapped them around myself.

"I owe you an apology," I began. "A proper one."

His brows pulled together. "For nearly getting yourself killed?" he asked roughly. "Because I'm not sure I'm ready to be gracious about that yet."

A choked laugh escaped me. "Add it to the list. But no. This is about the truth spell."

He went very still.

"Torin, I'm so, so sorry," I whispered. "I meddled with the one thing you value most—your integrity. I turned your own mouth into a weapon against your privacy. You didn't deserve that. No one does."

He looked at me for a long moment, eyes searching my face.

"I know you didn't do it on purpose," he said finally. "But aye, it's been ... a lot." His jaw flexed. "It's not that I mind being honest with you, Liora. I quite like it, actually. But I'd like it to be my bloody choice."

Tears spilled over. "You're right. And I want that for you too. That's why I'm here." I drew in a breath that shook. "There's a way to undo it. Properly. If you want me to."

He blinked, something like surprise flaring, quickly followed by guarded hope. "You can remove it?"

"Yes." I scrubbed at my eyes with the heel of my hand. "It has to be me. The original caster. There's a reversal spell. It'll ... unbind your tongue, so to speak." I winced. "Poor phrasing."

He huffed a soft laugh. "And if we do this ... there's no more magickal compulsion?"

"None," I said. "You'll be able to lie again." My stomach twisted. "Or not. But it'll be your decision."

He studied me. "And what does it mean for you?" he asked quietly. "If the spell goes?"

I blinked. "For me?"

"Aye," he said. "You've grown used to hearing exactly

what I think, whether I want to say it or not. If that goes, you'll have to trust me. Trust that if I tell you something, it's because I chose to. Not because I had to."

I swallowed, my stomach twisting. "I'd ... like that," I said honestly. "Terrifies me. But I'd like it."

He nodded slowly, decision settling over his features like a cloak. "All right," he said. "Do it."

Relief and terror crashed together in my ribcage. "Right. Okay. Um, stand still."

He obediently squared his shoulders, big hands resting loosely at his sides. The kitchen suddenly felt very small.

I stepped close enough that I had to tilt my head back to meet his gaze. My hands lifted, hovering uncertainly near his chest.

"May I?" I asked.

"Aye," he murmured. His voice had gone rough around the edges.

I laid my palms lightly against his sternum. His heartbeat thrummed steady and strong under my fingers. Closing my eyes, I pulled in a breath, calling up the feel of the original spell—the panic, the flare of power, the way it had snapped and latched onto him like a startled cat.

"Words I wound, I now unbind," I whispered, voice trembling but gaining strength as I went.

"By star and breath, by heart and mind.

By your consent and my regret,

I unbind this spell ..."

I hesitated, throat tight, then added, "From Torin Cattanach. By my hand, Liora Webster. Our fates reset."

Power shivered under my skin, running down my arms

in a rush. For a heartbeat, everything in the room hushed as if the house itself were holding its breath.

Then the air around Torin's throat shimmered, faint as heat off a road. Something that had been coiled there, unseen, unspooled with a soft pop, like a cork easing free. I staggered, lightheaded, and his hands closed around my elbows at once, steadying me.

"Easy," he murmured. "You all right?"

I blinked up at him. "Shouldn't I be asking you that?"

He flexed his jaw experimentally, like he was testing a muscle. "Feels ... lighter," he admitted. "Not sure how else to describe it."

Relief flooded me so hard my knees wobbled. "Try saying something you don't mean," I blurted.

His brows shot up. "Like what?"

"I don't know." I flapped a hand. "Something awful. Low-stakes awful. Not, like, manifesting your worst fears or something."

He considered, then cleared his throat, eyes never leaving mine.

"I hate trees," he said solemnly.

For a split second, I braced for the spell to recoil, for him to choke or for the words to come out twisted.

Nothing happened.

Then he grimaced. "Ugh. That felt wrong. But not ... magickally wrong. Just morally offensive."

A watery laugh burst out of me.

"All right, my turn," he said softly. "Test number two."

He cupped my face in his hands, rough thumbs brushing away the dampness under my eyes. His gaze searched mine, open and unshielded.

"I don't care about you," he said.

Something inside me flinched, even though I knew what we were doing.

He exhaled. "That was an easy test," he went on quietly. "Because it's a lie."

My heart thudded.

"Was it?" I asked, my voice thick.

"And I definitely don't love you."

My eyes filled as his hands slid down to my shoulders, then to my waist, pulling me in until my chest brushed his.

"Look at that," Torin said, his voice dropped low, his lips hovering just over mine. "Another lie."

My world narrowed.

"It is?" I gulped, my throat tightening as I pressed closer to him.

"Aye, it is. Liora." Torin brushed his lips softly over mine. "I love you."

No shimmer of spell light. No pressure forcing them out of him. Just a man, choosing to stand in a kitchen that smelled faintly of woodsmoke and herbal tea and saying the one thing I'd secretly, desperately wanted and had been afraid to hear.

"You—you do?" I croaked, because eloquence had left the building.

His mouth curved, tenderness flooding his eyes. "Aye," he said. "I do. I love your optimism and your tarot cards and the way you talk to yourself and your squirrel like it's the most natural thing in the world. I love that you leave crystals on my windowsills and that you're scared and you still run toward people in need instead of away." His voice went hoarse. "I love that you walked back into this town knowing what they used to say about you and decided to stay anyway. I love you, Liora Webster. Spell or no spell. Just as you are. That's the truth I'm choosing."

My vision blurred completely.

"Don't cry," he whispered, forehead dropping to mine. "You'll break my bloody heart."

"It's just—" My laugh came out strangled. "That's a lot."

"It's honest," he said simply.

I let out a watery breath. "Well, I suppose it's convenient, Torin," I said, voice shaking. "Because I happen to love you too."

His fingers tightened at my waist. "Aye?"

"Aye." A smile broke through my tears. "A ridiculous amount, actually. For a man who leaves muddy boot prints down the hallway and talks to trees more than people."

"They're better listeners," he murmured.

"I might fight them for that title," I said, and then I was laughing and crying and he was laughing too, relief etched into every line of him.

He dipped his head, brushing his mouth over mine in the softest kiss. Just a press of lips, a question.

I answered by sliding my hands up into his hair and pulling him closer.

The second kiss was not soft.

It seared.

His lips moved over mine with a hunger that had nothing to do with spells and everything to do with weeks of slow-building tension and fear and near misses. His hands spanned my back, splayed wide, anchoring me as my knees seemed to forget their purpose.

I melted against him, opening when he coaxed, tasting tea and something that was uniquely Torin. Heat flared low in my belly, curling through my veins. The kitchen, the house, the whole of bloody Scotland fell away until there was only the slide of his tongue across mine and the steady thud of his heart against my chest.

He broke away just long enough to murmur against my lips, "Tell me you're still sure."

"I'm sure," I whispered. "I'm so sure."

Something relieved and fierce flashed across his face. He kissed me again, slower this time, like he had all the time in the world to memorize the shape of my mouth.

A tiny chittering sound interrupted us.

"If you two are going to start making baby humans or whatever it is you lot do," Bracken announced, *"I'm going to need danger pay and some kind of tiny squirrel blindfold."*

I rested my forehead against Torin's chest, laughing helplessly.

"Bracken," I said, breathless. "Boundaries."

"Aye, well, consider them firmly established," he muttered. *"I'm happy for you and all that sentimental nonsense, but there's only so much tongue wrestling a lad can witness before he has to chuck himself into the birdbath."*

"I'm guessing the back door wasn't open for him to leave?" I said and Torin laughed against my ear.

"Um, nope."

Torin's chest shook under my cheek.

"Your familiar is a menace," he murmured.

"He's very emotionally invested in my happiness," I said primly.

"As am I, darling. As am I." Torin wrapped his arms

around me and gave me one of those sweet hugs where we just rocked back and forth in each other's arms, happy to just be.

For the first time in a very long time, even with a dragon in the loch and Kelpies at the shore and a whole village's fate tangled in glowing threads only I could see, my heart felt ... steady.

Loved.

Chosen.

Home.

Spell or no spell, disaster magnet or not, I was exactly where I was meant to be.

With my sister safe, a menace of a familiar, and a sexy tree man who loved me of his own free will.

The rest?

We'd weave it as we went.

EPILOGUE

LIORA

"I'm really not sure about this whole marshmallow on tatties thing." Agnes frowned down at the dish of sweet potatoes she was unwrapping. She darted a worried look over her shoulder at Sophie, who was overseeing the Thanksgiving proceedings with militant efficiency.

"Stuffing goes here. Green bean casserole next. Mashed potatoes. Sweet potato—" Sophie's head shot up as she looked across the restaurant until her eyes landed on Agnes. "Agnes? Did you make the sweet potato casserole?"

"Aye," Agnes said, lifting the pan in the air. "But are you certain it calls for marshmallows? I feel like you're having me on, Sophie."

"I promise, it's a thing." Sophie grinned and grabbed the dish from Agnes's hands.

"You could have just let me cook it all," Lia said.

"And what's the fun in that? Is it even Thanksgiving if you're not judging what dish someone brings?" Sophie arched an eyebrow and I bit back a laugh.

"There's the thankful and loving spirit we're looking for, dear." Lottie nodded briskly and Sophie laughed.

"Don't act like you weren't pleased when your stuffing won first prize at the neighborhood Thanksgiving potluck."

"As it well should have." Lottie sniffed and patted the pink feather fascinator tucked in her hair. "I do make the best stuffing."

"We'll see about that." Ramsay, Willow's gruff boyfriend who I'd only heard speak about ten words ever, glowered over his dish at Lottie.

"You don't scare me," Lottie said. "I won six years in a row. And one year it was against a man whose husband was a food critic."

Matthew whistled low in appreciation. "It's virtually impossible to beat a gay with food training and a flair for presentation."

"I saw him crying into his martini later that night." Lottie sighed with satisfaction.

"I had no idea Thanksgiving was so ruthless," Torin said, coming forward to hand me a glass of champagne.

We were gathered at Grasshopper, once again, but this time in far better spirits than the last time we'd all come here, dirtied, bloodied, and terrified for what the Kelpies had shown us. Though it had only been a couple of weeks since our run-in with the Kelpies and Zara's fall, a lot had changed.

And one of the changes was that I, apparently, cooked

now. Well, *we* cooked. Torin had taken one look at my panicked face as I'd stared down at the mounds of brussels sprouts and bacon and had taken pity on me. Together, we'd prepared roasted brussels sprouts with crispy bacon and gorgonzola, and I could only pray that it gained Sophie's approval.

"Liora?" My eyes snapped to Sophie's face, and I realized she'd said my name twice now. "The sprouts?"

"Right here," I said, rushing forward. I carefully placed the dish on the table and stepped back, heart pounding, as she lifted the corner of tinfoil and checked inside.

"You did great," Sophie said, beaming at me. "Looks roasted to perfection."

"Oh thank the goddess," I murmured, stepping back as she turned a laser eye on Orla and Finlay.

"Don't say you've let me down on biscuits now."

"Right, so here's the thing..." Orla said, stepping forward with a mutinous expression on her face. "Your biscuits are not real biscuits, so there was a tad bit of confusion—"

"You didn't..." Sophie sucked in a breath.

"Oh I have an idea what's coming." Willow exchanged a look with Lia, who only shook her head sadly.

"It's about to be a blood bath."

"What's happening?" Torin whispered in my ear, wrapping an arm around my waist and handing me back my champagne glass.

"I think Sophie's going to fight Orla? It's hard to tell."

"I've got money on Sophie," Lachlan said, coming up next to us. "She's efficient and terrifying."

"I don't know, mate," Munroe, Lia's partner and owner

of Common Gin, leaned in. "I've seen Orla on the job site, and she's scary good with power tools."

"As you requested." Orla raised her voice and uncovered her tray. "Biscuits."

Sophie sucked in a breath and we all leaned forward.

"Oh shit," Kaia said, turning to give Willow and Lia a knowing look.

Orla shoved her shoulders back and turned, presenting a tray of perfectly cooked shortbread biscuits to the room.

I released a sigh of relief.

"Those are lovely, Orla. Well done," I said, needing to fill the silence.

"It's the wrong biscuits," Lia hissed and I blinked at her.

"These are biscuits," Orla said, plopping the tray down on the table, her expression mutinous.

"Those are shortbread cookies." Sophie jabbed a finger in the direction of the table. "Biscuits are—"

"These?" Matthew strode forward and uncovered a dish full of what looked to be scones.

"Yes, these!" Sophie crowed and clapped her hands. Leaning up, she kissed Matthew's cheek and pointed for him to place his dish on the table with the dinner food. Scooping up Orla's biscuits, she gave her a look. "I'll just be putting these on the dessert table."

"You're welcome," Orla called loudly to Sophie's retreating back.

"For what it's worth, love, they're damn good biscuits." Finlay came forward and wrapped his arm around Orla's shoulder.

"I thought they looked lovely," I added.

"Nobody's going to complain about extra shortbread, I can promise you that," Archie barked from where he walked into the room carrying a massive turkey on a platter. "Out of my way, the lot of you. It's time to carve the turkey."

"I've never done a Thanksgiving meal before, but this all looks cracking, doesn't it?" Torin said, and I glanced up at him, my heart still doing that funny little flutter in my chest whenever I looked at him.

"Aye, it does. Aside from the marshmallow on sweet potatoes. I'm not so sure about that."

"I'll try anything once." Torin gave me a look that had heat curling through me. "Have I told you how pretty you look tonight?"

"Thank you," I said, my cheeks heating at his compliment. I wore a plum-colored wrap dress with my gran's brooch pinned at my shoulder. Two more opals had shown up after the battle, and I'd been told my challenges were complete. Sophie surmised that selflessly racing to Zara's side in the Kelpie attack and showing a genuinely contrite heart with Torin regarding what the spell had cost him had earned me my opals. The brooch itself looked as though the opals had always been there, the Celtic dragons curling around the three stones as if they were their eggs, and I couldn't help but wonder if there had been some link to my brooch and the dragon that had revealed itself from the shadowy depths of Loch Mirren.

"Have I told you how happy I am that you're with someone who compliments you?" Zara asked from where she sat, Mitch at her side, waiting for instructions on food.

"And you look beautiful as well," Torin added and Zara's smile widened.

"No need to flatter me, Torin, I already gave Liora my approval for you."

Zara had stayed with us for a week after her injuries were healed, and in that time, we'd come to a new agreement. She was going to be less critical of my choices, and I was going to be more understanding of why she'll never stop worrying about me. It felt like we were stepping into a new stage of our relationship, as sisters who respected each other as adults. I guess staring down mythological beasts together would do that to a relationship.

"What's this table?" Kaia asked and I turned from Torin, looking to where a long child's-height table sat next to the big table.

"Honestly? I'm not sure," I said, tilting my head at it.

"For all of our ... extra friends," Lia said, nodding as movement blurred past her and an array of dishes appeared on the short table. As if on cue, the door opened and in marched Gnorman, his arm tucked around Gnora's waist, both looking dapper in their finest clothes. Behind them trailed a veritable parade of animals. Two hedgehogs waddled in, followed by a crow hopping along, with Gloam behind them. Bracken appeared, racing in circles around the herd of dogs, who were, admittedly, on their best behavior and didn't give chase. Which was a miracle, considering Sir Buster was leading the pack and bristling with his usual barely contained rage.

Calvin, Willow's cat, sauntered at the back of the pack, unconcerned with the dogs in his presence, seemingly in conversation with a Scottish terrier named Oban.

"Honestly, it's incredible to see them all together," Kaia murmured.

They all stopped in front of their spots, like a well-trained parade, and looked expectantly at Sophie for instructions.

"Right, that's everyone here. Archie's carving the turkey, the rest of you, grab a plate and line up. Brice, can you get the food for our wee friends please?" Sophie ordered, and we all fell in line, grabbing our plates and heaping food on them, even though some of the dishes made me raise my eyebrows.

"Don't look at my sweet potatoes like that, Liora," Agnes said, glaring across the table at me. Graham sat next to her, and he leaned a shoulder into hers, his lips quirking in a smile as he studied his plate.

"It's just that marshmallows are a bit of a stretch for tatties, aren't they, darling?"

Agnes huffed, stabbing a marshmallow with her fork. "I trusted Sophie. But honestly, I've no idea what I made. This just feels wrong."

Graham leaned in, not crowding her, just close enough that his shoulder brushed hers. He studied the dish like it mattered. Like she mattered.

"You made something people are arguing about," he said gently. "That's usually the mark of a good recipe."

She snorted. "That's the mark of chaos."

"Mm. I've tasted chaos before." He picked up his fork. "Usually disappointing. This"—he took a bite, chewed slowly, then smiled, soft and unmistakably sincere—"is actually lovely."

Agnes waved a hand. "You don't have to do that."

"I know," he said quietly. "I still want to."

Her eyes flicked to him, sharp and guarded. "You're just saying that to be nice."

"No," he said, and there was no teasing in it now. "I'm saying it because you made it. And because you always think what you do isn't enough."

She looked back down at her plate. "Careful, Graham."

I watched the exchange in fascination, wondering just how much Agnes was hiding from us.

"I'm sorry. I didn't mean—" He shook his head. "Just ... I like seeing you proud of something. Even if it's marshmallows on tatties."

Agnes's mouth curved despite herself. "That might be the lowest bar you've ever set."

"I'd raise it for you," he said without thinking.

Agnes cleared her throat and leaned back, her gaze guarded. "Well, don't get carried away. I'll still be blaming Sophie if anyone dies."

"I'll tell anyone who asks that it was the best Thanksgiving dish I'd ever had, and that I'd eat it again any day of the week."

She shook her head, lips twitching. "You're impossible."

"Aye," he said softly. "But I'm on your side."

Across the table, Lia coughed pointedly into her wine. "You all are going to make me tear up into my wine."

Agnes and Graham spoke at once.

"He just doesn't like seeing me sad."

"She doesn't realize how good she is at pretty much everything."

They turned to each other, and despite whatever odd

tension bounced between them, they beamed at each other. They must have come to a truce of sorts, and I wondered if this was a Thanksgiving miracle.

And that was when the miracle ended.

It started with Bracken.

One second my squirrel was perched innocently on the edge of the low table, stuffing his cheeks with something suspiciously shiny, and the next—he bolted.

Straight across the floor.

Sir Buster's head snapped up.

"Oh no," I breathed.

Too late.

The dogs exploded into motion, as Sir Buster led the charge with a battle cry that could only be described as personal vengeance. Oban followed, barking wildly, with the others joining in, tails and ears flying.

"Bracken!" I shouted.

You'll never take my freedom!

The squirrel shrieked ... an impressive sound, honestly ... and launched himself onto the back of Gloam, who squealed and took off in the opposite direction, weaving between legs and under tables.

Plates clattered. Someone screamed. Lottie stood, clutching her napkin to her chest. "That's enough!"

"Get the dogs," Sophie roared, pointing like a general.

"I've got Sir Buster ... nope—" Lachlan skidded sideways as Sir Buster ducked under his arm.

Bracken made a daring leap for greenery that lined the walls, misjudged it entirely, and landed in the gravy boat.

Chaos peaked.

And then—

A *moooo* bellowed through the restaurant, halting everyone in their tracks.

Every head turned.

Hovering serenely above the dessert table, translucent and glowing faintly blue, Clyde blinked into existence, a spectral pie balanced delicately on his nose.

The dogs froze.

Bracken froze.

Even Sir Buster sat.

A collective silence fell.

"Is that a pumpkin pie?" Matthew whispered.

The dogs, apparently deciding that ghosts outranked squirrels, slowly backed away. Bracken took the opportunity to scramble up the greenery wall, chittering victoriously, gravy dripping from his fur.

Applause broke out. Actual applause.

"Well," Sophie said, straightening. "I guess that's Thanksgiving, then."

Eventually, the room settled. Laughter lingered like warmth in the air, the kind that settled into your bones. Torin squeezed my hand, and I leaned into him without thinking, my heart steady and full in a way it hadn't been in ... ever.

I looked around the table. At my friends. My sister, smiling and safe. At magick woven so tightly into the ordinary that it felt like it had always belonged here. At the low table, now calm again, where hedgehogs nibbled politely and the dogs pretended not to watch the squirrel.

And I felt it.

That quiet click inside my chest.

I was exactly where I needed to be.

My astrology business was growing—booked solid weeks out now. People were coming not just for answers, but for comfort and clarity, for a sense that the universe might be listening after all. My powers were intact, humming gently under my skin, no longer something to fear or fight, but something to live alongside.

For the first time in my life, I wasn't waiting for the other shoe to drop. Well, at least not until we figured out what to do with the Kelpies. But that was a worry for another day.

I lifted my glass.

"To gratitude," I said softly.

And as everyone echoed it back—laughing and clinking glasses—I knew this wasn't an ending at all.

It was only just the beginning.

Don't you think it's time for Bracken to find love? Read on for a fun scene where Bracken meets Hazel and Torin helps build them a home.

Join my mailing list and download the free bonus scene here

triciaomalley.com/free

Oh, and if you had any questions about Agnes and Graham? Just turn the page... :)

AGNES

"One does not simply walk past a shoe sale," Willow intoned, leaning back on the couch to lift her foot to showcase a slouchy low-heeled suede boot. The other women all cooed their approval.

"She got herself a pair of slouchy suede boots," Liora explained to Zara, who smiled out into the room.

"I love suede, it has such a soft texture," Zara agreed.

All the women of the Order of Caledonia, as well as Hilda, Lottie, and Zara, were gathered in the library at the castle. Between the busy holiday season, the fact that a freaking Beithir was living in the loch, and pretty much the heightened fear around life in general since our stand-off at the loch, we hadn't managed to get the women together as one. Namely because the men in their lives had become increasingly annoying, and almost never let any of them out of their sights. Even now, the lot of them were up in the games room, likely arguing over some sportsball match or another.

"How do you even have time to shop?" I asked, shaking my head at Willow. She was a seamstress, a clothing designer, and a psychic ... none of which allowed much time for shopping.

"Priorities." Willow laughed, running a critical eye over my outfit. I winced. I knew that look, which meant she was going to bug me about my clothes again.

"Don't start on me," I protested, throwing my hands in the air. So what if my jeans were paint-streaked? Loren Brae was a casual village and I had nobody here to impress.

"Oh, I'm starting." Willow reached for her sketch pad while the other women hooted in laughter. "You've been putting me off for a while now."

"I did the fashion show!" I protested, reaching for my glass of wine and taking a hasty sip. I didn't like being the center of attention, and it had taken everything in my power to don a dress of Willow's creation and walk the fashion show.

But Graham had made it better.

Even now, all these months later, my heart picked up speed when I thought about that moment when he'd seen me, all done up for the show, and his face had reflected everything that could never be between us.

Shoving those thoughts aside, I glared at Willow.

"I own a bookshop. And a pottery studio. I do not need a fancy dress, Willow. I'm not going to wear it anywhere."

"What you need is a date night outfit." Willow bit her lower lip as she focused on her sketch pad, ignoring my protests completely.

The silence drew out across the room, and I looked around as all the women studiously looked every way but at me.

"What?" I asked, exasperated.

"I think everyone is just fed up with trying to pretend like you don't want to jump Graham's bones," Kaia, a metalsmith who worked with all men and was as blunt as could be, grinned at me.

"I do not—"

"Och, you do. I swear I could drag Fin into a closet after watching you two pine for each other." Orla fanned her face. "It's like getting a contact high from your pheromones."

My eyes widened as all the women nodded in agreement.

"Seriously, Agnes. When are you two just going to bang it out?" Sophie asked, leaning forward in all her American earnestness. I'd grown to love her directness even while my cheeks heated at her question.

"Why do I feel like I'm suddenly the subject of an intervention?" I asked, shaking my head at the room.

This impossible group of women, bonded through magick and genuine friendship, all grinned back at me. It was the Order of Caledonia, almost complete, at their finest—not when they were battling Kelpies or keeping Loren Brae protected from harm—but when they were united, just like this, in friendship and support for everyone's idiosyncrasies.

Sophie was the first.

Her uncle had bequeathed her MacAlpine Castle, and she'd stepped into the role of the Knight of the Order of Caledonia and had taken on the almost impossible task of finding the other members of the Order while also trying to keep the Kelpies that ran amok in Loch Mirren at bay. And she did so with a relentless American optimism—once more into the breach and all that—that both intimidated me and made me admire her in the same breath.

In short order she'd found Lia, a kitchen witch, and hired her to run Grasshopper, the new restaurant at the castle. Shona, our garden witch, had come next, falling easily in line with Lia—the two of them sharing recipes and spells of a healing nature. Willow had come next, ready to design a specialty tartan for MacAlpine Castle. Orla had followed, our builder, and Kaia, a metalsmith, had joined her. Luck would have it that Faelan, Loren Brae's new vet and healer, had found her way here on her own, and Liora, the chartweaver, had returned to be with her sister, the two adding some key insights to the battle to subdue the Kelpies and restore Loren Brae to her might.

Each were strong women.

Each were opinionated women.

And all of them seemed to be of the opinion that I needed to jump one Graham Kincaid, owner of The Tipsy Thistle, my ex-boyfriend, and the man who haunted my dreams at night.

Not that I'd ever let him know that.

"Oh, Agnes," Willow gasped and heads swiveled to see where Willow drew on her sketch pad, but her eyes were unfocused, staring into the future.

She was having a vision.

"What do you see?" Shona asked, leaning forward.

Willow blinked, looking down at her paper, and then up at me, and I pressed my lips together in a tight line as Willow's eyes caught on mine.

Tears shimmered there.

"Don't..." I whispered, holding a hand up to ward her off. "It's not worth it, Willow. Let it go."

"Worth what?" Sophie demanded, leaning forward.

"Are you sure?" Willow asked, holding my gaze.

"It can't be. As you well know."

Silence drew out and then, because my heart was breaking, like it had so many times in the past, I got up and left the castle.

It didn't matter how much magick that incredible group of women had.

There were just some things that neither love nor magick could fix.

Are you all finally ready for Agnes & Graham's story?
Order Wild Scottish Fate today!

Fancy a wee drink and some grub in your favorite Loren
Brae pub? The Tipsy Thistle has its own line of
merchandise! Shop here - triciaomalley.myshopify.com

I wrote Wild Scottish Magic while ensconced in a charming room in Florence—sun pooling on old stone, church bells keeping time, and the scent of espresso floating through the shutters. The city's romance and beauty wrapped around me as Torin and Liora found their voices. Torin and Liora were a joy to bring to life, and I think Florence helped me listen to their stories more closely. Perhaps it's the way the streets bend toward surprise, or how music drifts from a piazza just when you need it, but their magic felt at home there, and their hearts did too.

And now, a peek at what's next. Wild Scottish Fate is waiting in the wings—Agnes and Graham's story at last. I'm thrilled to finally bring these two together. Their journey will draw a circle around the Order of Caledonia in a way that feels complete... but complete doesn't mean finished. Not yet.

There are more towns tucked behind the mist. More threads intertwined with Loren Brae. More unexpected connections ready to spark. If you've fallen in love with this world, take heart! I promise there are doors we haven't opened yet.

Thank you for traveling these worlds with me. Your notes, your laughter, your belief in a little wonder keep the magic of Loren Brae alive. Rest here a moment with Torin and Liora. Then look to the horizon with me. There's so much more to discover!

As always, Sparkle on!!!
Tricia O'Malley

STAND ALONE NOVELS

<u>Love's a Witch</u>

She's got runaway magic. He's got a town to protect. Too bad fate has other plans.

<u>Highland Hearts Holiday Bookshop</u>

As Christmas looms, and lonely hearts beg for love, I'm tossed into the world of magic and romance, aided by a meddling book club who seems more interested in romance than reading.

<u>Ms. Bitch</u>

"Ms. Bitch is sunshine in a book! An uplifting story of fighting your way through heartbreak and making your own version of happily-ever-after."

~Ann Charles, USA Today Bestselling Author

<u>Starting Over Scottish</u>

Grumpy. Meet Sunshine.

She's American. He's Scottish. She's looking for a fresh start. He's returning to rediscover his roots.

<u>One Way Ticket</u>

A funny and captivating beach read where booking a one-way ticket to paradise means starting over, letting go, and taking a chance on love...one more time

10 out of 10 - The BookLife Prize

CONTACT ME

I hope my books have added a little magick into your life. If you have a moment to add some to my day, you can help by telling your friends and leaving a review. Word-of-mouth is the most powerful way to share my stories. Thank you.

Love books? What about fun giveaways? Nope? Okay, can I entice you with underwater photos and cute dogs? Let's stay friends! Sign up for my newsletter and contact me at my website.

www.triciaomalley.com

Or find me on Facebook and Instagram.
@triciaomalleyauthor